CRITICS RAVE FOR JADE LEE!

WHITE TIGRESS

"An erotic romance for those seeking a heated love story."
—*RT BOOKclub*

"This exotic, erotic and spiritual historical romance is unique.... *White Tigress* is a fine distinctive tale of East loves West."
—Harriet Klausner

DEVIL'S BARGAIN

"Jade Lee has written a dark and smoldering story... full of sensuality and heart-pounding sex scenes."
—*Affaire de Coeur*

"[An] exciting erotic romance...."
—*Harriet's Book Reviews*

"A luscious bonbon of a sensual read—the education of an innocent: hot, sensual, romantic, and fun!"
—Thea Devine, *USA Today* Bestselling Author

"A spicy new debut...."
—*RT BOOKclub*

"Highly charged and erotic.... You won't be able to put it down."
—Roundtable Reviews

"*Devil's Bargain* is a definite page-turner...a must read this summer."
—*Romance Reviews Today*

ON THE VERGE OF GREAT POWER

"Joanna, what are you doing?" Zou Tun's words came to her from a great distance, and yet he sounded as if he were right beside her.

She opened her eyes, locking once more onto his gaze across the room. Distantly, she saw that his face was hot, his mouth slightly open. His breath came in barely controlled puffs. All these things she absorbed, let pass through her consciousness, then drop away.

"I want to know," she whispered, her voice gaining strength as her hands reversed their direction. "Where does the yin go? What is coming?"

"No," he gasped. "You are not ready."

Her circles were stronger now, and she felt the rush of the yin stroking hotter, stronger, brighter.

"Yes," she said feeling triumphant. "I am!"

Other books by Jade Lee:

WHITE TIGRESS
DEVIL'S BARGAIN

Hungry Tigress

JADE LEE

LEISURE BOOKS NEW YORK CITY

A LEISURE BOOK®

June 2005

Published by

Dorchester Publishing Co., Inc.
200 Madison Avenue
New York, NY 10016

ISBN 0-8439-5504-X

Printed in the United States of America.

Visit us on the web at www.dorchesterpub.com.

Hungry Tigress

9 January, 1896
Dearest Kang Zou,

Our distance weighs heavily upon me, my brother. The garden is dull, the birds are silent without your voice to wake them. Father reminds me that your studies take diligent care, but I see only that our beautiful family flower is incomplete without all its petals.

Have you attained Heaven yet? Can you return for the New Year's celebration? My poetry is ever dull without your help.

Your devoted sister,
Wen Ji

Decoded translation:

My son, you have been gone a long time without word, and powerful people have begun to ask me for a report. Our family's fortunes depend upon your success. Have you found the conspirators yet? Report immediately. Resolve this matter by the end of January and our family success is assured.

Your father,
General Kang

17 January, 1896
Dearest Wen Ji,

Alas, I cannot aid your poetry this day. Only constancy of purpose achieves the impossible, and my studies take much attention. The temple has a beautiful garden here, and whenever I gaze upon the plum flower, I think of you. But do not despair. Soon Father will choose a bridegroom for you and another flower will blossom in your heart.

Your brother,
Kang Zou

Decoded translation:

Apologies for the delay in report. I work day and night searching for the conspirators, but they are canny and difficult to locate. Do not hope for a resolution by New Year. Perhaps there is another means to restore our family's honor?

Your son,
Zou Tun

Pursuing knowledge serves only to increase our desires, thus creating hypocrisy and causing frustration. Pursuing the Tao eliminates intellectualizing and decreases desires. On the inside you will be pure and empty, and on the outside you will naturally adhere to nonaction and not engage in worldly affairs.

—*Lao Tzu*

Chapter One

17 January, 1898

No. No, no. No, no.

The word echoed in Joanna Crane's mind, the sound keeping beat with her mare's hooves. She knew she was being ridiculous; one could not outrun a parental edict. And yet here she was on an open road outside of Shanghai, running her poor horse into the ground.

No, Joanna was not escaping to join the Chinese rebel army. Because that would be silly and dangerous, even if those men were fighting for their freedom from an oppressive government. Just like her American forefathers, they were gambling their lives on a great and noble task, and she would love to fight alongside them.

But, no. She couldn't do that, even though she had the means of their support—both monetary and in the literature of great American thinkers. She could even translate it into Chinese for them without too much risk

3

to herself. In fact, she'd already started. She had her first scroll of Benjamin Franklin's writings already translated. Or paraphrased. She could do that, couldn't she?

No.

Why? Because her father forbade it. Because he had discovered what she was doing and confiscated her books. Because no man wanted to marry someone who read Benjamin Franklin.

Very well, she'd responded. She would marry. But whom? Not the handsome George Higgensam, an idiotic youth with more money than brains. Not young Miller nor old Smythee nor even pockmarked Stephens. Not any of the young gentlemen who had offered proposals over the last few years.

And why? Because her father had refused for her. Hadn't even asked her.

True, she had no wish to marry the men, but frankly she had no wish for her father to summarily dismiss them either. Especially without consulting her.

Didn't he see that she was wasting away? That without a husband or children to occupy her time, she was useless? Without a purpose or a cause to call her own, she was nothing but a pretty shell with nothing inside. Didn't he see that?

No. No one saw that but Joanna and her mare, Octavia, whom she was now riding without heed or focus. Which only proved what her mother had feared ten years ago: Shanghai made whites go mad.

It was no doubt proof of Joanna's staunch constitution that it had taken a decade for her mind to unbalance, but her reprieve was over. Obviously she was insane.

As if in agreement, poor Octavia—her eighth mare since coming to China—chose that moment to misstep. Joanna's mind was snatched away from her other problems as the horse's head dropped down to the dirt, jerking her nearly out of her saddle. As it was, Joanna banged her forehead upon her poor mare's neck, then had to fight to keep her seat while Octavia stumbled on an obviously injured leg.

Fortunately, Joanna had spent much of her childhood riding out one parent's intemperate mood after another and so was an excellent horsewoman. She managed to keep her seat and firmly, if a bit unsteadily, bring Octavia to a stop. Then she was off the heaving animal and doing her best to soothe the creature while praying the damage wasn't fatal. Her father did not pour money into damaged horses.

"It's nothing serious," she soothed as she began to gingerly feel about the horse's wrenched leg. "Just a strained shoulder. Truly. We'll have you up and about in no time."

But, of course, first she had to get the horse down. Meaning down in their barn, at home, inside the foreign concession of Shanghai, where the family's head groom would pronounce Octavia's eventual fate.

Joanna looked around, seeing nothing but open fields shielded by a few scattered trees and a long stretch of empty road. She frowned, mentally counting how many times "no" had gone through her head since she'd left. Exactly how far was she from Shanghai's gate? How long ago had she bribed the gatekeeper and outrun her maid?

She wasn't sure. But she knew it would take five times as long to limp poor Octavia back home. Guilt ate at her as she began the long, slow walk. Even the trees, growing thicker now, seemed to loom over her with disapproval.

Joanna sighed, seeing now that her mother's second prediction had come true: She was a spoiled miss with no thought to the consequences of her actions. Except, of course, that was the real reason she had come out here this day—because there *were* no consequences to her actions . . . ever. She was her father's showpiece, a hostess for his parties and a trophy kept in reserve for whenever he chose her husband. And because she was rich in this foreign land, she could do just about anything she wanted—within reason—and suffer no consequences whatsoever.

If she broke something, the servants replaced it. If she hurt someone, her father's first boy sent an expensive gift to make amends. If she acted wildly and impetuously, then there were maids and grooms aplenty to surround and protect her. Even now she knew that she would not truly have to walk the entire way home. Eventually she would catch up with her maid and a conveyance would be summoned. Naturally there would be bribes aplenty to cover the fact that an English foreigner had escaped to the proscribed territory, but that was simply money out of a never-ending coffer. It mattered little if Joanna's antics required a hundred or a thousand pounds—it was all the same to her.

She wondered if it was even possible for her to do something so heinous that her father's first boy couldn't buy her out of it. And if there was . . . would she do it? She immediately discarded murder. She wasn't so desperate to attract her father's attention that she would act violently toward anyone. Theft? The average Chinese was poor enough without Joanna taking from them. That would be cruel. And as for stealing from someone who could afford the loss . . . well, that was just silly.

There was always wanton licentiousness. She had seen a few of her friends choose that route. It relieved the boredom, if nothing else. But truly, she simply hadn't the inclination.

She would just have to support the Boxers in their rebellion against the evil Qin Empire. That was, os-

tensibly, why she'd chosen this particular route outside of Shanghai and then outrun her maid: She had
overheard the groomsmen talking about a group of
revolutionaries who were hiding out here. If only she
could find them, she would offer her services. If
nothing else she could supply blankets and food-
stuffs. And if she couldn't hand them a translation of
Mr. Franklin's writings, at least she could discuss with
them some of that great American's ideas. She'd read
all the great writers: Franklin, Harriet Beecher Stowe,
even the French philosopher Robespierre. But there
was only so much theory one could learn without
yearning to put it into practice. That was why she was
out here today. She was searching for a practice to fit
with all her ideals.

Assuming, of course, that they would even speak to
a white woman. That was always a risk in China. But
fortunately the revolutionaries would by definition
have more open-minded ideas. And probably they'd
be desperate for just the type of aid she could give.

But she first had to find them.

After getting Octavia home. After the poor creature
healed up. And after she arranged for another excuse
to make her way outside the gate. Assuming of course,
that the revolutionaries were really out here in the first
place.

Except . . . they had apparently just found her. She
didn't quite know when it happened; one moment
she'd been walking Octavia; the next moment she
looked up to find herself surrounded by the very men
for whom she had been searching.

Or at least, she hoped these were revolutionaries.
Right now they just seemed to be five rather dirty looking Chinese. Better to proceed cautiously, even if they
all wore the red shirts of the Boxers and white pants
now gone gray with dirt.

"Hello, new friends," she said in Shanghainese to the men surrounding her. "My horse has gone lame, and I would appreciate some help. You will be well paid for your efforts." Then she put on her most winning smile. Truthfully, it made her stomach clench whenever she did it. She called it her "empty-headed miss" look. But it was highly effective at times, especially around men.

Unfortunately, it was having no effect on these rather smelly Chinese. Normally such smells wouldn't bother her in the least. English or Chinese, men who labored tended to have an odor. But these men stank even more than usual.

One of them stepped forward, his heavy northern accent making him difficult to understand. "We don't want foreign gold."

That was unusual, she thought with a frown. She thought *everyone* wanted English gold. "I can pay in Chinese coin as well," she said smoothly. "If one of you would please ride to Shanghai, I am sure my maid will be somewhere on the road." When they didn't respond, she gestured to a break in the trees, where she saw at least one thick-limbed Chinese horse. Perhaps there were more. "That is your horse, isn't it?"

"I'd rather you be my horse!" one of them said with a leer.

Joanna paused, positive she could not have understood correctly. But when the largest man spit at her feet in disgust, while the others laughed not so politely, she began to rethink her conclusion. Had she just fallen afoul of brigands?

She grimaced at her own stupidity. Well, of course she had! Obviously these were not honest gentlemen intent on helping her. Unless, of course, she was right with her first guess. These might truly be the revolutionaries.

She smiled again, trying to appear more relaxed than she felt.

"Are you gentlemen Boxers? I have come most specifically to find you. I wish to aid your cause."

One man made a fist, then moved it in a very lewd way. "You seek Boxers?" he asked, and all his companions laughed.

She sighed. "I seek the Fists of Righteous Harmony. But if you men are not part of that *honorable* group, then perhaps I have erred. If you will excuse me." She tried to push past them, but they did not budge. Indeed, a small, wiry man with big fists pushed her roughly backward.

"What do you know of the Fists?" he demanded.

"I know they are wonderful, great men seeking to overthrow an oppressive government to gain freedom for all." She knew it was a risk saying such things aloud, but she had seen something through a gap in one of the men's shirts: a simple amulet with the crude outline of a man's fist. He was definitely a Boxer. Which meant all she needed to do was appeal to his political ideals. "I know, too, that the Righteous Fists have amulets that protect them from bullets. Like that one." She smiled, lifting up her hands in appeal. "I want to become a Red Lantern." She named the women who supported the Boxers.

The men stared at each other, obviously stunned that she knew so much. In truth, she was only repeating what she had overheard in servants' gossip and whispered confidences, but from the looks on their faces, she had guessed correctly.

And then, almost as one, all of them broke out laughing. Loud, mocking guffaws hit her like hard, cold rocks. "No ghost devil can shine red. It would kill them."

She swallowed, annoyed but not surprised by their prejudice. "Let me try. I will show you."

They laughed even harder. Their faces became crueler and more lewd with the sound. "We will try you. I think—"

"I have money," she interrupted, her voice rising in her nervousness. Clearly these were not the people she sought. "Do you wish money? I have only English money on me, but you are welcome to that. If only you will assist me to return to my maid, we will gladly give you much more in Chinese money." She held out her purse.

The biggest man slapped her hand, knocking the little pouch to the ground. "No devil money." He said the words, and apparently he meant them, but one of his friends wasted no time in snatching up the spilled coins.

"Then just what do you want?"

"Dead devils."

She pulled back in confusion. She understood his words, of course. The Chinese had many different names for the white people, and none of them were very complimentary. But why would they want to kill her? "I'm nothing here. A stupid girl, not even married. Killing me won't get you anything but more foreign devils with guns." She shifted, trying to look earnest. "I swear to you: Let me go, and I will convince my father to leave this country." It was a silly bargain, one she knew they wouldn't take. But she was rapidly running out of things to offer. She needed to buy time until she thought of something else.

Except they weren't really interested in the delay. The nearest one—a tall, thin man who smelled of garlic—grabbed her arm, yanking her sideways. She fought immediately, but her other arm wouldn't move; she had been grabbed and someone was yanking on her clothing.

She screamed. Indeed, she put all her breath and power into a sound that might carry all the way to Shanghai. But even that was cut off as she was hit— *hit!*—in the stomach. She gagged, her knees buckling.

Then another blow found her head, reverberating in her skull and fogging her mind over as . . .

As terrible things began to happen.

Then they stopped. They just stopped.

Joanna opened her eyes to see a dark whirlwind hurling her attackers everywhere. It was like a tornado—a dark, swirling force that picked up people and tossed them aside like so much paper.

Except that wasn't possible. God didn't work that way. And yet . . .

Joanna blinked, sliding backward and away in the dirt as she tugged her torn clothing together. What was she seeing?

A man. A Chinese man in dark pants and a white shirt. With a crude cap that flew off as he moved, revealing his bald head. He was fighting her attackers, but in such a way that she could barely comprehend his movements.

She had seen boxing. It was one of the sports her father enjoyed. But this was different. Her rescuer fought with a flat, open hand. And he used his feet. His hands chopped like axes; his kicks were like hammer blows. Next to him, Joanna's attackers looked like children's toys, blown over by the wind.

All was over in a moment. Her attackers scrambled away, running or limping as best they could. Within moments Joanna heard their horses thundering off in the distance. But her eyes remained fixed upon her rescuer. She still had difficulty seeing him as a man rather than a force. Especially as he spun toward her, his face tightened into an anger as dark as his black eyes.

Then he spoke—a low rumble in Mandarin Chinese. But she didn't know that dialect, and so she tried to ask him if he spoke Shanghainese. If he could tell her who he was. An angel? A Chinese magician? A revolutionary? They were ridiculous questions, but it didn't matter anyway as her mouth would not function.

And why was she shaking?

He looked her up and down, his gaze missing nothing. So powerful was his stare that she would have shrunk backward had she the strength. Instead all he did was bring her attention to the ugly scrape on her leg, another on her arm, and a raw gash on her chin. Her favorite russet habit was torn in a dozen places, and her honey-brown hair kept falling across her vision, bringing dirt and dead leaves with it.

She was a mess, and yet she couldn't focus on anything other than the man before her. He was stepping away from her, and she let out a sound—a terribly frightened, almost animalistic sound that she couldn't believe came from her own throat. But it did, though it made little difference to him. He simply kept moving. It was a moment before she realized he was walking to a rolled bundle of cloth on the ground nearby. He apparently just wanted to retrieve his sack, and his hat that lay near it.

She watched him pick up his things, his movements beautifully graceful, his gait a kind of rolling, balanced movement she had seen only on seasoned sailors. And yet his stride was different somehow; he moved in a way wholly his own.

She had questions, but still no voice to ask them. So she remained silent, though her muscles began to ache at the way she was curled into herself. Then, as she watched, the man unrolled a blanket from beneath his heavy pack. It was thin and coarse—a poor man's blanket—and yet she'd never felt better than when he wrapped it around her shoulders.

It smelled of him, she realized, and she inhaled deeply to further hold his power within her lungs. Her conscious mind identified Chinese herbs and the scent of fresh weather, though what exactly that meant, she wasn't sure. But mostly she closed her eyes and felt calm slip into her soul, a quietness she rarely experienced.

"Thank you," she said in Shanghainese. She hadn't even realized she'd spoken until she heard his question, this time in the dialect she understood.

"Are you hurt?"

She didn't want to answer his question. Truthfully, she didn't want think about the bruises or pains from what had just happened. But the memories came anyway, and she began to shudder.

"They are gone now," he said flatly. "I will keep you safe."

She looked up at him, her gaze drawn to his. She saw the dark pupils of his eyes expand and felt pulled forward, straight into him. He was looking at her with total attention—not even blinking as he seemed to press his strength into her. So she wrapped that thought, that feeling, around her tighter than his blanket.

"Promise?" she whispered. "You'll keep me safe?" Her voice was small in a way that embarrassed her. And yet she could not change it because she felt like a child, desperately in need of security. Or a woman who needed her rescuer—her very strong, male rescuer—close beside her.

Then she saw his face relax. For the first time since he'd appeared, he finally seemed human. He crouched down beside her. She watched him, her gaze never leaving his until they were nearly eye-to-eye.

"I *will* keep you safe," he promised. Then he put his hand on her shoulder. It was a simple gesture, but it seemed to surround her in a hot, strange wind so welcome to her chilled American soul.

She breathed deeply again, at last easing her grip on his blanket. "Thank you," she whispered. And a few moments later, she found she was able to speak normally. "I'm not hurt," she said firmly, as much to reassure herself as to communicate with him. "They didn't have time . . . You came before . . ." She swallowed, searching for the right words, but he stopped her.

"I understand." Then she felt his body shift as he looked around. "Is that your horse?"

Joanna looked in the direction he indicated, and she saw Octavia calmly sniffing the dead grass. The mare stood with her injured leg tilted up, and once again Joanna felt the bite of guilt. This one day's impetuousness had hurt her mare, endangered herself, and involved this man in a terrible fight.

"I'm so sorry," she whispered as she looked at her rescuer. "I've hurt her and . . ." She swallowed, seeing a swelling bruise on the man's jaw. "And you, too." She struggled to stand, determined not to cause any more problems.

He helped her up, but when she tried to give him back his blanket, the man simply shook his head. "You are not warm enough yet," he said. And only then, as he stood beside her, did she hear the undercurrent of fury in his voice. It was a low, steady anger that had been there from the very beginning.

"Your jaw . . ." she began, but her words trailed away when she didn't know what to say.

He frowned, touching his cheek as if only now realizing he'd been struck. "I will see to your horse." He walked quickly, speaking gently to Octavia in Chinese. Indeed, his words seemed to hold more warmth for the animal than they had for her.

Joanna abruptly stopped herself. What was she thinking? She couldn't possibly be jealous of her horse. Just because her rescuer had shifted his attention from her to Octavia? It was ridiculous, and yet honesty forced her to admit it was true. She wanted this man's attention firmly and completely on her. And what a spoiled creature that made her! After all, she was fine. Octavia was hurt.

And so Joanna went on her best behavior as she walked to her mare's side.

Octavia was often skittish, so Joanna was surprised when the horse didn't even blink as her rescuer began stroking her neck. He spoke more Chinese, his words low and too fast for Joanna to understand. But apparently Octavia did. The mare snorted once, then remained still as the man ran his hands across her injured shoulder, down her leg, then all the way to her hoof. His murmuring grew silent as he moved, and Joanna stepped back to give him more room.

She didn't think he had much experience with horses. His touch seemed hesitant and slow, not at all like the sure movements of the grooms her father employed. But Octavia seemed to like this man, even closing her eyes to half drowse as her twitching skin steadied and stilled.

There was nothing he could do to help Octavia; Joanna already knew that rest and poultices were the mare's best hope. She began to say so, but the man had such an air of attention about him that she did not want to break his concentration. So she waited in silence, watching and trying not to feel jealous as he lavished the mare with long, soothing strokes of his hand.

Joanna stared at the man's dusty bald head, her brain finally working enough to understand that he must be a monk. Monks were the only ones in China who were allowed to shave off their long queues symbolic of obedience to the Qin Empire.

She frowned. She didn't know of a monastery nearby. But then she saw that his head wasn't wholly bald. What she had initially believed to be dirt was actually the beginnings of hair growth, darkening his head with a soft fuzz. He must be traveling. That was the only reason new hair would be allowed.

She extended her hand, having the most powerful urge to touch the man's head, to feel the new hair. Or did she simply want to touch him? To reconnect with this most amazing man. Whatever the case, she stopped herself, curling her hands into fists to prevent so rude a gesture.

Then, suddenly, he was done.

He had been holding up Octavia's hoof, but now he set it carefully back on the ground. The horse shifted immediately, settling her weight upon the leg and snorting something that sounded like approval. Joanna stared, unable to do more than state the obvious.

"She's better!"

"Her qi is strong. She is a good horse." Then the man stood, resting his hand on Octavia's shoulder in much the same way he had touched Joanna a few moments before.

Joanna protested, "But she was hurt. Badly. I thought . . . I feared that my father—"

"She will heal." The man glared at her. "But you should be whipped."

Joanna reared back, shocked. It didn't matter that she'd thought the same thing just a moment before; he had no right to speak that way to her. "How dare you!" she hissed.

His eyes widened. Apparently no woman had ever spoken in such a way to him, either. But his surprise faded almost before she understood his reaction. Abruptly he was looming over her, his entire body taut with fury. "I dare," he snarled, "because she is a living creature of value. She is not a toy or a pet. And women need to be taught how to treat such beings before they destroy them with their stupidity."

"I know how to handle my horse!" Joanna snapped, more irritated with herself than with him. He stood barely an inch taller than her; his clothing marked him as one of the wretched poor, and yet she felt intimidated down to the very pit of her stomach. Intimidated enough that she was fighting back with every fiber of her being, despite the fact that she already knew she had acted irresponsibly.

So she turned her back on him. She lifted his blanket off her shoulders, folding it carefully as she spoke.

"Thank you for your assistance. If you provide me with your name and direction, I shall see that you are well compensated for your assistance."

"Give me your horse."

Her head shot up, his blanket tumbling awkwardly from her grip. "I beg your pardon?"

He stood with his legs spread, his arms folded across his large chest. "You wish to repay me. I wish for your mistreated horse."

Her gaze shot to her mare, who stood quietly at attention, not even eating the grass but waiting patiently, as if ready to be handed over. Joanna turned back to the man. "Octavia is not mistreated!" she snapped.

"If that were so, then she would not be lame."

"She is not lame!" Indeed, right now Octavia looked as if she could even bear a rider. Joanna wouldn't risk it, but the horse truly looked as hale as ever.

The man was apparently unswayed. "You owe me a debt. You said so yourself. I wish your horse. Nothing could be simpler."

"Nothing could be more ridiculous," she snapped. "You can't even feed and clothe yourself. You cannot manage a horse as well." And with those words, she picked up the man's blanket, awkwardly tossing it at him. He caught it midflight, quickly refolding it into a tight, smooth roll.

Then he shrugged. "I will see that she gains a good home."

"She has a good home now," Joanna retorted, finally gaining enough fury to gather the reins. She meant to pass beyond him, to move as fast as the mare could tolerate. But the man stopped her with a single outstretched hand. He didn't touch her, but she found herself unable to physically challenge him.

"There are Boxers nearby. Do you wish to be unprotected again?"

Her entire body clenched at his words, and her spine seemed to slick over with ice.

"Do you?" he pressed.

"Then you are not . . ." She swallowed. "You are not one of the Fists of Righteous Harmony?"

He straightened as if slapped. "I am a loyal Qin!"

"Of course, of course," she soothed. "But those men. They couldn't be . . ." Her voice trailed away. They couldn't possibly be the revolutionaries. Not when they'd acted no more honorably than a bunch of dirty highwaymen.

"They were," he said flatly. "And you are a fool to have thought differently."

She nodded, too sick at heart to argue. So much for her great vision of bringing American freedom to struggling Chinese. She certainly couldn't risk contacting those men again. The very thought left her as shaken and vulnerable as when he'd first found her. The only thing she could do to steady herself was to continue talking—arguing—with this man. If she kept talking, perhaps she wouldn't melt into a puddle of terror.

"Please, sir," she said as evenly as possible. "Come to my home. See that our horses are well cared for."

He didn't answer at first, and she found herself twisting uncomfortably as she waited. She did not want to be alone on this road. She did not wish to be left unprotected again. And despite his arrogant behavior, she had the strangest urge to stay near him, to learn more about him, to . . . She started, appalled at her thoughts. She most certainly didn't want to do *that* with him. But she did. Most powerfully so, it seemed.

Thankfully, he chose that moment to speak, cutting off her startling realization. "I will come," he said flatly. "But only to see that you are properly whipped."

Some people see only the surface of things, and with just a little knowledge they think they understand it all. It is the wise person who recognizes his ignorance, and it is the person who doesn't know he is ignorant that is the real fool.

—*Lao Tzu*

Chapter Two

Zou Tun cursed himself with every step he took toward Shanghai. Not even two weeks outside of the monastery and he had already lost his center, broken his vow. It was a simple vow, one most men kept without thinking. And yet for him, apparently he could not remain at peace for two weeks. Not even in the center of his mind, that place where all was quiet, where all made sense.

And he'd lost his peace because of a spoiled ghost woman.

He glared sideways at her, hating what he saw. He had never seen a female devil before. His experience with whites was limited to three Englishmen viewed from a distance in Peking. And, of course, all the stories of their atrocities.

But the woman beside him did not look like she ate children. Her teeth did not seem especially sharp, nor did her eyes shoot fire. And if she were truly very powerful, surely she would have defended herself from the

20

Fists. She had not. Indeed, she seemed no more than a weak and stupid rich woman.

He should have left her to her fate. He had vowed to not raise a hand in violence again. And yet he had reacted without thought, leaping to the ghost woman's aid without realizing the cost. And now he was saddled with her. She had attached herself to him as all ghosts did, feeding off his energy.

He ground his teeth together, the bruise on his jaw sending a shooting pain through the left side of his head—the side closest to her. *Let her feed on that,* he thought with smug anger.

Then he sighed, knowing he was being foolish. He had touched this woman, held her arm, and seen the horse she rode. She was solid flesh. And though she appeared strange, she was no more a ghost than he was. She was simply an uncivilized barbarian with a poor education.

He did, however, understand where an ignorant peasant could get the wrong idea. Walking this close to her, he noticed a kind of luminescence about her skin, a glow that could suggest the supernatural.

But there was no otherworldly coldness about her that he could detect. Quite the contrary. In her orange fabric, she seemed like a living flame, always moving, always shifting as she trudged beside him. In fact, even though she was clearly angry with him, she struggled to remain silent. Twice now she had opened her mouth to talk, then snapped it shut as she changed her mind. How long would her control last? Not long, he guessed. She was a barbarian after all, and a spoiled one at that.

She lasted longer than he expected, and in the end she said something totally unexpected. She apologized.

"I have been terribly rude," she began, her voice

even and low. "I have yelled and insulted you, and you have merely been trying to help. I know I acted rashly in coming out this far today." She sighed. "I fear I was in a bit of a temper. And I thought I could help—" She shook her head, cutting off what she was going to say. "In any event, it's possible that I would . . . if I were you . . . that I might also conclude—incorrectly—that I *usually* act this way. It's possible I might think that. If I were meeting me for the first time."

It took him a while to sort through her words, especially since she obviously believed he was in the wrong. Still, she appeared so earnest that he might have accepted her statement at face value. Of course, she didn't know he had been raised on the politics of the Peking court, where such ruses were commonplace.

So he turned, bowing slightly and appearing to accept her apology. Then, with a sweet smile, he straightened. "You spoke very nicely," he lied. "But you will still be whipped."

She flinched and he almost laughed. Next would come the tears and pleas, perhaps even a sly offer of various favors. Women would do anything just to get out of a richly deserved punishment. It was all very tedious.

Except this ghost woman did none of those things. Instead, when she'd recovered from her shock, she burst into laughter. "It must be a strange monastery indeed that teaches a monk that he can order a woman whipped."

Zou Tun frowned, thrown. Monastery or not, any man could inform another that his woman had endangered his horses. Surely even barbarians understood that. "You have done wrong," he said by way of explanation. "I will tell your owner such and you will be punished. And no amount of tears or begging will sway me."

Again her humor startled him, filling the road with a bright laughter. "I assure you, sir, I have no owner. And I will not be whipped. Indeed, I am growing quite anxious to introduce you to my father so that you may try to instruct him." Her expression sobered and her voice dropped. "No one tells my father what to do. Not with his buildings, his horses, or most especially"—she turned and pinned Zou Tun with a hard stare—"his daughter."

Zou Tun shifted, feeling unsure of himself when addressing barbarian customs. "It is a father's duty to discipline his daughter. How else will she learn appropriate behavior?"

The woman nodded, clearly agreeing. "Exactly. It is my father's job." She paused for effect. "Not yours." Then she waved her hand in his direction. "But please, don't let me stop you from trying. In fact, I am most anxious to see what his reaction will be. If nothing else, you will certainly gain his attention."

Zou Tun had no response. The woman's voice indicated that there was more to her words, but he did not understand her meaning. Instead he simply shook his head, speaking his thoughts aloud. "You do not behave as a woman ought."

She didn't answer beyond a shrug. And then, at last, he understood the problem. She was a barbarian, after all. She had not been properly instructed. So he decided to moderate his attitude. In truth, it would be a sadness to mar her beauty with the lash.

"Do not worry. I will advise your father to hire a tutor for you. You speak Chinese well enough. Your instructor will read you books on proper female deportment. It will be all you require to act appropriately in civilized society."

"It apparently didn't work for you!" she snapped.

23

Then she switched to her barbarian language, her words rolling like stones from her lips in a most unladylike fashion. All Zou Tun could do was shake his head in dismay.

"I have studied all the classics," he said when she finally finished her strange muttering. "It took many years." Then, when he saw her staring strangely at him, he hastened to reassure her: "You need not worry about such a thing. The books for women are simple and will not take long if you apply yourself."

She didn't respond, and he thought that perhaps she had calmed enough to heed his suggestion. He smiled placatingly.

"Truly," he said, "if you wish to live in Shanghai, you must learn these things."

"I have learned these things," she said slowly. "I have heard of your Confucius and have found him to be a highly intelligent man. And I have already read his instructions for women." She waved her hand, dismissing the sum total of a Chinese woman's education. "What I wish to know, though, is how a man of your . . ." She hesitated for a moment, then simply shrugged before continuing. "How a man of your low means could have obtained a classical education."

Too late he realized he was dressed in his simple monastic attire, filthy now from his many days of travel. Then, before he could think of a suitable answer, she pressed him further.

"And I have not forgotten your fighting either." Her voice shook slightly as she spoke, but it quickly steadied as she continued to study him. "You did not learn that in a rice paddy." She paused another long moment, and Zou Tun began to feel his skin prickle. She was thinking much too hard. "You have an arrogance unlike anyone I have ever met."

Zou Tun felt his breath freeze in his throat. It could

not be possible. She was a barbarian and a woman. She could not possibly know.

"You are not a common laborer, despite your attire. And you are Chinese. You spoke in the Peking dialect, didn't you?" She didn't wait for an answer. Instead, her eyes widened as her mouth split into a grin. "You are from the imperial court! My God, you are a real Mandarin, aren't you?"

He stared at her, shock robbing him of voice and sanity. She was a woman—a barbarian woman—and she had already guessed what no man had suspected for two years. "You are being fanciful, woman," he snapped. "I am a simple monk."

She clapped her hands together and released a crow of delight. "I knew it! I knew you were lying." Then she winked at him. "I'll give you a hint, Mandarin. The moment you tell a woman she's being silly is the very moment you've revealed your secret."

"There is no secret," he growled, desperately trying to regain some control. "Monks speak only with honesty."

"Ah," she said with a triumphant laugh, "but you're not a real monk, are you? You're a Mandarin disguised as a monk."

His breath stopped altogether, her words echoing hollowly inside him, for she had indeed spoken the truth. He was not a real monk. And he never would be, though he had tried desperately for the last three years to become one.

He looked away from her shining amber eyes, stepping from her with as much dignity as he could muster. His next actions would prove he was no monk more effectively than anything he had ever done. But even so, he tried to avoid his fate; he stepped away from her.

"You know nothing, woman. Do not reveal your ignorance by speaking further." *Indeed,* he silently prayed, *do not say anything more because such knowledge will get us both killed.* A family such as his had too many enemies. If his father's men didn't find him and drag him home, his enemies would happily assassinate him. Both would kill whomever happened to be with him at the time.

"Tell me what your name is," she urged, giddy from her secret knowledge. "No, wait, you'd only lie. Let me guess. You're not a simple blue bannerman. Or even red, yellow, or white. Your manner is much too elevated for such low ranks. You can't be a true official. Their entire power is in their title. Not a one of them would travel in secret like you are. They are too frightened of losing their position to even attempt the ruse."

"Not if there were some secret task. A mission so important . . ." His suggestion was ridiculous, he knew. Everything she'd said so far was absolutely correct, but he was searching for the last grain of rice in a cleared field. Anything that would keep him from what he had to do.

She was relentless, not realizing that every word doomed her. "Secret missions are often dangerous. Middle-ranking officials don't do dangerous things. They send others to do them." She narrowed her eyes. "But your education is a problem. No lowborn courier on a dangerous, secret mission would have read all the classics. You have. You're someone who has no fear of losing his rank, someone so high up in the political hierarchy that only the emperor himself could knock him down. But you're not an old, established general. You're young, which means . . ." Her eyes widened and he knew she had ferreted out the truth. "You're a prince. You have to be. You're one of the heirs to the—"

He reacted without thought, with reflexes honed by

years of study. He chopped her throat, a single blow that dropped her to the ground like deadwood. And as she lay sprawled at his feet, he heard her begin to gasp. He heard her wheezing horror in every struggling inhalation, knew her terror as she began to scramble backward, away from him, dragging her horse with her as if he could allow her to escape.

And all the while he stared at her, his own knees trembling as he knew the truth. He had failed. He was a failure. Like a black hole deep within him, the knowledge sucked his strength away as surely as he had just taken her breath. But he'd had no choice.

She could not be allowed to speak her knowledge. He could not let her tell anyone of what she knew. Women gossiped. Women told secrets, for what else did they have to occupy their time? Nothing. And even a barbarian woman's words could reach the emperor's ears. Or worse yet, her chatter could grab the attention of one of his enemies. There simply weren't that many missing princes.

So Zou Tun had to silence this foolish ghost devil. He had to kill her.

And yet, he knew as he watched her lose consciousness that he had not killed her. He should have. He still could. But something in him had softened his blow. Some weakness inside of him had averted his killing stroke.

She could not speak. Indeed, she might never make a sound again. But she would not die for all that her swollen throat cut off her breath. So long as she did not struggle too hard, so long as she remained still, in dreamless sleep, she would survive.

As would he.

Unless, of course, someone else discovered what she knew.

But now he stood in the middle of the road to Shanghai, a rich barbarian's horse beside him, and an unconscious, unkempt barbarian woman at his feet. This was not the way to remain inconspicuous.

But how to hide her and still perform his task?

He ought to simply kill her and her horse. Instead, he . . . he would wrap her in his blanket and carefully lay her across her mare, he decided. Fortunately the horse was still strong enough to carry her weight, though the animal's gait would be a little uneven. A good thing, because that helped disguise the creature. Add a misshapen lump on top, plus his tattered blankets, and with Heaven's blessing, no one would notice the excellent creature beneath.

The one thing he could not disguise was her saddle or clothing. She would have to be stripped of both. Except he had no wish to remove any of her clothing. Indeed, he had no wish to touch this foreign devil at all. Not because she appeared too hideous to him, but because she was so very different.

Zou Tun could strip a Chinese woman naked without even blinking. Breasts, legs, face—all were merely mounds of flesh, no more interesting than a tree or a sun-warmed rock. He had, after all, seen many, many of them, and would again. He was one of the potential heirs to the imperial throne.

But what about foreign breasts? White-woman legs? How would they be shaped? How would they smell, taste, and feel? He had no time to discover the answers, and yet he found himself dangerously interested. He would strip her without lingering, he decided. Without thinking. Without having the sight seared upon his much too distractable mind.

Not possible.

She was lying on her back, her face turned to the midmorning sun. He had to work quickly; he could not guarantee privacy for long. So he began unfastening the buttons that marched down the front of her garb. From neck to belly, he tried to unbind her clothing. Except his fingers were clumsy, his gaze often straying to the dark crescents of her eyelashes. They were dark brown curves, full and round, not angled into a sharp point like Chinese women preferred. Her breasts were also full and round, Zon Tun saw. They pushed upward despite her position on her back.

He pressed his hand flat upon her chest, relieved to feel the steady beat of her pulse and the regular rise and fall of her breath. She was a strong woman, already healing despite the damage he had inflicted.

He reached behind her, lifting her up to pull the dress off her shoulders. She was heavier than he expected, solid in a way that he found pleasing. This was not a woman who would break easily under any kind of pressure. Neither her body nor her mind would break, for hadn't she withstood an attack by members of the Fists of Righteous Harmony? She had withstood it and still maintained the intelligence to divine his secret. He had to admire such strength of character, even when it came in the most unlikely of places.

She wore a white shirt beneath her heavy riding clothes, and a strange binding contraption. He pulled the latter two garments apart as quickly as he could, only to reveal a soft cotton fabric that stuck to her skin, revealing the dark circle of her right nipple. The left nipple was hidden from his view by her dress, so he quickly stripped away all her unnecessary covering. Yes, both her nipples were darker than the surrounding flesh, both were pleasingly pointed and begging to be touched.

He stroked his hands across them, luxuriating in her shirt's soft fabric, the smooth slope of the rising mounds. He was most interested in her breasts. Would they be insubstantial in the way of ghosts? Or have the hard, shell-like covering of a devil?

Neither, he discovered as he slipped his hand beneath the soft cotton. Her breasts were warm and giving, and the nipples puckered beneath his touch. The only difference from a Chinese woman's was that these breasts were larger, fuller. Their weight was especially pleasing, and they were solid and large in his hand.

He liked these foreign breasts.

He abruptly stilled. What was he doing? Lingering over a foreign woman's teats? A helpless woman? He deliberately made his thoughts crude to shock himself out of his curiosity. This woman was repulsive, he lied to himself. He should be rushing through this task as quickly as possible.

And so he did. He pulled off her gown only to find ruffled white pants beneath. Female silliness—and yet he enjoyed the sight. He could not see that well, however, and indeed, he forced himself not to look too closely. But he saw enough. A dark triangle of curls, darker than the hair on her head. Full hips that would be excellent for childbearing. And long, muscular legs that ended in well-formed feet.

Very nicely formed feet, he realized. Not the deformed white lotuses Chinese women preferred, nor the heavier, darker feet of the Manchurian women of his own race, but pinkish white in color—as befit her rosy skin—and with tiny toes and a high arch.

Here, once again, he had to stop himself from being ridiculous. What did he care about a foreign devil's feet? He finished his task, stripping her of all but her white underclothes before quickly wrapping her in his blanket. Fortunately, with the removal of her strange binding device, her breathing became strong and steady.

He set her carefully atop the mare, which he darkened with mud and covered with his tattered bedroll. It caused a physical ache in his heart to blunt the creature's tail, but he could not allow the horse to seem well manicured in any way.

After tossing the woman's clothing and saddle to the side of the road, he led her and her mare across the country, deciding to enter Shanghai via a different route—one that wouldn't hold servants looking for a lost foreign girl.

His plan worked well. No guard questioned him, especially after he dropped a couple of coins into each man's hand. Better yet, the ghost girl roused long enough for Zou Tun to force a sleeping potion on her. She had not the strength to struggle, and she fell back and lay like the heavy sack of goods she was meant to appear.

Yes, all went perfectly. It was easy enough to hand the woman over to the head servant of the famous Tigress Shi Po. Easy enough, as well, to convince Shi Po's first boy that this was a barbarian seeker who wished to study in secret with the greatest Tigress in China. A few more coins and the young barbarian woman was quietly secreted away. By the time she regained breath and voice enough to communicate, he would be long gone. And at that point, any whisperings of the truth—hoarse or otherwise—would cause him no damage. With luck, they would assume she had changed her mind about studying and was making up tales to cover her impetuous actions. Weren't the white devils all liars? And why would a Manchurian prince abduct a white woman just to hand her over to a Tigress? It made no sense, and so the girl would likely keep silent for fear of laughter. Especially if she was returned home with no more damage than a bruised throat.

It was a feeble hope at best, but the only thing he could contrive at the moment. All that remained was for Zou Tun to deliver his message and the scrolls to Shi Po. Then he would return to Peking and to his part in the ruling of China.

He settled himself to stillness in the Tigress's waiting hall. But as the day wore on and his patience wore thin, his spirit became ever sicker. Irritation ran like poison through his veins, and he paced like a caged tiger in the tiny chamber. But not because Shi Po absented herself. And not because a barbarian woman had delayed his plans. Other thoughts intruded upon his solitude, and even a monk's peaceful contemplation yielded nothing but hot fury blowing in and out of his mouth.

It was time to return to Peking. He had this one last task to perform, and then he would return to his father's house. He would take off his monk's robes and kiss his mother's cheek. He would accept the tasks demanded of him by the emperor and would serve in a way that brought honor to his family name. He would do what was required of him by law and by honor. And he would think no more of full white breasts or blood-stained scrolls. He would not hear the screams of his brethren nor the chattering of a barbarian woman with uncanny intelligence. And he would not—ever—allow himself to be distracted from his life path.

Yes, he would bring honor to his father and his family, as was his duty. After fulfilling this last promise to Abbot Tseng, he would return to Peking no matter how much his heart sank at the thought.

He composed himself once again to await the Tigress Shi Po. Another hour passed. And then another hour. Servants brought him tea, and the sun dipped low in the sky. Soon he began to pace again, and to curse and wrestle with his thoughts more forcefully than any man against any tiger, male or female. And still he found no relief. No way to discharge his task. No way to call for the mistress of the house, a woman without the intelligence to understand that it was not her place to keep a man waiting—even one dressed as humbly as he.

At last, Shi Po's husband appeared. The man—Mr. Tan Kui Yu—bowed deeply before Zou Tun, his large frame clumsy and yet no less earnest as he apologized for the delay. He had not been informed a guest waited.

Zou Tun responded as politeness dictated, indicating that there had been no insult. Both men knew they awaited the Tigress Shi Po, and once again, Zou Tun ruminated on the folly of any religion conferring its highest honor upon a woman.

"She studies night and day now," Mr. Tan murmured, and Zou Tun was surprised to hear a note of worry in his voice. Then the man frowned and scanned him from head to toe. "If you come to learn, I fear you will be disappointed. She will not teach another. Her own immortality consumes her now." Was there also a note of censure in the man's voice?

"I fear I have been unclear, Mr. Tan," responded Zou Tun with barely concealed impatience. "I have brought a gift to the Tan family." He hesitated only a moment. During all his pacing, he had not thought to plan for this. It was an evil way to bring such news to a family, disguising it as a gift. But such was the only way to avoid unwanted imperial notice.

The Tigress religion was a bizarre, relatively harmless offshoot of the true path, though many in China believed it to be a deviation more perverse. And so Zou Tun steeled his emotions to silence as he drew a set of scrolls from his bag. The weight of the parchment felt triple what it should, but there was no help now for that. He reverently set the heavy scrolls before him on a low table. That such sacred texts should go to a bizarre religious sect bothered him. But he had promised the dying abbot that he would deliver these scrolls to the man's sister, and so he would do, even if the woman was leader of a strange cult. Besides, he thought with a shrug, better the texts remain in Tigress Shi Po's hands than in the Emperor's court.

"This comes from far north. From your wife's brother, I believe."

Mr. Tan's eyes widened as he saw the dark stains marring the parchment. Both men recognized blood. Mr. Tan's gaze landed heavily upon Zou Tun.

"You bring evil tidings into my home," he said softly. To his credit there was no condemnation in his voice, merely sadness. Then he turned slowly, as if with an old man's aches. He used a muted hammer to strike a small gong. A liveried servant appeared, bowing almost to the floor.

"Bring your mistress here," Mr. Tan said. "Tell her . . ." His voice trailed away as he gazed at Zou Tun's face. Specifically, at his long, straight, *Manchurian* nose. "Tell her we accept an imperial gift."

The servant's eyes widened in shock, and Zou Tun again sighed. Twice now in one day someone had seen through his disguise. Twice now someone had looked past the dirt and his clothing to see what none other had guessed.

"I am merely a poor monk," he said in a low, urgent voice.

Mr. Tan bowed deeply to him. "Of course. Please allow me to call for some fresh tea."

And in this way Zou Tun's protests were silenced, and the great Tigress Shi Po was summoned.

In China, ladies did not often appear before men. But in this household—when the lady led an entire religion—some customs had to be relaxed. And so the two men waited, speaking little before a side door opened and a willowy form appeared behind an elaborately carved divider. It was a "modesty screen," and Zou Tun knew that the great Tigress stood on the other side.

Mr. Tan wasted no time. He turned to Zou Tun. "Please tell me what has brought such a"—he swallowed—"a rare gift to the Tan family."

"I am the last of the students of Abbot Tseng Rui Po." Zou Tun hesitated, unwilling to go on, but he knew he owed it to his former mentor to say the rest without flinching. "The emperor discovered that the Shiyu monastery harbored and trained evil revolutionaries from the White Lotus Society."

Behind the divider, the Tigress Shi Po gasped in horror. In these troubled times, the emperor did not tolerate rebellion of any kind.

"The soldiers came at night," Zou Tun continued, his blood pounding as he struggled for control. "Abbot Tseng Rui Po died with these cradled in his arms. He asked me to bring them to you."

Mr. Tan reached out but did not actually touch the the stained yellow scrolls. "How did you come to survive?"

It was a natural question, and one that Zou Tun expected. Still, it was difficult to answer, and to his shame his voice trembled as he spoke. "I am often troubled at night. I left the monastery to visit a barren place where I tried to meditate. It is a secluded grotto, hidden from view, and sound comes strangely to it. By the time I understood what I heard, it was too late. I could not stop it. Nor could I save any of my brethren."

He had tried, though. He had rushed nearly to his own death, and all to no avail. The last of his fellow students were executed without explanation or mercy. And he could do nothing but watch. And hide.

"After the soldiers left, I found the abbot and these scrolls. He told me his sister's name, asking me to . . ." Zou Tun paused, rephrasing his words to maintain appearances. After all, no woman could hold power. Such was unnatural. And so he could not suggest that Mr. Tan's wife was so bizarre a creature.

"The abbot said his sister knew the great leader of a secret religious sect—Shi Po. To honor my teacher's last request, I have taken the burden of delivering these texts to this great leader."

Mr. Tan simply shook his head. "I know nothing of these things, but perhaps my wife can assist."

It was an obvious lie, but a necessary one. Zou Tun nodded, his task complete. But before he could stand, the unheard-of occurred. Before he could do more than press his hands to his knees to rise, the wife of the house emerged from behind her screen.

She was a small woman with an imposing presence. Her hair was pressed in the Manchurian style: wrapped around a slim board that lay flat upon her head. Fresh flowers adorned the board, chrysanthemum and lotus, each costing a fortune at this time of year. Pearls dripped from her ears, and a single red dot graced her lower lip. Though dressed in the height of female fashion, to Zou Tun's mind Shi Po appeared more masculine dragon than feminine tigress, with a hardened skin rather than a soft, womanly heart.

And yet he could not deny her beauty. Indeed, she was as youthful as the morning dew and as magnificent as the evening sunset.

He bowed without thought, acknowledging her as he would his own abbot.

"You were with my brother when he died?" she asked. Her voice was soft, a sensuous whisper that skated across his skin. And yet her words brought a chill rather than the warmth they should have.

"I could not save him," he replied, his gaze seeking the floor in shame. The soldiers believed the abbot a leader of insurgents so did not grant him a quick, easy death. Instead, the great man was left to die slowly— painfully—choking on his own fluids.

"You could have taken these scrolls," she continued. "Set up your own school. That is the normal way of such things, is it not?"

It was. But he could not. "I am . . . not worthy." He was also expected back in Peking, though he was delaying his return as long as possible.

Then she stunned him by touching him. She reached out and lifted his chin with long nails that scratched. His gaze flew to hers, and he remained frozen in shock at her unwomanly behavior. And yet, how many times had Abbot Tseng done just this? How many times had he scrutinized Zou Tun and found him wanting?

Many times. And once more such was done by his sister. After a long, hard breath, Shi Po released Zou Tun's chin, turning away in disgust. "No," she spoke with angry disdain, "you are *not* worthy."

Zou Tun bristled. He was a Manchurian prince, one of the most likely heirs to the Dragon throne. How dare a woman pronounce him unworthy of anything? She was unworthy of tying his boots. . . .

His thoughts spun away into silence. Zou Tun recognized the childish rantings of pride. For all that this Tigress was a woman, she had the power and strength of her brother, the abbot and mentor Zou Tun had cherished. Her disdain was not to be taken lightly.

But before he could phrase a question, the Tigress spoke again, her voice clipped and hard. "Do you wish to become worthy?"

Zou Tun froze, his heart trembling inside his chest. He could not deny the longing her words produced. To study the sacred texts. To continue his quest for enlightenment, even immortality. Such was a temptation that tormented him night and day.

But he was a Manchurian prince. Such things were denied him at a time when China was threatened by enemies within and beyond her borders. Zou Tun could not indulge fantasies. No more than a woman could choose her own fate.

And yet, looking at Shi Po as she stood before him, he could well imagine that anything was possible. That a woman could lead a religion. And that he, a lost Manchurian prince, could find peace.

But it was not possible, and so he shook his head. "I have performed my duty to my teacher . . ." he began.

"Your duty is to learn, and yet you turn away like a frightened child." She stepped close to him, her head bowed in the traditional position of a respectful, subordinate woman. But there was nothing submissive in her attitude. Indeed, because he was still seated, she was staring down at him as if he were a weevil in a rice bowl.

Slowly he stood, frustration bleeding into his voice. "Do you seek to instruct me, woman?"

"I seek to enlighten you, monk." Then she shook her head, stepping away from him as she would a muddy path. "I cannot discharge your task, monk. I know nothing of this Tigress Shi Po."

Zou Tun jerked forward, his hands clenching into fists. If she would not accept the scrolls, honor demanded that he continue to search for the Tigress who was right here. Who must accept the scroll in order for his task to be complete.

With effort, he relaxed and controlled his temper. "If you do not assist me," he pressed, "I cannot even discharge my task. I will be dishonored."

She simply shrugged, not bothering to look at him. Then she turned, her eyes narrowing as she pinned him with her regard. "You have learned the yang fire from my brother. Who will teach you of the yin?"

Yin. He knew she referred to the female power, the essence of femininity that must be balanced in every soul—man's or woman's—before one could reach enlightenment. Could it be that she had already seen his lack, understood why his training had faltered?

Impossible. This was a woman. And yet, who better than a woman to see a deficiency of yin?

"I must discharge my task," he muttered, more to himself than anyone else. In truth, there was no reason for his urgency. His father would quickly point out that honor demanded he return home, not remain with some woman in unnatural study of obscene rituals—for wasn't that the essence of this Tigress religion?

He didn't know. And yet, could he refuse such an opportunity—to study with a woman who had trained two immortals? For that was what the abbott had said: His sister, the Tigress Shi Po, had trained two immortals who had since departed for their heavenly realm. Who better to lead Zou Tun on the path to immortality than one who had already taught others? Even if she was a woman.

Shi Po moved to Zou Tun's side, her voice a whisper. "Do you wish to learn, monk?"

"Yes." He answered with the truth because that was how one always answered a teacher.

"Then you must stay."

He trembled; he could not help it. Imperial pressure to return was very great. "How long?" he whispered.

He knew better than to ask; enlightenment came when it would, when the heart and mind were ready. But mostly enlightenment came when one opened one's eyes to the truth. And even the great Tigress Shi Po could not say when a man would be ready to do that. Her answer was as predictable as it was surprising:

"As long as your stamina holds out."

He nodded, puzzling through the different meanings of her words. He had learned a little of the Tigress religion from his abbot. Where the Shaolin used celibacy and strict physical disciplines to smooth the path to immortality, the Tigresses used sexuality in a riotous, indulgent chaotic quest for the divine. Though how such a thing was possible, he could not fathom. He would learn, he supposed.

The thought drew a predictable response from him: His dragon, the organ between his legs, poked up its head.

Before joining the Shiyu monastery, he had entered into the bedroom battleground with relish. The idea of doing so again—and in the name of enlightenment—woke the lascivious side of his nature.

"One more thing," added Shi Po as she stepped back behind her screen. "You have brought a white barbarian to learn from me. *She* will be your partner."

Zou Tun's eyes shot up, anger whipping through him. "Do you seek to shame me?" he snarled.

To the side, Mr. Tan reacted for the first time since his wife's entrance. He growled low in his throat, his eyes narrowing significantly. But there was no other response, for Shi Po had disappeared behind her screen.

Mr. Tan's demeanor changed and he began to apologize, stammering as he tried to explain. "I am sure, sir, that she did not . . . I mean, she cannot know . . . She does not expect—"

"Cease," Zou Tun said, his voice low and heavy. "She can and does." Then, when the man obviously did not understand, he explained, "She wishes to test me, Mr. Tan. If I am a true seeker, I will take what knowledge I can—even from a white barbarian."

Mr. Tan nodded, albeit slowly and with a severe frown. Zou Tun could not tell if the man understood the rest of Shi Po's intent, the oldest and most powerful of court practices: blackmail.

No, the Tigress religion was not approved by the imperial court. If Zou Tun revealed the nature of Shi Po's practice, if he suggested it was immoral in any way or brought unwanted imperial attention to the Tan household, Shi Po would reveal that he had studied with her. And not only that he had studied with her, but that he had performed strange rites with a ghost barbarian as well.

Practicing with a Chinese woman might be forgiven, especially as he was a Manchurian prince. But not even the emperor himself could ignore relations with a barbarian woman. If revealed, Zou Tun would be killed—if he was lucky. Other, more gruesome possibilities existed, especially if he was left alive as an example to others.

His path was set. Especially since his bringing the white woman here was already enough to damn him. Shi Po could see him killed for that alone. So, honor and enlightenment aside, Zou Tun would study with the barbarian woman. It was that, or be revealed as a deviant traitor and die.

1 February, 1896
Dearest Kang Zou—
New Year's has come and gone, and you have not returned home. No celebration could lighten my spirit without your presence. Worse still, Father searches diligently for my bridegroom, but he

delays in the hope that you can assist him. Pray, brother, can you not cease your studies for the short time it would take to visit us?

Your devoted sister,
Wen Ji

Decoded translation:

Son—

Time is slipping away and I grow impatient. Delays are costly, and I am anxious to take your report to the emperor. Can you give me an answer soon?

Your father,
General Kang

10 February, 1896
My sweet sister, Wen Ji—

The air warms, and I have begun to think of your garden. The mountain air is still cold, but I sense the coming spring. It teases me, just out of reach, and yesterday I pricked my finger on a thorn. Still, I know there will be fruit soon. And flowers. And much rejoicing. But not yet.

As for the matter of your bridegroom, Father has always been most intelligent in his choices. Trust him, my sister. You will be well married soon enough.

Your diligent brother,
Kang Zou

Decoded translation:

Dearest Father—

I have not forgotten my duties to you. I am nearing the conspirators, but they are suspicious and dangerous. I cannot move too quickly. As for our family fortunes, my father, you have always been most canny. Surely there is another path to the emperor's favor? All cannot depend exclusively on me.

Your diligent son,
Zou Tun

When the gale-force winds come, it is always the big tall trees that get blown over, while the pliant little grass just sways back and forth. That weakness overcomes strength seems obvious.

—Lao Tzu

Chapter Three

Joanna opened her eyes slowly, her body cold, her mind dull. The first thing she saw was wood. A wall. An unfamiliar wall of dark wood right next to her face. She was lying on a lumpy pallet with coarse sheets and a thick blanket that had slipped below her shoulder. That was why she was cold—because nothing covered her shoulder.

Nothing covered her *bare* shoulder. In fact, her entire body was bare. Naked. Beneath the sheet and blanket she was completely unclothed.

And her throat hurt like the very devil. She tried to swallow, but that produced a soft mewl of pain. Or it should have been a mewl of pain, but it came out as a kind of gurgle that scraped with hot needles against her throat. Abruptly all her breath stopped. She cut it off but the pain lingered, a low burning that made her close her eyes again. Whatever had happened to her was not in the least bit pleasant, and she wanted it all to go away.

It didn't, of course. Instead of disappearing, her

memories began to return. One by one they lined up for her perusal despite all her efforts at dismissal. Why couldn't she wait just a moment longer before dealing with what had happened to her?

She remembered the fight with her father. She remembered feeling trapped like a bird in a gilded cage and not wanting to sing at all. So she'd gone for a ride—a wild one to vent her anger. She'd been looking for revolutionaries with a strange thought to join them. Well, not a strange thought. She had been thinking of such ever since reading the letters of several American revolutionaries. Wouldn't it be nice to be part of a movement like that—to help the tide of freedom overwhelm a country?

So she'd gone looking for the people the English called Boxers, whose name actually was the Fists of Righteous Harmony. Then . . .

It all came rushing back: Octavia's wrenched shoulder. The revolutionaries who weren't revolutionaries at all, at least not how she thought of them. They had acted more like bandits. They had—

She leapt right over that part, to her rescuer: the tall Chinese man with hands as fast as lightning. She remembered him being handsome as well, his eyes hypnotizing. And his touch had been gentle as a summer's breeze on her shoulder. And on Octavia's as well. She remembered his voice as . . . as haughty and arid as a desert wind. And yet, the thought of him warmed her. Not in a tender way, but heating her blood as she recalled his demand that she be whipped!

She began to shift on the bed, intending to sit up. Then the rest of her memories intruded. Her discussion with him on the walk back to Shanghai. And her deductions: The man was a prince, an heir to the imperial throne.

And he had hit her!

She sat bolt upright, alarm crackling through her. Pain tightened her throat, cutting off her breath. He had hit her, and she had stopped breathing! Just like now, she had gasped and sputtered and choked until she'd died.

She stilled. She breathed in light pants, only gradually realizing her hands were on her throat. She hadn't died, she told herself. She had lost consciousness. And she would lose consciousness again if she didn't control herself. The flesh beneath her fingers felt hot and swollen, but not bloody. Perhaps she was only bruised. She had to remain calm.

But she couldn't breathe! She closed her eyes, focusing. But her heart was pounding and she had to breathe! She inhaled, trying to calm herself, but succeeded only in creating more pain, more panic as the bite of cold air clawed at her throat.

A male voice sounded in her ear. Soft, low, and in Chinese, it came to her mind as so much gibberish. Her entire focus was on her throat, on breathing slowly and quietly. But, God, the pain was unbearable!

Then she felt a hand. Warm and large, it touched her shoulder and infused heat throughout her body. It calmed her racing heart but did little to soothe her throat. Or perhaps it did because the pain began to fade a little. And with the easing pain, the tightening in her chest loosened. Her shoulders dropped a little, and air flowed through her raw throat. Slowly, like water through a narrow, dirty tube. But it flowed.

"You must not panic or you will harm yourself further."

This time she could translate the Chinese words. So she nodded her understanding, even as the man's voice continued.

"I have taken away your voice but not your life. If you struggle, that will only make things worse. You could cause enough swelling to suffocate yourself. If you wish to live, you must remain calm."

She whimpered in frustration, and pain lanced through her. *No sounds,* she told herself. No sounds at all—or she'd die for sure.

Again the man spoke, the ring of authority hardening his tone. "Do not use your throat. Do you understand me, barbarian? It could kill you. You must remain calm or you will d—"

She whipped around, flattening her hand against his mouth. Didn't he understand that threatening her life did *not* induce calm? If he would just be silent for a moment, she could regain control of herself. If he would just stop talking, if the pain would just ease up a bit, if she could just close her eyes in silence for a moment . . .

Her panic faded.

Her pain receded. A bit.

And finally her breath returned—albeit in a stuttering flow through a raw, agonized throat.

Only then did she focus outward. Only then did she open her mind to what her senses were telling her. She was on a bed in a small room without even a window. She was naked to the waist, since the sheet and blanket had fallen away from her. And she had her hand over a man's mouth. A Chinese man.

The Chinese man. The Mandarin who had hurt her in the first place.

She squealed in fear, scrambling backward as fast as she could. Except the squeal released another firestorm of agony in her throat, closing off her breath again. She ended up curled on her side, her body clenched in a tight ball of horror. She didn't know what to do. She didn't know how to help herself. She didn't know anything but fear and pain and—

"You are safe here. Do you not remember my pledge

to keep you safe? Do not fear, barbarian. You will not be harmed."

She opened her eyes enough to glare at him. His assurances meant nothing. If it weren't for him, she wouldn't be in this position right now. She wouldn't be gasping for her breath. She wouldn't be . . .

Well, she might have been severely hurt by the bandit revolutionaries. In fact, hadn't they said they wanted to kill her? Hadn't they been about to do just that? This man had stopped them. If it weren't for him, she would probably already be dead.

She frowned, trying to sort through her confusion. Obviously the Manchurian didn't want her dead. He already saved her life once, and was now warning her to remain calm so that she wouldn't choke. Therefore he did not intend to kill her.

But there were worse things than death. And one of them might just involve being locked naked in a tiny room with a depraved man. She relaxed her arms from about her knees, lifting her head enough to inspect the man beside her.

He looked much as he had before. He wore loose peasant clothing, had a serious face—cleaner than she remembered—and the dark, fathomless eyes of a man who kept secrets. And that was when she remembered *why* she'd been hit in the throat.

He was a Manchu—most likely one of their princes—traveling in secret, probably on a dangerous mission. And she'd figured it out. And, idiot that she was, she'd *told* him her deductions. That was when he'd hit her throat, knocking out her voice and her breath at the same time.

She bit her lip, wanting to talk but knowing better than to try. She had no wish to revisit that kind of pain again. Instead she slowly straightened, intending to

48

find a way to promise him she wouldn't tell. His secret was safe with her. Honest.

Except her movement recalled one more fact to her attention: She was naked. On a bed. With him.

She sat up, wrapping the sheet about her. She pulled it and the blanket tight and glared in question at him. Why exactly was she naked?

Apparently he wasn't immune to shame. His tan features flushed with embarrassment; then he slowly stood, easing off the bed and onto a simple stool nearby. There was a table as well, covered with scrolls, but he ignored them. And behind the table was a small washstand and a dressing screen covered with an elaborate painting.

"Are you feeling calmer now?" he asked.

She nodded, but did not for one moment lessen her glare.

"You are perhaps wondering about your clothing." He glanced around the room. "Perhaps even about where you are and what is going to happen." He sighed. "Unfortunately, that will take some time to explain."

She lifted her chin, folding her arms more securely across her chest, trapping the blanket where it was. As far as she knew, they had plenty of time.

"If you can remain calm, I promise to explain things as best as I can." He paused. "But first, are there any . . . any body functions you wish to take care of? Any pain—other than your throat—that needs attention?"

She hadn't been thinking about that. Up until now most of her focus had been on breathing. But now that he mentioned it, she did need to use the necessary. She straightened, glancing about the room.

There was nothing she could use, unless it was behind . . .

"You will find what you require behind the screen,"

he acknowledged as he extended his hand. "There is clothing there as well."

She took his hand reluctantly, but it was the easiest way off the bed while still keeping the sheet and blanket around her. He gave her as much distance as he could, supporting her hand as she climbed down, then released her immediately afterward.

She crossed the tiny room, ducking behind the screen as her urgency increased a hundredfold. She barely got the sheet unwrapped in time. And then she received another shock—one that made her cringe in horror, not once, but multiple times as the implications sank in.

She was hairless. It was all gone! And not from her head; that was neatly braided in a queue down her back. It was her *other* hair. Gone!

At first she thought it had fallen out, that something had made it just disappear from her body. But that, she realized, was ridiculous. It had been shaved off. Someone had spread her open, taken a razor, and neatly, carefully shaved her clean.

The very thought gave her chills. Who would do such a thing? And why? The *when* was obvious: She'd been unconscious for who knew how long. But why? And what did it mean? What was going to happen to her?

The questions spun in her mind, creating a clutter that threatened to break her control. But she dared not risk choking again. So she modulated her breath and tried to think clearly.

She didn't have any answers, so—obviously—her first step was to get some. If she was a prisoner, she would have to find a way to escape. If the Manchurian was a depraved monster, she would have to find a way to defend herself. Simple. Easy. And not something she could accomplish while hiding naked behind a privacy screen.

Carefully she cleaned herself up, checking her body

for any other changes. There weren't any, except for the lack of hair. So she finally straightened, searching for the clothes the Manchurian had mentioned.

But there weren't any. Not real clothing, at least. There was nothing except a flimsy silk robe of the darkest burgundy, which, in truth, was quite beautiful. It slid onto her body like . . . well, like silk—all slippery and cool in the most sensuous of ways. The design was interesting as well. It was of a tiger climbing up a mountain, not down out of a tree, as in the traditional design.

Another robe rested beside hers. This was a larger one, obviously meant for a man. It was dyed blue, and it displayed in green thread a mountain dragon slipping in and out of the clouds. An interesting pairing, she thought. A tiger climbing a mountain. A dragon slipping in and out of clouds. Truly, she wondered if these things had been placed here by chance, or if there was some meaning. Perhaps . . .

"Miss Crane?" came the Manchurian's voice from the other side of the screen. "Miss Joanna Crane, are you unwell?"

Perhaps, she thought with a sigh, she was simply avoiding what awaited her on the other side of the screen. But it was time now. She took a deep breath and tied the robe securely about her waist. Then, before she emerged, she grabbed the other robe. Its dark blue belt might be useful. As weapons went it wasn't much, but it was all she had. And as luck would have it, both robes had pockets. She quickly slipped the tie into one and did her best to disguise the bulge.

"Miss Crane?"

She would have said something, but she couldn't. Still, the urge to speak was difficult to suppress. So she stepped quickly from behind the screen, smiling slightly to indicate she was fine.

51

He inspected her from head to toe. His eyes didn't linger anywhere in particular, but she couldn't help wondering about the hair. Did he know? Had he been the one to do it? Her face heated in embarrassment, but she quickly pushed that aside. Anger would serve her better, and so she held on to that emotion, pushing her fears down as much as possible.

"You are unhurt?" he asked, his voice cool and detached.

She nodded, then passed him, heading for . . . where? He was sitting in the only chair in the room. He abruptly stood, crossed behind the screen, and grabbed the chamber pot. Without another word he picked it up and carried it to the door. He had to pause to unlock it, pulling a key out of some secret pocket within his clothing. He accomplished the task quickly, opening the door and setting the chamber pot outside. Joanna had a brief glimpse of a sunlit hall, and the faintest scent of incense was carried to her upon the soft notes of a Chinese lute. It was a strange thought, but then this was a strange place.

Then the Manchurian was back, carrying a tray of something steaming in a small bamboo container. She might have escaped right then. She might have made it out before he set down the tray and relocked the door. But her stomach was rumbling, and she was suddenly starving as she caught a whiff of the sweet meat dumplings she was now sure waited within the bamboo container. So Joanna stood quiet, reasoning that there was little she could accomplish in a robe and with no voice.

Besides, the Manchurian had promised to tell her what was happening. She settled in the chair—his chair—and awaited her meal and explanation.

She was not being polite. Indeed, she was well aware that in Chinese society the woman often stood while the man ate. But she was not Chinese, and he might as well begin to accept that now. In her society, if anyone was going to stand it would be her jailer—for that was indeed how she had begun to see him. After all, he was the one with the key.

He turned, frowning slightly at her position and attitude. But she simply lifted her chin, so he shrugged, choosing to sit across from her on the bed. Indeed, he reclined in such a negligent pose that she began to think he had the better seat. And that he looked very handsome in that pose. His muscles, though lax, were clearly defined. His chest was obviously broad, and his eyes—those damnable dark Chinese eyes—seemed even more intense than before.

"Are you hungry?" he asked.

She nodded, unsettled by her thoughts. He offered her a bowl of white rice and chopsticks. She took them greedily, but he did not immediately release them.

"The sleeping potion will sometimes make one's stomach sensitive. Please eat slowly."

She nodded in understanding. Then she looked down at her bowl. What she had initially believed to be rice was actually more like rice porridge. Or mush. How was she supposed to eat this? And with chopsticks?

She looked up at her jailer. His bowl contained fine Chinese rice. It was stickier than most Caucasians preferred, made for eating with chopsticks, but was of obvious good taste and texture. He was eating with relish. Then he deftly nabbed two steaming dumplings from the bamboo container and dropped them into his bowl.

Joanna leaned forward, looking for more of the succulent-smelling dumplings, to find the container now held only sauces of a variety of colors: mustard yellow, thick reddish brown, even a thin, oily orange. But no dumplings.

Of all the greedy pigs! she thought with disgust. There had been two dumplings—one for each of them. Well, she refused to be denied so wonderful a treat. She set down her bowl, reaching for the teapot. It was Chinese tea; she recognized the scent. Likely it would have tea leaves swimming in the brew, but she'd tried it before and it was actually quite pleasant.

She smiled sweetly at the Manchurian and filled two cups. Then, contrary to her upbringing, she did not hand him the tiny porcelain but left it on the tray. He smiled his thanks, leaning forward to take his cup. When he did so, she neatly plucked one of the dumplings from his rice bowl.

He noticed her action immediately, and his eyebrows shot straight up on his bare forehead. Joanna simply lifted her chin, smugly raised the dumpling with her chopsticks—no mean feat—and dropped the whole thing into her mouth.

It tasted heavenly. The meat was sweet and tender, the dough a perfect, fluffy accompaniment. Obviously this household had an excellent chef and a large purse. Even she, with all her father's money, had trouble finding meat this tender.

And then she swallowed.

She hadn't forgotten her tender throat. Indeed, she was excruciatingly aware that she must keep each and every breath a shallow, calm flow of air. But there had been so much else to worry about that she had forgotten to think ahead regarding swallowing. No meat, no matter how tender, would pass through her throat without the most severe pain.

And severe pain was exactly what she got. Severe enough to make her gasp, dropping her food bowl as she gagged. And gasped. And whimpered. A cup of tea was pressed into her hands.

"Drink. It will help," the Manchurian urged.

Joanna didn't question. She brought the nearly transparent porcelain to her lips and sipped the hot, soothing water. For that was exactly what it was: steaming hot, greenish water that eased the constriction in her throat. She didn't care that it tasted vile. Nor did she care that, as she drank, the back of her mouth and tongue grew numb. Numb was exactly what she wanted. And as the pain eased and her breath returned, she began to understand what she'd just done. She'd stolen food that she couldn't eat and been properly repaid for her efforts.

She would have apologized. She would have said something, but of course she had no voice to speak. So she simply looked at her lap in shame and frustration. If she could talk, she would have demanded an explanation by now. If she could talk, she would have stomped to the door and screamed until he unlocked it or someone came to rescue her.

But she couldn't do any of those things. She couldn't even eat her favorite food when it was brought on a beautiful platter to her door. All she could do was sit there and feel miserable while waiting for an explanation that obviously wasn't coming.

At that thought, she lifted her gaze and glared at her captor. She didn't know if he could understand her thoughts. Indeed, he appeared supremely indifferent as he calmly pressed her bowl of rice gruel into her hands and returned to his lounging position on the bed. She tried glaring at him some more, mentally sending thoughts of fury his way. But they had no effect, and in the end her own growling stomach forced her to eat her rice paste.

It was a daunting meal, a lumpy white paste that looked as appetizing as wet clay. But she was starving, so she lifted her chopsticks and tried to scoop up a bit. She had learned the use of chopsticks when she'd first gotten to Shanghai. Her Chinese nanny had taught her, and Joanna still occasionally enjoyed private meals where she used them. But scooping up wet paste on two bamboo sticks was beyond her current skills. She barely got any food at all, and was nearly sobbing in frustration when her captor released his own frustrated sigh.

Abruptly setting aside his food, he quickly stepped outside the room. But he didn't actually leave. Instead, he gestured to someone and waited quietly for that person to join him.

Joanna didn't move. She simply waited, choosing to watch rather than struggle uselessly with her rice paste. Her jaw dropped in shock as a stunningly beautiful girl stepped up to her captor, head bowed.

The girl's pose was all that was subdued about her. Her skin glowed, and her eyes were alight with intelligence as she glanced coyly inside the room at Joanna. She and the Mandarin spoke quickly, in voices too soft for Joanna to understand. Then the woman bowed and quietly slipped away, returning moments later. She carried a single Chinese soup spoon of the finest porcelain, obviously for Joanna's use. She handed it over, bowed, and retreated.

In short, the girl did nothing remarkable—merely fetched a spoon. But Joanna watched, feeling mesmerized by the willowy grace with which she moved. The girl seemed to flow through space, as if her entire being harmonized with her task, with her environment, and with herself.

Indeed, that perhaps was the true source of the girl's beauty: simple elegance of motion, rather than of face or form. Objectively speaking, the girl's features were not particularly remarkable. In fact, thinking back, Joanna thought her nose rather small and her eyebrows thick. But the peace radiating through her gave the impression of surpassing beauty.

Without thinking Joanna stood up, wanting to go to the woman. She wanted to talk to her, to learn how the girl maintained such a wondrous appearance. But before she could do more than stand, her captor closed the door and returned, spoon in hand. Joanna looked mutely at the door, and he shook his head.

"You cannot go out, Miss Crane. You and I are fated to stay in this room for a long, long time, I am afraid."

Joanna blinked, the heaviness of his words hitting her almost as forcefully as his meaning. He sounded as if he dreaded the coming days. But why? What were they to do in this chamber, locked together?

She let out a tiny gasp of alarm, but he was gentle as he pressed the spoon into her hand.

"Do not be afraid. In truth, you and I are richly blessed. We are to learn the secrets of a very exclusive sect of Taoism. We are to study together, to seek enlightenment."

She narrowed her eyes, reading his expression. His body seemed heavy and dull. Indeed, if she hadn't understood his words, she would have guessed he was speaking of death or some excruciatingly unpleasant task.

She set down the spoon, choosing to remain standing as she stared at him. Then, very deliberately, she folded her arms across her chest and shook her head. She made her movements slow and very firm so he would understand. She would not study anything with him. Certainly nothing that required parts of her body to be shaved. What he did was his own affair, but she would not participate.

Indeed, she absolutely demanded to be returned home.

He settled back on the bed, reclining not so much with ease as exhaustion. Joanna frowned, glaring at him, trying to make him understand. When he returned to toying with his food, she actually stamped her foot to gain his attention. She stomped her bare heel. No reaction. Twice she stomped. Even a third time, hard enough to jar her bones all the way to her hip.

Nothing. In the end she stomped to his side, folded her arms with crisp, hard movements, then shook her head no.

He looked at her, his expression dark and empty. "I understand your anger, Miss Crane. Indeed, I share it. But there is nothing we can do but make the best of this situation." He straightened, coming to stand directly before her. "You will not be going home. You will not be speaking with anyone." His voice caught on those last words, and he had to clear his throat before he could continue. "You will learn to accept the situation as it is and hopefully benefit from the experience." He sighed, leaning back on his heels as he, too, crossed his arms over his chest. "There is nothing we can do to alter this path. And anger serves no one."

He waited a moment, arching a single brow, his expression amazingly flat. She continued to glare at him. He casually leaned down and picked up his rice bowl again, then took his time returning to his place on the bed, bending his body and unfolding his legs across the mattress.

"There is one benefit to the Tigress sect," he commented, leaning back on the pillows. "The beds are much, much better than at the monastery." And with that, he smiled.

No, she decided, perhaps it was more of a smirk, although he seemed to be mocking himself more than her. And then he applied himself to his food.

Joanna stared, unable to understand what could

make this man—this Manchurian prince—simply accept imprisonment without so much as a whimper of protest. With his fighting skills, he could break out in no time. She stepped forward, touching his thigh to get his attention. His leg muscle twitched beneath her fingers, shifting like a living, powerful thing. But then it stilled as he slowly raised his gaze to her.

She lifted her hands, doing her best to imitate his fighting. She had it completely wrong, of course, and must have looked like an idiot. But she hoped he understood her gestures. She pointed to the door. Would he fight their captors and escape?

He shook his head. "I have made a vow against violence. I do not fight. At all."

She arched a single mocking eyebrow. He had fought well enough against the revolu—the bandits.

"I do not fight at all—unless I am overcome by stupidity."

She lifted her chin at his insult. It was not a stupid thing to rescue her!

"If I had simply stepped aside, if I had ignored your situation as I had vowed, then I wouldn't now be here. I wouldn't be trapped in this room with you, about to be instructed in practices I believe are useless."

She might have believed him. He certainly sounded angry and bitter enough. But he was the one with the key to the room, which she indicated by pointing her finger. He could escape anytime he wanted—with or without the use of violence.

"Yes, I have the key," he acknowledged. "And without it you can go nowhere." He straightened, setting aside all pretense of eating. "But there are more ways to trap a man than a simple lock and key. I hold the key to this room. Someone else holds the key to my prison."

Joanna stared at the man, seeing his rigid body, his

darkened expression. The lighting was not good in this room, sunlight filtering only partially through thin ventilation holes next to the ceiling, but in some ways that made things clearer. It gave shadowy outline to his hardened form, delineating not only his powerful muscles but the almost casual way he draped his body. There was anger there, to be sure. But also an underlying acceptance. That conflict seemed to make his body rigid and dark.

Only two possibilities existed. The first was that he truly was trapped by more than just a closed door; something else held him here, something he could not fight. Though Joanna found it hard to imagine what could keep a prince captive, she was certain that there were things he might fear. Perhaps he spoke the truth.

The other possibility was equally plausible. What if he secretly preferred it here? What if he had no interest in accomplishing his other secret mission or whatever it was he should be doing? That would explain his casual acceptance of captivity. She could well believe that a plush bed and beautiful Chinese servants were infinitely better than what awaited him in the outside world.

So was he trapped? Or was he a willing captive? She almost wanted to stay long enough to find out. Almost. But not enough to give up her freedom or her reputation. She had already been gone too long. There were ways to hide a couple days from the gossipmongers: an illness, a visiting friend, a solitary mood, for goodness' sake. She was certainly known for her shifts in temperament. And she had used such excuses to cover a variety of excursions to Chinese and Caucasian scholars. Even to speak with missionaries or statemen—all those people traditionally denied gently bred women unless strictly chaperoned.

But the Mandarin looked like he intended to stay

for weeks, if not months, and that simply wasn't possible. With a sweet smile, Joanna leaned over and grabbed the cooling teapot. Heading for her teacup, she pretended to begin to pour. Then, while he was still relaxed, she threw the tepid water at him. It wasn't hot enough to harm him, but it would startle him long enough for her to grab for the key. Then it would be a quick two steps to the door and freedom.

That was the plan, at least. And it started out well.

She surprised him—of that much she was certain. But that was as far as it went. He gasped only slightly. He moved even less. Brown water dripped down his head and into his eyes. It looked like the action even cut off his breath for a moment. But his only physical movement was to grab her hand as it went to his pocket. That was all. He didn't put his hands up in defense of his face or to clear his vision. He didn't even shake his head. He simply grabbed her hand and twisted, awkwardly torquing her arm around and forcing her to drop slowly to the bed.

She landed in a ponderous heap on the mattress, her eyes wide and her breath wheezing painfully in and out of her throat. He followed her down, still moving with slow, conscious intent. He wanted her to know he was stronger, cleverer, more dominant, and the message came through loud and clear. He settled his weight upon her, pinning her down. She bit her lip to restrain a cry even as she felt her belly quiver in delighted response. His male organ thickened against her, and she tried to shove him away. But far from flinging him from her, her legs seemed to soften, to accept. It wasn't possible. He was being horrible. And yet, her traitorous body didn't seem to care.

He let his face close the distance between them so that when he spoke, his breath heated her lips. "I had thought to give you more time," he said. Tea dripped from his hair into her eyes. "But obviously you are of stronger constitution than I expected." He made the compliment sound like an insult. "Therefore," he drawled, lengthening his words to make them very distinct, "it is time to begin your education."

So saying, he reached above her head. With movements too fast to follow he adjusted her position on the bed while still holding her down. She fought as best she could, but it was a losing battle—not only with him, but with her breath. She couldn't throw him off her without exciting herself. And the moment her inhalations deepened, pain flared, her throat thickened, and her airflow became severely restricted. In the end there was little she could do but breathe steadily.

By the time that battle was won, she had lost the fight against him. Raising her head a bare inch off the mattress, she suddenly realized the horrid truth. She was tied spread-eagle to the bed.

Our souls are transparent. Like mirrors. Through judiciously wiping away the blemishes on our souls, we will naturally come to understand the things around us.

—Lao Tzu

Chapter Four

Zou Tun pushed himself off the barbarian woman, sickened by what he had just done. He was not in the habit of tying up any creature, much less a woman. But she had to understand that there would be no escape—for either of them.

He pushed himself to his feet, still feeling the heat of her burning into his body. How could such a creature ever be considered a ghost? She seemed more substantial than most women he knew, with the exception of the dowager empress. Of course, to compare that lauded woman with this barbarian was ridiculous—and yet he could not help himself. The two had the same fire within them, and he did not like the idea of restraining such energy, no matter what the reason.

But he had no choice, and so he secured her bonds before drying the tepid tea off his face and clothing. It had been a bold move, throwing the drink at him and trying to grab the key. Bold and surprising enough that it would likely have worked with a different man.

Jade Lee

But he had been trained in fighting at the Shiyu monastery. He knew how to read the tensing of muscles and the sly look in a man's eye. Even so, she had surprised him enough that he was now wet.

Irritated with himself, and with her for causing such strange thoughts, for pushing him outside of his center, he stomped to the door and opened it. A girl was waiting, and he passed on a request to see the Tigress Shi Po. He was anxious to begin his training, which meant beginning the barbarian's as well. The sooner they began, the sooner this would end.

He waited impatiently at the door, passing the time by rubbing irritably at his new-grown hair. He had not yet decided if he would keep his shaved head or allow his Qin queue to regrow. And here, yet again he was showing unusual indecision. Was he a monk or a Qin heir? He wasn't sure, except to know it would be extremely difficult to be both. Indeed, he had spent the last few years trying to be both, only to end up with dead brethren, a captive white woman and a conscience so mired in guilt that he could not think straight.

That was why, he supposed, he had allowed the Tigress to trap him here. He could not return to Peking in this state of indecision. His enemies would eat him alive. So he was hiding here, "forced" into useless training while he decided what exactly he wished to do upon his return to Peking.

Because he had to return. He owed it to his father and his country to forgo the monastic life and his personal dreams of enlightenment. He was a Manchurian prince and he could not indulge himself in religious frivolity at the expense of his country. He would not.

At least, he would not for much longer.

He took a step into the hallway, his annoyance

growing. He was forbidden from wandering about the large compound. That the Tigress lived in such wealth made him sneer. True religious sects disdained creature comforts as a distraction and temptation. But what could one expect from a female cult that glorified sexuality? Merely this: a focus on the lowest forms of comfort with complete ignorance of the higher possibilities.

Still, he was not above enjoying a comfortable bed or soft cotton sheets. Given his training at the monastery, he believed he could quickly master any tasks here. He would view the time as a restful vacation before returning to the capital. Fortunately, he was disciplined enough to enjoy his surroundings even when they included a barbarian.

Shi Po joined him, a servant girl following her. The Tigress moved gracefully as always, her beauty undeniable. But Zou Tun had seen the coldness within her, and so he felt no desire at the sight of her lithe figure.

"You wish to begin?" she asked, her voice low and melodic.

He nodded, gesturing behind him at the barbarian. Mindful that Shi Po believed the woman had come seeking the Tigress training, he said, "Her throat injury pains her greatly. I had to restrain her to keep her from causing further harm to herself."

The Tigress looked past him, a single brow arched. "She is violent?"

He shook his head. "Not generally. But the pain is significant," he lied. "I assume there are ways to begin training despite her circumstances?"

The woman nodded, then held her hand out to the side. The servant girl quickly handed over two scrolls, bowed and withdrew. The scrolls were then passed to Zou Tun.

"You must first purify yourselves. The instructions are written here for both you and her." Shi Po tilted her head slightly, indicating the other scrolls she had given him. "I assume you are able to read these?"

She was toying with him, seeing if she could insult him. She knew quite well that as a royal Manchurian, he would be able to read.

"Your kindness is unmatched," he drawled. "I am well able to read your secret texts, but I fear the barbarian will not be able. You will have to send someone to read them to her."

She raised an eyebrow as if in shock. "Oh, sir. All my girls are occupied with their own studies. They cannot spare the time. Nor would I ask them, as they are not knowledgeable in matters of barbarians. I am afraid you are the only one I would trust with such a task."

He barely restrained himself from growling at her. Why had he not just walked by when the Fists attacked the white woman? For whatever reason he had helped her, and now he was trapped. Naturally the Tigress Shi Po would force him to train the white barbarian; blackmail wasn't possible unless he was the one who touched the white.

Behind him he could hear the woman struggle with her bonds, her breathing controlled but no less furious. He knew she was trying to gain the Tigress's help, to silently communicate her situation. It was just as well that he was being forced to begin her training. Who knew what the Tigress might understand, even from a mute barbarian? Especially one as intelligent as Joanna Crane.

"Very well," he snapped. "I will call for you if I have any difficulty." And then, with a rudeness that belied his court upbringing, Zou Tun tried to shut the door.

The Tigress stopped him, her slender arm holding it open with a strength that startled Zou Tun. "Do not rush this process, Mandarin," she said, her voice hard. "Moving too fast will ruin it." She glanced disdainfully at the bed. "Especially with a restrained creature."

He nodded in understanding—a single, short movement—and then forcibly pushed her out. It was bad enough that he would have to purify the white woman himself. He would be damned if he allowed this she-devil to watch.

He stomped back into the room, unrolling the first of the new scrolls as he did. The text was simple, the pictures graphic. He understood their meaning and purpose. It was merely the thought of performing such actions that repulsed him.

Or should repulse him.

He set down the scrolls, turning toward the woman lying so open before him. Her robe covered her body a bit, though it would take nothing at all for him to strip her naked. Still, she remained covered now, only her ankles and a bit of one calf showing. Her bare feet remained in full view, white and pleasingly formed. But it was not her feet that would occupy him now.

He would have to touch her breasts, directly above her yin center. His hands actually twitched at the thought. He had touched her once before, but not with the intention of purifying her. He had been curious to discover her texture, her substance, and had learned she felt as warm and soft as any woman. So why was he anxious to do so again?

It was merely his baser self returning. During his time at the monastery, he had ruthlessly quelled the animal in his spirit. Every man had one, but the Shaolin subjugated that creature, channeling it into their fighting skills. But given the tiniest measure of space—such as when Zou Tun had indulged his curiosity on the road to Shanghai—it returned with full vengeance, demanding all manner of depravities.

And now he would have to give it even more space, allowing himself to touch this woman's breasts—to stroke them, to massage them, to purify them. But it would be a cold task, a necessary one done with no more interest than he would empty a chamber pot or set a man's broken leg. Such was his plan, and his only hope of returning to his center.

He sat down beside his bound charge with a determination rarely seen in even the most devoted of monks. "I must purify your yin now," he said slowly. "Yin is your female essence, your womanly energy. Time and coarse living have dirtied it, aging your body and muddying your true purpose of merging your energy with a man's. Therefore, it must be cleansed. Do you understand?"

She had gone absolutely still when he settled on the bed. Indeed, he feared she had stopped breathing. Her eyes were trained on his face, her stomach muscles rippling with tension as he spoke. Clearly she understood his words. If not, she knew he intended to touch her in ways that were not usually appropriate between strangers.

"I take no joy in this task," he stated, praying that such would be true. "I intend to complete it as quickly as possible. Do you understand?"

The woman shook her head, but not because she didn't comprehend. She was afraid, her panic making her breaths fast and shallow. She began pulling at her bonds, struggling ineffectively but with great strength. And when he lay the flat of one hand on her breastbone, her struggles increased to an absolute frenzy.

He knew better than to fight her. A mind caught in a panic had to be waited out. Quietly. Patiently. Eventually she would tire and see that he meant her no harm. Still, it was excruciatingly hard to sit impassively by, one hand pressed gently against her beating heart, while her legs and arms flailed uselessly at her bonds. Indeed, if she continued to struggle, he worried that she might cut off the blood to her hands and feet. The leather straps were meant for gentle restraint, and yet could still do harm if one struggled too fiercely.

Fortunately for the white woman, her throat pain quieted her long before she damaged her hands or feet. She had to stop struggling to breathe without great pain. And focusing on that alone eventually stilled the frantic tempo of her heart.

"This exercise is not meant to hurt you, Miss Crane," he said, surprised at the rough timbre of his voice. "It will increase and purify your yin. There will be no pain. This I swear," he said. Though in truth, he knew little about a woman's yin. "But for your own health, you must remain calm." He hesitated. "Perhaps I can help you find your center—that place inside you of perfect peace."

He didn't know if he could do it. He had never aided a woman before, much less a barbarian woman. But things would go much easier for both of them if he could. So he closed his eyes, willing his own peace to slip into her body, his own inner quiet to silence her terror.

He felt it work. Beneath his hand her breathing eased. A moment later he knew she had accepted what would come. There were no words to describe the moment, only a certain knowledge that she had bowed her enormous pride to the inevitable.

He opened his eyes and was startled to see a single shimmering droplet slip from her eye. A tear, and then another, from the other eye. And more. They came in a steady stream without sound, without wails, without even the stuttering sobs he'd heard from many women he knew. It was a single silent tear followed by others.

All he could do was stare, watching the silvery trails merge into her hair.

In the sacred Shaolin texts of Lao Tzu, the master spoke of the weak overcoming the strong. Of how water in its formless, harmless state gently penetrated and overcame the most solid of barriers. So too had this woman's tears dissolved Zou Tun's iron will.

It was a message to him, her tears, that he could not conquer her resistance by force. That her nonaction was indeed more powerful than his determination. And he could not continue this action without completely abandoning the Tao—the middle path—by which all monks lived.

He withdrew his hand.

"Perhaps you are not strong enough for this exercise yet," he said. He sighed, once again feeling frustration eat at him. Now seemed the perfect time to begin. She had to accept her situation. Her struggles had ceased, and she lay docile upon the bed. Now was the absolutely perfect time to begin, and yet he could not. What a weak child he had become, when the sight of a ghost woman's tears swayed him from his course! And yet, much as he railed at himself, he knew that she had vanquished him.

He would not touch her without consent. So he turned to the second scroll, resolved to begin his own exercises.

Like the text on female yin purification, the yang ritual was equally explicit. Zou Tun cringed at the thought of performing such tasks in front of a white woman, but he knew it was necessary. If they were to become partners in this training, then she would have to grow accustomed to the sight of his dragon. And since he could not purify her, he needed to begin purifying himself. Still he paused, turning to the woman to explain.

"Since we cannot begin cleansing your yin, I shall have to start on my yang. I will not touch you, as this is not for you. But it would be helpful if you do not distract me during the process. It is very complicated," he lied. In truth, it was very simple. It was merely the control of his dragon that would be difficult.

She nodded in understanding, and so he took a deep breath, steeling himself to begin his task. He stood, excruciatingly aware of her eyes upon him, and slowly stripped off all his clothing. He did not have much. His shirt was wet anyway, so it was no loss to remove its clammy fabric from his body. His socks and boots were an equal pleasure to remove, as Shanghai was warmer than the north, and his feet appreciated the gentle air.

But then it came time to pull off his pants. He heard the woman hold her breath, obviously startled by his intentions. His back was to her, but he knew how she looked. Her eyes would be wide with maidenly shock, while underneath would be a woman's sly glee. All women enjoyed seeing a man at his most vulnerable—naked and hard, aching for what they offered.

Fortunately, he was not at his full length, and given this humiliating situation, he was not likely to be. Possibly never again. So he resolved to be a man, to accomplish his task whatever the cost. And so, with a stiff back and angry gestures, he untied his belt and let both pants and rope fall to the floor.

Before he lost his nerve he turned around. Let her look her fill. Let her reveal the sly character inside her female breast. Then he would have no interest in her at all, for he would see that this was just a woman like any other. Less than any other woman, in fact, because she was a barbarian.

That was his plan. Except, when he turned to face her, to let her look her fill, he saw no maidenly horror. Not even a sly superiority. Instead, she revealed a simple and unabashed curiosity.

As he stood there, naked before her, her eyes narrowed in study. She looked at him completely, from the top of his dark head all the way down his chest, and finally, ultimately, to his jade stem. He could not tell what he thought, and she had no voice to tell him. So he stood there, watching her study him with an intensity he had seen only in the most dedicated of students. Indeed, her gaze moved with a doctor's care over his entire form while she tilted and strained her head one way and the other to apparently see from a better angle.

She even wet her lips unconsciously, her tiny pink tongue bringing them to a glistening sheen. He did not believe she had lascivious thoughts; her manner was much too scholarly. And yet his body seemed to respond as if she were the most alluring seductress.

And under her scrutiny, his stem thickened and lengthened. His dragon had decided to appear, pushing its head out in hunger.

"I will begin the exercises now," he said, his voice tight with self-consciousness. Taking the seat opposite her, he sat down, his legs wide for better access. He placed the scroll on the floor, narrowing his eyes in the dim light to make sure he read the instructions correctly.

"'That which is exhausted will be renewed,'" he read aloud.

With his left hand, he stroked his thumb from the base of his stem all the way to its dragon head. It was stimulating, of course. The exercise was designed to strengthen his resistance to just such activities. Fortunately, he had plenty of practice quieting his mind no matter what was happening to his body. Usually he ignored pain, not eroticism. No one could train as a Shaolin without pain. Nor could they sit without moving for twelve hours without learning to ignore great discomfort. But essentially the techniques were the same. And so he accomplished the seventy-two left-handed strokes without much more than a flushed face and a fully extended dragon.

It was only when he switched to repeat the process with the right hand that he began to experience difficulties. He had to shift positions slightly, adjusting his right elbow as he switched hands. That naturally broke his meditative state, and for the first time since he began, he again grew aware of the white woman watching him.

She didn't make a sound. Indeed, he doubted she had moved. But her eyes caught his, and when he met her gaze, he could not look away.

She had been watching his hand movements; he was sure of it. But not anymore. Now she looked at him, her focus intent, her face flushed, and her breath coming in soft, shallow pants. It was one thing to perform physical movements while maintaining a meditative state. He had mastered such things during his fighting exercises even before entering the monastery. But to stroke one's jade stem while a woman watched was something else entirely.

He could not return to his isolated thoughts. He could not imagine himself in a quiet center of stillness. She was there. In his center. In his circle of peace. And no silence could be found between them even as neither said a word.

Her expression was no longer accusing. He could detect no lingering anger that she was bound to the bed. Even her intellectual curiosity had faded, though he still saw sparks. She was not even absorbed by lascivious thoughts, though her body was obviously excited. Indeed, as he watched and continued his right-handed strokes, he saw her lips grow redder, glistening as she wet them again with her pink tongue. The silk covering her breasts fluttered as she breathed, and Zou Tun could not resist letting his gaze slip to the temptingly jiggling soft mounds.

But even that could not hold him for long. His gaze returned to her face. To her eyes, as she watched him watch her. And all the while, his dragon flushed larger and fuller in its hunger. A hunger for her.

He felt his groin tighten, and he knew he was close to release. He knew he could not contain himself much longer. And still, he could not look away. He could not see anything but this white woman's eyes of polished bronze.

What was she thinking? Did she like what she saw? Did she want to touch him? To taste him? Those thoughts spun in his mind when all should have been quiet. Images came as well, adding potency to the sound of her soft breathing.

Her legs twitched on the bed, her silk robe slipping open the tiniest bit as she moved. She stilled immediately, but the damage was done. Zou Tun's eyes jerked to a tiny sliver of white thigh visible in a crack between the folds. The fabric was trembling slightly with her breath, holding his gaze, teasing his mind with thoughts of what lay beneath. Would she be as warm as a Chinese woman? Given the heat that pulsed in the tiny room, he could not believe she would be cold.

He closed his eyes, trying to block out the sight of

her, struggling to regain his focus. He brought his attention back to his task, appalled to discover that he no longer stroked his dragon with one thumb, but gripped it in a full fist. He stopped, shifting back to using his right thumb, but his dragon clenched in protest at the sudden change.

And then her scent penetrated his focus, unique and distracting as nothing else could be. He knew the smells of men in all their varieties—sick or healthy, in ecstasy or drunkenness. Through odor Zou Tun had been able to identify a man's state by the time he was eighteen. Women, too, were no particular challenge. Mongolian or Han, young or old, in heat or in menses, he had made a catalog of such scents long before he'd found the peace offered in the Tao.

But this woman was different. And her scent was not covered in flowers or doused in opium. Her scent gave a honeyed taste to the air, fogged his mind with pepper spice. He opened his eyes, knowing her smell was more deadly to him than the vision of her flushed body. But sight did not stop her olfactory assault, and the perfume of her continued to fog his mind.

Once again he met her gaze and gripped his dragon. He tried to return to study, to the practice of this most bizarre Taoist path, but he could not find the meditative peace he sought. He tasted her on the air and saw the fire blazing in her eyes. Witch fire. Ghost-people flame. It seemed to consume his mind.

In her eyes he saw intelligence, curiosity, and a desire that had her body twitching beneath her robe. Some part of his mind registered the slight widening of her legs, the tremble of her belly and even the jiggling of her breasts. He knew what happened, absorbed the evidence of her arousal, but his attention stayed on her eyes: liquid bronze, shimmering in firelight.

His body clenched. His center was lost in the mists of those eyes. He was with her, and with one quick flash he leaped the distance between them.

Or so he imagined. In truth it was his yang, leaping forth from his dragon's mouth. White flame leaped forth as it had not done since before he'd entered the monastery. And with it went his yang power—not poured into the white woman's yin, but spilled uselessly onto his hand and the floor as if he were a boy seeing his first powdered breast.

He stared down at his hand, humiliation burning through his trembling body. What had he done? How could he fail at this simplest of tasks? And then, without warning, the bedroom door burst open.

Or so it seemed. Thinking back, perhaps he'd heard knocking. He'd ignored it, wanting only the roaring that preceded the dragon fire. It mattered little. The Tigress Shi Po stood before him now, her dark eyebrows arched in disgust.

He could not look at her. Indeed, he could do little but reach for his tea-stained shirt and use it to clean up his shame. This most simple of tasks was for the lowest practitioner, and he had not accomplished it.

"It is as I feared," Shi Po said, her voice low and sad. "My brother's monks have no discipline."

Zou Tun wanted to defend himself. He wanted to explain about the white woman and her witch fire. But he did not. Whatever the ghost woman's power, he was the one to blame. Only empty men blamed their failings on a woman, and he was not so. He pressed his lips together and waited while the Tigress sniffed the air with a wrinkled nose.

"Impure. Both of you." She advanced farther into the room. "Immature yang. Polluted yin." She waved at a servant who held a tea tray just outside the door. "I feared as much. I brought tea to restore you."

The servant entered, quietly setting her tray on the single table tucked behind the chair. Zou Tun did not speak. There was nothing to say. He waited like an errant child while the servant poured the tea and then bowed out of the room. Then, with a tightened jaw, he quickly downed the liquid though it burned his throat.

Shi Po crossed the room, going to the ghost woman's side. "You have not begun with her," she accused.

"No," Zou Tun responded. "She is not yet ready."

The Tigress curled her lip in disdain. "She is more than ready. Her body cries out in pain. Her blood swims with pollutants." She turned, looking pointedly at his dragon. "You feared your reaction should you touch her." She nodded to herself. "A wise man knows his limitations." She sighed and rolled up her sleeves. "Very well. I will do it this time."

Zou Tun straightened in alarm, but it was nothing compared to the white woman's reaction. Though it must have pained her, she whispered a harsh cry. She shook her head, fighting against her bonds, straining her arms and legs as she had not done before. Earlier, Zou Tun had feared for the woman's hands and feet. Now he feared she would break her wrists. Already her skin was discolored from bruising. Blood would soon follow.

"She grows frightened whenever someone nears," he said, moving toward the Tigress.

Shi Po shrugged. "Do not fear for my safety. Those bonds are stronger than they appear. They will not break." She reached down and flipped open the top of the girl's robe. One pert breast stood out stark and white.

Then Zou Tun did the unthinkable: He broke his vow against violence once again. Striking as a snake would, he snatched the Tigress's hand and held her still when she tried to pull away.

77

"Miss Crane does not wish to learn today." With his free hand, he pulled the ghost woman's robe closed.

Shi Po's eyes narrowed. "All animals fear what they do not understand." When Zou Tun still did not release her, her gaze froze him. "Can you not feel her sickness? She needs to be purified even more than you do. This is the only way with those who cannot learn."

"She is a barbarian, not an idiot." He glanced down at the white woman, seeing the way she panted fast and frightened. Yes, she looked like a terrified animal, but he knew she was smarter than most Chinese women he had met. That shallow panting was the only way she could manage her panic without passing out. It gave her the air she needed to breathe. "Her injury is greater than it appears," he admitted.

"Her fear is great, and you are too tenderhearted to do what is needed," Shi Po accused.

Zou Tun frowned, turning back to the Tigress. Something in her tone was different; something lay beneath her words that he did not understand. Then another voice cut in from the door. A deep voice. A man's voice, low and questioning.

"Do you wish her to be initiated as you were? In violence and in pain?" It was Kui Yu, the Tigress's husband. His questions were soft-spoken, but no less powerful.

Zou Tun still held Shi Po's slender wrist, so he felt the sudden tension and anger that radiated from her. Her eyes narrowed, and such was her fury that Zou Tun's hand loosened in surprise as she rounded on her husband.

"You dare interfere in my instruction?" she hissed.

Zou Tun grew even more surprised. Women never spoke in such a way to their husbands! Certainly not in public. In Peking such a woman would be whipped or hanged. And yet Kui Yu did not respond with anger. Instead he simply smiled a warm, almost comical smile. Indeed, Zou Tun might have thought the man an idiot if not for the intelligence of his words.

"Of course not," he said lightly. "I know nothing of this practice and would not dream of interfering. I am simply home early and wished to share tea with you. The day is dull without your beauty before me." He flicked an almost disdainful glance at the white woman. "Is this not our guest's partner in practice? Surely it is his task to purify her. You need not sully your hands with her."

Then Kui Yu reached out, gently lifting his wife's hand out of Zou Tun's hold before escorting her to the door. But she would not leave. Not before she gave one last acid glance over her shoulder.

"The ghost people fill themselves with death. For her own sake, that girl must be purified. And I will not allow such sickness in my house any longer." She pinned Zou Tun with her angry stare. "Tell me now if you cannot do this."

Beside him, the white woman stiffened in fear, but Zou Tun knew better than to argue. Miss Crane would begin her exercises whether or not either of them wished it. So he bowed his head to the inevitable.

"I will accomplish what is required."

Next, the Tigress turned her acid stare on Joanna. "You went through much to come here. I don't know why, nor do I care. Heaven has offered you a boon. Purity, health, perhaps even enlightenment can be found within these walls. Accept his attention now while your throat heals. Then, when you are ready, you may choose again. Enlightenment, or the sure steady withering of your body. You need not become a hag, white woman. But you will soon if you are not purified."

Zou Tun turned to see Joanna stiffen on the bed. Her eyes were wide, and he could see her gaze hopping from the Tigress to the servant. Both were beautiful, graceful women, both testaments to the restorative power of the Tigress regimen. Did Joanna Crane consider accepting this practice? he wondered. Surely not. Surely she was too intelligent to believe sex and enlightenment could be found together. And yet, he could not deny the simple lure of beauty. What woman would not wish for that?

He could see that Joanna wanted to speak. She stretched up from the bed, her eyes alight with intelligence. But there was no more time as the Tigress's husband interrupted once again.

"I grow thirsty, my wife. Do we have any more special tea? The kind with ginger and lily?"

Shi Po turned, frowning slightly even as her features softened. "Lily? There is no such thing as ginger and lily tea. Chrysanthemum flavors your tea, my husband. With other spices that only I know."

"Ah," he said, as they began walking down the hall. "I have no head for such things. Without you, I would probably drink mud and grass and be miserable."

So they departed, leaving Zou Tun and Joanna Crane alone in the room. Zou Tun quickly closed and secured the door, though obviously the Tigress had a key. Still, the locked door gave them some feeling of privacy, especially as he made sure it was stuck fast.

Then he turned, mentally scrambling for his own calm center so that he would have the strength to accomplish his task. He crossed to the white woman, slowly sitting down at her side.

"You understand that the Tigress feels these things. She will know if you do not perform her exercises."

The woman nodded her head—once—showing that she did indeed understand what was happening.

"I cannot let you leave. No more than I can run from here. Therefore, I must do this thing."

She swallowed, and he saw tears swim in her bright bronze eyes.

He reached over, lifting the relevant scroll off the floor. "They are simple exercises. You can see that they will not harm you."

He opened the scroll to show her, but from her tied position she could not see the text. The room was too dark, with the only light coming from high above. Even so, she obviously tried to read. Her eyes narrowed, and Zou Tun watched her focus flick from the written words to the diagram. Still, he knew she could not see much, and so he let his hands drop, bringing the parchment to his lap.

"I wish to untie you."

Her gaze had been following the scroll, even though she could not read it. At his words, her focus snapped to him.

"Shi Po is not a fool, and neither is her husband. There will be guards posted outside our door. You will not be able to escape even if you manage to move past me. Do you understand?"

He watched her expression droop, and knew he had guessed her intent. She still nursed plans to escape. "Do the ghost people keep their word?"

She blinked, then nodded vigorously.

"Many men have spoken of how the ghost people are as inconstant as the wind that blew them here. They promise with all goodwill until the mood strikes them differently. They are prey to their own bestial natures, and cannot control their actions. Is this so?"

Her frown became fierce. She vehemently shook her head.

"I believe it is so," he said firmly. "I believe the ghost people have such weakness, just as many of my countrymen do." He paused, making sure she gave him her full attention. "You also have shown yourself to be subject to your whims."

She opened her mouth to object despite her injured throat. He pressed a finger to her lips to keep the sound inside.

"You injured your horse because of such a whim," he reminded her.

She pressed her lips together, clearly disagreeing. Then, to his surprise, she nodded.

"Ah, so you do agree?"

She shrugged, clearly unwilling to give him complete victory. And for some bizarre reason, that made him smile.

"Very well. You have shown that you can learn. Learn this: We must purify your yin. For your own health as well as for further practice. The process will take many days."

Her eyes widened at the word *days*, and she shook her head in refusal.

"Yes. Days. But the sooner you are purified, the sooner we can begin the training and the sooner this captivity will end. I have no more interest in remaining here than you, but it is necessary."

Her eyes narrowed in anger. He did not care. It was the truth. He could not leave, and he could not allow her to return to her fellow barbarians until he was long gone. Therefore, she had to stay with him as his partner in this bizarre religion.

"I offer you a bargain. I will untie you if you will agree to remain here. Otherwise I shall leave you bound. Even worse than that, I shall demand a different partner," he lied. "I do not know who will purify you then. Shi Po will have the choosing, and she is not a tender woman."

The barbarian did not respond, but her very stillness told him she understood her choices exactly.

"Will you make this bargain with me?" he asked. "Will you accept the training from me? Without struggle?"

She didn't respond at first. Instead she stared at him, her eyes narrowed. Her gaze felt heavy upon him, as if she were weighing his worth and his honesty against those of some unknown stranger chosen by Shi Po.

Then Heaven intervened to assist her: A noise sounded from just outside the door. It was not a loud sound, merely the shuffling of tired feet. Zou Tun saw Miss Crane's eyes cut straight to the door, and he knew her thoughts. She wondered if the person outside would help or hurt her. Was the guard there to keep them locked inside? Or could he be turned to assist her?

Zou Tun decided to answer her questions. Without another word he grabbed the cold tea tray and unlocked the door, pulling it as wide-open as possible. Just in the hallway, standing right outside the door, was not one, but two heavily armed guards. There was no surprise on the men's faces when they looked inside and saw a ghost woman chained to the bed, merely a smirking envy. One of them took the cold tray from Zou Tun's hands.

Zou Tun shut the door, cutting off the men's leering looks. He walked back to the bed.

"Choose now," he said. "Will you make this bargain with me? If I untie your bonds, will you accept what I must do?"

She cast one last look at the doorway, her dismay evident. She did not want one of those men to touch her. And so, with a sigh, she nodded her head. She would accept his bargain.

Without another word he unbound her hands and her feet, helping her to sit as she tried to rub feeling back into her wrists. He waited patiently, knowing neither of them wished to proceed. Still, he was excruciatingly aware of the passing time. How long would Shi

Po spend with her husband? How long before she came to inspect their progress?

He did not know, but he feared her reaction if they did not begin soon. With a voice as gentle as possible, he turned to Miss Crane.

"We must begin now. Please remove your robe."

> *5 March, 1896*
> *Dearest Kang Zou,*
>
> *A great evil has befallen me! Terrible demons have killed my darling songbird. Oh, my brother, she was singing so sweetly, but then with a great boom her song was silenced. When I rushed to see my darling bird, it was an old, shriveled thing, a most despicable creature that once had given me such pleasure. How horrid for such a young bird to be struck down needlessly.*
>
> *My only explanation is that I called these demons of death to me. My melancholy at your absence has given me such grief that I drew evil to me. Oh, please, dear brother, can you not come home for a short time to save me from the ghosts that must now be drawing ever nearer?*
>
> *Confucius speaks of the natural family order. Ours is out of balance without your presence.*
>
> *Your grieving sister,*
> *Wen Ji*

Decoded translation:

> Son, great evil threatens our country. My battles against the white barbarians have gone very badly. The enemy has some ghostly magic that destroys our brave soldiers. The Chinese fall like old, shriveled

men at the mere sound of the white people's booming guns. Without a success soon, our family name will be forever struck from the emperor's mouth.

You must bring me word of your success. Our only hope lies with you.

Do not forget your obligations to family and country. A dutiful son and a good Manchurian would accomplish your task speedily.

> Your anxious father,
> General Kang

30 March, 1896
Dearest Wen Ji,

I grieve with you, and tremble that such terrible ghosts should threaten our family garden. Is there no defense against these monsters? I have made offerings in your name and pray ceaselessly for your welfare.

The climate warms slowly here in the mountains, and my studies proceed even more weakly. But I have found great wisdom here, amazing wonders in the writings of Lao Tzu. Though I fear for you constantly, my soul is learning peace for the first time. My heart toils ceaselessly toward enlightenment, and I spend long hours striving to walk in harmony with what is natural. I wish that you could join me here, learning from the abbot's wisdom. But of course, such things are impossible.

But perhaps Heaven will smile upon us yet, dropping the impossible into our hands.

> *Your hopeful brother,*
> *Kang Zou*

Decoded translation:

Dearest Father,

I grieve that the battle against the barbarians goes so badly. Is there nothing you can learn to fight them? I have made offerings to Buddha for your welfare.

I have made little progress finding the conspirators. But I have discovered great knowledge among the monks. The Tao brings peace and joy to my heart, and I spend much time striving to walk a true monk's path.

I wish to show you these things, to teach you as I have been taught. But of course, as a general, you cannot afford such luxury. Still, if I earnestly devote myself to my studies, perhaps Buddha will bless our family with good fortune.

Your devout son,
Zou Tun

Everyone is selfish and has desires. If we wish to rid our-
selves of selfish desires, we must first engage in self-
examination, and then we must purify and empty ourselves.
If we can understand ourselves, overcome ourselves, be con-
tent and persevere, then we will have attained the Tao.
—Lao Tzu

Chapter Five

Joanna knew the time had come, long before the Mandarin said a word, but her mind had still not fully
come to grips with the situation. She was locked in a
room. Her throat had been hurt so that she could not
make a sound or even breathe deeply without great
pain. And some woman was making her and this man
both do some kind of exercises that involved manipu-
lation of one's most private places.

The concept was bizarre, the situation even more
so. And yet here she sat while a man calmly informed
her it was time to take off her robe. She had heard
about these kinds of deviants. There were whispers
and rumors of girls trapped and sold into sexual slav-
ery. Though her situation did not exactly fit what
she'd heard, she supposed that was what had happened to her.

Indeed, it would be what everyone would assume
had happened to her, whether or not she escaped with
her virtue intact.

Unfortunately, her reputation was not her most immediate problem. Captivity. Injury. Great pain. All these were more pressing.

She was tempted to embrace a fit of histrionics, to allow the pain to knock her unconscious so that she would not have to endure whatever was coming. Indeed, unconsciousness seemed like an excellent option right then. Too bad she wasn't in the least bit interested in being senseless.

It was stupid, really, and Joanna felt a grave disappointment in herself for her cowardice. The bald truth was that she was too afraid to force herself to black out. What would happen to her? What would be done? To what would she be subjected? She found she didn't want to be blind and deaf in addition to being mute. She might miss an opportunity to escape—or a clue to this bizarre situation.

To make herself unconscious would be to surrender to hopelessness. And she could not give up that easily. Which meant she had to stay awake. Which meant . . .

She had to take off her robe.

"No," she tried to whisper. But pain cut off the sound before she could do more than shake her head.

The Mandarin's eyes grew hard. "You have promised, Joanna Crane. Do you wish to be tied up again?"

She shook her head. She could accomplish nothing when bound. Instead she pointed to the scroll. Perhaps if she knew what was to happen, she would be better able to choose. After all, she could always knock herself out with a few deep breaths, right? So perhaps if she could see the scroll, understand what made those women so beautiful . . .

He handed it to her, spreading it open upon her lap. "You see," he said in the same low, soothing tones he had used to calm her horse. "I shall read it to you so you understand there is nothing to fear."

In truth, she could read the text relatively well on

her own. After a decade in this country, she had learned a great deal. But the more he spoke aloud, the longer the delay. So she nodded, smiling slightly by way of thanks.

"'That which is old will become young again,'" he began. "'That which sags will become firm. The lotus will bloom and dew will glisten like pearls among the petals.'" Then he pointed to a picture of a naked woman sitting with her right leg bent. "You must sit like this with your foot pressed against your cinnabar cave."

She frowned, not sure she understood.

"Cinnabar cave," he repeated slowly. "It is there. At the juncture of a woman's thighs. We call it such because of the unique scent."

Joanna felt her face flush with embarrassment. No one had ever shown her pictures such as these, much less discussed them with such frank honesty. But the Manchurian continued, moving on to a picture of a woman with her hands on her breasts.

"'For purification, circle the breasts seventy-two times, starting in the center, then moving outward. Rehabilitation begins by moving the hands in the opposite direction, starting at the outside and moving toward the center.'" He stopped reading then, but Joanna did not. She continued to scan the words, trying to understand.

Then she felt the man's hand gently lifting her chin, forcing her to look into his eyes.

"Do barbarians put great store in a woman's purity?" he asked. Then he frowned, shaking his head. "Not purity. Virginity. Do you barbarians prize a woman's virginity?"

She managed to nod, even though her face was flaming.

"We Chinese do as well. That is why Tigresses do not

allow a man's dragon ever to enter their caves. It distends the opening and steals her youthful fluids."

Joanna blinked, completely lost. She glanced back down at the scroll, touching the sketch of a tiger—no, a tigress—stretching its body down the page, appearing just as a small cat would when waking from a nap. The pose was evocative, and had drawn her eye from the beginning.

"Yes. The women here are called Tigresses. The men are Dragons. The best, I believe, are called Jade Dragons. We are to learn their practice."

Her gaze shot back to his eyes, her question obvious. *Why?*

He hesitated, and she could read his inner debate on his face. Would he tell her the truth or not? She was about to become mutinous in demanding honesty when he shrugged his shoulders, apparently deciding on the truth.

"I am here to discharge a debt, and the Tigress Shi Po named this as my punishment."

Joanna's eyes widened. This training was his punishment? But if he saw her question, he did not answer. Instead he reached forward, taking her hand casually.

"You are here because I cannot release you. I cannot allow . . . certain people to know that I am here. And so, as long as I am in Shanghai, you must remain here and silent."

She straightened, wishing desperately that she could speak, that she could find the words to convince him that she would say nothing. But of course, he knew that. She pressed her hands to her throat, then to her mouth. She couldn't say anything. Didn't he understand that?

He nodded. "Yes, that is why I shut off your voice box. So you could not speak." Then he sighed. "But you can read, can't you? And write?"

Her hands slipped away from her mouth, and she

began to deny it. But before she could shake her head, he stopped her by again touching her chin. He held her steady, his eyes seeming darker than the black ink on the scroll between them.

"Do not lie to me, Miss Joanna Crane. It will poison the trust between us; then I fear we will never finish the training. We will be trapped in this tiny room for the rest of our lives."

She frowned, knowing that could not be true. By now her father surely knew she was missing. Likely he would bring guards into every home and brothel in the whole of southern China. And he would not stop until he found her. All she needed to do was survive until he arrived. Survive and look for her opportunity to escape.

Meanwhile, her companion's fingers gripped her chin even tighter. "You are hoping for an opportunity to escape. That is only natural. But I am your single ally in this place. You may be able to hurt me, but you cannot run from them."

She studied his expression closely as he spoke, and she read no lie in his face. But he spoke as if the women—the Tigress and her guards—were her enemy. Perhaps they were his enemy, but she had done nothing wrong. Nothing but speak rashly on a road outside of Shanghai. And yet, she didn't know what he'd told the Tigress about her. What exactly would they do to her if she escaped him? Who was more dangerous? More sincere?

"This I swear to you, Miss Joanna Crane: I will not hurt you. I will not take your virginity. I wish only to practice this religion with you until we both may leave. If you treat me honestly, I will remain true to this vow. But if you lie to me, I will not object when the Tigress sells you to a perfumed garden, where you will be addicted to opium and sold to the highest bidder. Do you understand?"

Joanna swallowed, knowing he was not lying to her. Even worse, she suspected he spoke the truth about her future as well. This was not a brothel such as she had heard of. And if she did not want to go to one of those, then she would have to make the best of it here. With him.

She nodded, though her eyes were blurred with tears. He did not let them fall. Instead he gently wiped them away with his thumbs.

"I like it that you wear no paint," he commented, surprise lacing his voice. "It allows me to see you are flesh and blood, not ghostly spirit. It will make this easier on us both."

She blinked, startled and annoyed by his comment. Did he truly think she cared whether he wanted her in cosmetics or not?

"Much better," he said, a smile softening his features. "You have much fire in you. You should not diminish it with tears."

It took a moment for her to understand. When she did, she could not believe she had heard correctly. Had he been teasing her? So that she would not cry? But why?

"I am not a monster, Joanna Crane," he said gently. "I am—"

Who? She cut him off by abruptly pressing her hand against his chest. Then she mouthed the word again. *Who? Who are you?*

He hesitated. Clearly he did not want to tell her the truth. Especially as he had gone to such pains to hide his identity. But he was no monk; that much she had already figured out. And so she began guessing, mouthing the words as best she could.

Imperial?

He didn't answer, but then he didn't need to. She

trailed her finger down his long, straight nose. He was definitely Manchurian. Probably of the royal line.

Prince?

He grabbed her hand, pulling it away from his face. "No-Name. You may call me Monk No-Name."

She grimaced at him, but he did not pause. Instead, with a quick, businesslike air, he put her hands against the edges of her robe.

"Remove it so that we may begin."

Her time had run out. He would allow no more delays. Indeed, as she hesitated, he put the scroll aside and pushed at her legs so that she would adjust her position.

"You need not remove this covering, so long as you sit correctly." So saying, he held the fabric closed even as he pushed at her right knee.

She accommodated him as best she could, bending her leg so that her thighs fell open. He kept the robe closed so that nothing was exposed. Nothing he could see, of course. But she still felt it. She felt the air and the bedsheets. She felt her hips tilt and her unmentionable area—the area that no longer had hair—tingle with unaccustomed awareness.

Her face flamed even hotter, but no tears blurred her vision. Instead she focused on her anger. Anger at him—Monk No-Name—who had brought her to this place. Fury that an imperial prince tried to hide his own identity, and yet did it so badly that a wandering stranger could figure him out. And pure rage that any man, much less an incompetent imperial spy, could simply order her to open her legs and bare her breasts.

And yet, here she was doing it. She bent her knee and allowed him to push the heel of her right foot tight against her groin. The area was hot against her foot—hot and wet in a way she had never experienced before, but she knew when it happened. She had grown moist as she watched him with his own purification rite. And now she was still wet and pulsing as he pushed on her heel. The change in her body made her even angrier.

"You must expose your breasts," he stated firmly. Then he added in a softer tone, "Find your center. It will make everything easier."

She didn't understand his meaning, but then she didn't care. Instead she glared at him, wishing she truly had fire in her eyes. She would burn him to a crisp where he sat. She would . . .

Fanciful dreams would not serve her now, so she abruptly cut them off. He was reaching forward to strip her, but she slapped his hands away. He pulled back, his anger growing, but she didn't care. He needed to understand. She wasn't refusing the task, but she had to do it on her own. Of her own choice. And with her own hands.

She swallowed and, with shaking hands, slowly pushed her robe off her shoulders. It slid easily down to her elbows, especially as she was tucking her arms tight around herself, still trying to keep herself covered. But that was silly. She would have to have it off if she intended to perform the circles. She would have to take her arms completely out of the sleeves.

She took a breath—not too deep, especially as her tears had tightened her throat and cut off her breath. She didn't want that. Not yet. Not now. Not when she had just gained some measure of control.

She steeled herself to act. Her whole body trembled as she moved, but she slowly, inevitably, pulled her arms out of her sleeves, allowing the fabric to pool at her waist.

She was naked from there up, in front of a man who

was not her husband. At that moment her courage
failed her. Her head was bowed so that the long curls
of her hair fell down before her face. Her bare arms
clutched her exposed chest, and she was folded in on
herself almost to her knees.

No matter what she said to herself, she could not do
more than that.

She felt his hand, gentle and soothing upon her
shoulder. "This is a small room, and I cannot leave it.
But I do not need to be here, directly in front of you."
She felt his weight lift off the bed and the whisper of
the air as he moved behind her. "Perhaps if I sit here,
with my eyes closed, this will be like bathing for you.
In the privacy of your own chamber. Only instead of
your body, you are cleansing your yin. Would that be
better for you?"

His hand had not left her shoulder even as he
walked around her. And though her back prickled at
the shift of air and space behind her, his hand kept her
grounded. His warmth kept her sane. In the end she
was able to nod, straightening by slow inches as she
tried to hold his thought in her mind.

I am in my own chamber. I am alone. I am simply washing.
She thought the words to herself over and over, but
no matter how she tried, she could not convince herself of the illusion. The truth was that she was *not*
alone. He was with her. And she was naked and . . .
and touching herself.

"Your body is like ice," he murmured from behind
her. "I am not even touching you, and yet I can feel it."
He sighed. "Miss Crane . . . Joanna. Please, this is
merely an exercise. Like sitting up or walking. An action of the body. There is no shame in it, and though
your modesty does you credit, it will not serve you
now."

She had no response to that, even if she could have

spoken. Perversely, his voice—his very presence—made what she needed to do easier. She was able to straighten further as he continued to speak, his voice conversational.

"Many women in China believe their bodies are meant to be adorned, to be beautiful, to be appreciated by men but never touched. As if they were a flower that can only be viewed. Touch it, and it withers and dies. But I have never seen the sense in that. Our bodies are part of ourselves. Tools, if you will. And if the tool is pleasing, then all the better. But like all tools, the body must be maintained. It must be attended to, honed, and perfected."

He leaned forward, his breath a hot wind in her ear that sent shivers down her spine.

"In this, perhaps the Tigresses are correct. A body must be touched. Even the flowers are ministered to by the bees and butterflies, by a gardener's hand, by a child's delight. Perhaps a woman's body must be touched as well to find its full purpose."

She knew he would touch her then. Her back tingled with his presence long before she felt the brush of his fingertips.

"I wish to help, Joanna. I wish to make this process easier for you. To help you learn it is not evil, merely a new avenue of study. I have no lewd interest in your body. My desire is only to make you more comfortable. Miss Crane, *may* I assist you?"

Joanna almost smiled at his formal tone. He sounded as if he were offering her a hand out of a carriage or to be her escort to a party. But he wasn't offering anything so proper. And the thought of his hands on her body brought . . .

Brought what? Tears to her eyes? Nonsense. Fury into her soul? No. Not anymore. She had seen the Tigress Shi Po and believed that woman to be the real enemy here. In this she believed in Monk No-Name. He truly wished to help.

She felt him place both his hands on her back, right between her shoulder blades. Then slowly, ever so gently, he widened them, letting his fingertips trail across her shoulders and down her arms until he encircled her with his heat.

"Chilled hands will only frighten your yin. It will shrivel in the cold, trapping the pollutants inside."

So saying, he cupped his hands around hers, lifting them slightly as he tried to warm her. But her chill came from deep within and could not be heated so easily. He waited there a moment, letting her grow accustomed to him. She felt the calluses on the outside of his hands, the roughness of his skin, and the exquisite gentleness of his touch.

"Let me guide you," he whispered, and so he slowly pushed her hands to her chest, setting her fingers on her breastbone.

She was not ready for such things, and she shrank backward, away from her hands still cupped in his. But there was nowhere for her to go except back, deeper into his arms. She wanted to shy away from him, too, for his upper torso was still naked. His chiseled, strong chest was still bare for any to see. And she *had* seen. And she liked what she saw.

But a pleasing picture was one thing; having a man's naked chest pressed against her bare back was something else entirely. And so she tried to grow tiny, shrinking away from his chest behind her and his hands in front. Except they weren't his hands. They were her own. He only guided her. And so, in the end, that was where she allowed the touch.

She straightened, to pull her back away from him, but the motion pressed her breasts into her hands. Her tiny hands, surrounded by his much larger ones.

His large hands, which neared her flesh but did not quite touch. Unless she moved quickly, unexpectedly.

So she didn't. She sat excruciatingly still while his large hands guided hers.

"We must do seventy-two circles this way," he said. And he moved their hands upward from the center bone to separate over the tops of her breasts. Then he guided her hands to the sides, drawing them open as they traced the gentle swells to the fullness underneath.

Joanna felt only her own hands touching her breasts, but it was his heat, his breath, his power that moved her. Their hands flowed above, around, and then below her breasts, lifting and massaging what had up until now simply been fleshy attachments to her body, a pair of fatty mounds of less importance than her legs or arms.

But that was not how they felt now. After first one circle, then another and another and more still, she began to feel her skin, her breath, her center like two tiny flames just beneath the surface. And with each circle the flames steadied. They didn't grow, but they ceased to flicker. What had been two unstable glimpses of light settled into tiny coals of the dullest red—warm, but not burning. Giving heat but not fire. That was how her breasts felt. As if they were the outward symbol of those two tiny coals.

Seventy-two.

The Manchurian's hands stilled, stopping in the center of her chest between her breasts. Joanna blinked, startled to realize she had relaxed backward into his arms. That his head rested next to hers, their cheeks almost touching but not quite, especially as he was taller than she, his arms longer than hers, and his legs were bent awkwardly at her back.

"You must change your leg position now," he murmured.

She had forgotten how she sat, her right leg bent so that her foot pressed against her groin. Except as she had shrunk from his hands, she had slid backward, so her heel no longer pressed tightly against her.

"It must be hard to keep the pressure against the cinnabar cave," he said as he looked over her shoulder. She was still covered, but he must have understood what had happened. "If you press your back against my leg, it will help to hold you steady."

Twisting around, she realized now that he sat much as she did. One leg extended to the floor, but the other was bent, giving her a solid, straight support to brace against. She glanced up at his face, studying his expression, fearing what she might find there. But his features were relaxed, his face smooth and simple and completely impassive.

Could a man remain so calm when nearly touching a woman's breasts? Her old nanny would say no, but looking at this man, Joanna could believe it. Whereas her mind and heart were still churning with turmoil, his gaze remained calm and quiet.

Whatever his true identity, he certainly appeared as asexual as a monk. Or perhaps he was a man who had found that center he spoke of.

She let her gaze slip down to his nether region. She knew what a man's anatomy was. And if she didn't, he had displayed it for her an hour before. But his position pulled his loose pants away from his body. He could be ready to expel his white liquid again, and she would not know. So her gaze traveled back to his face as she once again tried to read his intention.

"If I wished to ravish you, Miss Joanna Crane, I would not have untied you from the bed." His voice was an ironic drawl, as if he mocked himself and her in the same sentence. But then his tone deepened, and all traces of humor—sarcastic or otherwise—disappeared. "I have promised to protect you to the best of my ability. I will not break my word."

She took another long breath, another long look to search for any lie in his body or face. There weren't any. And so she nodded, smiled her thanks as best she could, and readjusted her position. She pushed her body toward him so that her lower back pressed hard against his shin. Then she lifted her braid off her shoulders, coiled it, and repinned it in place.

She felt him reach forward, helping her to pull her left leg tight to her body. She did not want to tuck it close, but he was insistent.

"You must stop the flow of energy there. It is not time."

So she helped him tuck her foot against her . . . what had he called it? Her cinnabar cave. It was a startling thing, this hardness of her heel against a place that felt soft and moist and open. She thought she would not like it, but there was pleasure in the sensation, so she allowed him to pull her leg even tighter.

"Your hands are still like ice. It was not as serious before. The first circles can be cooler, as they disperse the pollutants. But now we are stirring the fire. Coldness will not aid you here."

She looked down at her hands, once again cupped within his larger ones. They appeared so pale, so tiny against his darker, tanned skin. Clearly this monk had spent a great deal of time outside. And just as clearly she could see how the superstitious Chinese would call her a ghost. Her hands did indeed appear insubstantial next to his.

And as she watched, he lifted her hands, brought them close to her mouth. "Blow on them," he instructed. "Warm your hands."

She did as he bade even though she knew it would not help. Her chill came from her soul; her hands would not warm until her internal heat returned. And in time he realized the truth as well.

"My hands are warm," he said, his voice careful. "I do not wish to frighten you, but I can perform this exercise for you. If you wish me to help."

She knew she ought to object. She knew she ought to do a lot of things, beginning with having stayed at home so long ago. So what was one more mistake in a legion of mistakes? If these exercises must be performed, then let them be done correctly. In a way that would not cause harm.

She nodded, slowly allowing her hands to slip from his.

"Close your eyes," he instructed. "Lean back against me and simply be without thought or emotion. If you feel pleasure, allow it. If you feel fear, accept it. They are all parts of you that can occur without changing you. Allow your emotions to exist and you will learn that without resistance they will flow through you, leaving you in peace. Do you understand?"

No, she did not. But she was willing to try. And so she lied, nodding her head even as she closed her eyes.

"Breathe," he instructed, his words becoming a slow monotone. "In. Out. In. Out. Steady. Calm. Unafraid."

Then he began.

His touch startled her, but not as she expected. She had thought having a man caress her would make her excruciatingly uncomfortable, sort of how one tolerated a fitting for new clothing. Awkward. Possibly embarrassing. But mostly just something she had to endure until it was over.

But this went far beyond that. This was a man's hands on her breasts. First two, then three, then four

101

fingers pressed against the bone between each breast. Then he began circling, moving underneath and around, then above and between. It was a steady flow, but in an ever-narrowing spiral.

"Breathe," he ordered, and the hot puff of his breath against her ear made her gasp.

"Steadily."

She nodded, knowing what he wanted but unsure she could comply. His hands were moving higher, narrower, circling toward her nipple, and the feel of that made her squirm.

"Remain still!"

This time his voice snapped her back to attention, but it was excruciatingly hard to obey. Her breasts seemed to be throbbing, but not evenly. The beat followed in the wake of his hands, pulling tighter with his every narrowed circle.

She did not want him to touch her nipples, and so she breathed in as deeply as possible, trying to push his hands wider. But then she had to exhale, and as she did, his circle tightened again. This was so bizarre. And yet it was no different from when she'd performed the circles. No different except in direction. And the spirals. And that his hands were like hot wind, blown steadily over the coals behind her breasts.

With his ever-tightening circle, the coals grew redder, radiating more heat, more power, more . . . everything. Joanna didn't know how to comprehend it. Didn't know how she should feel about it.

"You are resisting," he said, his words matter-of-fact. "It will stop the flow and cause more problems. Embrace your confusion. Accept the fear. And then it will pass from you."

Embrace confusion? She was confused. There was no embracing it. Accept the fear? How did one accept being afraid? She was afraid. She didn't want to be. So she . . . she fought it.

That was what he meant. So she grabbed hold of his wrists, holding his hands still while she struggled with the panic caused by breasts suddenly alien to her body. She held his wrists still, feeling the steady beat of his pulse beneath her fingers, but mostly feeling his heat, his patience.

His calm.

Easy for him to be calm. He didn't have some person making his body swell and throb. Except he had swelled before. While she watched. And that memory did more to distract her than anything else.

"Do not run to other thoughts. Stay with your body. Stay with what is happening here. Hiding only clogs the qi flow."

She frowned in irritation. She'd never hidden from anything in her life. Unfortunately, he must have taken her expression to mean something else, because he began to explain.

"Qi is the Chinese word for energy. It is both male and female. Yang for male, yin for female—"

She shook her head, cutting off his annoying explanation. She twisted, looking back at him and seeing his clenched jaw, though his eyes remained impassive. She strongly suspected she wasn't the only one who was trying to distract unwanted thoughts. But that would not serve either of them.

She had read enough of the yin text to know that she was supposed to focus on purification with the first seventy-two circles, then the rising tide of yin. Well, water imagery didn't work for her. It never had. So she decided to stay with the thought of coals, burning hotter with each breath and with each circle.

That was what she would embrace. Not fear, not

embarrassment or even confusion. Those were necessary evils to this situation. She would make the exercise as effective as possible, and thereby end it as soon as possible.

So she took a deep breath—or as deep as her sore throat allowed. And as she exhaled, she released the Mandarin's hands, allowing him to begin again. All the while, she held the image in her mind—hot coals. Hot yin coals. Yin fire, burning beneath her breasts.

God, she was on fire. Her breasts, her ribs, her entire body crackled with heat. She arched her back, giving her breasts as much room as possible, as much air, as much space as she could while his hands continued to stoke hot circles of energy into them.

Again his hands narrowed, the spiral winding tighter, closer, higher. Now she found she didn't inhale so deeply, countering his movements. Instead she exhaled all the way, wanting his touch to rise closer. To touch her nearer.

She wasn't even sure where she wanted him to go. Her mind was consumed by the fire, by the flow of his hands, stirring the energy around and around. Higher. Hotter.

What was she straining toward?

"Seventy-two."

She didn't say the word. Someone else had. Her Mandarin? His hands had stopped moving, his fingers pressed just to the inside of each tightened nipple.

But she didn't want him to stop. She wanted more. She wanted to know—

Why was the Tigress Shi Po standing over her?

Why does heaven dislike "bravery in firmness"? Who knows the reason? The way of nature is to win without contending, to reply without speaking, to have things come without calling, to plan without worrying. . . . We should take nature as our example and dispense with firmness and contention.

—Lao Tzu

Chapter Six

Zou Tun's body flushed with anger. How dared the Tigress enter his bedroom unannounced? How dared she look at him and Joanna Crane as if they were bad food that even dogs would not touch? And how dared she stand in silence, judging them as she would—

—a student? Evaluating them as an instructor did her pupils?

No. Her thoughts were more calculating. More intricate. What was she thinking?

It did not matter. She would not act so again.

Joanna was just coming back to herself, her body still trembling with the power of her yin. And what sweet power it was, burning like a white star such as Zou Tun had never experienced. He reached forward, grabbing the sheet to cover her as quickly as possible. The Tigress had no need to see such beauty. It demeaned Joanna somehow. And Zou Tun greedily wished to keep her for himself, not even sharing her with the woman who claimed to be their teacher.

Such were not the thoughts of a holy man, but Zou

105

Tun did not care. He was too angry with Shi Po's intrusion to think straight.

The Tigress stepped closer, her eyes narrowed. She studied them more thoroughly. No doubt she saw Joanna's flushed cheeks and reddened lips. Zou Tun knew that beneath the sheet, the white woman's hands were tightening into fists. But even more important, she was beginning to curl into herself, drawing tighter against Zou Tun and farther away from the Tigress.

"Why have you disturbed us?" he demanded, his voice low and hoarse.

Shi Po stiffened. "It is my right to inspect my students."

Zou Tun gently shifted from beneath Joanna and firmly stood before the Tigress. She was small in stature, much smaller than he'd expected, given the power of her qi. But he was not intimidated. Instead he did his best to tower over her, making his demands absolutely clear even as he blocked her view of Joanna.

"I care not what you do with your other students. You will not enter here without our permission. Never again."

"This is my home," she hissed. "You are my guest."

"Then accord us the honor of guests and do not walk uninvited into our bedroom."

Her eyes narrowed, and for a moment he felt the power of her rank. He felt menaced by a tigress. And yet he refused even to blink.

"There is a great commotion in the barbarian territories. It seems a ghost woman has gone missing."

Zou Tun heard Joanna shift on the bed, her attention obviously caught. Fortunately she was still mute. Before she could say or do anything, he spoke, doing his best to distract Shi Po.

"Who can understand what goes on with barbarians?" Irritated, Shi Po slipped to his side and stared at

Joanna. "Do not toy with me, monk. They are searching for this girl. Why? What evil have you brought to
my home?"

"No evil. But if it frightens you, release me and her.
I will see that she is returned to the barbarians."

On the bed, Joanna nodded, obviously wanting exactly what he offered. But Shi Po did not leap at the
suggestion, as he hoped. Instead she reached out, her
hand hovering inches above Joanna's breast as if feeling the air there.

"Her yin runs so clearly. And after only one session."
Joanna shrank from Shi Po's sharp fingernails, but
could not move away. Instead the ghost woman closed
her eyes, fighting mutely as the Tigress gripped her
chin, lifting her flushed face to the lamplight spilling
in from the hallway. "These barbarians are strange
creatures. Perhaps their lack of civilization makes
them closer to their elements. Perhaps—"

Joanna clearly had enough of the inspection. She
suddenly jerked her head out of the Tigress's hands,
pushing to her feet, sheet still clutched to her chest.
Her bearing was regal as any imperial consort's, and
with firm steps she made for the open door.

For a moment Zou Tun almost believed she could
make it, that this reddish-haired barbarian woman
wrapped in a sheet could walk right out of the Tigress's
home without anyone daring to stop her. But someone
did dare, and it wasn't Zou Tun or the Tigress. It was
Kui Yu, the Tigress's husband, sauntering in.

"Oh!" he exclaimed, as if he had intended to find
the dining room and simply missed. He blinked and
focused on his surroundings. "My apologies," he said
to Joanna as he blocked the exit. "But my dear, you
simply cannot leave like this. Your dress looks like a
sheet."

Joanna pointed to the door, indicating she wanted

to leave. Even from the side, Zou Tun could see the shimmer of tears in her eyes. She had been pushed too far, having lost both her freedom and her voice in less than two days.

Kui Yu gathered her arms together, holding her hands in his. "I see this often, you know. My wife thinks I don't, but I do. All the new girls are frightened at first, even though they chose this path." He shook his head. "It is a confusing thing, this becoming a Tigress. How much more disturbing for a barbarian with no training in our Taoist ways? Still, I will tell you what I tell all of them."

He smiled warmly at her, even daring to brush a curl from her face. "You must think about what you are returning to and what you are giving up. Here you will not be mistreated. You will be taught a skill with which to fascinate your husband, keeping him enthralled throughout your life together. You have a chance to become immortal and be revered by all. But most important, you will learn peace, my child. A quietness of the soul that comes from walking the Middle Path." He tilted her chin so that she looked directly at him. "Can your life at home offer you as much?"

Joanna nodded her head. *Yes,* she indicated. Her home offered her as much.

Kui Yu patted her hand. "Ah, that is merely fear talking. In any event, it is too late for you to leave today. There are many dangers in Shanghai at night. Fortunately we have sturdy servants to keep us safe here." So saying, he gestured to the thick-chested brute who stood guard just outside the door. Then he turned back, tweaking Joanna's chin and smiling in a fatherly way. "Think on it tonight and see how you feel in the morning. If you still wish to leave, I will assist you." He extended his hand to his wife. "My heart, the evening shadows grow long, and my thoughts dull without you to lighten my cares. Please leave our guests to their tasks. Even great Tigresses must rest."

As if pulled by her husband's will, Shi Po glided forward and took Kui Yu's hand. But she didn't leave. Instead she frowned at Joanna, tilting her head slightly. "What is it about these barbarians that makes their yin so strong? It is a puzzle that must be sorted out."

"Of course," agreed Kui Yu in an affable voice. "But not tonight. It grows late."

Shi Po nodded, moving with him as if an obedient wife. But her words carried even as she shut the door. "I wish I had seen Ru Shan's pet before they left. Now I have only this ghost to study."

Then her voice was lost, leaving Zou Tun to watch Joanna fight with the door—first trying to open the lock, then banging on the wood hard enough to make it tremble. It made no difference, of course. He had heard the snick of the bolt after Shi Po left. And even if the door were unlocked, the guard still stood outside. Her struggle was hopeless.

As was his own.

He dropped on the bed with a sigh, watching until Joanna came to the same realization. She did so slowly, her body weakening, her arm tiring enough to stop pounding on the door. Then, a moment later, she would gather herself together and begin banging again. Twice he watched her go through this process: allowing hopelessness to take hold, her spirit weakening until she gathered herself together again and pounded her small white fist against the door. She was obviously praying someone would finally listen to her.

But they didn't. Only Zou Tun watched, and in the end he could stand it no more. He stood, gently touching her arms.

"They will not listen tonight, Joanna. But perhaps Kui Yu will help you tomorrow." It was a lie, for he could not allow it to happen. Even if she could convince Kui Yu to release her, Zou Tun could not allow her to leave. Not while he was bound by Shi Po to remain. It was dangerous enough if the Imperial soldiers found him and dragged him back to his father. It was even worse for everyone if his cousins—his competitors for the throne—discovered him. They would think nothing of razing the entire household.

Yet she needed something to hold on to, so he murmured that tomorrow would offer new possibilities.

She didn't want him to touch her. She shook him off many times. But he was persistent. And gentle. And in the end her tears forced her to stop. He watched her crumple and sink down against the doorway. He knew now that she had at last realized her situation. She now accepted that they were both prisoners here and would not be released anytime soon. Up until now she had been playing at understanding, pretending it was a game.

Now she knew. And her sobs wrenched his heart.

He gathered her in his arms and carried her to the bed. She did not resist, even when he curled his body around her. It was cold at night, even in the southern city of Shanghai. With only a single blanket between them, the shared body heat was welcome.

And besides, even if she did not need this comfort, he did. He closed his eyes, trying to appreciate his first bed since the burning of the monastery. His body should be glorying in its gentle pillowing instead of the cold, hard ground.

But he could not enjoy himself. Instead he drew his only pleasure from the soft woman in his arms, the beautiful Joanna Crane, barbarian ghost whose yin had been like molten silver flowing around his soul. It had not been a physical sensation as much as a mental image, but it had persisted the more he purified her yin.

He was a monk with three years of training—three years of discipline in mind and body, of a slowly quieting soul and a learned willingness to hear the messages of the divine. Yet in that time, he had heard nothing. Not a word. He had found only a peace that calmed him, that invaded his very spirit as no political intrigue ever had.

But now her. Joanna Crane. Ghost barbarian. Her purity had flowed through him, warmed him, brought him a divine whisper that three years of dedicated study had not. Could it be that this bizarre female sect, this Tigress cult, knew something the ascetic Shaolin monks did not? Could it be that the discipline of Paochui fighting and the study of ancient texts were not enough to attain enlightenment? That exalted understanding required the combined energy of female yin and male yang to catapult one somewhere that his abbott's celibate students had never been?

He did not want to think it possible. And yet he could not deny that he had felt more than simple lust when purifying Joanna Crane's yin. He had felt the whisper of the divine.

Which left him in a quandary. He had intended to stay with the Tigress for a few days, a week at most. He had intended to learn what he could from her and then escape. Seven days' respite. Seven days to assuage his conscience with regard to his old master. Seven days to decide how to proceed once he returned to Peking.

Seven days would have been plenty of time for these tasks. He'd even planned to return Joanna to her home, should circumstances allow. But seven days were not nearly long enough to achieve enlightenment.

Worse, he knew that pure yin was as rare as a phoenix

feather. Certainly none of the women he had known before were close to what he found in Joanna. He had no understanding if all white women flowed as sweetly, but she was the only woman he had access to now. And she could very well be a key to enlightenment.

None of this made any sense to him: that a female cult could have answers that the Shaolin did not. That a ghost barbarian could lead an imperial prince to enlightenment. And yet fortune came in many disguises. He would be a fool to release something for which many spent a lifetime searching.

He had to keep her. He had to pursue the Tigress teachings in earnest with Joanna. And yet he had to return to Peking to face his responsibilities there. If she were Chinese, he could marry her and take her wherever he willed. But she was a ghost woman, one of the barbarians who were poisoning his country with opium. He could not marry a ghost woman. Neither could he take her as concubine or even a pet. These things would be considered heinous for a commoner; for an imperial prince, such a crime would not only see him killed, but would likely destroy his entire family.

No, he could not take Joanna to Peking with him. And so whatever enlightenment he desired, he had to find it now, here in Tigress Shi Po's home. While outside the imperial forces moved ever closer.

With that unhappy thought, he resolved himself to sleep. The morning would require study such as he had never before known.

Joanna felt warm for the first time in a long while. The sensation was so pleasant that she deliberately kept her eyes closed and her mind blank. She knew something waited, something ugly that would surface the moment she came to full consciousness. So she tried to postpone the inevitable; she concentrated exclusively on the enveloping heat, giving it names and images as she drifted in and out of sleep.

It was like a hot breeze on a chilly night.

It was like fuzzy mittens on a winter's day.

It was like a strong, hot man wrapping her between his powerful thighs.

She jerked, shocked by her thought. But what brought her to full consciousness was the hideous truth: She *was* surrounded by hot man. Hot, nearly naked man. And she was nearly naked as well!

She sat bolt upright, her gasp shooting needles of pain down her throat. And that was when the ugly reality hit, when she remembered everything she hadn't wanted to remember, when she knew where she was and that she'd slept all night with a man.

His eyes were open as well, but he did not move. He merely watched her, his expression calm, his body tense.

Joanna opened her mouth to say something, but the pain in her throat prevented it. No, not the pain in her throat. Words did not come because she had no idea what to say. What did one say to a half-dressed man in one's bed? Especially when circumstances prevented one from screaming about damaged virtue and male perversions.

Of course, her virtue wasn't truly damaged, was it? And as for male perversions, there hadn't been any, had there? She groaned slightly, closing her eyes and trying to sort through the past two days. It had been only two days, hadn't it? She wasn't sure. Maybe three. She had been unconscious for part. Asleep for another. And in between, she had been . . .

Her face heated with shame. She'd touched her breasts. She'd let him touch her breasts. And she'd watched him as he touched his . . . his . . . what had he called it? His *dragon*. She'd watched him, and she'd touched and been touched. And she'd hated it.

Well, not really. She *ought* to have hated it. In truth, she . . . well, she didn't know what to think. She counted herself a logical girl. Focused. Scientific, almost. Someone who objectively analyzed situations and came to rational conclusions. And her logical, rational mind told her that she was still cataloging the experiences, learning what she could until she found a means to escape.

That was all she felt, she decided. Scientific curiosity. And a hedonistic pleasure.

She dropped her head into her hands with a soft moan—or what would have been a soft moan if she'd had working vocal cords. What really came out was a gurgled rasp. She was thankful the Manchurian spoke before she could work herself into a true state of hysteria. And his words, amazingly enough, were exactly what she needed to hear.

"I have a plan," he said. "For escape. But I will have to find the right time."

Her head jerked up and she focused on his words.

"It will take me a bit to arrange. But in a week, maybe a little more, we can escape this place." He slowly pushed up from the bed. The blanket dropped away, revealing the large, muscled expanse of his bronze-skinned chest. She blinked, trying to force herself not to stare, but his body was so . . . so . . . alive. And close. She could even touch it with her fingers. His naked chest.

"But you must help me," he continued, as if she weren't staring at his chest. At the way his body tapered down to a tight belly and . . . Was he wearing pants underneath the blanket? Had she been wrapped in legs covered in fabric? Or had they been naked male legs on her bare flesh? She didn't remember. She was dressed in a robe. Or at least half-dressed. But her robe had bunched, leaving her legs exposed.

She shook her head. Truly, it made no difference how they had slept! But for some reason she desperately wanted to know.

"Joanna?"

She blinked. Then she blinked again, but made herself keep her eyes closed. Looking at him wasn't going to help her understand anything. Well, maybe she'd learn more about male anatomy, but yesterday had brought enough of such lessons. She didn't want to know more. Did she?

She ruthlessly cut off her thoughts. He was saying something to her. Something important, to which she really wanted to listen. Really. But was he wearing pants?

Stop it! Just stop it! she ordered herself. *Get out of bed. Stop thinking about clothing. Just get on your feet and think.*

She did, though with a reluctance that made her movements clumsy and stupidly slow.

"There is no need to be alarmed," he said as she finally put her bare feet on the cold wood floor. The shocking temperature steadied her even more, and she was able to scramble backward until she pressed her back against the privacy screen.

"Do you need to use the pot?" he asked.

She did, but she needed him to keep speaking even more. So she shook her head, gesturing that he should continue with what he had been saying. Whatever it was. She awkwardly began straightening her robe, putting her arms back in the sleeves, tying the belt tight.

"How is your throat this morning? Does it pain you?"

She nodded, her eyes drawing together into a frown. His voice seemed strangely thick now, deep and coarse instead of his usual smooth tones. Could he be getting sick? Was she going to be infected by some foreign disease? Was she . . .

He shifted position on the bed, straightening as he lifted onto his knees, simultaneously tossing the blanket aside. Joanna breathed in a long, fortifying breath. He was wearing pants. She didn't know if she was pleased or disappointed. All she really knew was that her burning question was resolved. He wore pants. She needn't think about it any longer.

"Will you help me with an escape plan?" he asked, his voice taking on an edge of frustration.

She nodded, getting hold of her thoughts. Yes. She very much wanted an end to all of this . . . unsettlement.

"Good, because what I want will be difficult, but it is very important. Absolutely necessary." He paused, clearly waiting for her acknowledgment. She gave a quick nod. "We need to accept the training. Not just accept it but embrace it. Completely. Without reservation."

She felt her eyes widen, her thoughts too chaotic to make sense. She was filled with a clutching panic.

He must have seen it on her face. He must have understood her reaction, because he was quick to rise from the bed and move to her side, taking her arms. She pushed backward, away from him. She wasn't prepared for him to touch her. She couldn't think when his naked chest was right there next to her, his lean body gloriously displayed.

Unfortunately, all that was behind her was the privacy screen, that beautiful bamboo construction with its lovely garden scene. Lovely, of course, if one didn't look too closely at the actions of the figures beneath the greenery. Either way, the screen was directly behind her, and she flattened herself against it in an attempt to escape.

The screen was not heavy enough to withstand her weight. She knocked it backward and it fell, banged against the wall, and then began to slide down, its base nearly taking her feet out from under her. She tried to recover, of course. Tried to step away, not toward him, but to the side.

But he didn't let her go. The urgency in his voice had infected his movements, and his hands now gripped her. She tried to fight him. She began to struggle in earnest. She wanted away. She wanted out. She wanted . . .

But there was nowhere to go. Not with the screen underneath her feet and this man surrounding her. She was losing her balance. Something painful cut into her ankle. She couldn't find purchase. He was holding her so tightly. He was . . .

Picking her up.

She kicked at him. She hit his face as best she could. She drew her knee up hard so that it connected with that same broad chest at which she'd been staring. She heard his grunt of pain, but then his hands tightened around her. She tried to scream, but all that came out was a painful squeak that sent shooting pain straight up her throat and into her brain.

Then suddenly she was free. Falling.

No!

She landed safely on the bed. She flattened her hands on the mattress, doing her best to gain her balance as she glared at him. The Manchurian stood over her, large and intimidating, while one hand rubbed the red kneeprint on his chest.

"I do not wish to hurt you," he growled. "I have no interest in taking your virginity from you." He huffed, and his hands dropped to his hips. "Joanna Crane, listen to me! To escape we need to appear as if we have embraced this teaching. We need to truly do it with a whole heart."

She opened her mouth to object—to scream, to say something, anything—but he held up his hand to stop her. She would have ignored it, but any sound hurt, debilitating her further. So she bit her lip, forcing herself to remain calm. Rational.

He continued to speak. "The Tigress practice does not take one's virginity. Only your yin. Your purity will not be harmed."

She arched a single eyebrow. She was not so naive. Naked bodies touching meant a loss of purity, period. Virgin or not, this Tigress training would taint her honor in the eyes of any potential husband.

He continued. "Perform all the exercises. Learn the teaching. Be my partner in this training, and I will arrange our escape."

She narrowed her eyes, showing her doubt.

"Within two weeks."

She shook her head.

He grimaced. "A week. One week. Cooperate with the training for one week. That will give me enough time to arrange an escape."

She stared at him, her thoughts finally clearing as she absorbed his words. She understood what he proposed, but did she trust that he spoke the truth? Her gut told her yes, she could trust him. But her mind was not so sure. Wasn't he the one who struck her and dragged her to this unholy place? Wasn't he the one who walked around pretending to be a monk when anyone with eyes could see that he wasn't one? Wasn't he the one . . .

Who had spoken honestly and openly about their situation. He had touched her kindly, explaining that it was necessary. This Tigress Shi Po had some hold over him. And there was no love lost between those two. But did that mean Joanna could trust him to create an escape?

She didn't know. But then, reason pointed out that it didn't matter. She had no other options except to hope for the help of the Tigress's husband. Either way, the Manchurian was correct. The appearance of cooperation might afford them greater leniency, more options.

Slowly Joanna nodded, agreeing to his proposal. But she had one condition. She held out her hand, fingers outstretched, palm flat.

He frowned, not understanding.

She mimed her request, indicating his pocket, taking out the key and unlocking the door. Then she pointed again. The key. She wanted the key to the door.

She could tell he didn't like the idea. She already knew that all men—English or Chinese—wanted control. Well, she would not cooperate unless she retained control of the door.

"But there is still a guard," he countered. "You cannot escape with him standing there."

She shrugged. She would deal with the guard later. The first obstacle was the locked door.

He hesitated, so she folded her arms, glaring at him to make her position clear. She would not cooperate unless he handed over the key. And he was obviously reluctant to do so. Too bad. She held firm.

He pulled the key out of his pocket, but did not hand it to her. Instead he held it just out of her reach. "You will cooperate fully?" he asked. "You will do what the Tigress instructs?" She hesitated, and he was quick to reassure her: "Your virginity will remain intact. Of this I am sure."

Again she thought over her options, trying to see every angle. It seemed she didn't have much choice, and so she nodded. To all appearances she would be the best student the Tigress ever had.

A thrill of excitement coursed through her, at once both enjoyable and disgraceful. Truly, she wasn't supposed to be intrigued by what she was about to learn! But she wouldn't be human if the prospect didn't interest her. After all, she did find this man attractive. Exactly what was she about to learn? About her own body? About his?

She smiled, and he pressed the key into her hand. A loud banging echoed on the door.

Joanna scrambled forward, working to unbolt it while, behind her, the Manchurian tensed and rolled onto the balls of his feet. She knew he was fully alert, poised for whatever danger waited on the other side. She slowed her movements, glancing back at him to be sure. At his nod, she pulled open the door.

The Tigress Shi Po stood there, her expression impassive even as her keen gaze scanned the room. "It is time for lessons. You will both come now."

> *20 April, 1896*
> *Dear Kang Zou,*
> *Your studies sound interesting, but of course they mean nothing to me. The sun is darkened and all is in turmoil here. And without my songbird, I am ever melancholy. Even Mother pines without word from you. She refuses to eat and has torn her clothing.*
> *Father is choosing between bridegrooms now. But all are old or fat or poor, so I do not know why I must marry any of them. A woman's choices are never her own. Return home soon, brother, so you may find a young, handsome choice for me.*
> *Your frightened sister,*
> *Wen Ji*

Decoded translation:

> Dear son,
> Your studies have no bearing on the family disaster. Our humiliation at the hands of

the Japanese is a terrible tragedy. Especially after losing to the white barbarians. But it was inevitable, since I am forced to fight with ill equipped, uneducated, frightened troops. We will soon lose everything without your help.

Return home immediately with news of triumph against the insurgents. Otherwise, I fear for not only our family but the entire country. More and more these invaders steal from us without punishment. And China has fewer choices than an ugly girl.

Your impatient father,
General Kang

3 May, 1896
Dearest Wen Ji,

My heart grieves at the choice Father faces. And I am aware of the trials that our mother faces daily, though I believe she is stronger than she appears. But all is not lost. The scrolls of Lao Tzu speak of the wisdom of nonaction. Of the end of struggle. Can you not look for peace in times of turmoil? Truly, the wisdom of Abbot Tseng surpasses ordinary understanding.

Ever hopeful,
Kang Zou

Decoded translation as understood by General Kang:

Dearest Father,

I have heard of the dangers facing China. News has reached us even here in the mountains. I also remember my responsibilities to both family and country, but know you will find a way through your difficulties soon. Remember that the great teacher Lao Tzu counsels nonaction. Abbot Tseng has taught us that there is great wisdom in the end of struggle.

Your bewitched son,
Zou Tun

All ideas and values are established by people, and value judgments come through comparisons. But the way we look at things must constantly change, and thus our value judgments must constantly change. So when dealing with beautiful and ugly, being and nothing, difficult and easy, long and short, high and low, front and back, etc., take them lightly and don't let them cause you trouble.

—Lao Tzu

Chapter Seven

Joanna kept her eyes open as the two "servants" led her from the bedroom through the Tigress's large compound. It was only the two guards, but both were very large and apparently intent on following orders.

At least they had allowed Joanna time to dress in loose-fitting pants and a utilitarian shirt before escorting her to her lessons. Otherwise she would be walking through this rather beautiful place dressed in just a robe.

Having seen only her own room and the hallway outside, she hadn't realized how very large the compound was. What she saw now was a house in the front, and beyond that, presumably, the street. That would make the building to her right the main building, where guests and others visited. But behind that was a long, rectangular garden surrounded by five other buildings—two on each side and one on the end. That made for six buildings in total, all dominated by the Tigress Shi Po.

How had this powerful woman lived in Shanghai

and Joanna never heard of her? The question was ridiculous, of course. Joanna and all other foreigners might make China their home, but they certainly didn't interact with the natives. Most of her fellow Caucasians barely even noticed the Chinese who drew their baths, cooked their food, and even managed their homes. The Asians were simply servants, and China was a vast playland of opportunity where anyone could make a fortune.

A great scholar or a rich empress could live right outside the foreign territories and not one of Joanna's friends would know about it.

The thought humbled and shamed her. How long had she lived in China without even noticing the vast country of people who surrounded her? And worse, she was counted as an expert on the Chinese by most everyone she met. After all, she could read and write in Chinese, had been raised for nearly a decade by a Chinese nanny. She listened to the servants' gossip whenever she could. What more could there possibly be to know?

A great deal, obviously, and so Joanna kept her eyes and ears open as their sandaled feet stepped down beautiful multicolored pathways that meandered through a large garden. To her right she caught a glimpse of large, shimmering goldfish in a deep pond. To her left a songbird fluffed its feathers in a cage. But nowhere did she see any sign of the Tigress's husband, the kind man—Kui Yu was his name, she'd been told—who had offered to help her leave should she so wish this morning.

Well, she did wish. But she could hardly say so with two guards around her, the Manchurian behind her whom she'd just promised to obey, and the Tigress Shi Po waiting somewhere to "begin her lessons."

So she followed behind the guards, keeping her eyes and ears open while her heart fluttered in her chest. Exactly what kind of lessons were in store?

She glanced beside her. She didn't even know his name, but somehow the faux monk had become her most trusted ally. And right now he appeared calm, arrogant, and completely in control. It was only when he caught her eye that she saw a flash of uncertainty.

He quickly masked his nervousness with a soft smile. He was trying to be reassuring, which was a silly gesture. The guards were huge men armed with knives. Even with his impressive fighting skills, they were in danger. Especially since more guards stood at the opposite side of the garden.

Still, she was calmed by his smile, and she did her best to return his gesture with equal bravado. She even managed to hold the expression until they stepped into a ballroom.

In truth, the room wasn't a ballroom; it was simply that so many people were crowded into it that that was immediately what Joanna thought of. Especially as the room was devoid of furniture beyond a couple of plain chairs pressed against the side wall. The floor was wood, polished smooth. The walls had simple banners, but she had no time to decipher their words. Instead she spent her time looking into the faces of the dozen or so beautiful women clustered in a tiny knot at the center of the room.

They were talking excitedly, their Chinese words making the room sound more like a marketplace than a ballroom. But when Joanna entered, they all fell silent, turning in one body to inspect her. Or perhaps, Joanna realized, it was not to look at her as much as her man.

She stiffened at the thought. He was not *her* man,

and yet she felt ridiculously possessive of him—though he had taken her voice from her. She even refused to be separated from him as she met the curious gazes of each and every woman in the room.

They were of varying ages, these Tigress students—for that was what Joanna assumed they were. The youngest was perhaps barely into her teens, but the oldest seemed well into her forties. Their hair was bound simply with a cord, leaving the long, straight locks to trail beautifully down their backs. Each woman—even the oldest—had golden, youthful skin that shone almost as bright as their dark eyes. Some wore makeup; some did not. Some had rich clothing; some wore threadbare attire. Some had their feet bound, as was the Chinese custom; others did not.

All noticed her possessive attitude and their reactions ranged from stunned surprise to angry disdain.

Joanna understood. She had survived too long in Shanghai society not to recognize the symptoms. She was looked upon as a barbarian, a beggar, and a fool. She had no right to a Chinese man, much less this one, though she wondered if any there recognized her companion's true identity.

In any event, there was little time for further assessment. The Tigress Shi Po entered the room, walking slowly on her bound feet. She wore the same loose-fitting clothing as everyone else, only on her it appeared stately. Beautiful. Inspiring.

The other ladies immediately dropped to their knees, kowtowing before her. Joanna, of course, did nothing. She was not Chinese and had no interest in banging her head upon the floor for her jailer. So she stood, as did the Mandarin, while the guards faded back toward the door.

The Tigress surveyed the women as they straightened, arranging themselves in rough lines but remaining with their eyes lowered, their heads bowed, out of respect for their instructor. She did not move until all was situated; then she flowed smoothly forward, coming to stand before Joanna. Her eyes were cool, her chin lifted. She inspected Joanna, and though Joanna wanted nothing from this woman, she felt her heart begin to pound inside her chest. She was acutely aware of her disorderly braid, her ill-fitting clothing, and every other fault in her body and soul.

Indeed, it took an act of will to stand straight and tall, looking the Tigress in the eye, but Joanna accomplished it. She used her pride. The Chinese thought the whites were barbarians. Let them see an American woman who could match them eye-to-eye.

As if understanding the unspoken challenge, Shi Po smiled. A slight tilt appeared on her lips, a spark of amusement in her eyes.

"Very well," she said in a melodic voice that nevertheless commanded everyone's attention. "We will see today if a ghost barbarian can learn." She pointed to a place in the last line. "You will stand there. Watch. Learn. Do, if you can."

Her challenge rang out in the room, and Joanna lifted her chin, determined to meet whatever task was set her. At one time she might have folded her arms and refused to cooperate, but she had just promised the monk that she would do what she could to appear docile. So she took her spot.

Meanwhile, Shi Po moved on to stand before the monk. "Exercise of the body trains the mind. As a Shaolin, you understand this, yes?"

He nodded.

"Then you may perform your tasks over there." She gestured to the side of the room, an area empty of all except two more servants who stood framing a paper window. Then she glided back to the lines of women.

Clapping her hands, she called out, "Qi strengthens with each stimulation."

As one the women echoed her words.

Then Shi Po spoke again. "Swallowing from above and quivering from below gathers the qi."

Again the women repeated the words.

"Continual refinement of these will harmonize the qi.

"When the qi circulates, illumination will occur.

"The ancients said, 'Ingest the dragon to move the tiger, absorb the dragon to illuminate the tiger.'"

The lecture continued for twenty minutes while Joanna strained to understand. She could follow the words, but much was strange imagery. What exactly was a Tigress's dew? Or a dragon's cloud? Obviously these women knew, and Joanna felt a keen desire to find out as well.

Then, just as quickly as it had begun, the chanting ended. Shi Po cried out, "Tigresses, twist your tail downward." With a loud snap, the woman clapped her arms straight down against her sides to press her hands against her thighs. All around Joanna, the other women did the same. As one they inhaled, drawing their palms together in front of their hearts. Then each moved her arms in three graceful circles about her face and head, each circle growing larger until the third ended in the first position. Without pausing, the movement became a figure eight, flowing easily as the women's bodies and arms adjusted.

Joanna spared a moment to watch, seeing that the oldest student's body seemed nearly as supple as that of the youngest. She tried to think of any white woman who could move as gracefully. She could not. Corsets and bustles did not encourage flexibility. But what tiny waists these ladies had! It was only now, as their figure eights became twisting Ss, that she realized how trim this exercise could make the body.

The women continued with their movement for some time, at last pausing at the bottom of the motion. All the ladies had become flushed, and the cool room had heated considerably. Joanna thought they were finished, but in a moment Shi Po called out again.

"Tigresses, twist your tail upward."

And so they began again, only this time their palms traced a figure eight that had sprouted another loop. The ladies' hands, pressed firmly together, wove in and around their knees, their torsos, then their heads before looping back the other way. It was a beautiful sight, and Joanna nearly lost herself in simply admiring the three rows of women, all demonstrating supple and toned bodies.

After two more circuits, the women finally stopped, drawing their hands back to their chests before finally allowing them to drop back to their sides.

Joanna expected that every one of the ladies would be short of breath. Indeed, looking at the class, she saw that a few of the younger women were panting. Not so the older women, and certainly not Shi Po. Especially not Shi Po, who turned steely eyes on Joanna.

"You will do this with us now," she said. Then she straightened, looking disdainfully at her younger students. "Tigresses, twist your tail downward."

So it began. Joanna did her best to keep up. After all, she was younger than most of the women here, she was reasonably fit from her daily horseback rides, and she had even studied basic anatomy. She ought to be able to perform a simple series of loops and swirls without difficulty. The pattern couldn't be difficult to master.

But it was. Her hips would not go in the right direction, her balance was always threatened, and her hands would not stay pressed together. Some of the ladies hadn't even tied their hair, and their locks remained a beautiful shimmer down their backs. Joanna's braid flopped into her face and stuck to her sweaty skin.

She performed the full exercise three times, the last two with Shi Po standing behind her constantly flicking a finger into one body part or another. By the end, the Tigress had put both hands on Joanna's hips to steady her as she finished. Then, gasping through her strained throat, Joanna finally put her hands to her sides and silently thanked God she was finished.

Except, she wasn't. Shi Po stood in front of her, waiting. Joanna frowned, wondering what the woman could possibly want when the other ladies were breaking apart to sip from little teacups on a tray. Without thought, Joanna licked her parched lips, desperately wanting a drink. But when she moved toward the tray, the Tigress snapped at her.

"No! Tigresses twist their tails *four* times." Her eyes narrowed in speculation. "Unless you are too ill for this?"

Nothing on earth would induce Joanna to admit weakness now. She straightened her body and resolved to perform the exercise one last time—without the benefit of following anyone.

It was a miserable experience. Even remembering the patterns, she constantly forgot her elbow movement or hip position or head placement. The only thing that made it bearable was that most of the class was not watching. Instead, their gazes slipped across the room to the monk and his Shaolin exercises. By the time Joanna finished, all but herself and Shi Po were in a rough semicircle, all ogling her Mandarin.

Shi Po noticed it immediately. How could she not when her entire class was practically drooling? Not that he wasn't a beautiful, sweaty man. Tired and irritated as she was, even Joanna couldn't keep her eyes away from her pretend monk as he performed what looked like a mixture of dance and abrupt fighting moves.

He was smooth and controlled. His gestures were powerful. And his muscles rippled beneath his skin in a beautiful dance. He was man in all his glory. And yet he was so much more.

Because what stood out to Joanna was not his sculpted muscles, his bronzed skin, nor even the elegant grace with which he moved. What truly fascinated Joanna and drew her like a moth to a flame was his eyes, that dark, penetrating stare that seemed to see right through her. He had pure purpose in each and every movement, as if his entire being were caught in his practice. And that entire being, focused on his one task, created a center of power and energy that overwhelmed as much as it beguiled her.

In a word, he was stunning. Joanna felt her mouth grow dry with hunger.

"Behold the Shaolin priest in all his glory," called Shi Po without a trace of mockery. Indeed, she sounded admiring, even jealous. "What amazing qi. Purified male yang in all its power, strengthening a qi that radiates like the sun. He can destroy his enemies with such power. Topple stone walls with a single blow." Then her voice dropped. "But he cannot attain Heaven with it. Without our female yin, he is chained to this earth."

Shi Po's words rang through the room. The monk gave no indication he heard. His movements did not stop, though sweat was pouring off his body in a steady stream. And then, with a graceful pulling motion, he finished his work. He drew his hands together at his heart, and—as the Tigresses had earlier—let them flow down to his sides. Only then did he look at the women who surrounded him.

"When body, mind, and spirit are in harmony, when

131

they move as one without thought or distraction, then I am indeed in Heaven," he said.

But the Tigress Shi Po shook her head. "You are in harmony, Shaolin. A wondrous and powerful place to be. But you are not in Heaven. Only we can take you there." She stepped forward, her head canted slightly as she inspected him from head to toe. "I could show you the way. As could many of these other women." She arched an eyebrow in challenge. "Do you wish a different partner?"

Joanna stiffened, fear turning her blood to ice. Was she about to be tossed aside? Would he abandon her? What would be done to her then?

The monk locked gazes with her, obviously thinking through the Tigress's offer. No shift in his body or expression told her that he understood her fears, that he would not push her aside for another. If Joanna could talk, she would have. Indeed, she stepped forward to interfere. But the only sound she could make was a soft mewl, a high, kittenlike noise that would not help her. She did not want to appear weak in front of these women, and so she kept silent and waited. As, indeed, did everyone around her. The other students had shifted at the Tigress's comment, arraying themselves in a variety of subtle positions. All of them were trying in their own particular ways to catch her monk's attention.

Joanna cast a panicked look about her. Many of these women were stunningly beautiful. All of them were skilled in things that Joanna didn't understand. What man could refuse that? What man would chose a virginal ghost woman over a skilled courtesan?

Her monk, apparently. He didn't even glance at the other women. Instead his gaze shifted from Joanna to Shi Po and then to the floor. He bowed slightly. "You selected my partner two days ago. It is a poor student who discards his tutor's choice."

The Tigress's eyes narrowed, and Joanna felt her icy stare. "But attachment hinders flight to Heaven," she stated. She began to walk forward, around the monk. "Love of gold you have obviously overcome. Envy of property and status . . ." She shook her head. "These things you have discarded."

Joanna's focus sharpened. Obviously the Tigress knew the monk was not what he seemed.

"But what of lust of woman?" Shi Po challenged.

The monk arched an eyebrow at her. "My purity is clear in this."

All around him the women tittered. Even Shi Po allowed herself a smile. "A man locked in a monastery without temptation is not pure, Shaolin. He is merely lacking in opportunity." She stepped closer.

Joanna watched her monk's nostrils flare with the Tigress's scent. She watched his eyes narrow and shift, following Shi Po's willowy movements. There was no doubt about it: Shi Po was not only beautiful but a true seductress.

Still, the monk did not move. He did not so much as lift a finger as the Tigress seemed to stalk him, moving closer and away, near enough that he caught her scent, but then back far enough that he would have to work to catch her.

And still he did not move.

"How will your purity fare when your dragon hungers and the white clouds press for release?" Shi Po stopped directly before him, her body taut with challenge. "Your strength failed you yesterday, and that was only an exercise."

"There is no shame in falling," he countered, his voice and body apparently at ease. "Only in not standing up again."

The Tigress reached out, extending one long nail to trace a delicate pattern across his chest. She took her time, and though Joanna could not see any meaning in the shapes she sketched, she could see the woman's intent. Shi Po was toying with him, challenging him in a cold but very interesting way.

"You *will* stand up again, Shaolin," she said, her voice a sultry purr. "Again and again and again. But wisdom can be found only in remaining up and staying strong. I wager you will fall by choice. Because you enjoy it. Because the pleasure in it is stronger than the qi that holds you back." Then she pushed him slightly, pressing her nails into his chest.

If she thought to move him, she failed. His body did not sway; his muscles did not even ripple, though tiny spots of blood welled beneath her fingertips. Instead she pushed herself away, causing her first ungainly movement Joanna had ever seen.

"Partner the ghost woman then," she said with a clear note of pique. "You have no more substance than she." And with that Shi Po clapped her hands, calling the other women to attention. "Tigresses, invert!"

The whole scene seemed to start over. To the side, the monk returned to his drills. In front of Joanna the Tigresses began more exercises that she could barely fathom, much less perform. They arched over backward until their hands touched the floor. They bent the other way, folding forward until their heads were between their knees.

Joanna did as best as she could. But by the time they shifted to the floor, she was completely lost. She simply was not flexible enough to bring both ankles behind her head. Neither could she curl her body so far forward that her chin rested on her crotch.

She tried, though. She attempted all and was reassured to see that many of the other women could not do them either. But Shi Po could, and with a grace that left Joanna feeling an unwelcome twinge of envy.

Whatever her faults, Shi Po could perform amazing physical feats.

Finally the class was over. A servant brought in cold water, which Joanna viewed with desperation. She stepped forward, already anticipating the cool relief for her parched throat, but two women cut in front of her, and a third grabbed her arm, holding her back. She would have jerked away, angrily pulling from their restraint, until she saw what was happening.

The water was for the monk first. Everyone waited upon his pleasure. Unfortunately he hadn't yet noticed what was happening. He was standing, his body a tall, sleek line beaded with sweat. He was not panting and his eyes were closed, and yet he had the air of a man working hard. All eyes were drawn to him.

Then it happened. In the space between one exhalation and the next, he threw off all his energy in a whirlwind of lethal force. Just as when he had first fought off her attackers, his hands and feet moved faster than Joanna's eye could follow. Imaginary foes fell like rain.

All around her the women gasped in awe. Joanna, too, was impressed, but this time she watched more closely, saw more than before. As before, she noticed his focus, his intent. And she tried in her limited ability to see the body movements, the flow of hand and leg.

Then she entered a different place. She didn't know what brought it on—likely exhaustion from her own exercises. But whatever the cause, she began to feel his energy. And without thought she walked forward, directly into the whirlwind.

It was suicide, this mad step into the lethal spin and kick and punch. And yet she had no fear. She sensed his power and would know when the wind gathered in him to explode in her direction.

It was coming. She felt it. She could not see it, but

inside her heart she sensed it—so long as she did not think too deeply. She simply walked, approaching steadily. Soon she stood just outside of his reach.

He could extend his blow. She knew that if this were a true fight, his fist would find her, knock her aside like the wildest of tornadoes. But this was practice, and he would not unbalance his power—his qi—enough to reach her.

He continued his spinning kicks and the wind began to gather. She felt it draw him back just before he exploded forward. His fist was the point of the arrow, his body the shaft and the bow. He put all of his force into a single thrust directly at her face.

It stopped an inch short of her nose. She didn't flinch.

She watched as his eyes widened in surprise, his awareness of his surroundings returning enough to find her there.

He drew back with a startled gasp, and she watched as his eyes narrowed, fury building behind his expression. She recognized his thoughts. He was angry at how close he had come to hurting her, obviously doubting his own control. And so, before that same power was unleashed in temper, she bowed slightly to him, then gestured to the side. To the water. To the parched women waiting patiently on his pleasure.

He frowned, and she could tell he was struggling with orienting himself—first to her presence, so close to his practice, and then to the other women waiting on him. Slowly his arm lowered; his body drew into itself as if gathering what remained of his strength.

All waited, holding their breath to learn what would come next. What would he do? Even Joanna trembled a bit inside. She, too, had come back to herself. She just now realized how close she had come to taking a lethal blow. And yet outwardly she remained calm, her appearance poised.

Or so she hoped.

He bowed—once to her, then a second time to acknowledge Shi Po. It was a formal gesture meant to convey respect and thanks. But it was also a slap of disdain, for he acknowledged the white barbarian before the Tigress who housed them.

All around, the women gasped again. Indeed, with all their sighing and gasping, Joanna was rapidly coming to think of them as a Greek chorus. But her attention was more on the monk before her and the Tigress who imprisoned them. And when the monk moved to get water, Joanna accompanied him. As was the custom, she waited until he drank before taking her own cup.

The water was heavenly, as cool and sweet as she had imagined, and a welcome relief to her still-raw throat. It was almost as delightful as the knowledge that in taking her drink before Shi Po, she had declared her status as guest and not prisoner to all who stood around them.

Truthfully, it was a ridiculous gesture. The reality was that she was a prisoner, and so was the monk. But his show of respect to her over Shi Po warmed her heart as had nothing else. And so she smiled as she drank, her eyes meeting his in a moment of shared joy.

Then it was over.

Shi Po glided forward. The other ladies slid behind her in a line, apparently from most accomplished to least. But since Joanna had already drunk, Shi Po switched the order, gesturing to the youngest of the ladies at the back of the line to come forward and take her water first.

This threw the girl into confusion, as it was obviously not usual. Indeed, the entire line fell into chaos as each lady tried to guess and relay what was supposed to happen next. All the while, Shi Po's lips pressed into a tighter and thinner line.

Score one for the imprisoned barbarian! Joanna thought. Especially as she watched her monk's eyes sparkle with silent delight.

Unfortunately, her victory was short-lived. The line sorted itself out. The women drank their water, and Shi Po was soon back in control of the situation. She barely even glanced at Joanna as a servant brought a long silk case. The other women obviously knew exactly what was happening, and they quickly arranged themselves in a rough semicircle. Clearly the Tigress was about to teach, as she pulled a long, slender scroll from the pouch.

Joanna glanced at her monk, but his face was impassive. He stood casually, his weight balanced on the balls of his feet. Taking her cue from him, she decided to stand, too, neither part of the class nor too distant from it.

Shi Po began to speak.

Modesty wins adoration. By doing things for others, you can accomplish your own ideals.

—*Lao Tzu*

Chapter Eight

The Tigress began simply. Folding her feet beneath her, she bowed her head and spoke.

"Sex is a powerful force. Like a wild horse, it must be trained and harnessed before use. Most religions ignore the wild horse, preaching total abstinence in the hopes that it will disappear." She lifted her head, looking directly toward the monk. In return, he nodded his head, acknowledging her statement.

"I tell you this," she continued, her gaze hard. "The horse does not leave. And if it does, you have lost a most powerful ally." She turned back to her class, her tone softening as she settled into the rhythm of her speech.

"The Tigress tames the horse. She masters it slowly and gently, first by familiarizing herself with its body. This allows her to understand how the horse moves. Second, she learns by feeling the horse, by touching all its aspects so the horse becomes accustomed to her presence. In this way the Tigress learns how the horse thinks. Then, lastly, she becomes one with the horse so that she can mount it and ride it to Heaven. Only in this way can a Tigress—or a Dragon—find immortality."

Joanna listened to Shi Po's voice, half mesmerized by its cadence. The fluid tones of her words were like beautiful music, their meaning nothing to the beauty of their sound. But to lose herself in the sound was to miss the point. So Joanna focused, making an effort to understand.

Unfortunately, she realized, like many religions the Tigress cult spoke in metaphors. Shi Po's words were beautiful, but in the end there was no obvious practical application. How did one "feel one's sexual nature"? "Touch all aspects of it as one would a horse"? It wasn't possible, and so Joanna sighed, bored.

Then Shi Po unrolled a scroll, and in bold black ink was a drawing of a male organ. Beside it, and of an equal size, was a man's face. He was smiling normally, but there was a glint in his eye. In truth, it was not an unattractive image of a man's face. But beside it was the other drawing, and that other drawing was large and colored and so . . . very, very there.

No one moved. Not even the monk, who had flushed a dark red. And into the silence Shi Po continued her instruction, unrolling her scroll inch by inch to reveal a long succession of images, one after the other, of the man's organ growing and his face becoming pinched and red.

"This is a man's dragon," Shi Po said. "See how it hides in its tunnel, shy and withdrawn. And see here the man's face. Though he appears content and restrained, he is always aware of the dragon. Like the wild horse, his dragon constantly torments him, waking him from sleep, filling him with lust whenever a beautiful girl walks by." The Tigress lifted her chin, turning to look directly at the monk. "Is that not so?"

Everyone twisted, even the guards, all looking to see

how he would respond. Most men would have flushed a brighter red. Joanna's father probably would have stammered out some sort of hot denial, adding that this topic was inappropriate for discussion. The monk's color calmed and his expression became somewhat amused, and he bowed his head slightly.

"A man's dragon is a fearsome beast that he must learn to control," he said.

"Control?" Shi Po challenged. "Or hide? Only to have it roar out of its cave at the slightest provocation?"

Joanna recalled the monk's exercises from the previous night. Indeed, his dragon had pushed out into his hand, seemingly demanding attention.

But the monk merely shrugged. "Each man manages his dragon in his own way."

Joanna's gaze settled on his face, studying his expression closely. She longed to ask him questions. How did he manage his dragon? Just how powerful was its hunger? Was a woman's tigress equally demanding, once awoken?

Unfortunately, Joanna could not ask these things. And Shi Po was apparently uninterested in pushing further. Instead the woman returned to her lecture and her series of pictures. She described the dragon's stages, along with the depicted facial expressions. She explained how the dragon pushed out of its cave, longing for a drink from the pool inside a woman's cinnabar cave. She pointed out the places where the dragon was most sensitive, and how it finally contorted and spewed white cloud.

She pointed to places on the diagram where the dragon could be pushed to interrupt cloud flow, and she explained that it took a man of great power and focus to control his dragon.

"Such a man," she said, "would be a truly intimidating creature—a jade dragon. Such a man, when waking his dragon, stirs the yang fires, making them hot and strong. But by keeping his natural essence inside of him, he maintains his yang power and grows stronger each time his dragon stirs." Shi Po smiled, her gaze again finding the monk. "But few men have such discipline. And so we Tigresses catch their power, taking it into ourselves to strengthen us, to make our horses hardy enough to carry us to Heaven."

Leaving the poor man to wither and die, Joanna thought. It was an odd idea, and obviously not true. She knew relatively little of men's dragons, but she did understand that few men died of carnal relations. If they did, some of her father's friends would never have made it through their adolescence.

Still, Shi Po's attitude brought on the thought. It was as if sexuality were a means of conquest where the woman gained every time a man lost. And Shi Po, apparently, had bested many, many men.

The lecture continued. Or rather, the challenge continued, as Shi Po once again drew all attention to the monk.

"Do you have that power, monk? Can you hold your yang essence within you, or has your qi withered and died from neglect?"

All about the room, the women tittered. No man would claim his strength had withered from neglect, and yet yesterday he had been unable to contain his dragon cloud. Hearing the laughter, Joanna guessed everyone here knew of his failure.

Still, the monk did not appear disturbed. Instead he bowed slightly to Shi Po, his voice respectful even if Joanna was close enough to see that his eyes were not. "Only a fool would claim greater wisdom than his teacher, especially on his first day of instruction."

Shi Po frowned; then she too dipped her head. "You

speak wisely, monk, for in learning to control the wild horse, you men have much work to do." She lifted her chin, a coy smile on her face. "Our young Tigress cubs require a demonstration. Will you make yourself an example for them?"

The monk's expression finally broke. Joanna watched as his eyes widened, emotion darkening his skin. And as the Tigress's meaning sank in, Joanna felt her own jaw drop.

Did she mean he was to demonstrate what was in the diagrams? To show himself in all those separate states as Shi Po brought him to the point of releasing his dragon cloud? The thought was appalling. And intriguing. Joanna felt her face heat with equal parts shame and interest.

Meanwhile the monk swallowed, words momentarily deserting him. The Tigress grunted in satisfaction. "See here the untrained reaction. Though his dragon may be roaring in his belly for release, the civilized man denies its existence. But any man who denies the power of his dragon can be used by it, controlled by it, and dominated by it. See our ghost barbarian as well. Her shame floods her face and she longs to flee, and yet the Tigress within her salivates with hunger."

Joanna stiffened at the statement, appalled to realize Shi Po spoke the truth. She was ashamed. And she was titillated. She wanted to see the monk's dragon again. She wanted to know what he was like just before release. But not so interested that she would embarrass him like this to learn the answers! Indeed, she was appalled by the way their so-called teacher was treating them.

But then, Shi Po wasn't really their teacher; she was their jailer. So Joanna straightened, lifting her chin and putting on as much aristocratic disdain as she could summon. Let them call her a barbarian and try

143

to humiliate her. She wasn't the one making sport of another.

Too bad her show of defiance was ignored. Shi Po began speaking again, and attention shifted back to her. "The Tigress knows a man's dragon and a woman's tigress are just that wild horse that needs to be tamed. There is no shame in understanding it. In enjoying its beauty. In trying to ride it. There is only use and the ultimate goal: immortality. Riding the horse to immortality."

It was a mixed metaphor to be sure, but one that made sense to Joanna. And it apparently made sense to the many women there. One particularly lovely girl stepped forward, bowing before Shi Po.

"I will demonstrate for the cubs," she said, her voice melodic and soft.

Shi Po nodded, but her eyes went once again to the monk. "How old do you think Little Pearl is?" she asked.

Beside Joanna, the monk frowned, his eyes narrowing. "Seventeen," he judged, and Joanna agreed, though she would have guessed slightly younger. Perhaps as young as fifteen. There was such an air of sweet youth about the girl, she had to be in her teens.

"Little Pearl turned thirty this New Year."

Joanna started. It couldn't be. And yet, the girl—the *woman*—nodded her head in agreement.

Beside Joanna, the monk also narrowed his eyes, clearly disbelieving. But all around them the ladies bobbed their heads. And then, one by one, they stepped forward, giving their ages. Not all of their years seemed completely preposterous, but all were beautiful women with youthful skin and supple figures.

That alone was remarkable enough, if one believed their statements. But something else struck Joanna, something she had been aware of from the first moment she had seen these ladies, but only now began to comprehend: Each of these women had a quiet strength about them. All of them spoke and smiled and moved with innate confidence, as if they had a focus in life, a purpose that brought them serenity.

Indeed, of all of them, Shi Po was the one who seemed the most disturbed, the most agitated in her surroundings. Which seemed odd, as she was unquestionably the most beautiful, the most graceful of all.

How Joanna longed for innate confidence. How she wished she had the simple assurance that she was on the right path, that she was being taught the secrets she needed to accomplish whatever it was she was supposed to do with her life. These women had that. However bizarre their beliefs, they clearly knew peace. And beauty.

"You are interested, aren't you, barbarian?"

Joanna's gaze cut to Shi Po, to the challenge she saw in the Tigress's posture. It was fortunate that her throat was still too injured to answer, for indeed, she didn't know what to say. To blush and turn away would be to admit she feared her own inner tigress. But to step forward and claim interest in these secrets would be too bold, too rash a step. She was intrigued. But did she truly wish to embrace this strange religion?

Shi Po smiled. "Come then, barbarian, and stand beside me. We will watch Little Pearl as she practices with her green Dragon."

Joanna hesitated, unsure what to do. Then the monk touched her lightly on the back. He didn't speak, but one glance at his face and she understood. She could go with the Tigress and it would be safe.

Why she trusted his unspoken comment, she wasn't sure. But she did, and so she slowly moved forward, walking beside Shi Po, who led the class to a dark and rather shabby-looking building in the back of her compound. Everyone followed except Little Pearl. That young woman disappeared through a side doorway, her steps as silent as they had been confident.

Shi Po led them all into a tiny chamber dominated by a bed. The center area was lit with many bright candles that gave off a cloying perfume, but the surrounding walls were shrouded in darkness and several thick tapestries. It was a cozy room obviously meant for a rendezvous, and one look at the tiny space told Joanna that they all would not fit inside.

Except they did.

Moving with a silence that stunned her, the ladies slid surreptitiously behind the tapestries. They disappeared on all sides, and when they were gone the wall hangings fell back into place, their heavy fabric stilling with a speed that surprised her. Stepping forward, she pushed one hanging aside to see a tight line of women staring back at her. They all stood like statues, and the room was obviously much larger than it appeared.

"In here, barbarian," called Shi Po from behind a tapestry. "And remember to be as silent as a ghost." Then she grinned at her joke, even as she pulled Joanna into the recessed alcove. It was only when the tapestry dropped back into place that she saw the truth.

The fabric was laced with dozens of tiny holes through which an audience could view the chamber. She turned, looking over her shoulder at Shi Po, her unspoken question obvious. The Tigress nodded, gesturing.

"A Tigress must practice. She often finds green Dragons, men who wish to release their seed to her without thought to their immortality or even their youth." The woman paused, shifting slightly so that she had a better view inside the chamber. "And sometimes other Tigresses watch. To learn." She shifted her gaze to Joanna. "There is much to be discovered here, barbarian. If you have the wit to understand."

Joanna swallowed, knowing the Tigress spoke the truth she believed. There was a great deal here to be learned. But to what point? Immortality? Her Christian upbringing told her that immortality came only from God, after death, through a belief in Jesus Christ. Now these people believed it came through sexual skill? And though she knew no logical reason, she had a vague feeling that watching someone else perform sexual acts was somehow immoral.

And yet, despite all Joanna's uneasiness, Shi Po's earlier words were clear in her head. She did have a sexual nature. Didn't everyone? And what if she wanted to explore it? God would not have made carnal relations pleasurable unless He meant them to be enjoyed. And what if there *was* something spiritual to be learned from sexuality? What if—

A tap on her shoulder made her jump, scattering her thoughts like so many leaves in a storm. She jerked sideways as she turned and nearly fell forward into the tapestry. But strong hands cupped her elbows, holding her steady.

The monk.

He smiled reassuringly at her, and she took a deep breath, steadying herself. On her opposite side she knew the Tigress Shi Po watched everything they did, so she lowered her eyes, trying to appear shy and demure. But what she felt inside was a pounding in her heart and a rushing of her blood. Especially because, on the other side of the tapestry, the door opened and Little Pearl escorted a blind man into the room.

He was filthy, his hair matted, his clothing torn and wretched. Even his feet were encrusted with mud. The stench of the man made Joanna's eyes water and her skin crawl. But it wasn't until he scratched himself that she saw the worst. In truth, it embarrassed her that she had been so focused on the dirt that she hadn't fully seen the man. But she saw as he tried to scratch himself: He had no hands.

He didn't have unformed limbs, as sometimes happened with children. She had seen beggars who never developed hands. Their arms narrowed to a smooth point. But not this man. His arms were adult-sized, flowing smoothly down to what should have been normal wrists and hands. Except on him, his hands had been cut off. Abruptly. Cruelly.

The sight turned Joanna's stomach.

Little Pearl was bringing this man for intimate relations? She couldn't possibly! And yet one glance at the Tigress Shi Po, and Joanna knew it was true. Beautiful Little Pearl was undressing the blind man. She was gingerly pulling off his grimy shirt and untying the rope about his waist before tugging his coolie pants free. He stood before her, his only clothing a matted cloth about his loins and the dirt that encrusted his entire body. And she was going to . . .

Joanna blinked, unsure she was seeing things correctly.

Little Pearl was bathing the man.

With a bowed head and reverent touch, she was gently cleaning the wretched man's body. Starting with his face and using numerous cloths, she was brushing at his sores and slowly revealing clean skin. He seemed now human, where before he had been more like an animal.

Servants came and went, bearing away the man's clothing, bringing fresh water and clean cloths. And when his body was free of filth, they brought a razor and soap so that Little Pearl could shave his face and head. Now Joanna understood the need for the heavy scent, for as the man's body was cleansed, the perfumed candles covered all stench. And with each entrance and exit of the servants, fresh air filled the tiny room.

In time, both the man and the room became clean.

Little Pearl spoke little as she worked, her focus on the gentle slide of her hands, the smooth glide of the razor as she cut away the man's matted hair. Not so the man, for as she worked he began to speak. At first he called her "great mistress" and begged for a crumb of bread. The servants had brought that, too, and in between her ministrations, Little Pearl fed him fruit, bread, and sweet tea.

Then, as his stomach was filled, he began to call her an angel, wondering if he had died. She indicated he had not. She explained that he was in a hospital, where she was caring for his ailments.

And then he began to speak of his life. He had been a great servant once, he said, for a rich Manchurian family in Peking. He had a wife and four children and was greatly admired by all, he said. Until one day his master had entertained an important eunuch of the dowager empress. The eunuch had been drunk, crashing about without thought or care. In his drunken stupor, he had broken a valuable vase of the Ming dynasty. But rather than take responsibility for his crime, he had blamed it on this man, this servant, claiming that he had seen him in the act of thieving.

The story made no sense, and his master knew it. But such was the fear of the Qin Empire, such was the terror in which these people lived, that the master had no choice. The servant's hands were chopped off. Worse, because of the anger and bitterness in the servant's eyes, the eunuch had demanded that his eyes be put out as well.

All this was done, but in one thing the master was merciful. Though the servant was tossed out to beg for whatever life he could find, his wife and children had remained at the great house, cared for, because of his years of honorable service.

He had a little money, and so this man had made his way to Shanghai, where his brother lived. But blind as he was, he had no way to find his brother once in the great, teeming city. And so he now survived off begging as best he could.

Joanna strained to understand his story, spoken as it was in thickly accented Shanghainese. Even when the words made sense to her, she wondered at their truth. She knew that the Chinese prided themselves on their civilization. With their great culture that spanned five thousand years, the Chinese were using parchment and ink when the Europeans were still squatting in mud huts. And yet, that this story could be true . . . It turned her stomach.

She turned to the Manchurian by her side, moving with infinite care so as not to disturb the tapestry or catch the attention of the Tigress beside her. The monk saw her shift immediately, his gaze meeting hers in the tight space. He knew what she was asking. Could this story be true? Could a loyal servant be blinded and mutilated just because a powerful guest visited?

He didn't answer with words, but his eyes slid away and down, his sadness as evident as his shame. *Yes,* his silent motion said, *yes, the story is likely true.*

Joanna's great anger returned. She swelled with the righteous fury of an oppressed people. She felt as she had not since coming to this strange place. Her hands clenched with fervor. She would help these poor people. As the Americans had thrown off the British, so would she help the Chinese throw off their monarchical oppressors.

But how? How would she do this with no voice and no way to escape this strange compound? And once she escaped, how would she join the great revolutionary movement? Her last attempt was what had landed her here. What could she do, a white woman in this land of both great beauty and great evil?

She had no answers, and her mind continued to churn, her eyes following Little Pearl and the mutilated servant. Little Pearl had finished shaving the man's head and face. She had washed his sores and fed him while he told his story. And now, as his words dwindled to silence, Joanna's rage quieted as well. Her eyes opened to the peace that seemed to surround the man even as Little Pearl moved lower down his body.

"I will shave you here now," she said softly. "It is the only way to remove the vermin."

"No!" The man shrank back, trying to pull himself away. "I am too ugly for your eyes."

"I am a nurse," Little Pearl lied. "I do this to help you. Please," she urged when he still tried to withdraw. "Allow me to care for you or I will be in great trouble with my mistress."

Only the threat of her suffering calmed him. Slowly he allowed her to ease his arms away and gently strip him of his breechcloth. It was stiff, yellow, and stuck painfully to his skin in places, but Little Pearl did not hesitate. Nor did she rush. She eased the dirty cloth away before discarding it, then began to wash and shave the area.

Joanna watched closely, her attention fixed not on the man but on Little Pearl. She could not believe that such a beautiful young girl would act so subservient to a dirty beggar. Even in the United States, where all men were created equal and Christian generosity was a virtue, Joanna did not think she could find a girl of Little Pearl's age and beauty who would so happily and gracefully perform such tasks. And yet there was only purity in her movements and gentleness in her touch.

It was humbling to watch, especially knowing that Joanna would herself not be so giving.

And then Little Pearl began her other ministrations.

Joanna had seen it coming. As Little Pearl moved and cleansed him, the man's dragon had grown larger and fuller. It was smaller than she expected, certainly smaller than her monk's. But it was there, poking its head out of its tunnel, its mushroom face just as pictured on the scroll.

Joanna couldn't tell when exactly Little Pearl changed the manner in which she handled it. Her ministrations always had a kind of caress, but bit by bit her hands fondled more than cleansed, stroked more than shaved. And the blind man closed his eyes, a sigh of blissful contentment upon his face.

"Does this bother you?"

It took a moment for Joanna to realize who spoke. She'd been so absorbed in what was going on that when the monk whispered in her ear, she was confused. But then he cupped her elbow and continued.

"If this is offensive, I will try to remove you. I swore that you would not be harmed."

She frowned, wondering what exactly he meant. She could not look at him. Shi Po was too close, and he was taking great pains to make his words barely audible.

"Does this frighten you?" he pressed.

She shook her head. No, the sight did not frighten her. No, she did not wish them to risk life and limb in attempting an escape at this moment. And no, she was not harmed in the least by watching Little Pearl's act of kindness.

Joanna was humbled and awed.

She bowed her head, surreptitiously taking the monk's hand. She felt the calluses and the warmth that were part of him, and she held on tight, keeping him from making any ill-advised moves. Then she watched as Little Pearl opened her ruby lips and mouthed the beggar's dragon.

There had been pictures of this act in Shi Po's scrolls. Pictures and labels and explanations. But those were nothing compared to watching a beautiful woman in the act.

It took little time. No doubt the man had not had such tender care in many years, if ever. And he had been well stimulated by the cleaning process. Still, Joanna was fascinated. His face looked as if he were in pain. His eyes scrunched shut and his breath came in gasps. And when the beggar's breath suddenly stopped and his body went rigid, Joanna thought for a moment that he had died.

But he hadn't. His dragon spewed forth its milky cloud, and Little Pearl consumed every drop. In this way, Joanna knew, the Tigress took in the Dragon's yang, making herself stronger while it weakened the man. Or so Shi Po taught.

But looking at the beggar, Joanna didn't see him as weakened. Only happy. Blissfully happy, with closed eyes. Moments later his breath settled into the deep pattern of a man asleep.

Another person whispered into Joanna's ear. It was Shi Po, her soft voice still managing to hold danger. "Little Pearl will complete her service by finding this man's brother. In such ways, a Tigress honors the yang that sustains her."

Joanna nodded, beginning to understand the beauty of their philosophy. She remained silent as the others began filing out of their hiding places, bowing respectfully to Little Pearl as they passed. The monk and Joanna also bowed before joining the rest of the women outside in the courtyard.

Shi Po followed, walking with the stately arrogance of any queen, and Joanna spared a moment to wonder if she had also ever served as Little Pearl did, with a maimed beggar or other man of low status. She couldn't imagine it, and yet the tenets of their religions clearly called for such.

But she wasn't given much time to contemplate as Shi Po gestured to all the women. "You understand your tasks," she said.

They nodded, bowing deeply to her. Then they scattered, and soon only the Tigress, Joanna, and the monk remained in the courtyard. And the guards, of course. But they were at a distance, out of earshot.

The Tigress turned to Joanna, her eyes narrowed in clear challenge. "You have seen what you need to learn. Will you accept your teaching? Speak now with a clear heart, for I can spare no more time for a barbarian whose presence is not her own choice." And with that she glared not at Joanna but the Manchurian.

It took a long moment for the information to sink in. But then Joanna realized exactly what had been said: *a barbarian whose presence is not her own choice.* Shi Po was acknowledging that Joanna was a prisoner. But not the Tigress's prisoner. The monk's.

A wave of hot rage surged through her. She spun on her heel, disbelief warring with the obvious truth. He had made her believe they were both prisoners, that the Tigress held them captive. But now, looking at the guilty flush to his features, she knew that wasn't true. She had been held by his command. And the Tigress's hateful attitude toward her had been no more than the all-too-common Chinese disdain for a barbarian who had invaded her home, required her services, and challenged her authority at every turn.

And all because the monk demanded it.

Joanna tasted anger, bitter and harsh in her bruised throat. A throat he had damaged. But before she could give expression to her fury, he took her hands, his voice low and intense.

"I have not lied to you," he said. "I *am* a prisoner here. And because I am here, you are as well."

She tried to shake off his grip, but he held her too firmly. A moment later he released her, his hands falling to his sides.

"I cannot allow you to leave and perhaps speak of my presence. I cannot risk that," he said. He shifted his gaze back to the Tigress. "Unless, of course, you will release both of us."

Shi Po shook her head. "You are here to learn, monk."

"I have been here for two days, in the same room as a white barbarian. Even your students have seen this. That is ample evidence to damn me, Tigress. You have your blackmail material. Why will you not release me?"

Joanna frowned, desperately trying to follow both his words and the conversation's undercurrents, even as the Tigress waved her guards away.

"You have great skill, monk. You have demonstrated control, power, and vast knowledge." She stepped forward, her entire body a challenge. "My poor servants would be no match for you."

Joanna glanced at the retreating guards, seeing their awkward gait, their lack of power and control. She didn't need the Tigress's next words to realize the truth.

"You can escape at any time."

The monk did not answer. His gaze dropped. And

then the Tigress asked the question that was pounding in Joanna's brain.

"Why? Why would a Qin Mandarin stay in the home of a Tigress? Why would he help purify a white barbarian despite the cost to his reputation and his life? Why would he *hide* here, in my home?"

As if against his will, the monk's gaze slid to Joanna. He looked at her, and she saw anguish in his eyes, a pain and a hunger that she could not comprehend.

Beside her, the Tigress echoed her confusion. "You want this woman. Why?" When he did not answer, Shi Po shook her head. "No, if you wanted her, you would have taken her. She has been in your room for two nights. You are not here because of her." Her eyes narrowed. "And you are not here because of me." She reached out, using one long finger to touch his chin, anchoring his gaze. "Why *are* you here, monk? What do you seek?"

If Joanna had seen anguish in his eyes before, there was nothing in them now. Nothing but an emptiness, carefully hidden behind a placid exterior. The Tigress exhaled in disgust.

"A fleeing man sees nothing but the tiger behind him," she said.

"Then it is fortunate that I have a Tigress to distract him," he countered.

Shi Po pushed him away, her disgust clear. He didn't move far. Indeed, a block of granite could not have appeared more solid. And so the Tigress shifted her attention to Joanna.

"What is your decision, barbarian? Do you want to stay and learn? The exit is there." She gestured to a shadowed opening in the gate at the back of the courtyard. It was made of dark stone and shrouded by trees and the house. But it was undeniably an exit, and no guard blocked her path.

She turned to go to it. She was sick to death of Chinese strangeness. Days ago her only thought had been to help the oppressed poor throw off the yoke of a corrupt dynasty. She had found revolutionaries, only to be assaulted by them. Then she had been rescued by one of the Qin leaders, only to have her voice stolen before being herself trapped in the home of a religious cult leader. Words like *blackmail* and *purify* had been used with regard to her, and she understood none of it. She *wanted* none of it.

And so she would leave. She even took a step toward the door. But she did not go farther. She stopped, an image holding her in place, mesmerizing her. She saw Little Pearl ministering to the maimed beggar. The two were surrounded by candlelight, and Joanna had watched as a filthy, wretched man became clean, then drifted off onto a quiet, peaceful sleep. But most of all, she felt the peace that surrounded the two. A peace of mind, a peace of purpose, and a peace that she longed to experience herself.

Was this what the monk had called her center? If so, then it seemed well worth pursuing. It was worth risking everything to find.

She didn't even realize she was speaking until she heard—and felt—the rawness of her voice. "I want to learn," she said.

The pain of speaking nearly undid her. It seared through her body, and yet that felt right somehow. It was a cleansing of herself, a dedication of purpose that should come with pain. Because she already knew this would change her entire life. And so she pushed even further, speaking again with a conscious will, even knowing the agony she would cause herself.

"I must . . . write Father." Her father was likely beside himself with worry—he and most of the foreign consulates with him, for he would rouse them all to find her.

But Shi Po shook her head. "You cannot contact anyone from your old life. Not until your training is over. I cannot have outraged barbarians storming my door."

Joanna shook her head, already anticipating the problem. "Deliver note. In secret. He will not hunt you."

The Tigress reached out, drawing Joanna around so that they faced each other. "How can you be sure?"

It was a good question, but Joanna did not have the voice to explain. Instead she swallowed, forcing herself to say one last thing. "I trust you. You must trust me."

The Tigress waited a moment, her eyes narrowed to the point that she truly resembled a stalking beast. But before she could speak, her husband appeared.

"I will see that the message is delivered," he said.

Both Shi Po and Joanna jumped, surprised. But whereas the Tigress seemed to grow angry, Joanna bowed her head in acknowledgment and thanks. The husband—Kui Yu—smiled warmly; then his attention shifted to the monk, who stood like stone beside her.

"What of you, Mandarin? What of this evil you bring to my house, and how will you make amends?"

There was a silence, a squaring off of these two men, and the women faded into insignificance. But not for long. Shi Po straightened, moving to take her husband's side so that they faced the Mandarin together. The monk cut his gaze to Joanna—a flicker only, but in it she saw a quiet plea. Would she take his side against them?

She nearly laughed at the thought. He had lied to her, betrayed her, even taken her voice away. And yet the hunger in his eyes weakened her. She saw pain and wished to soothe it.

But not enough to overcome his betrayal. She straightened, stepping backward away from this struggle she did not comprehend.

The monk turned back to the Tigress and her husband. When he spoke it was in a low tone appropriate to a supplicant. "I will earnestly learn what you have to teach, great Tigress. And then, when I have mastered what I can, I will take my knowledge to the dowager empress on your behalf. Though I believe she has already heard of your work." He swallowed. "Isn't that what you wanted from the very beginning?"

Kui Yu did not answer. Instead he tilted his head to his wife, his expression unreadable. "Is this acceptable repayment, Tigress?"

Everyone waited while Shi Po considered. She drew out the pause, as if there was much to weigh. And perhaps there was. Further exposing her cult religion to the leader of her country could be no small thing. In fact, it was likely a very dangerous move—but also one that could bring her enormous imperial favor—and the fortune that came with it.

In the end, Shi Po inclined her head. "I accept you as my true student, Mandarin. And the white barbarian as well. Go and practice what you have learned today." Then she graciously accepted her husband's arm and began to walk away.

It was only after she had taken a step that Joanna realized what had just been said—that she and the monk were to practice. Together.

Rushing forward, Joanna scrambled to a place in front of Shi Po, stopping her and her husband in the middle of the path. She had no voice to speak, but she bowed deeply before them and hoped the reason for her agitation was clear.

The Tigress frowned. "There is a problem, barbarian?"

Joanna straightened, but only halfway. She kept her head lowered respectfully, even as she cast a significant glance at the Mandarin.

"You do not wish to practice with the monk?"

Joanna nodded, relieved to have gotten her message through.

"He has betrayed you, imprisoned you, and stolen your voice," Shi Po replied. "And yet such evil deeds have turned out most fortunately for you. You would not be my pupil without his efforts."

Joanna froze, her relief fading. Shi Po stepped closer, using her favorite method of gaining someone's attention. She extended a single, sharp-nailed finger and poked it underneath Joanna's chin. By exerting the slightest pressure, she forced Joanna to straighten and look her in the eye.

"Did you not see how Little Pearl served today? How she honored the yang giver?"

Joanna nodded, her belly tight with anxiety.

"A Tigress possesses all things save one: a man's yang. For it to be of use, that must be given willingly and with a pureness of intention. The monk has much to atone for with you, so he will give of himself completely. And you, barbarian, must learn to forgive. In that way you will honor his yang gift." Shi Po leaned in, her eyes cold as she pressed her point. "And in serving him, you will learn to forgive."

The Tigress straightened, slowly adjusting so that she seemed to bow to her husband, her posture subservient. In return, he smiled, his eyes shining with a love that momentarily stunned Joanna.

"Address yourself to service, barbarian," Shi Po said. "For in serving he who has wronged you, you may gain all." And with that final statement, the Tigress and her husband walked away.

> *17 May, 1896*
> *Dearest Kang Zou,*
>   *Your Abbot Tseng sounds like a wise man. Could he come to my wedding? Shall I send a carriage for you both? The family is most anxious to meet him.*
>
>

Your happy sister,
Wen Ji
>

Decoded translation:

> Dearest son,
>   Is Abbot Tseng the leader of the insurgents? Is that why you mentioned him in your letter? Shall I send soldiers now to kill him and the other rebels? I will tell the emperor of your report.
>
>

Your pleased father,
General Kang
>

> *30 May, 1896*
> *Dearest sister,*
>   *Send no carriage! Do not tell the family that he is coming. There is disease in the monastery, and we are all too sick to travel. Fortunately the abbot is a wise man and a great teacher. He is showing me the ways of the Shaolin. I am growing stronger with every moment in his presence. I am sure my offerings and prayers are stronger now. They will help you more.*
>
>

Your earnest brother,
Kang Zou
>

Decoded translation as understood by General Kang:

> Dearest Father,
> Do not send soldiers! Do not tell the emperor anything! There is danger throughout the monastery. Fortunately the abbot is helping me. This religion is a wonderful breeding ground for strength and power. I am definitely bewitched by it.
>
> > Your prayerful son,
> > Zou Tun

A wise person understands that the great Tao of the universe lies within one's own heart, and that it isn't necessary to run around in search of it.

—*Lao Tzu*

Chapter Nine

Zou Tun stood mountain-still as he waited to see what Joanna would do. But though his exterior remained quiet, inside a whirlwind of fears churned. He could see that she was furious. And truthfully, she had a right to be.

But that didn't mean he wanted her anywhere near his dragon. Not in this frame of mind.

Unfortunately he had little choice in the matter. If he wanted to pursue this learning—and he most definitely did—then this was the woman who needed to be his partner. He wasn't sure when or how he'd come to that conclusion. It was more of a feeling than a knowledge. But he had long since learned to trust the internal nudges of his spirit. Indeed, it had saved his life not too many days ago. And so, if it directed him to a white barbarian woman—even a furious one—then he would obey.

Assuming, of course, that she wished to continue.

She turned to him, her eyes narrowed, her lips pressed tightly together. He had been surprised when she spoke. He knew her throat was still swollen, and he had not thought she could withstand the pain enough to speak. But she had. And now she was likely suffering the consequences.

"I can ease the pain in your throat," he offered. He tried to make his voice soothing, but his nervousness betrayed him. His own throat felt tight and painful, almost as if he, too, had suffered her injury. Fortunately she didn't shy away. Instead she fixed him with such a glare that he felt his belly tremble.

No woman had ever intimidated him. But this woman—the woman who would soon be touching his most intimate places—could freeze his blood to ice.

He swallowed, knowing he had to make amends but unsure how to begin. "You wish an explanation of my actions. I will give one to you, as well as an apology. But I have need for secrecy, and we are standing in an open courtyard. Please, will you come to our chamber?"

She folded her arms across her chest, her eyes still icy cold. Then he watched in dismay as her gaze flicked to the darkened gate. She was thinking about leaving. He almost grabbed her. He nearly lifted her up in his arms to carry her to their bedchamber, where he could make his explanations. He did not want her to leave, and he feared another kidnapping was the only way to keep her by his side. But his reason kept him still. Violence of even the gentlest sort would not aid him now. She had to decide on her own.

And so he stood still, his breath barely flowing through his constricted throat.

He had a moment—in truth, an eternity—to realize how far he had strayed from the Tao, from the Middle Path. He was a Shaolin monk, sworn to a life of virtue and quiet harmony with nature. And yet here he was running from his father's soldiers, hiding from his father's enemies, training to harness his dragon's power, and barely restraining himself from abducting a barbarian woman in order to allow his dragon full rein between her thighs.

What had he come to?

His spinning thoughts came to an abrupt halt as Joanna sighed. He could tell from the way her entire body sagged that she had decided to stay. And though he had no ability to reason out her thought processes, he was able to give thanks to Heaven for her decision.

Without even looking at him, she spun on her heel, leading the way to their room. So stiff was his body that Zou Tun didn't immediately move to follow her. Instead he felt himself smile, his body softening as the grip of his fear eased.

She was such a magnificent woman. Barbarian or not, she was pleasingly formed, more intelligent than most men, and she walked with a regalness equal to the most arrogant imperial courtier. Magnificent. He could do much worse than spend many days in study with her.

He caught up with her easily. For all that she walked briskly, his legs were longer. Still, she pushed past him to enter their chamber first, her gaze flicking angrily past him. He grinned at that. He couldn't help himself. Now that he felt confident that she would stay, he found her anger pleasing. He had never wanted an imperial wife, a woman who bowed and spread her legs without thought, her only interest in his seed. This woman he would have to work to gain, to coax her into pleasure even if it was part of the Tigress teachings. And so he resolved to do just that: to woo her so that they could advance to the highest level of practice.

He shut the door, his immediate goal clear. She was standing in the middle of the room, her anger a palpable thing in the tiny space, so he put on his humblest expression and bowed deeply.

"Please allow me to fix the injury that I have inflicted upon your body," he said, his tone excruciatingly formal. "It will not cure the damage to your throat, but it will allow for speedy healing."

He stepped forward, but she took a hasty step back, clearly shaking her head to say no.

He paused, confused. "I will not harm you. I slowed the healing process earlier, so you would not tell my secrets. But now I understand the grave harm I have caused you. Please allow me to return the qi to your throat so you can heal quickly. Naturally." He paused, searching her tight expression for some kind of softening. "You should be better within a day, maybe two."

She gave no reaction. But again when he stepped forward, she shook her head.

He stilled, confused. She should be anxious to get her voice back.

"You do not trust me," he guessed, and from her wry expression, he knew he was correct. "But if I wished to harm you further, I would have done so long before this. You have agreed to remain here in seclusion with me as we learn the Tigress teachings. I trust you not to talk about my identity." In truth, he believed no such thing. But as her partner, he would never leave her side. There would be little opportunity for her to talk with anyone other than himself. "Please, allow me to help you."

She arched a single eyebrow at him, clearly showing she did not believe him. He sighed.

"How can I gain your trust?"

She thought for a moment, then unfolded her arms enough to point to him.

"Me?"

She nodded.

"What do you want me to do?"

She shook her head. Then, when he still did not understand, she pointed to herself.

"You?"

She nodded, pointing to herself again.

"You. What about you?" When she grimaced in response, he continued speaking out loud as he thought. "You. You are Joanna Crane. You—"

She nodded vigorously, interrupting his words.

He frowned. "You are Joanna Crane?"

Again she nodded. Then she pointed to him, and at last he understood, though his heart sank at her meaning.

"You want my name. That is how you will trust me?"

Again she nodded.

He bowed his head, anxiety filling his throat. He tried to weigh his options perfectly, but he could not. There were too many variables, too much to guess. Except for one thing: One glance at her face told him she would accept nothing less than his true name.

He could give her a false one, of course. He could name any one of a dozen high-ranking Mandarins. She would not know the difference. And yet part of him longed to tell her the truth. Part of him was sick to death of hiding his real name, his real soul.

He delayed, though he could sense her anger growing every moment he remained silent. Indeed, he could feel the heat in the air around them. He lifted his head, speaking his thoughts out loud.

"You must understand," he said. "I have hidden my identity for so long, the name seems like it belongs to someone else. It is not me at all."

He looked at her, and she appeared to be listening, her expression softening with his words. But not softening enough. She still would have his name.

"Zou Tun," he finally blurted. "I cannot tell you my banner name, but my name is Zou Tun."

She nodded and mouthed the words, *Thank you*.

He looked away, expecting to feel sick worry in his

167

belly. But instead he felt a loosening, an easing of his pain. Frowning, he turned back to her, but he didn't have anything to say. Only questions whirled in his mind. Why would telling her his true name give him relief? And why would her smile appear like an angel's blessing?

He moved without thinking, extending his hand to her throat. She was in pain. He could feel it, but only as a twinge of guilt. Closing his eyes, he used his will and his monk's training to restore the flow of qi to her throat. She didn't fight him. Just the opposite; she lifted her chin, giving him greater access.

And when he was finished, she smiled and whispered, "Thank you."

"The fault was mine. The remedy my burden."

She frowned, taking hold of his hand and drawing it back to her throat. Then she spoke, though still in a bare whisper. "How?"

He shrugged, doing his best to explain. "The Shaolin monks teach of the body's energy and call it qi. The Tigresses divide that energy into male yang and female yin. But either way it is qi. It flows like a river and can be diverted in a similar manner—away from a place in the body like your throat, or back to its natural course." He paused, shifting to sit on the bed. "As to how such things are done, the mind controls them. I merely will it to be so and focus all my attention upon it. The change happens as I will it."

She frowned, clearly not believing that was all there was to the process. And for some reason he grinned. He remembered his own similar reaction some years ago, when he'd first joined the monastery.

"I swear to you, it is that easy. In truth, the harder one makes it, the less effective it is. A man's mind is everything. It guides his power, and it will move another's qi as well."

She stared at him a moment, obviously thinking through his words. It was a strange feeling having a woman consider his words so carefully, so clearly. Especially since he knew she weighed his words not only for logic but also for intent. She still did not fully trust him.

"I have no reason to lie to you," he answered, hearing the note of pique in his voice.

She continued to regard him with a clear and steady expression. Only one woman had ever dared to look at him in such a way, and it was disconcerting to feel the same attention from a white barbarian as he had from the dowager empress. Indeed, he was beginning to feel as if Joanna Crane and Empress Cixi had more in common than either would appreciate.

Rather than follow the direction of his thoughts, he decided to shift his attention.

"We must continue purifying your yin," he said, trying to keep his expression bland. He had no wish to reveal to her how much he sincerely wanted to assist her with the task. And yet she must have sensed it, because she shook her head. Instead she gestured to his jade stem.

He hesitated, wary of her mood. Did she intend to hurt him when he was most vulnerable?

As if in answer to his thoughts, she settled onto her knees before him, just as Little Pearl had done for the beggar. She brought a basin of water and a washcloth over, then bowed her head and appeared as subservient as any Chinese female. But was it a ruse? Could he trust her?

She lifted her gaze, her right eyebrow arched. This, too, was part of her challenge to him. She would not trust him unless he trusted her. And so he nodded, steeling himself to take the risk.

"You understand that you are not to draw my essence out like Little Pearl did," he warned. "You are to press upon the *jen-mo* point to prevent the dragon cloud."

She nodded. She had indeed been listening during the Tigress's lecture.

He swallowed. He knew he had to do this. He knew, but . . . Straightening his shoulders, he made his decision. With quick movements he stripped off his shirt and pants. He stood naked before her, his muscles taut with anxiety. His dragon hid in fear.

She had been wearing a soft smile of victory. He had seen it, for all that she tried to hide it from him. But now, as she gazed up at him, her challenge faded. Her eyes widened and her hands shifted restlessly in her lap. He knew he was an impressive sight. It was not vanity that made him think so; it was simply excellent food as he'd been growing and the monastic exercises he practiced so devotedly. Still, he could not stop a masculine surge of pride at the admiration in her eyes.

"What do you wish me to do?" he asked, thankful that his voice remained level, as if he were not still trembling with tension.

She gestured to the bed, and he complied, lying down on his stomach because he was too wary to lie on his back. Then he closed his eyes and prepared for the worst. Even in this position she still had access to vulnerable places. But he had resolved to trust her, and so he did his best to relax.

Tepid water hit his skin, thick drops that made him flinch. And then the washcloth. She held it firmly, pressing too hard as she scrubbed his back. He said nothing, but in his mind he wondered if she intended to treat his jade stem with equal fervor. The pain might very well be unbearable.

But then she gentled, her hands growing tired. Or perhaps she realized that his back would soon be raw if she continued as she had. In any event, she began to stroke more than scrub, to soothe more than cleanse. And Zou Tun exhaled in relief until his thoughts pushed into his mind.

Was this a ruse?

No, he answered himself. This was a Taoist challenge and a metaphor for life. Worry for the future only destroyed the present. A man who walked the Middle Way neither concerned himself with what was to come nor with worries about what might have been. He contented himself with the present. And so Zou Tun took another deep breath, and with his exhalation he resolved to enjoy the experience without any thought beyond it.

So began his meditative exercise. Another breath helped him attune himself to his surroundings. He felt the scratch of the sheets beneath him, heard the creak of the mattress as Joanna Crane moved, but mostly he felt the gentle stroke of a beautiful woman's hands. He heard her breath and felt her movements, easily synching his rhythms to hers. The water was tepid, the cloth rough, but where she moved, his body heated. And when she passed by, the flesh cooled and eased.

Then, as sometimes had happened before, pictures began to form in his mind. Imagination or true awareness, he was never sure which, allowed him to see her even though he lay on his stomach with his eyes closed. He saw her flushed from her exertions, her hair clinging wetly to her neck. Her eyes were bright, unusually so, and she focused completely on her task. She had begun with his back, moving on to his arms. Now she washed the fingers of his right hand, gently easing the cloth between each as she stroked his calluses.

He wanted to curl his fingers around hers. He wanted to entwine himself with her, holding her tightly to him in the most basic of ways. And yet he wanted more than that—a meeting of minds, perhaps, though the thought of wanting intellectual connection with a ghost woman felt completely bizarre. But in meditation one accepted everything—every thought, every image, and every feeling no matter how strange, in order to allow them to pass through.

Zou Tun remained lax, accepting all she chose to give without pushing her for more. And soon she finished with his arms and hands and moved to his feet.

As a cosseted imperial bannerman, Zou Tun had received many baths: from his mother when he was young, from servant women as he matured. He still remembered the experiences as pleasurable and potentially erotic, depending on his age and the intention of the woman who assisted him. But this experience was different. This bath was intended to be stimulating. Yet he was *not* supposed to pursue the woman. Unlike the beggar, he was to accept her ministrations, allow her to take him to his peak, then *not* release his seed.

So it was that no matter how relaxed she made him, no matter how much her touch coaxed his dragon to rear its head, he found himself settling deeper and deeper into his meditations.

Until she asked him to turn over.

He knew the instruction was coming, indeed, had been preparing for just this moment. But as he settled on his back, his focus was interrupted. His dreamlike state dissolved into the very present experience of her kneeling beside him, of his legs and feet still cooling from the stroke of her cloth. His dragon was no longer afraid but poking proudly out of its tunnel.

He looked at her, seeing that her face was flushed and her eyes were half closed, as if she, too, mediated as she worked. She had loosely braided her hair away from her face, but her breasts swung free, her nipples pointed against the slightly wet fabric of her shirt. If it weren't for the quiet in her face, he would have thought her aroused.

"Take off your shirt," he ordered.

He didn't understand where the command came from. The last thing he needed was to be more stimulated, to see the rosy blush on her ghost skin. But he was angry with her for being so disinterested when he could not breathe, when his dragon danced with her every stroke even though she touched only his chest.

"I wish to see your breasts." He kept his voice cold, trying to discomfort her. If he roused her anger, she would change her methods and he could keep his honor intact.

But she wasn't bothered. She merely looked at him, meeting his gaze with a calm, flat regard. He saw a rapid pulse beat in her throat. Her heart was not as calm as her face. She merely dipped her head and boldly lifted off her light tunic. Then she was bare to the waist, her rose-tipped breasts within a short hand's reach from him.

His dragon reared in interest.

She arched a single brow at him. A challenge? Clear as day. Could he retain his yang fluid despite her determined attentions?

He curled his hands into fists. He was a Shaolin monk, trained to the highest level in Paochui. He had spent thousands of hours disciplining his mind and body to the Middle Path. He would not let any woman, much less a ghost barbarian, rip him from that. He would allow her to stimulate him; she would heat the fire of his yang to boiling, but he would not release. He would use it and her yin to gain enlightenment.

He closed his eyes, looking away from her to focus on his breath. Only his breath.

The caress of cool water prickled his fevered skin. And the brush of one pert breast came against his arm. Her lips gently pressed against his belly.

His eyes flew open. A kiss? That had not been part of Little Pearl's example!

"Why did you do that?" he asked, his voice harsh.

She was licking her lips, tasting them even as they became redder, wetter, and curved by the faintest of smiles. "Wondered," was all she said.

Wondered what? What he would taste like? Or what it was like to kiss a man? Either way, it made Zou Tun release a frustrated growl. He wanted to grab her. He wanted to drop her on the bed and plant himself deeply inside her. He wanted to do it fast and hard and in a way that only beasts acted.

And wasn't that the point? He was a beast. Or he could be. But he wanted to be an immortal. Or at least an enlightened man. And so he would restrain himself. He would learn to master his desires in the only way possible: with a woman, and with stimulation.

He closed his eyes again, willing his body to relax, forcing his breath to steady. It didn't work. Especially as Joanna began to wash his legs. Starting at his feet, she cleaned him with water, the rough brush of fabric as erotic as anything that he had ever felt.

He knew it was only a game of the mind. He had been washed before and not indulged in sexual activity. It was only because that act was denied him that his entire being focused on her. She was leaning across him, washing the leg farthest from her so her bare belly pressed against him. Her skin was soft and smooth—a woman's skin.

He inhaled deeply, trying to clear his mind. Instead, that brought her scent to him. She was aroused. That odor meant only one thing. And yet, there was more to it as well. It was Joanna's scent and hers alone. And her face and body formed in his mind whenever he closed his eyes.

He wanted to move, wanted to arch his hips, wanted so many things. He had been uncomfortable before. He had sat in meditative poses while his hips or his knee or some part of his body burned with pain. He had been able to look beyond it, to see that the pain, the hunger, the desire—all of it was only a part of who he was. It was only a small fraction of his consciousness.

But this desire was not isolated to one part of his body. It was all-consuming. It throbbed through his entire being. It was *him*.

No! He was more than this. He was more than his desire. Even as her cloth began to touch him, began to cleanse between his thighs and the soft underbelly of his dragon, he could be more than this.

Except that he couldn't. Her touch conquered his mind. It aroused his body. It tormented his soul.

And then she set the cloth aside.

He didn't dare open his eyes. The sight of her lips coming down around his dragon stem would be too much. But he couldn't stop himself. He wanted to see what she looked like as she touched a man's dragon— probably for the first time.

He had expected her eyes to be hooded, shrouded in shyness. They weren't. Her eyes were wide-open, her head tilted to one side. She had used the washcloth on his dragon. But now she reached out, her touch hesitant but her interest clearly engaged.

With one finger she stroked his dragon head, darker now as it thrust fully forward. He felt the stroke like the touch of lightning searing through his body. His hips jerked; his dragon spit—but just a little: the single pearl bead that Tigresses prized so very much.

She had been unprepared for his reaction, so she drew back. Her expression was open as she studied his body. But what thoughts were swirling in her mind, he couldn't fathom. What did a ghost woman think when presented with an imperial dragon?

Apparently she thought it was funny. Her lips were curved in humor. He was sure of it. Then, as he watched and as she began to play with his dragon, her lips drew into a full smile. She touched his tip, swirling the bead of moisture around. Then she pulled her fingers to her lips, closing her eyes to smell the dragon pearl. She opened her mouth, extending the tiniest tip of her pink tongue to taste it.

The sight nearly undid him. Zou Tun felt his dragon contract, pulling together in preparation to throw his seed.

"Stop!" he ordered. "Stop it now!"

It took a moment for her to understand. First she whipped her hand away from her mouth. Then he gestured, and her eyes widened. She comprehended: He wanted her to press on the *jen-mo* point, to stop the flow of his dragon cloud.

She moved to help him, but her hands were uncertain, her fingers fumbling. At another time her nervous movements would have made his dragon retreat in fear. Not this time. His dragon knew it was her hands and touch. It stretched for her, aching for her caress no matter how abrupt.

She lifted the dragon's soft belly, painfully jostling the twin houses of his dragon cloud. Then, mercifully, she found the spot. She pressed in hard with her middle finger, holding back the cloud in the place where—on a woman—the child would emerge. Stopping the energy flow from there cut off the power that fed his dragon.

She held her finger in place, her hand naturally cupping his dragon's belly. It was a war of needs.

Above her hand his dragon still strained, loving the caress of her hand but needing the qi power she had removed. In his mind, as well, he fought bestial hunger, straining to stay on the Taoist path to immortality. In his mind he knew he must stay on the Middle Path, but his dragon and the heat of her breath across his belly drew him to the surrounding jungle.

Until his need eased. Until his dragon starved enough for him to draw his mind and his body back to the Tao.

He took another deep breath, trying to block her scent from his thoughts, and slowly released his rigid control.

"Thank you," he breathed.

Opening his eyes, he found her studying him again, seeing everything from his flushed face down to his curled toes. She looked at all of him until her gaze finally returned to his face. And as their gazes locked, she slowly withdrew her hand.

The brush of her fingers against his stem brought his dragon instantly back to life. But even that faded as he focused on her eyes. Her beautiful eyes, like polished bronze. He let himself get lost in those eyes, searching and finding the fire that seemed to light them from within.

So mesmerized was he that he nearly missed that she was moving over his dragon again. That her ruby lips were opening. And that, inch by inch, she was drawing him into her mouth.

He groaned. He could not help it. The moist, slick slide of her tongue across his dragon head made his eyes roll back in ecstasy. He knew what his task was now. He knew he was to allow the stimulation to draw his mind upward to Heaven into immortality. He knew this, but his mind would not go. His thoughts remained earthbound. With Joanna.

No matter how much he struggled, no matter how much he tried to ignore the curl of her tongue, the pull of her kiss, and the—sweet Heaven—grip of her hand around his stem, his dragon became everything he was, and her lips his entire world.

He felt his dragon muscles tighten. He knew the white heat consumed his mind. He fought, railing against it, but it was no use. It was too overwhelming.

She was too powerful.

And he was . . .

"Help!" he cried even as he thrust forward, deeper inside her mouth.

She was there even before the sound faded from the room. She lifted from his dragon, her fingers quickly finding and pressing the *jen-mo* point, stopping the flow of qi until his buttocks relaxed and his breathing slowed.

He opened his eyes, even though the power of his dragon fire still pounded in his blood, demanding release. He found what he sought immediately—her eyes—and he settled into the shifting colors there. Her pupils were large, their dark circles reminding him of the dusky points of her breasts. But around those pupils, around those dark centers, there remained a shimmer of blue and green. The colors of sky and earth. The whole world was right there in her eyes.

And with that expansion of awareness, the grip of his hunger eased.

"Thank you," he whispered, his voice hoarse.

She arched a single eyebrow at him, her eyes narrowing. "Feel powerless, Zou Tun?" she rasped. Then she shifted her hand off the *jen-mo* point to the place where she held—and squeezed—his dragon. Her grip wasn't strong, but it held the threat of much more force. "Your body is beyond your control?" She shifted her fingers, massaging the twin houses of his cloud. With the qi flow restored, his dragon thrust into her hand, despite the denial of his thoughts.

Then she smiled. It was an angry, harsh smile, filled with the power of her position. And with his vulnerability.

"You did this to me," she said, her voice strengthening despite the pain it must have caused her. "You took my voice from me. My freedom."

And then her other hand began to move. Slowly at first, stroking his dragon stem up and down. She smiled, her red lips widening.

He knew what was to come. She was going to milk his stem, pull the dragon cloud from him, take his yang seed into her body, where she would use it to gain immortality for herself. She would take his power—and a year of his life—and there was nothing he could do about it. Her body would grow more youthful, her soul would step higher to Heaven, and he would be discarded. He would become a used thing of no more importance than that beggar.

He shook his head, unable to form a thought, unable to do more than beg for mercy. But her hands were relentless, the heat of her breath on his dragon head even more so. Heedless of the danger, his entire body began to clench. White-hot lightning poured through his mind and body.

"No. Please," he begged.

She simply shook her head. Then, as he watched, she opened her mouth, extending the tip of her pink tongue. He watched her move, his breath already suspended, his Taoist control shattered.

Her tongue touched his tip. And in its one long, meandering stroke, he lost all control. His dragon thrust into her hand, pushing as far into her mouth as he could.

But she pulled away. Her mouth, her face, her entire body separated from him. Except for her hands, which continued their maddening rhythm.

Her message was clear: He would not control even the manner of his yang loss.

And then, with a soft, almost gentle smile, she moved her thumb. The thrust of his hips had revealed all of his dragon head, leaving the underside fully exposed. Her thumb touched it, the most sensitive ridge just behind the head.

His body exploded. Mind, heart, and soul—all flew from him in the roar of dragon fire. Over and over his dragon roared, disgorging his essence. So powerful was his loss that he had no doubt he had lost a year of his life, a year of his power, all for her use.

Except her mouth was not on his dragon. She did not catch anything, but let his seed spill uselessly— wastefully—onto his belly.

When his breath returned, when some measure of consciousness formed in his weakened body, he slowly forced his eyes to open. She had taken away her hands, removing them from his body, casually wiping her fingers clean while he struggled to think.

His gaze slid down to his belly, where his essence lay. "Why?" he whispered. Why had she not taken his power into her body? Why had she not used him as a Tigress would, for her own betterment?

Her demeanor remained calm, her expression relaxed, and she pushed up from her position by his side. As he watched, she straightened to her full height, her white breasts still gloriously displayed before him.

"Why?" she said, her words mocking despite their raw sound. "Because I have no use for any part of you."

The Tao produces myriad things, lets nature take its course, and is selfless and unprejudiced. Rulers should take this as their model, governing through nonaction and silence and living at peace with the people, which in the end leads to a naturally tranquil society.

—Lao Tzu

Chapter Ten

Joanna pulled on her shirt, pleased with the afternoon's work. Not only had she found out her monk's name, Zou Tun, but she had also made her position clear. She was a strong American woman who would not be lied to. She didn't need him. She needed . . . Her thoughts trailed away, as she was unsure how to finish.

She needed something. But it wasn't him. And so she'd shown him.

She would have completed the gesture by walking out of the room, but truthfully she didn't know where she'd go. Though she worried about her father, she didn't want to go home. Her whole idea several days ago had been to spend some time away, to help mastermind a great revolution against an imperial oppressor. She hadn't expected to land here, but then, she hadn't expected the revolutionaries to attack her either.

Which meant what? At the moment it meant that she wanted to learn what the Tigress Shi Po taught. It meant that she would stay here, even performing certain exercises with certain men that left her insides quivering and her hands unsteady. She would stay even if her face remained flushed and her blood seemed to pulse, pulse, pulse throughout her body.

This was something she wanted to learn. She wanted Little Pearl's peace. She wanted to find her own center. Even if it meant she had to remain here with Zou Tun to get it.

She walked to the door, pulling it open to retrieve a tray of food. Beside the tray lay parchment, ink, and a brush. It would be difficult to write a letter to her father in English with the Chinese brush, but she would find a way. Assuming, of course, that she could figure out the words to use.

Behind her she heard her monk—no, she corrected herself. She heard Zou Tun moving about, no doubt cleaning himself up and covering his shame. Listening to his movements she couldn't suppress a smile.

She had bested him! A man who could fight off five determined revolutionaries, a man whose body rippled with power and dominance—he was a man who was, after all, still just a man. One who could be bested by the simplest of techniques, in the simplest of ways. The way of the Tigress.

And though Joanna's father would be horrified by her actions, she didn't care. What she was learning here was power. And it was a power that could be learned nowhere else. So she intended to grasp it with both hands . . . so to speak.

"You are very pleased with yourself." His words startled her. She hadn't forgotten his presence; in truth, she was excruciatingly aware of his every move, his every breath. But she hadn't expected him to speak so calmly about anything, least of all what had just occurred. He was supposed to be hiding his shame or blustering in embarrassment. Not calmly evaluating her mood.

Still, she had decided on this course, so she would not run. She turned, facing him square in the eye. And then she allowed her most brilliant, smug grin to grow upon her face.

"Do all ghost people take such pleasure in humiliation?" he asked.

Her grin faltered but did not fade. Instead she simply shook her head, and pointed a long, angry finger at him.

He nodded. "Yes, I deserved such treatment. And I accept it as appropriate punishment." He folded his arms across his bare chest. He had not bothered to put any clothing on at all, but had come to his feet, his glorious body challenging her by his simple ease with his own nudity. "But I do not know if ghost people remain trapped inside their anger, reveling in another's anguish"—he lifted his chin—"or if they dispense punishment and move on. Is my humiliation complete?"

She swallowed, the last of her grin fading. His question was reasonable, and she was a reasonable woman. She saw no point in bearing grudges, especially as her point was made. The Tigress had selected them to be partners. She could be the bigger person and move past his transgression to a larger place. A better place. In the name of Christian charity or Tigress betterment, she would not hurt him any further.

She dipped her head. "I believe we understand each other." The words hurt her damaged throat, but she felt them important enough to say aloud. And he apparently agreed, because he too smiled. Warmly. Hugely. And in such a way as to make her incredibly wary.

"Excellent," he said as he reached for the tray of food. "Then I suggest we enjoy our meal." He extended his chin toward the paper and ink. "You intend to write your father?"

She nodded, looking dumbly at the writing implements in her hand.

"Good. We shall eat. You shall compose your letter. And then we shall begin *your* exercises."

He spoke the words casually, as if the plan were of no more import than whether they went for a ride on horseback or in a carriage that afternoon. But she caught a glimmer of malice in his eyes. Or was it anticipation? Or maybe it was just the simple pleasure of eating after so much exertion. He certainly was popping steamed dumplings into his mouth as if he were starving.

But if he was starving, why did his eyes linger on her? Why did his attention center on her breasts, which were modestly covered? And why had she not thought that he would want revenge?

Even if she thought the matter over, even if he stated he deserved and accepted his punishment, did he really mean it? Or did he intend to strike when she was at her most vulnerable?

He didn't speak, though he obviously understood her anxiety. He was starting to smile. More than smile, in fact. His grin grew and grew. It was there on his face when he offered her a bowl of rice. It was there in his movements when he shifted on the bed, offering her a seat. And it was there in his entire demeanor when she declined, choosing instead to try to compose her letter to her father.

There really wasn't any choice in what she wrote. Only one thing would quiet his fears, keep him from rousing the entire country searching for her. Still, she hesitated to write it with the monk right beside her, his enjoyment of her discomfort a tangible presence in the room. Her only comfort was that he probably couldn't read English. So she made quick work of her letter, folding it and setting it outside their door. She knew the Tigress's husband would see it delivered.

Which left her alone, once again, with the consequences of her actions: Zou Tun with an unholy grin on his face.

Rather than deal with him, she decided to eat. She didn't have much of an appetite—or so she thought. In truth, the moment she lifted the egg soup to her lips, she found herself ravenous. It was all she could do to keep herself from gobbling the food like a beast.

And all the while, the Mandarin just watched, his dark eyes glittering, his mouth pulled wide into a too-happy smile.

Then, abruptly, the food was gone. Her letter was written. And Zou Tun was clearing away the tray with large, cheerful movements.

He said, "The Tigress does not stint on food. I find that an excellent thing in a hostess, don't you?"

Joanna smiled, nodding because that was the polite thing to do. And wasn't that a ridiculous thing? Remaining true to good manners when she was about to . . . about to what? What exactly were they about to do?

She looked at him, and her question must have been obvious in her face because he slowed in closing the door, his good humor evaporating.

"You are nervous, wondering what is coming next. Correct?"

She didn't really want to admit to being nervous, not after her great show of independence, but it was the truth and so she nodded.

"We will work on your breast circles. Your yin is surprisingly pure." He paused, obviously thinking. Then he shrugged as if he had decided. "Even if it were not, I cannot stay in this location for much longer."

She frowned.

"A week more, at most." He sighed. "I would love to tease you, to pay back a little of the humiliation you just served me."

She straightened in alarm, but he was quick to reassure her.

"But we haven't the time. And even if we did, I would not have hurt you." He extended his hand, lifting her chin to see his earnest expression. "I meant it when I said I accepted my punishment from you. I deserve much worse, but am pleased that the anger is over between us." He searched her face. "It *is* over, is it not? Your voice is returning. You grow stronger with every breath."

She bit her lip, knowing what he said was true. Her voice was returning. But honesty forced her to say a little more. "There is still some anger. I cannot just will it away."

He released her chin, his manner equally grave. "That is natural, I suppose. But you will not let it interfere with our task, will you?" His question was part challenge.

It was a challenge she was more than willing to meet. "*I* am not petty," she said firmly, using her expression to ask the same question of him.

"And neither am I," he returned. "Therefore we will begin." He hesitated, still searching her face. "I know that enlightenment cannot be rushed. But I hope that we can pursue it aggressively." His expression intensified. "Do you agree?"

"Aggressively?" she whispered. Her throat was burning.

"I will not hurt you. But sometimes the awakening of a woman's yin, especially that of a virgin, can be unsettling. You will tell me if you become too agitated to continue."

She nodded, still very unsure of his meaning.

"Good. Then as you have drawn out my yang, I will open the flow of your yin."

He reached for her shirt, but she stopped him, her hands gripping his wrists with all her strength. "How?" she rasped.

"I will suck on your breasts." When her grip did not ease, he smiled gently at her. "It will not hurt. This I swear." When she still did not release him, he shifted slightly, fighting her enough to touch her face. "I will stop the moment you request it. I swear this by my honor and my name."

She waited. When he did not continue, she pressed him. "What name?"

He sighed, a sound that came from deep within him. But in the end he spoke, his voice a bare whisper. "Kang. My name is Kang Zou Tun. And now you know enough to get us both killed." He sighed. "I have many enemies, Joanna. And after three years in a monastery, I do not know who wishes me dead. Indeed, that is why I am hiding right now. To decide upon my course before I return to Peking." He focused hard on her. "Do not betray me. You cannot imagine the consequences."

She lifted her chin. "There are worse things than death."

His eyes abruptly widened, stark terror blowing through him. He grabbed her arms. "Do you plan suicide because of what we do here?"

She blinked, startled by his sudden vehemence. His eyes flew to the door, where her letter sat outside.

"Is that what your letter was—a note of farewell?"

She frowned, not understanding his tone, much less his words.

"Answer me!" he exclaimed. "Do you plan suicide?"

"No!" she exclaimed, pushing him away from her. She knew she hadn't the strength to force him away, but he released her nonetheless. "No," she repeated more firmly when his gaze did not waver.

"You will not kill yourself for honor?"

She stared at him, her stunned disbelief obvious. And then she watched as he nodded, his breath easing out of him, his body slowly relaxing.

"Of course," he said to himself more than her. "You are a barbarian. Such a thing would not be in your—"

"We know about honor!" she snapped. Her words were loud despite the constriction of her throat. "I will die for important things. Freedom. Justice." She released a small laugh at her own expense. "I wanted to join the rebellion." She focused on Zou Tun. "Now I want Shi Po's power."

He reared back as if slapped. "You would aid a rebellion? Against me?"

She would have laughed at that. She would have given him an entire lecture on the arrogance of thinking he embodied an entire empire. But her throat could not stand the pain, so she simply gave a single dip of her chin.

She watched him grow icy cold.

"I should kill you where you stand."

She swallowed, telling herself she was not afraid. That he would not hurt her. But her heart fought her words, which came out as a rasping whisper. "The beggar. Would you kill him, too?"

She hadn't said everything, but she knew he understood her meaning. Little Pearl's beggar had been maimed and cast off, all on the whim of a court eunuch. This monk could not possibly support such atrocities. And yet apparently he could, because he slowly settled onto their bed, his words more sad than guilty.

"The eunuchs are bitter and angry."

She walked over to face him, her stance making her opinion clear: No matter how angry or bitter men became, such abuses should not occur.

He did not look at her. "There are traditions, Joanna Crane. Ways of life that have lasted for thousands of years."

And that was when she saw it: not angry defense, not even passionate denial, but simply a soul-deep sadness. Like a black well with no bottom, an endless source of pain and grief. All in the name of tradition.

"You know," she finally whispered, awe and shock cooling her temper. "You know the empire will eventually fall."

He looked up, his expression fierce—not with denial, but with a crazy hope. "The people will not rebel against the Son of Heaven."

She snorted in laughter. The Son of Heaven was too young, and too much in the shadow of his mother, the dowager empress. She was the one who ran China. "They will rebel against a woman," she said softly. "Of what importance is a concubine?"

He looked away, and she knew he struggled with his own thoughts. He seemed to be at war with his arrogance. On the one hand, Manchurians were raised with the certainty that they were descended from Heaven. That nothing evil would happen to upset their position of power. And yet the rational part of him knew the truth—that no people would bear the oppressor's yoke indefinitely. Eventually they would rise up. And why not now, when a woman ruled China and the west brought the constant example of independence and freedom to their very door?

At last he shook his head. "Empress Cixi is . . . strong. If anyone can hold China against the barbarian hordes, it will be her. And her son."

He believed it. Joanna could see that in his body. Or perhaps he hoped with every fiber of his soul that it was true. And yet he was here, studying Tigress and Dragon teachings rather than sitting at his emperor's side, helping to make a difference.

"Why are you here?" she asked, wincing at the pain in her throat. "What will you do?"

He didn't answer. Or perhaps he couldn't answer, because he didn't know. He simply shook his head, his gaze remaining distant, his expression infinitely sad. And in the end he looked up, straightening his spine as if steeling himself. "I am here to help release your yin, Joanna Crane. Prepare yourself."

She wasn't surprised by his command. Indeed, she'd known he would end the conversation soon. He was too conflicted to allow her to probe his wound so easily. And there *was* a wound there; she just didn't know what it was. But she would know, eventually. Because she wanted to know, and he needed to tell.

But not now. Now was her turn to feel the yin river. And—if she was very strong—she would ride it to immortality.

She slowly drew her shirt over her head. Her breasts bobbed as she moved, and she was excruciatingly aware of his eyes on her chest. But this was what she wanted, she reminded herself. And indeed, her breasts were already peaking in preparation for his touch.

"Let me sit behind you," he said. "I will adjust our position when it is time."

She nodded, watching with increasing anxiety as he settled with his back against the wall and his legs spread. He was still gloriously naked, his dragon resting at his crotch like a thick, heavy rope. It didn't frighten her anymore. After what she had done earlier, she now knew it was a living thing, hot and pulsing to the touch. And from what she could tell, it seemed to have its own mind, stretching for attention when it wanted it and hiding away when it did not.

"Do not be afraid," he said, opening his arms so that she could settle between them.

She nodded rather than spoke. She was wondering if she too had a part of her body that could rule her, that could come alive as his dragon had. With the right touch, the right caress, would her breasts feel like his dragon? Or was there another place? Another—

She cut off her thoughts, forcing herself to turn away from the sight of her monk and focus on her exercises. There was already a wetness between her legs, a throbbing that made her wonder if that was the place of her dragon. But she was not given time to think as Zou Tun helped her sit between his legs.

Grabbing hold of her hips, he pulled her bottom tightly against his dragon. She felt it like a hot brand behind her, burning into the base of her spine. It wanted her. And she wanted . . .

"You should take off your pants. They will not be comfortable."

She jerked slightly, turning to face him. She couldn't speak. Her throat was too hot, too painful. But her question was clear nonetheless. Why? Why should she take off her clothing?

"It will make you more comfortable," he repeated. Then he closed his eyes. "I won't even look. And you can cover yourself with the sheet. But there should be no fabric between your heel and your cinnabar cave."

She didn't respond. She hadn't the voice or the words, only a fluttering panic like a stuttering flame that twisted and contorted right behind her chest.

"You will feel more comfortable," he repeated a last time.

She stared at him. His eyes were closed, his body relaxed. His *naked* body was relaxed.

He did have a point, she realized. Obviously he had felt more comfortable without the interference of clothing. And indeed, she did not like the idea of rough fabric pressed so intimately against her cave. But to completely undress? She didn't know if she could do it.

And yet what choice did she have? If she wanted to learn the Tigress's power, she would have to undress eventually. She had looked at the Tigress scrolls. There had been little time, but she had unrolled one, scanning its pictures, reading what she could. She knew that there were deeper intimacies to come. More . . . openness. The things she had done to Zou Tun would be repeated for her.

She knew this. So why was she delaying? If she wanted to learn, then she would have to disrobe.

She did. As quickly as possible. Then she scrambled into the bed, pulling the sheet up to cover herself as high on her waist as she could.

And yet she felt her nakedness like a brand. A tattoo. A loud declaration to the world of what she was. But she had no name for it. She wasn't a tigress. Not yet. She wasn't ashamed, either. Well, not exactly. She wasn't even her father's daughter anymore. Not since leaving home.

Now she was . . . what? A naked woman in a Mandarin's arms. But what did that mean? Who *was* she?

The questions twisted in her mind, heating and coiling with the flame that churned inside her. They made her feel ill, these questions, this fear. This nakedness.

Until she felt him touch her. His hands settled quietly, gently upon her shoulders.

"Try to breathe steadily. Find your center in your mind."

She hadn't even realized her breath was coming in

192

jerky gulps until he spoke. But with his warmth upon her shoulders and his quiet words, she began to calm herself. She focused on steadying her breath, and in time it calmed the frantic beat of her heart.

Was this her center?

"I will not force this upon you, Joanna Crane. If you want to change your mind . . ."

She shook her head, quickly and with force. Then she spoke, the words more important than the pain. "I want to learn."

"So be it," he responded. His hands began to move ever so slowly down her arms. "You must pull your right leg in. With your heel . . ."

She remembered. She pulled her leg up, but she could not get herself settled. She felt clumsy, the sheet uncooperative as it continually tried to slip off her hips. Her hands became frantic, her breath once again stuttering and gasping.

Until, once again, he touched her. This time his hands slid all the way down her arms to still her trembling.

"Why are you shaking?" he asked. "Is it shame?"

She shook her head. She knew she ought to feel shame, but truthfully, she did not. So much was denied to women. All over the world they were treated as less than a person. That she had found a way to give herself power was not a shameful thing. That it might be a key to something so much larger was glorious. So no, she did not feel shame exactly.

"Is it fear of what is to come?"

Joanna hesitated, then once again shook her head. She was not afraid of the future so much as curious about it. Or perhaps *nervous* was a better word. But very, very interested.

"Joanna Crane. I do not understand. Why—"

193

"Change." She said the word. She rushed it through her lips, wishing she could explain herself more completely. She wanted to become this new thing, this Tigress. Her life had been so terribly unfulfilling before. And yet she shook with fear of taking the next step. She felt terrified and anxious and excited and confused all at once. And she could not explain it to herself, much less to him.

He seemed to understand. He patted her hand, and his voice took on a lighter tone. "The Chinese have a very large book. It is called *I Ching, The Book of Changes.* Many poems, many words are devoted to the changes that happen in the heavens, in our worlds, and most especially in our minds." He reached up his hands, casually adjusting her braid. "There is one that I think fits you."

She twisted slightly so she could see him. She had heard of *The Book of Changes,* but knew very little about it.

" 'The Arousing.' It is also called 'Shock and Thunder.' Would you like to hear it?"

She nodded, latching onto his words as a way to steady herself. Perhaps they would help her understand her own needs.

" 'Shock brings success,' " he began. " 'Shock comes—oh, oh! Laughing words—ha, ha! The shock terrifies for a hundred miles, and he does not let fall the sacrificial spoon and chalice.' "

She remained silent after he spoke. The words were beautiful, but she didn't understand them.

"It means that shock comes from God. It is always terrifying. But laughter and joy come as well."

"Spoon?" she asked. "Chalice?"

He nodded. "Ah, you have seen the crux of the poem. When you remain centered, holding the spoon and cup of your faith, then you can embrace joy without being overcome by terror."

She tilted her head, thinking about his words. Could it be true? Was her terror of something profound? Something godly?

This wasn't what she had been taught. Christianity wouldn't agree with much of anything she'd learned here. But Zou Tun's words felt right, that God could be revealed within her own body. And that the revelation would be . . . unnerving.

"Do you understand?" he asked, his voice gentle.

In answer she scooted back, settling her spine against his chest and pulling her right heel in tight against her groin. As she feared, the sheet slipped away from her hips. Looking down, she could see more of herself than she wanted. And yet the sight of her own body did not upset her anymore. Especially as she tried to see God within her body, the divine in her heart.

With that thought held inside her, and with Zou Tun enfolding her, she steadied her heartbeat, and the twisting flame inside her grew calm.

"Ready," she whispered.

He nodded. "Close your eyes. Find your center. I will begin."

She did as he bade. Somewhere in her thoughts was the reminder that she could perform these breast circles on her own. She didn't need his hands on her body, his fingers starting just outside her nipples, pressing a long, pleasurable spiral around her flesh. But she said nothing, forcing her thoughts to center on her breath. And on the feel of his hands.

It was nicer with his touch, easier to think about her breathing. And the feel of his large, calloused hands made her shiver with delight.

His movements were exquisite, the pressure gentle enough to soothe, hard enough to be substantial. As her breathing deepened, she pressed harder against his hands, her body rocking forward against her heel. Without conscious thought, they began a rhythm: forward as he circled her nipple, backward as the circle expanded and her breath deepened. She'd exhale as his hands returned to a point just beside the center, and both he and she rocked forward again.

"Seventy-two," he whispered. She hadn't realized he was counting out loud. His breath was a hot echo of the fiery press of his dragon below, against the base of her spine. But now his circling stopped as she leaned back against him, her breasts a heavy, full weight upon her chest.

"I will reverse the circles now. This will draw the yin forward like a rising tide. After seventy-two spirals, I will lay you down on the bed and release it. Are you ready?"

She nodded, her breath too hot against her lips to speak.

"Change your leg position first."

She had forgotten. And, curiously, she did not want to move. But he helped her, reaching forward to lift her knee while she extended her stiff leg. There was a wet sucking sound as she moved, and her face heated with embarrassment. A hot lick of fire shot up her belly.

She was quick to move then, adjusting her position so that her other foot pressed deeply against her groin and the sheet again covered her. But she could not deny the feeling of moistness, and her embarrassment made her duck her face away.

"Your dew is plentiful and sweet-smelling. That is an excellent thing, Joanna Crane," Zou Tun said.

She didn't know how to respond, so she said nothing. She allowed him to gently pull her back, and they once again settled into a rhythm.

It was a simple movement, really. They began with her relaxed against him, slightly reclined, his fingers in the same position as before—at the top of the bone between her breasts. As she exhaled, his hands slid lower, underneath. It was only on their rise—when his hands were on the outsides of her breasts—that she began to inhale. And with that breath, he pressed forward, rocking her against her heel. His hands circled closer and higher.

He always stopped this spiral just before touching her nipples, no matter how much she strained for his touch. And then he would reset, pressing her back until she once again rested against him.

Except it was never completely like at the beginning. It was as if each cycle pulled or pushed or drew something from her. With each circle her breasts seemed to fill, expanding as they had never done before. And as his hands spiraled to her peaks, so too did her energy—her *yin*—until it began pressing against her nipples. The yin waited there, just behind the dark, tight disks of flesh. And no matter how overburdened she felt, she could not release that tension.

Still Zou Tun circled, drawing more and more of her power. Below, her heel continued to press rhythmically against her groin—harder with each cresting thrust. She did not do it consciously, and yet she knew it was happening. She felt the tension in her thigh as she drew her leg in tight. And she knew whatever was occuring below was creating more yin, infusing it into her blood so that Zou Tun could gather it and pull her to her peak.

In truth, the imagery was not so clear in her mind.

She simply felt full, and with each circling, each press, each near touch, she felt even fuller. And she did not want it to stop.

Was this what Zou Tun felt like when his dragon expanded? When it pushed out of its sheath? She felt his organ against her bottom, thicker, larger, harder than before. She knew she could make the dragon rain again, but she would not stop what she was doing. She wanted to feel her yin release, just as she had released his yang.

"Seventy-two," he said, his voice hoarse and breathless in her ear. Then he pushed her forward so he could step away from her. His movements were abrupt and ungainly, jostling her so that her heel slid from its position, pushing deeper inside her than ever before. She moaned at the exquisite feel, even trying to intensify the sensation.

"Lie back," he said. Then, before she could comply, he began helping her down, straightening her leg despite her protests.

"So full," she whispered. She wasn't entirely sure what she meant. Only that her blood was rushing, her breasts were throbbing, and there was a largeness to her body. The expansion felt amazing and frightening and wonderful all at once.

He didn't respond with words. Instead she felt him cup her right breast, shaping it, drawing it upward toward him. She arched as he did, her hips shifting restlessly on the bed. What did she want? She didn't know.

She tried to be analytical. She tried to understand these feelings as she would understand a text on philosophy. But the sensations were too overwhelming, the tide too high for her even to breathe.

And then he put his mouth on her nipple. His lips were wet, his tongue rough. When he sucked, he pulled her entire body with him.

Lightning shot through her. White-hot fire pulsed

from his mouth—sucking, sucking, sucking—and to a point that throbbed between her thighs. It was like she had a thick dragon of her own, but this one was inside her, hungry, greedy, and alive.

He continued to suckle, and with each pull against her nipple Joanna's hips bucked. Her back was arched, her entire body bowed as she thrust herself toward his mouth. And still there was no relief, no release. Only a building of pressure within her body and mind.

She gripped his arms tighter. She didn't remember grabbing hold of him, but now she held on as if he were the only answer. She wanted something. She needed it as much as she needed her next breath.

And yet it would not come. The coiled beast within her would not release.

At last he opened his mouth, drawing away. Cold air hit her breast, sending another tremor along her spine, making the dragon writhe within her.

"I will try the other side," he said, and she had enough consciousness to hear the desperation in his voice. "I will take a little time to prepare you better."

She didn't understand. Even as he stroked and pulled at her breast, she had no thought to how she could be better prepared. She *was* prepared. She was more than prepared. She was desperate.

She felt his weight settle on her as he shifted position. Her legs were pinned down—open—but her only thought was for his mouth. His lips. He had to . . .

He thumbed her left nipple. He rolled it between his fingers and tugged it. She thrashed on the bed, her movements echoing the coiling twists of the dragon inside her. It was huge now, a beating monster that filled her entire chest.

"I will suck now," he said. "Once very hard. To open the gate."

"Now," she gasped. "Yes. Please, now." She arched her back, thrusting herself toward him as much as she could. She didn't need to push far. His head descended, his lips clamped on, and he sucked.

One hard, painful pull.

Inside, her beast shot forward, only to slam against the pain. Joanna screamed at the agony, which mingled with the burning misery of her raw throat.

This wasn't working. This wasn't working! She had no thought beyond that, even as he settled once again to his rhythmic suckling. But it wasn't working.

Bang! A door slammed against the wall.

"What are you doing?" It was the Tigress Shi Po, demanding something in a high, angry voice. "Stop this at once!"

Zou Tun abruptly released her, his body weight pulling off of Joanna with a suddenness that left her gasping.

"She isn't ready, you fool."

Joanna whimpered. Nothing made sense. And yet she knew whatever was happening, whatever wrong thing Zou Tun had done, she didn't want it exposed by Shi Po. She scrambled backward with shaking limbs, drawing the sheet against her chest, pressing it there as if a swathe of cotton could hold back the squirming dragon inside her.

Zou Tun helped. He shifted off the bed, standing to face the Tigress while still shielding her from view. But when he spoke, his voice was thick and guttural, as if he had as much trouble as she did in forming words.

"She wished to release her yin."

Even from her position on the bed, Joanna could still see the Tigress. She wrinkled her nose, sniffing the air. "As you released your yang?" She sneered.

Joanna saw Zou Tun's back muscles ripple at the insult, but he did not deny it. Instead he folded his arms across his chest. "She understands your teaching. She wants to learn."

"Your barbarian whore understands nothing."

Joanna shifted to her knees, fury burning through her. But it was nothing compared to Zou Tun's reaction. He shot forward, grabbing hold of the Tigress's arms with both hands. His grip must have been painful, because it bit deep into her flesh, and he raised her up in the air as he spoke.

"She is no whore!"

"Then why do you treat her as one?" Shi Po shot back. "Why were you lying between her thighs, your dragon poised to strike?"

Joanna frowned, doing her best to calm her raging blood. She needed to find the rationality to remember what had happened, to recall . . .

He *had* been between her legs. Her legs had been spread and his hips had been pressing her down, his dragon . . .

She did not remember his dragon. She did not know if he had been ready to plunge it into her. But if he had been ready, if he had wanted to take her virginity, to . . . to use her as his whore, she knew that she would not have stopped him. She would not have known what was happening until it was too late.

Meanwhile, Zou Tun had set the Tigress back on the floor. Releasing her arms, he straightened to his full height.

"I would not have done that."

The Tigress shook her head. "You had no control of yourself." She glanced disdainfully at Joanna. "Neither of you did." She folded her arms and glared at Zou Tun. "She is not to blame. She is a barbarian with no understanding of the qi power. But you are a monk, trained in the Shaolin way. You know what pure yang can do." She stepped forward, lifting his chin with a single sharp fingernail. "I tell you now that yin and yang combined are a thousand times more potent. They become a beast that can only be ridden, never controlled."

She shifted to look at Joanna. "You have hurt her this day, monk. As you have been hurting her from the very beginning." Her gaze shifted back to Zou Tun. "What preys upon you, monk? What gives you such pain that you must release your anger on a naive ghost girl?"

Zou Tun did not answer. His pain was too deep for him to explain it to one such as Shi Po. Joanna knew that, even if the Tigress did not. So while the woman waited for an answer, her impatience becoming palpable, Joanna drew herself together. Though neither Tigress nor Zou Tun paid the least attention to her, Joanna pushed her shaking body to stand, wrapping the sheet tighter around her body.

Then, before she could think about her action, she stepped between the two.

"I understand," she said. It was all she could manage.

Neither of the two so much as blinked. They were completely consumed with each other. Or perhaps not, because Zou Tun extended his hand, holding Joanna back when she would have stepped closer.

"The Tigress is right," he finally said. "Enlightenment cannot be rushed. If it is, we will end up rutting like beasts in the field. What we do here is supposed to be more."

Joanna shook her head, wishing she could explain. Now that her mind was clearing, she wanted to ask questions. But all she could do was shake her head and repeat what she had said before.

"I understand."

The Tigress turned to her. "You understand what, barbarian? That it felt good?"

Joanna shook her head.

Beside her, Zou Tun's eyes widened. "There was pain?"

She rolled her eyes in frustration, paused, then shook her head.

"No pain?" Zou Tun repeated, his eyes searching her face.

"There was a little pain," Shi Po translated. "But there was also pleasure, yes?"

Joanna nodded.

"That is natural. Your yin is not yet pure enough to flow without pain."

Joanna nodded again. But this was not what she wished to discuss. She turned to Zou Tun, pressing her palm flat upon his chest. "I . . . understand," she rasped out one last time.

Zou Tun wrapped his hands around hers, holding her tight to his chest. But his frown showed his confusion. Again the Tigress filled in the gaps, her voice less angry. "She understands *you.*" Her eyes sharpened on Joanna. "Is that correct? You understand his anger?"

At last. They had finally figured out what she was trying to say. Except Zou Tun was shaking his head.

"She cannot," he said. "She does not know."

"It does not matter if she understands," the Tigress snapped. "It is the gravest of abuses to take advantage of another. Are you no better than a bitter eunuch?"

Zou Tun's gaze snapped to the Tigress. "I did not mean to cause harm. I thought she was ready."

"You thought. Because you are an adept in this practice," she sneered. "You can tell when a girl's muscles are prepared. When her mind is focused and her body is strong enough to manage the yin river."

Obviously Zou Tun was *not* an adept in these things, and so he bowed his head in shame. Though it likely cost him a great deal of pride, he continued his bow, dropping to one knee in an imperial kowtow. "How do I repair the damage?"

Joanna ached, her eyes burning to see him so shamed. She wanted to pull him to his feet, wanted to tell him she was not harmed. But her voice prevented it. And her mind told her that she did not yet know the extent of the damage. Because she, also, was new to this, she did not yet know what was true.

Shi Po sighed, her sharp eyes taking in Joanna's distress and Zou Tun's shame. "A burdened man cannot ride a tiger, and no monk—Shaolin or Jade Dragon— can reach Heaven while a worm eats at his insides. Root out your pain, monk, and seek to make amends."

She waited until he nodded. Then she shifted her gaze to Joanna. "Continue your exercises. He has accelerated the process, so you must be extra careful to remain pure of mind and body." Then she drew two stone balls linked by a short chain from her pocket. The first was small and made of jade. The other was nearly twice the size of the first and made of polished marble. "Put the small one inside your cinnabar cave. When you can stand upright for a thousand heartbeats without it slipping out, then you will be ready to experience the yin river."

She turned to leave, pausing at the door to throw one last instruction over her shoulder.

"He must not touch you until then."

21 January, 1898
Dearest Father,

I write this with a heavy heart because I know it will cause you pain. I did not intend such a thing by my rash actions, but I know now that it was inevitable. I am deeply sorry for that. How-

ever, please understand I am happier now than I have ever been.

I am married, Father—to a wonderful man who brings me great joy. And with him I am learning such an amazing thing that I cannot express. There is a beauty in what we are learning, a joy and a peace that I have never seen before. I never even imagined it was possible. Oh, Father, I so wish to remain where I am. And even if you were to find me and drag me back, I would escape. I would—I must—stay here to learn more.

Please stop your search for me. Please send your men home and devote yourself to finding your own happiness.

And please be happy for me. Because I was searching, and now have found. And life is glorious!

> *Your loving daughter,*
> *Joanna*

Modesty wins adoration. By doing things for others, you can accomplish your own ideals.

—Lao Tzu

Chapter Eleven

Joanna exhaled with relief as the Tigress left. She dropped back down onto the bed, sighing because her legs were still weak, her strength uncertain. But as she sat, she studied the two balls in her hand, feeling their cool polished sides and even testing the strength of the chain.

It was very solid. She need not fear it would break or separate from the stones.

Zou Tun remained on one knee, his head bowed, his right fist pressed to the ground. It took a long time before he moved, but eventually he raised his gaze to hers, watching her with that dark, serious stare that seemed to go right through her.

"Why did you say you understand? What do you think you know about me?"

Joanna looked at him, seeing the fear in his eyes, but also recognizing guilt, worry, and even hope. She did not have the voice to tell him that she knew a great deal about men's pain. That she had seen the same tortured emotions in her own father ten years before, when her mother died in his arms. And she'd seen it every day since, lurking behind the quiet determination in his demeanor.

It did not matter the source of one's pain. She knew that Zou Tun suffered. And she knew, as well, that he was struggling through it as best he could. Sometimes that meant lashing out, hurting people when one least intended. She understood, forgave, even as she took steps to ensure that he would not harm her again.

He surged forward, stopping an inch before her. "What do you know?" he demanded.

She didn't flinch, but she braced herself. If he hurt her now she would leave. She would walk out of the room and demand a new partner. But everything inside her told her that he would not touch her. Not in anger. Not even in his pain. She remained right where she was, vulnerable on the bed.

When she did not answer his bellowed question, Zou Tun collapsed. He seemed to crumple inside himself as if a tornado had blown through his soul, leaving him behind to flutter uselessly to the floor. He did not sob, though she guessed he wanted to. Instead he simply sat and stared sightlessly into space.

"What do *you* know?" she asked, her voice as gentle as she could make it.

He didn't answer. He just shook his head, his lips pressed tightly together.

She leaned down, curling her fingers beneath his arms and pulling. His gaze lifted to her, startled and confused. But she just shook her head and tugged. Now was not the time for words.

Eventually he moved, half pushing to his feet, half allowing her to roll him onto the bed. They didn't speak at all, yet they moved as one. With her encouragement, he crawled onto the bed, resting on his side, his head dropping wearily to the pillow. Then he opened his arms, and she slid into place there, her back against his chest, her body enfolded in his arms.

She barely could tug the sheet over their bodies, but once the fabric settled across them she closed her eyes. His breathing had already steadied. Hers was rapidly meshing with it.

She had a fleeting thought before sleep claimed her completely. It was an image, really, a vision of her monk. Zou Tun stood proudly before her, his body gloriously naked, his shoulders thrown back in pride and power. His head sported a Manchurian queue, a beautiful fall of thick, dark hair. But he was trembling, struggling to stand firm. It took a moment's study to realize why his strength was failing, but eventually she saw.

He was wounded, though not in the physical sense. She studied his body, and she could see no cut or wound. Instead she saw a golden shimmer of energy. It surrounded him in glory, she thought. Except it was not glory. It was not God's radiance. It was his own power, seeping away, draining like water from a sieve. She could not see why it slipped from him. She only knew that it did.

And that he would die if it continued.

Joanna was slipping away. She was leaving him.

Zou Tun tried to tighten his arms, to keep her with him, but his mind was too fogged by sleep, his limbs too heavy to move. So he struggled to wake, to force his limbs to obey. By the time they complied, it was already too late.

She was out of bed.

He opened his eyes, seeing only darkness, hearing the muffled sounds of a city settling in to rest. It was night, which meant that they had slept through the late afternoon and evening.

As he was still orienting his thoughts, a sudden flare

of light cut through the room: a candle lit by Joanna, so she could find her way behind the privacy screen.

He released his held breath. She wasn't leaving him; she was using the chamber pot.

He let his eyes drift closed again, listening to the sounds of life in Shanghai. Even in this wealthy, secluded area, he could still hear the people—laughter or bellows, revelry or pain. He could hear horses clopping down the street, the creak of wheels or the slaps of feet. Even if the sounds weren't truly there, he heard them in his mind.

He hated it. Peking was worse, of course. Noise and busyness, power and treachery—all made their own sounds, filled the air with clutter.

And nowhere could he find the whisper of the wind or the gentle rhythms of a peaceful forest at night. No animals burrowed nearby and no water flowed crystal-clear within a half hour's walk. All around him for miles was noise. Human noise. And he wanted it to end.

He looked at Joanna, outlined by the candle against the privacy screen. She was a beautiful sight, his Joanna. She remained naked, so he could see her entire long and muscular body in silhouette against the screen. Her breasts were high and well formed, her hips sweetly rounded, and her legs the kind that could wrap around a man and hold on for life.

His dragon stirred, his body ready for the most primal of needs. But that was the only part of him that moved. The rest of him remained still, his mind focusing on the beauty of this healthy woman, not the lust that wanted to dominate his thoughts.

Why had she not returned to bed?

He could tell from her movements that she had completed her business. So what was she doing?

As he watched, she held out the two connected stone balls. She tested them, feeling their weight. He knew what she was supposed to do. The Tigress had instructed her to hold the smallest one inside her for a thousand heartbeats. When she could do that, she would be ready to experience the yin flow.

Did she plan on trying it now?

She did. As he watched she widened her legs, then awkwardly curled into herself as she brought the smallest ball up toward her cinnabar cave. The larger one dangled through her fingers, swaying with her movements.

Zou Tun lifted his head off the pillow, wanting to see more. But his movement made the bed creak and Joanna froze.

"Zou Tun?" she called. Her voice was a low whisper.

He said nothing, pretending to be asleep so that she would not feel awkward. It was not something with which a virgin would feel comfortable. Certainly not the first time.

He heard her sigh; then she returned her attention to her task. And as he watched, she proceeded.

He saw her shift uncomfortably, and the ball immediately slipped out.

She sighed again, and the sound was enough to make his dragon rear with interest. But Zou Tun remained still, his breath suspended.

She tried again. This time she seemed to understand better what to do. She straightened, her legs slightly spread, her cave and belly muscles no doubt tensed to near breaking. Indeed, as he feared, he saw her shudder. It was a large movement that shook her entire body, most especially her shoulders. Which naturally set her breasts to bouncing—and his dragon to dancing. He had to clench his belly to prevent his lust.

Except he wasn't supposed to stop his lust, was he? That was part of the Tigress's teaching. He needed that lust. He needed the power of his desire to mix with Joanna's yin. So he stopped his struggle against the inevitable.

His dragon was awake. Fighting it served no purpose. He accepted the sensations as it straightened and hardened, poking its head out from its sheath. It wanted to see Joanna. Very well; so did he.

He relaxed, accepting the churning power of his sexual hunger, but he did not move toward Joanna. Instead he simply allowed himself to watch. And appreciate.

She tried once more. Apparently her shudder had relaxed her muscles enough that the small ball had again slipped free. So she was experimenting, obviously becoming more comfortable with the act of pressing the ball within her.

Again a shudder racked her body. This time the ball did not slip free. This time she was able to straighten, her legs still spread.

Zou Tun began to count heartbeats. His own heart was pumping hard, as hers was likely to be. Their counts would match closely enough.

Fifty beats.

One hundred beats.

Two hundred beats.

Her shoulders were beginning to relax. He could see her confidence growing.

Three hundred beats.

She shifted slightly, readjusting her feet. And with that movement she turned toward him. He could see her standing there, legs spread, with the other ball trembling where it hung between her thighs.

Lust slammed through him hard enough to stop his breath. He had never seen a more erotic sight. And yet he did not act. He felt the hunger surge in his blood; he even allowed thoughts and images of hot and sweaty love to flow through his mind. But he kept his body still. He did not allow the images to consume him.

His lust remained fierce, but it was not the whole of his thoughts, the complete dominance of his being. It was merely a part of him that he would control.

Five hundred beats.

Joanna was beginning to strain. He heard her breath—small panting gasps that added fuel to his dragon fire. Another shudder shook her body—a smaller one, but a tremble nonetheless. And just as before, her breasts danced with the movement.

Beautiful. She was so beautiful.

He lost himself in the perfection that was Joanna, her body and mind. He worshiped both the woman who stood before him, struggling with a new exercise, and the woman of his memory, who was as passionate about discovering his secrets as she had been to learn this new religion. She was smart and capable and had a smile that burned like a warm coal inside his frozen chest.

Seven hundred beats.

She would not be able to hold it much longer. He could tell that the larger ball was slipping lower, threatening to pull the smaller one out. It bobbed there as she fought the weight, drawing it higher with her muscles . . . only to have them fail. The balls slipped free, dropping to the floor with a heavy thud.

Seven hundred and eighty-six beats.

Zou Tun was impressed and pleased. She was nearly ready, even though she had no experience with these things. Truly, she was an amazing woman.

He heard her cleaning her hands and the balls, refreshing herself with a towel before stepping out from behind the screen. He knew she was moving from a bright place to a dark one, so she would not be able to see that his eyes were open. But he had no wish to lie to her, even in so little a thing as to pretend he hadn't seen. So he spoke, his voice slightly grating.

"You are very strong."

She froze. He thought for a moment that she would deny it. She simply shrugged.

"Horseback riding," she said, her tone low but pure. Her throat must be feeling better.

"Yes, I suppose that makes sense. Some of the muscles must be similar. But . . ." His voice trailed away.

"Some are different."

She remained standing before him, completely nude, her body a sweet temptation even in the darkness. To distract himself, he gestured to the door. "Our dinner is probably out there. Are you hungry?"

She nodded, then quickly ducked behind the screen. He watched as she slipped on a robe, then stepped to the door. As she opened it, Zou Tun noted that the door was unlocked. It was also, from what he could see, unguarded. They were free to leave if they so chose.

He didn't move, except to don loose pants, before returning to the bed. She joined him there, setting the tray of food between them.

They ate in silence. The food was cold, the tea lukewarm, but the atmosphere remained relaxed. Soothing. And he found his dragon liked her all the more for the companionable silence.

He turned his thoughts elsewhere, wanting to learn of this woman. After all, she knew more about him right now than anyone alive.

"How long have you lived in Shanghai?" he asked, surprised that his throat was still scratchy even after drinking the tea.

"Ten years," she answered. "We came from Boston. In the United States."

He nodded, pleased that he knew where that was. And he found himself even more interested in what her life was like. "You must have been young when you left. Do you remember?"

She smiled, her face growing softer and even more beautiful. "I remember noise. I remember my father's anger because we were poor. I had a favorite tree that I would climb when my parents' arguments were too loud. I would hold my brother, and we would play finger games until it got too cold and my mother came looking for us." She sighed. "That's what I remember most—holding my brother when he was sleepy, and my mother finding us when it was all over."

Zou Tun frowned, unable to fathom a family of such open dissension. "In China, women do not argue with their husbands."

She glanced at him, obviously startled. Abruptly she burst into laughter. "Of course they do. I have heard them in the markets—husband and wife bickering like angry birds."

He stiffened, lifting his chin in disdain. "Any woman who does so disgraces herself and her husband! A wife's first duty is to maintain harmony within the home. She cannot do that if she cannot hold her tongue."

"No disagreeing with a husband?" Again humor laced her tone. "Let me give you a suggestion, monk. If you wish for such harmony in your home, do not marry a woman who knows her own mind." She grinned at him. "But I wish you luck in finding one."

"You," he snapped, "would not be a peaceful wife."

She did not take his insult, but merely shook her head, her smile still warm. "No, I most certainly would not."

"Your husband would be constantly fighting off bandits, nursing your horses, and searching the woods for wherever your whim took you next."

Her smile died, the light in her eyes fading equally quickly. When she spoke, it was softly and with an edge of hurt. "Tell me that you have never taken the wrong path, never made a bad choice."

He opened his mouth to defend himself, to say that he had never done anything as stupid as leaving his home unprotected to seek out bandit revolutionaries. But the words died on his tongue. Because, of course, what he had done was much, much worse. And so he looked at his hands, feeling the weight of guilt pulling at his shoulders.

"I am being churlish, striking out at you when it is my own shame that consumes me. I apologize, Joanna Crane. I have treated you most unfairly."

She watched him, her food forgotten in her lap. Then she spoke, her voice hesitant, as if she were unsure. "I had a dream about you, Zou Tun. A frightening dream that I cannot seem to dismiss."

He shifted uncomfortably, anxiety tightening his belly. His countrymen put great store in dreams, but he had always found them to be unreliable, their content usually self-serving. And yet he could not deny a whisper of cold fear that blew through his soul.

"I saw you in my dream and your qi was leaking out of you." She frowned. "No, it was worse than that. It was pouring from you, and if you did not stop the loss immediately, you would soon die."

He frowned, trying to understand the purpose behind her words. "Someone was taking my qi?" he asked, wondering what enemy she wanted him to fight.

Again she shook her head. "No. There was no enemy. Just you. It was something about you that was . . . unplugged. Like a wound that wouldn't close. Only, instead of blood you were losing energy. Power."

"That is an ugly dream," he said, annoyed by her obvious ploy. Truly, she must think him a half-wit to fall for such a thing. But she was the one who'd been caught. Her next words would tell him exactly what she wanted. He leaned back, doing his best to sound sincere. "I do not wish to die. What must I do to end this loss?"

She sighed. "I do not know. I have only just learned that people can have such things as energy. Yin and yang as parts of a larger force called qi? These things are strange to Westerners." She raised her eyes to his. "I assumed you would know the meaning. Isn't there any folklore or something, stories about how to stop qi from draining away?"

He frowned. He was well versed in all the classics. He knew nothing of such stories. Worse, he could not determine Joanna's purpose in telling him this dream. Why would she say such a thing without having an idea how to effect change?

"I do not know of anything like that," he finally said. Was she being coy? Would she tell him now what she wanted?

Apparently not. She shrugged, dismissing her story. "It was only a dream. I am sorry I brought it up."

He stared at her. What drove this strange woman? "Why do you hate us Manchurians?" he asked.

She reared back, shock on her face. "I don't hate you. Why would you say that?"

"Why would you risk your life to join the Fists if you do not hate us?"

"We have already discussed this. You know of the abuses of your government."

He leaned forward, pressing his point. "Yes, I do. Better than you." He reached out, taking her hand as he tried to divine the truth. "But you are not Chinese. You have not been oppressed by the Qin Empire. Why would you risk everything to fight for peasants?"

She pushed off the bed, clearly agitated. He could

see how the fire in her soul tormented her, pushing her to do things she did not think through. Her movements were tight, her voice high and angry. And her words made no sense.

"Have you never thought of righting injustice? Of fighting for freedom no matter what the cost? Liberty is not just a thing of the body. It is a thing of the soul. Who will fight for the shackled souls if not those who are already free?"

She was slipping into English, her words incomprehensible to him. But he had heard enough to recognize passion that meant little in any practical sense. So he waited until her blustering had finished. When she finally stopped speaking, when she turned to him like a toy that had stopped spinning, that was when he spoke.

"We do not shackle any person. And if there are shortages, privations, and poverty, it is because of reparations demanded by you Western barbarians."

"You killed our missionaries!" she shot back.

"We did not wish for them to come here. You forced us to accept them into our country. We cannot help it if the peasants do not want them here, preaching their foreign God."

She rounded on him, her mouth open, her jaw beginning to work. But no sound came out. And if words were coming, he stopped them, raising his hand with the weariness that seemed to perpetually fill him.

"I will not debate this with you, Joanna Crane."

"Why? Because I am a woman? Because you know I am right?"

He shook his head. "Because I do not understand these issues. I never have."

She reared back, obviously stunned. Indeed, he was startled as well. But once started, he could not stop himself from explaining further.

217

"I am merely speaking what I have been taught. You are as well. Neither of us understands the situation well enough to know true answers."

She dropped her hands to her hips, standing before him like a vengeful spirit. "Do you doubt what you have seen? Do you think that beggar lied about what happened to him?"

Zou Tun shook his head. "No, I do not think he lied." He raised his gaze, pinning her with the force of his beliefs. "But I also know that the system of eunuchs has been in place for thousands of years, long before my people conquered this country two hundred years ago. I know that China is a land long on tradition, and no change comes about easily." Then he pushed off the bed, coming to stand directly before her. "And I also know that Empress Cixi fervently wishes these things to change. She and her supporters all want to make China better for even the smallest peasant."

Joanna frowned, folding her arms across her chest. "The dowager empress cares only about feeding herself. About her jade boat and her jewels."

It was a good thing that he heard uncertainty in her voice; there was a time when he would have killed anyone who dared utter such a thing. But he was older now, wiser in the understanding that nothing in politics was as clear or simple as one might wish.

"You are merely echoing what you have been told. But I have met the dowager empress. I have spoken with her, and I tell you what you think is not true: She is a great lady with great dreams for China."

He watched her eyes widen with awe. "You have met with the empress?" she breathed.

He didn't answer directly, choosing his words with care so that she understood. "I am a man, not a eunuch," he said firmly. "And no man is allowed within the women's quarters of the Forbidden City, certainly not to speak with a lowly concubine. Such a thing would be treasonous. Punishable by death."

She leaned back, rolling her eyes at the intricacy of Chinese politics. "She is running the country, Zou Tun. To not see her . . . How can you support such a system?"

Again he spoke without heat or passion, trying to make her understand. "A woman could not possibly lead a country, Joanna Crane. The emperor is the Son of Heaven. He has been in power for nearly a decade."

"But—"

"But, but, but, but, but! You do not understand our country, Joanna! You foreigners know nothing of our ways, and yet you demand reparations and send more missionaries. And you, Joanna Crane—a barbarian woman—seek to join those who fight against us? Why? Why would you risk your life when you do not even understand the simplest things in our government or our traditions?"

She stared at him, momentarily silenced. Then she lowered her eyes, her voice soft but no less passionate. "Do you not understand the ideals of freedom and justice?"

He sat back down, frustration bleeding away his strength. "Ideals are beautiful things. I was raised on the Confucian ideals, and they are powerful. But when a person risks his life in a revolution, he is either striving for something he desperately wants or running from something he truly hates. You cannot desperately want justice or freedom for China. You know little of our people and our ways. So, Joanna Crane, I ask you again—why do you go so quickly to fight my government? What are you running from?"

He did not expect her to answer. She had already shown more spirit and intelligence than most men of his acquaintance; he hardly expected her to have a stronger moral character as well. And no man or woman wished admit to their failings.

But once again he found that he knew nothing of barbarians, and even less about their women. She slowly dropped onto the bed and drew her knees up to her chest, resting her chin atop them. But what was most arresting was her eyes. The only light in the room came from a single candle, and that one flickering flame cast her in a strange glow. He could well call her a ghost person now, because her eyes were haunted and her voice a dry whisper.

"We were not wealthy before, back in America. My father worked hard, but he could not find a way to make himself rich. And we knew that it would be even harder back in England, where my grandfather was born."

"So you decided to come to China."

She nodded. "My father had a cousin who had already made a fortune here. He convinced my father, and my father . . ." She sighed. "My father packed us up to come to Shanghai. My mother did not want to leave, but my father insisted."

"That was his right. He is the man and must find a way to feed his family."

Joanna shrugged. "It was clearly the best choice for him. He's made more money here than he could in ten lifetimes where we were."

Zou Tun hated that a barbarian could do such a thing in his country—gather wealth like so many grains of rice—when many of his own people were starving. But he knew enough not to begrudge her father. Would not his own people, if given the chance, leave home for the promise of great wealth just past the ocean?

But when he looked at Joanna, he could see that she

was not happy with the outcome. "What happened?" he asked.

"My mother and brother . . . the passage was hard on them. My brother became ill on the boat. My mother soon afterward. They did not live more than a week on Chinese soil."

"Travel is often hardest on women and children," he said. It was a stupid statement, poor comfort at best, callously cruel at worst. But he had no understanding of how to comfort the grieving, and he knew from experience that even the best words did little to ease pain. So all he could do was reach out to touch her hand. She gripped his fingers, her strength surprising, as if she suppressed great pain.

"Let me hold you, Joanna," he said softly. "If you wish, we could begin your exercises again. Those first seventy-two circles are meant to soothe and calm pain. Especially female pain of tears and loss."

She turned to him, her expression almost amused. "How like a man to want to escape pain by *doing* things." She shook her head. "I would think a monk would know better."

"You seek solitude?" he asked. He well understood the need, but he had not thought she would desire it.

"No," she said gently. "I buried my mother and brother ten years ago. Their loss was terrible and painful, and all sorts of other things I can't even name. But they are gone and I am at peace with their deaths."

He nodded. "At least you still have your father, and he you."

"Yes, we had each other. And he had his work. And that brought money, which brought more things and more people and more"—she shrugged—"of everything into our lives."

He frowned. "Is that not what you wanted? Wealth?"

She laughed, the sound bitter. "He wanted money, Zou Tun. I wanted my family. So I clung to him, and he showered me with things."

He did not understand her tone. "You were unhappy?"

She lifted her head, looking at him with serious eyes. "What do wealthy Manchu women do with their time? How do they spend their days?"

He frowned, never having considered the question.

"Do they read? Do they study science? Do they help with the work of the government?"

He reared back, appalled. "Most cannot read. They spend their days . . ." His voice trailed away. What worthwhile thing did they do with their days? "They paint and gossip. They worship Buddha and play spiteful tricks on one another."

She stared at him, her expression clearly expectant. But he didn't understand. Women were generally silly, spiteful creatures. They enjoyed such entertainments. Didn't they?

Apparently not, because Joanna simply shrugged. "I am a terrible artist, and I have not been able to devote myself to religion. Even if I did, my father—and your government—would never release me to work with the poor. He fears for my safety."

"Rightly so!" Zou Tun said, a little more hotly than intended. "But what of a husband? Surely you can bear children by now. And you are not ugly or deformed. Why have you not married?"

She trilled a false laugh. "La, sir—how you flatter!"

He grimaced, annoyed with her frivolity. They had been speaking seriously, and now she wished him to flatter her? Before he could respond, she sobered, interrupting his thoughts.

"You have said that Papa and I have each other. That is true. He has me. He owns me. I am his greatest prize in an entire mansion full of prizes." She looked at her hands, extending her fingers as if to look for a ring. "No man is worthy of me, and so I am trapped with Papa. I have no purpose except to be beautiful, no thought except how to please my father. At least, that is what he thinks."

Zou Tun gaped at her. "Is that not what all women want? To be praised for their beauty? To bring honor to their homes?"

She groaned, her head dropping against the wall with a dull thud. "Would *you* be content with such an existence, Zou Tun?"

He straightened, insulted. "I am a man!"

She laughed once more, the sound soft and angry. "Then I am a man as well, because I cannot stand to live there one minute more."

He leaned forward, needing her to understand. "Do you think it would be different with those bandits? I tell you truly, if they do not kill you immediately, they will spread your legs and use you until you are dead of their attention."

She flinched at his words, but she did not deny them. She had already admitted that choice had been a mistake. Instead she looked about the room, her expression wistful.

"I am here. Learning things my father would consider sinful." She glanced at him as if confiding a great secret. "When this is all done, I don't know that he will take me back. I am a tarnished prize now."

Zou Tun well understood. Wrong as it was, many fathers would bar the door to their children. "I could never do such a thing to my child. Even a foolish girl child. Perhaps your father loves you equally well."

She smiled, a wistful look in her eye. "Perhaps," she said, though she did not sound as if she believed it. "Either way, I am not sure I wish to return. There is so little for me there, and the world is a very large place. I do not want to be locked away again."

"You are not afraid?" He could barely understand such a bizarre woman, who did not tremble at the thought of being separated from her protectors.

She laughed in response, and this time the sound was freer. "Of course I am afraid. But I am nothing at home. At least out here I have the hope of becoming more." Her eyes seemed to sparkle. "I might even become immortal."

A month ago he would have laughed at the thought. How preposterous to think a barbarian could become an immortal. But he had heard whispers of other immortal women. And one was a barbarian, by all accounts. And though he originally considered this Tigress practice a silliness thought up by silly women, he was beginning to doubt himself. Little Pearl's radiance was hard to deny.

Joanna Crane was a woman of amazing logic and bravery, very manly in such matters. And yet, when he looked at her, even with her knees curled up against her chest, he could think of her only as a woman. An intriguing and beautiful woman.

"So you wish to pursue this," he said gently.

She glanced at him in surprise. "I thought that was obvious."

He shook his head. "I mean to its end point. With dedication and commitment."

She frowned, still not understanding what he meant. Slowly her expression cleared, her body uncoiling. She glared at him. "You thought I wasn't serious? That this was a casual whim, the actions of a bored little girl?"

His gaze slid from hers even as he defended himself. "You were blown here by fate. By your mistake and then mine. Perhaps it is easier to stay here than run home. Perhaps to do so is less frightening than an angry father."

· "Perhaps," she said firmly. "But that is not why I chose to stay." She shifted onto her knees, her breasts bobbing beneath her robe. "There is something here, Zou Tun. Something I wish to learn. I have already read some of the Confucian classics. I have learned a little of Buddhist philosophy. It was hard to do so. No one would help me. No one thought it appropriate for a woman. But I wanted to know, Zou Tun. And so I studied as much as I could alone. I read what I could find and what I could translate. But this . . ." She gestured to the room, toward the entire Tigress complex. "This is something I can study. This is something I wish to know."

He watched, seeing the passion that burned within her. A bright flame, it was steadier and stronger than he had ever thought to see in a woman, much less a ghost woman. "What of your politics?" he challenged. "What of the revolution against the oppressive Qin Empire?"

She hesitated, her shoulders drooping slightly. "If I thought I could help, I would consider it. If I thought I could make the world more just, freer, then I would do what I could, no matter the risk."

"But it is not your fight."

She sighed, reason finally making her agree. "I could not help China even if I decided to." Her chin lifted, her gaze hitting him with a near physical blow. "But that does not explain you, Kang Zou Tun. You are a Manchurian, a member of the ruling race who has met with the dowager empress." She folded her arms across her chest, looking at him with a seriousness he could not ignore. "I have told you why I ran from my home. What about you? Why are you here instead of in Peking?"

He didn't answer. Indeed, he couldn't. Not when shame and failure rode him so hard that he could barely breathe. And yet, facing her was like standing before the dowager empress. Joanna had the same force of character, the same manly intelligence, the same qi strength. If he could not answer this barbarian woman, how would he ever face Cixi? Either her or the emperor.

He didn't know. He had no answers for Joanna or himself. He had nothing except the flat certainty that he needed to find his solution quickly. Time was rapidly running out. Before long he would be standing before his father, the general, and the emperor.

Then what would he do?

The Tao created the myriad things, and after their creation, they must still preserve the spirit of the Tao and act in harmony with the Tao. We, too, should be yielding and act in accordance with nature.

—*Lao Tzu*

Chapter Twelve

He wasn't going to answer her; Joanna could see it in his face. He had no intention of sharing his innermost thoughts with a barbarian woman. Well, that was just too bad. She had just bared her heart. And her breasts, for that matter. If he wanted her to trust him, he would have to learn to share.

She leaned back against the wall and stared at him. "Let me make it easy for you, Zou Tun," she said, her voice excruciatingly dry. "You're still working on gaining my trust. This isn't helping."

"And how long will I be paying that debt, Joanna Crane?" he shot back. "Will I forever be acting as your slave in order to gain your trust? Forever—"

"I didn't ask you to be my slave. I asked for a simple answer—to the very same question you threw at me not so long ago. Are all Manchurians this prickly?"

"Yes! We are not accustomed to being questioned by women. And certainly not—"

"Not barbarian ghost women," she finished for him. "Yes, I know. But you know what else? I am sick to

227

death of everyone thinking I am stupid or insubstantial or uncivilized just because my skin is whiter than yours. So how about this, monk? You will start thinking of me as your equal, or you can walk out that door right now and find yourself a new partner."

He reared back as if struck. She could tell the thought of a woman as an equal had never before occurred to him. To his credit, he didn't immediately deny the concept. She wondered if it was a measure of his openness to new ideas or his desperation for her as a partner that held his tongue. Either way he sat there, mouth open, while she sighed in disgust. It seemed she spent her entire life trying to prove to someone that she wasn't an idiot. That she was capable of so much more than they thought. She took a deep breath, launching into her defense one last time.

"I saw through your disguise, didn't I? When no one else had."

"There was another," he whispered, his voice tight.

She shrugged. "Fine. One other. Out of how many?" She leaned forward. "I have a quick mind and a willingness to learn. How many of your countrymen—men or women—can claim that?"

He nodded. "It is true you have shown . . . unusual intelligence and curiosity."

"Damned by faint praise," she murmured. Then she decided to take a different tack. "You obviously think I'm capable of being a fit partner for you. In fact, you seem to want me over all those other ladies. Even the Tigress Shi Po." She frowned. "Why is that exactly? What do you see in me that is not available with all those other women?"

She could see he had even less desire to talk about this than about his reasons for being here in the first place. His expression darkened and his face seemed to twitch, as if he wanted to strike something. Indeed, his entire demeanor darkened, became more threatening. But she was not intimidated. He had once promised to keep her safe, and she believed he would now keep to that vow.

Besides, he obviously wanted her for some reason. He would not discard what trust they had already established.

"You might as well stop with the evil eye. I am not intimidated."

He frowned. "I was not trying to curse you. And contrary to what the peasants believe, Shaolin monks do not practice magic such as the evil eye."

She blinked. She had meant the phrase as an expression, not as truth. But she could well believe that a superstitious peasant would think fighting monks capable all sorts of things. She shifted to her knees, facing him. "Zou Tun, why do you wish to partner with me above all those other, more experienced women?"

He sighed, and she could tell that she had won. "I trust you," he finally said.

She shook her head. "There is more."

"Trust is no small thing, Joanna Crane. I do not know those women. I do not know their purposes in pursuing this training. I do know that the Tigress Shi Po desires political power. She leads women into the pursuit of immortality by a means not accepted by all. It would be an easy thing to see imperial forces destroy her and her followers."

Joanna shuddered, pulling her blanket about her shoulders as if it could ward off the chill of his words. "Destroy her? Do you mean kill her?"

"I mean kill her and all her family. I mean they would execute all of her followers and their families. And seize all of their fortunes, no matter how small." He gestured to the compound outside. "The imperial treasury is perpetually short because of barbarian demands. The empire seeks funds any way it can."

Joanna felt her eyes widen. "You would do that? You would expose her just because she teaches women about their bodies? And about men's bodies?"

If Zou Tun's expression was dark before, now it became angry. "I would do no such thing," he snapped. "But others would. And she risks a great deal by bringing me here."

"So why has she done it?"

"Because having me on her side could also be a great boon, a great safety for her."

Joanna was silent for a while, absorbing his words and the political maneuverings he described. It was a world she did not understand. In truth, she did not want to understand it. To think of hidden purposes all the time, to search for gain and loss with every breath, every action—it was too . . . cluttered a life. And she pitied him for having to endure it.

"Is that why you are here? To escape the . . ." How could she phrase it? "All the machinations of power?"

"Of course not!" he snapped, though she could detect a trace of panic in his expression. "I am a Manchurian bannerman! I would not hide in a woman's skirts just to avoid the running of a country!"

Odd how the more defensive he became, the surer she felt that she was nearing the truth. "Is that what you are doing?" she pressed. "Hiding in a woman's skirts?"

His back went ramrod straight. "I am pursuing immortality as a Jade Dragon. What is it," he asked, "you think we are doing?"

She almost laughed. Still, she answered him. "I am learning what no American woman has ever been taught. Indeed, this is a philosophy that no American man or woman has ever conceived of before."

His eyes narrowed. "So you believe it is possible?

You believe you can reach Heaven through these practices?"

She hesitated, wondering what she believed. She had been raised in the Christian church. She shuddered to think what her priest might think of what she was doing. "My faith has always been a cold thing, bringing no comfort and little strength."

"Do not mistake the pleasure of the yin tide for God, Joanna Crane. That would be a grave mistake."

She agreed. "But why would God give us bodies, give us the pleasure and power in the yin tide, unless it had a purpose?"

"Attaining Heaven?"

"Why not? I overheard some of the women talking this morning. They said two of Shi Po's students achieved it. They became immortals." She raised her chin, daring him to deny her next statement. "And that one of them was an Englishwoman."

"I heard that as well."

"So you believe it, then. You think it is possible."

He took his time answering, but when he did it was with a gravity that surprised her—more than surprised her; it instilled in her a sense of awe. And a purpose.

"I do believe it, Joanna Crane. And more than that, I believe I can accomplish it with you."

"Why?" she breathed, not realizing she spoke until the word had left her mouth. "Why with me?"

He shook his head, as if he weren't going to answer. But then he spoke, his words haunting in their intensity. "I have studied the Middle Path—the Tao—for many years. It has brought me peace and courage when I felt lost." He sighed. "But never has it brought me strength."

She frowned. "But your body has amazing strength and power. You defeated five attackers with ease."

"Not strength of body. Any man can train to attain that. I mean a different kind of strength." His gaze shifted to focus on her face. "An immortal kind of strength. The kind of clarity that takes a man to Heaven."

"Then why—"

"Because I have felt it with you already, Joanna Crane. A taste. That very first time I assisted you with your exercises, I felt it then." He raised his hands in a gesture of uncertainty. "I had thought all yin was the same. Much as all women are the same."

She snorted, unable to let that statement pass. "All women are not the same."

"No," he agreed softly. "In this I was a fool, for you are nothing like the women I have known. I do not know if that is because you are a ghost barbarian . . ."

She shook her head, correcting his impression. "Even among my people I am exceedingly unusual, Zou Tun."

"Then it is as I suspected. You are unique. And your yin, Joanna Crane, is most potent."

She did not know what to think of that. Was she to feel flattered that her womanly essence was rare? She didn't think so. After all, she'd had no participation in the making of it. It was simply part of her, like an arm or a leg. And yet perhaps that was not so. "Yin is not just a part of our bodies, is it? It is an essential part of who we are."

He nodded, his expression thoughtful.

"So who I am, what I think, and what I do, all play into my yin. Into its creation and its purity, yes?"

"Of course. It is the same with yang. It is the pure essence of who I am as a man. My education. My training. My deeds." His voice broke slightly on his last word, but he did not explain.

"Then I am pleased that my yin is so strong. It suggests—"

"Yes, Joanna Crane," he interrupted. "It says that you are a strong, amazing woman."

He spoke flatly, with little inflection, but there was awe in his eyes—and a kind of hunger.

"So that is why you want me?" she asked. "Because I am strong? And amazing?" She liked hearing that word and was vain enough to repeat it.

"That is why I wish to partner with you. And why together I believe we can reach Heaven."

"Because your yang is as powerful as my yin." It was not a question. She had felt his strength, his masculinity. At times it was overwhelming.

He did not answer. His silence was acknowledgment enough.

"Very well," she finally said. "We have a mutual goal. I suppose we had best get back to the business of pursuing it."

He remained still for a moment, as if gauging her sincerity or strength of purpose. Whatever it was, he must have found her acceptable. A moment later he lifted their tray and set it outside. Then he turned to her, his stance almost militaristic.

"I made a mistake before, pushing you before you were ready. I will not do that again."

Joanna nodded. "Shi Po said you must not touch me. Not until I can hold the balls—"

"Yes, I know."

"I am nearly to a thousand beats."

He grinned, and the sight made him appear suddenly boyish—in an incredibly handsome way. "This, too, I know."

"Very well, then. I suppose we should do the exercises. Do you want to go first?"

He hesitated, and she wondered for a moment what he was thinking. "We are not to touch each other. Agreed?"

She nodded. "Of course."

"Then let us strengthen and purify ourselves at the same time."

She paused, realizing how much she would miss his hands on her breasts, his caresses during her exercises. But she knew he was right. And there was no point in his watching her or her watching him when they would not be able to help. To touch. To learn.

Still, she felt strangely shy at the thought of touching herself in the same room as him. That he would be doing his own exercises added to the strangeness. And the excitement.

"Joanna?"

"Yes," she said quickly, before she could change her mind. "Yes. We will do this at the same time. But on opposite sides of the room."

Her hands shook as she pulled off her loose shirt, but from excitement, not nervousness. She'd enjoyed watching his face as he performed his exercises. More specifically, she wanted to see his eyes again, feel them lock onto hers, and again know that connection between them. Whether or not he spilled his seed—and she knew he wasn't supposed to—she wanted to feel that electric pull when he touched himself.

That she would be touching herself at the same time made her toes curl in anticipation.

She settled herself on the bed, her back against the wall. But as she began to curl her left foot to her cinnabar cave, her robe gaped and tugged. It was time, she realized, to stand completely naked before him. She had once before. She could do so again.

Her gaze lifted to his, seeing the dark, swirling pools of his eyes. Slowly, while he watched her without blinking, she slipped the robe from her body. It pooled at her feet. And as it did his nostrils flared and his eyes darkened. She could already tell that his dragon peeked out in interest, and she felt a womanly thrill at her power.

She straightened, her gaze never leaving his as she climbed onto the bed. Then, hardest of all, she widened her legs completely so that she could curl her left heel against her cinnabar cave. The area was already wet, her heel a welcome roughness. She settled it in tight.

All the while he watched her, his gaze a tangible presence, his breath a hot whisper in the darkness.

She was settled. And so, apparently, was he. His hand gripped his dragon in the specific hold shown on his scroll.

Joanna lifted her hands, pressing them to her breasts, again in the manner in which they had been taught. What they hadn't been taught was to time their breaths, to move with one motion—one circle synched with one stroke—while their eyes held each other's as warmly, as wondrously as if no space separated them.

The first seventy-two strokes were meant to be soothing. They weren't. With each breath Joanna took with Zou Tun, she felt her yin tide rise. But with each circle that lifted and molded her breasts, the fire burned hotter just above her heart.

Her mouth felt dry, so she wet her lips. Even from across the room she saw Zou Tun's body jerk. His gaze left hers to fixate on her mouth, and his buttocks tightened and raised him in his chair.

"Joanna . . ." he said, his voice thick and low. She didn't know if it was meant as a plea or a warning, but she didn't care. Already the yin tide was flowing like hot lava through her.

She felt the need to move. Arching her back, she

pressed her breasts into her hands. Her head dropped backward and her groin pressed forward, grinding into her heel. A flame shot from that location, coiling about her spine like a greedy serpent. All too soon she felt the serpent's mouth settle, clamping hard on the yin center just behind her breasts. The power tightened in that line, gearing a hot, trembling course that linked her cinnabar cave to her breasts.

She hadn't felt this much power before, this much desire. So she experimented, starting her next circle right on top of her nipples.

One touch, one tweak, and her body convulsed. She tried to maintain her focus, tried to analyze her feelings, but words wouldn't come. They were always wrong. She knew her heart pounded, her breath came in hot gasps. But more than that, her entire chest felt full and fiery, her mind restless with the energy of it all, and her focus would not remain.

"Seventy-two," she lied. In truth, she had no idea how many circles she had performed. She knew only that she was finished with soothing strokes. She wanted to build, to push, to increase this burning tide.

"Joanna, what are you doing?" Zou Tun's words came to her from a great distance, and yet he sounded as if he were right beside her.

She opened her eyes, locking once again onto his gaze. Distantly she saw that his face was flushed, his mouth slightly open as his breath came in barely controlled puffs. Below, she saw his dragon, large and dark red, stretching toward her. His hand no longer held it in the correct position, but he gripped himself tightly.

All these things she absorbed in the distance, letting the thoughts pass through her consciousness, then drop away.

"I want to know," she whispered, her voice gaining

strength as her hands reversed their direction. "Where does the yin go? What is coming?"

"No," he gasped. "You are not ready."

Her circles were stronger now, and she felt the rush of the yin stoking her hotter, stronger, brighter.

"Yes," she said, feeling triumphant, "I am."

She wasn't guessing. Indeed, there was no room in her mind or body for doubt. There was only yin, pulsing hot and powerful in her blood. It built within her, and she did everything she could to make it burn ever brighter. Her circles did not end short of her nipples. Each spiral ended tighter, with a pinch and a pull that kept her blood humming in higher and higher notes.

She was ready. She was more than ready as she rocked forward, pressing her cinnabar cave hard against her heel. A few more spirals. A few more rolls. Soon. Yes!

Something gripped her wrists, jerking them away from her body. She resisted, tightening her arms, trying to draw them back, but she succeeded only in pulling herself up, lifting her hips off her heel.

"No!" she cried, fighting the restraint. She had enough consciousness to open her eyes. She saw Zou Tun towering over her, his dark eyes blazing with worry. She didn't care. The tide was so high, the nameless peak so close. "No!" she cried again, twisting hard to break his hold.

It didn't work. He still held her, but the sweat on her arms made his grip slick. He was struggling, so she redoubled her efforts.

"Joanna!" he cried, but she did not listen. She was fighting him with everything she had, all the pent-up power of the yin tide, still surging within her.

"Joanna!" he tried again, and she curled her legs up, planting them hard against his chest. Then she shoved with all her might.

He cursed, twisting his chest so that her legs slid aside, their force wasted in the air. Then he used her momentum against her, jerking her hands above her head so that her body abruptly straightened in the air.

She dropped hard onto the mattress, her teeth rattling in her head. Then, before she drew breath to scream, he was atop her, pressing her completely flat. He landed with a heavy grunt, and she meant to kick him, to throw him off, but his legs hooked over hers and his hips ground down in an exquisite weight that made her entire body shiver.

"Joanna," he gasped against her ear. "You are not ready."

She shoved hard at him, her body tingling wherever they touched. "I bloody well am!" she exploded.

"It is sex, Joanna. It is not the practice. It is merely sex."

She shook her head, not wanting to listen. But what little movement her head made, it was nothing compared to the shift and roll of her body as she tried to dislodge him. His hardened dragon pressed into her belly, and she heard him groan with the sensation.

"You do not understand, Joanna," he said, his words half plea, half moan.

"I feel the yin," she said, her voice a low vibration she felt echo through him. "I feel it." She shifted to look him in the eyes. "I want to know where it leads."

"Orgasm," he said.

She frowned, not knowing the Chinese word. "Orgasm?" she repeated, testing it.

"The yin peak," he explained, beginning to lift his chest off of hers as her struggles ceased. But as the air touched her breasts, she moaned with loss. The tide was ebbing away, the lava cooling, leaving behind a darkened space.

"I want to feel it." She curled her hands into fists. "I want to know it!"

"It is only sex," he repeated. "Not Taoism."

"So be it," she answered hotly. Then, to emphasize her need, she pressed her hips forward, ramming herself as hard as she could against his dragon. He growled at the power of her thrust, but she continued to speak. "You know what I seek. You know what this is."

He nodded, and she could see he fought with his desires.

"Can you show me?" she asked. "Can you show me without . . ." How to say it?

"Without fucking you?"

She flinched at his hard word and the violence it implied.

"A monk is still a man, Joanna. You tempt me too far."

"But that is practice, is it not? To raise your desires but not give in to them?" She didn't know what she was saying. How could she be asking this of him? How could she want him to do this with her? And yet she did. She wanted to tempt him. She wanted to feel what others felt. And if that meant—

"You would risk your virginity?"

She swallowed. Was that what she risked? Did it matter so very much? Hadn't she thrown away everything else already?

"Can you teach me and still control your dragon?" She looked deep into his eyes, searching for understanding. "Can you control yourself?"

She felt him shudder, a tension and release that felt exquisite against her body.

"Zou Tun," she pressed. "Can you hold to your teaching while I abandon mine?"

He didn't speak, but she felt his conflict as he

thought. She knew—as he must—that she was determined on this course. She had felt the hot pulse of yin and would reach its crest one way or another, whether or not a Tigress did such things. Just once she needed to know.

"Yes," he finally whispered.

Her gaze sharpened, and her heart trembled even as the yin began once again to heat. "You will show me?"

"If you are sure." He didn't wait for an answer. Instead he pushed himself off of her. Shoving away, he pulled himself to his knees between her legs. With a quick jerk, he pulled her thighs closer. Her hips were lifted off the bed, her knees bent over his shoulders, and her cinncher cave spread before his face. Still his eyes were trained on her, his expression hard, his mouth pulled into a hungry smile. "Are you sure, Joanna Crane?"

She swallowed. Then, before she could speak, she felt his hands move. He had been lifting her bottom, adjusting her weight upon his shoulders. Now his hands curved inward, and she gasped in surprise as she felt his thumbs slide toward her cave. Flowing from her bottom upward, they delved ever deeper, widening and opening her folds such as no one had ever done.

She was wet there. The yin dew, the Tigresses called it. And she saw him inhale deeply, taking her scent into him, murmuring his pleasure in a low hum against her leg. And still his thumbs rolled slowly forward, pressing deeper, opening her wider.

"Be sure, Joanna, because once I begin, I will not stop until you give up all your rain."

"Will it hurt?" she gasped.

He smiled. "Yes."

"I don't care."

He grinned, his expression almost regal. "As you

wish." Then he lifted her hips and pressed her against his mouth.

It didn't hurt. That was her first and last clear thought. It didn't hurt, but it wasn't entirely painless either. The moment his tongue touched her, pressing and exploring, Joanna began to tremble. Or perhaps not tremble so much as tighten and pulse. The lava flow flared white-hot, but with a rhythm, as if a distant drumbeat echoed in her blood.

She felt her legs tighten across his shoulders, press her closer against him. Her body arched, and her head and neck began to ache where she was rigid against the mattress. But her mind barely registered those things. Her attention was focused *down there* as his thumbs spread her open, giving his tongue room to roam in a strange figure eight: a wider circle around her cave, but then a tight loop higher, at a place that burst into a single, burning flame. And with every tight circle, he pushed that little blaze higher and hotter into her body. Already licking the cord that ended in her breasts, the flame seemed to expand. It radiated down her legs, which were gripping him so tightly. It roared through her blood so that even her fingers throbbed with its pulse.

But there was more. She knew it. She felt it. That fire, that flame, had not reached its zenith. If only he would not do a full figure eight. If only he would stay at the top circle, the tiny loop. Right there. Oh, God, right there.

Then she felt something different. Something hard. Something . . . His thumbs. Both of them pressed inside her cave. Opening, widening her. Her legs would not go farther open, but she tried anyway. She wanted to be split open. She wanted anything, if only he would circle her flame just a few more times. Just enough. Until she felt . . .

His thumbs moved together inside her. Inside. Then out. Inward, then they withdrew. It was a tempo that almost matched the sound in her ears. But it was too slow and too little. If she had breath, she would have begged him for more. As it was, all she could do was arch into his stroke, silently begging again for his tongue.

He shifted his thumbs. Where before they were simply penetrating her, this time they pressed inward and held, pushing against the cave walls such that she felt the pressure almost to her belly. They stayed there, massaging and pushing in a tight circle. She didn't understand what he was doing. The pressure crossed the flame, almost as if cutting it off.

But she had no breath to ask. And he was busy—finally—pressing his lips to her body once again.

The crosswise pressure continued, but it added something else. It seemed to push the source of the flame toward him, making it more open to him, so that when his tongue at last spiraled in, he had plenty of room, plenty of space to push and toy with that wonderful place.

Yes!

Her legs trembled, her breath rasped. And then . . .

The flame exploded.

A flash fire burst across her skin, and she screamed with the joy of it. But there was more. Her mind expanded with the power. It soared through the fire and beyond, even as her body bucked in Zou Tun's arms.

And it was beautiful.

Even as it ebbed, it was sublime.

She sighed happily, still floating on that beautiful yin sea. She felt cradled in its warmth, surrounded by it and Zou Tun, who continued to cradle her body, her legs now lax in dangling over his shoulders.

"*That* was sex," he said, his voice a low rumble against her thigh.

She grinned, too lost in languor to comment. He was settling her down on the bed, shifting his body. Soon she was flat on the mattress, or near enough to it. They had not adequately moved the blanket, so now it lay bunched underneath her hips, lifting her cinnabar cave higher on the bed.

She would have closed her legs then, would have moved to a more modest position, but he was still between her legs, lying on his belly, his legs extended beyond the bed. His face remained where it had been, a few inches above her cave, his smile as radiant as it was smug.

Then he touched her, wrapping his hands underneath her thighs, lifting them so that she bent her legs, her knees moving up in the air. She didn't like the shift, and she murmured a vague protest. The sensations were discordant, like tiny little fires flaring and dying randomly about her body.

"Zou Tun," she murmured, wanting to push him away but having no angle from which to do so. "Stop. I understand."

He nodded, his hands sliding in long strokes along her inner thighs. "You understand sex. But now you must learn practice."

She frowned and lifted her head, doing her best to look at him. "Practice?"

"The only way to ride the yin tide, to direct it to where you want it to go, is to experience it over and over until your mind can control it."

"Wh-what?" she stammered. She had no mind to comprehend his words, much less control anything.

"The yin tide is a tigress that you must ride," he reminded her. Then he grinned. "I have great stamina,

243

Joanna Crane. I will give you many hours of practice."

"Many hours—" Her words ended on a gasp. His stroke on her thighs kept rising higher until his thumb began another slow figure eight around her cave.

"Many, many hours," he repeated. Then he leaned down and began his kiss.

23 June, 1896
Brother,

I have told everyone that you will bring the abbot to my wedding, and Father is most anxious to meet him. The date draws ever nearer, but the myriad preparations are confusing me. My temper grows short and even my summer garden brings me no peace. I fear I begin to sicken. Only your swift return will ease my heart.

Have all the brothers recovered from their disease?

Your anxious sister,
Wen Ji

Decoded translation:

Son,

The emperor is pleased with your progress. I have a few details to finish, but then I will be able to act against the monastery, especially as I now have Abbot's Tseng's death warrant from the emperor. You must return home immediately or you could be killed in the confusion.

Have you identified the rebels? Or should we kill all the monks in the monastery?

Your anxious father,
General Kang

7 July, 1896

Sister, you cannot wed so soon! You are too young. And certainly you should not marry someone old and feeble, whom you despise. Life for you must be very confusing indeed. But here, all is at peace. The disease is gone. The brothers are all busy with their studies. And Abbot Tseng is a great spiritual leader with no political leanings at all. Indeed, I am sorry to tell you that I will not be returning home for many, many months. Even years. It is beautiful here. And peaceful. Not a place for any unpleasantness at all.

Tell father I want to live my life here as a Shaolin.

I pray constantly that Father makes no more moves to wed you to someone ugly.

> *Your earnest brother,*
> *Kang Zou*

Decoded translation as understood by General Kang:

Father,

Please do not attack the monastery. The action would be hasty and ill-advised. I understand that my messages have been confusing, but rest assured that I have things well under control. The brothers are busy plotting rebellion. Abbot Tseng hides his plans well. Indeed, he is so devious that I plan to study him longer. It may even take years.

I pray constantly to make you proud, Father.

> Your earnest son,
> Zou Tun

The sea of desires is difficult to stay, but if you cannot rid yourself of desires, you will surely drown. A person with uncontrollable desires will not only be unable to feel satisfied or comfortable, but conversely, will feel pain and will harm his sense of self.

—Lao Tzu

Chapter Thirteen

Joanna woke slowly, her body coming awake by painful inches. Sweet Heaven, she was sore. That should have made her irritable, but truthfully nothing could dim the delicious glow that warmed her.

Last night had been incredible. The yin tide had been overwhelming and unmanageable, but Zou Tun had been extraordinarily patient—and exquisitely capable of all sorts of interesting things. She lost track of how many times he had let the tide recede, allowed her to catch her breath, only to bring the sensations back, to raise the fire inside her again just so she could try again to ride it. And again. And again.

She stretched a hand behind her, searching for his warm presence. But he wasn't there. Cracking open her eyes, she saw him sitting beside her studying the Tigress's scrolls.

How wonderful that there were things written about these experiences! How marvelous that her partner understood them so well. And how ridiculous that no one in her own culture had ever thought to share them.

Surely married women experienced this yin tide. Surely they knew about these incredible feelings. Surely they . . .

But that was where Joanna's list of "surely" stopped. Because even with her little experience with men, she knew that most would not be as patient as Zou Tun. Most men would not have spent hours upon hours pleasuring her while their own dragons remained large and hungry and completely ignored. And, of course, most men would not be now sitting beside her studying texts on how they could use the experiences to attain Heaven.

Which meant she was most fortunate in her choice of partner.

She smiled, extending a hand to touch him. He turned to her immediately, an unspoken question in his eyes, but she was feeling too languid to speak. She simply wanted to stroke his beautiful skin, watch the planes of his angular face, and revel in the knowledge that he was her partner.

"How are you feeling, Joanna?" he asked, his voice strangely rough.

"Happy," she said. Then he touched her, a long stroke across her cheek, and she closed her eyes to better appreciate the sensation. "What's wrong with your voice?"

"It is punishment for removing yours. My voice will return when I have earned your forgiveness."

"I forgive you." She didn't even have to think about it. Last night was worth a thousand days of silence.

"Thank you," was all he said.

She smiled, delighted with the feel of him stroking her skin so tenderly. But in time his caress stilled. He remained connected to her, his hand a wondrous weight upon her shoulder, but she knew his attention had returned to the scroll.

She grinned in understanding. She, too, had many questions she hoped the parchment could answer. So she opened her eyes, loving the way his brows pinched when he read, even as the lines about his mouth smoothed into a slight, curving smile.

"What does it say about the yin tide? About what happened . . ." Her voice trailed off as she tried to find the words. She had experienced something last night, during that first time and then again later. Perhaps the dozenth time he had brought the yin tide back up to overwhelm her. For a moment she had been carried somewhere else. She had gone someplace . . . sublime.

But before either of them could say more, the door burst open with a rush of frigid air. Joanna gasped as she scrambled to cover herself, and even Zou Tun seemed to be startled. He spun around, his body crouching into a fighting stance. But soon they both relaxed.

It was the Tigress, standing in the doorway with her eyes narrowed. She studied them.

"You had sex with her," the woman accused, her eyes angry.

Zou Tun straightened, his clothing creating a soft shirring sound as he moved between Joanna and the Tigress. "I did not," he answered coldly, though his words were thick and short, as if speaking pained him. "We practiced." Then he shifted uncomfortably. "She practiced."

"She was not ready," Shi Po snapped. She moved forward, but Zou Tun blocked her path.

They would have stood that way forever, glaring at each other, if Joanna had not shifted to her knees, wrapping her blanket about her, though its texture chafed her already abraded skin. "I was ready," she said as she gently pushed Zou Tun aside.

The Tigress's eyes focused upon her like the pricks of a sharp needle. "You are in pain."

Joanna met the Tigress's gaze, shrugging slightly. "It was worth it."

Her flat statement seemed to reassure the Tigress, but Zou Tun spun around in surprise. "You said it didn't hurt. You—"

Joanna pressed her hand to his lips, cutting off his words. "I have no regrets." She smiled slowly. "And many questions." Then her eyes shifted to the Tigress. "The yin tide is overwhelming. How does one ever learn to ride it?"

Shi Po's answer was as predictable as it was enlightening. "A great deal of practice, young cub."

"But in the end," Joanna pressed, "what awaits us?" Last night she had felt the power of a Tigress, felt it grip her in its mouth and shake her. But there had still been that moment of something else: that glimpse of sheer ecstasy that held a hint of so much more. If only she could learn to control it. If only . . .

"I will send you a tea for the pain," answered Shi Po, interrupting her thoughts. "And texts beyond what you have already been given." She gestured to the scrolls that lay open and forgotten beside the bed. "You may come to me after you have finished those. We will discuss your conclusions then."

But as Joanna looked at the writing beside her, Zou Tun pulled away. He dropped to one knee in another imperial kowtow. "I have erred greatly, Tigress. I thought she was ready for the next step. I did not realize there would be pain." On his last word, he cast a quick glance toward Joanna, but she could not tell if it was in accusation or worry.

Either way, Shi Po would have none of it. She leaned

down, curling one long fingernail beneath his chin, tilting Zou Tun's head upward so that he looked her in the eye. "Did you force her?"

"Of course not!"

"Is she your pet?"

Again he exclaimed in hot denial, "Of a certainty, no!"

"Then why do you take responsibility for her actions, monk? Does she not choose for herself?"

He hesitated, clearly thrown.

Shi Po elaborated. "With choice comes responsibility, monk. Do not steal it." She shifted her eyes to Joanna. "Do you understand?"

Joanna nodded. She did understand. Last night's activities had been her choice. If she suffered a great deal of stiffness because of it, she had only herself to blame. But even more, she now realized that the Tigress teachings were more than just physical experiences, more than just a yin tide to set her mind afire; they were a way of life.

She was only now beginning to understand the physical and emotional demands required to walk this Tigress path. Last night her mind had been unprepared for the tumult of yin, and it nearly drowned her. This morning she knew that her body had not been completely ready either. She would need hours of mediation to discipline her mind, hours more physical exercise before she was ready for the next attempt.

But now, more than ever, she was committed to her course. Even if it took a lifetime of study, she wanted to experience that perfect moment. She wanted to find Heaven again, and know how to remain there as long as possible.

Joanna lifted her chin, meeting the Tigress's stare. "Is there another class today? I am most anxious to attend."

The Tigress nodded, her movements graceful as she

accepted Joanna's decision. But it was Zou Tun who captured Joanna's attention. His sigh was loud and deep, and he shifted to face her. His gaze transfixed her, and she read hope and fear mixed there.

"Are you sure, Joanna?"

She grinned. "I have never been more sure of anything." She looked up at the Tigress. "I want to learn this. I want to become an immortal. And I will devote my entire life to learning."

Silence greeted her statement. From Zou Tun she sensed great relief and joy. But the Tigress Shi Po sank slowly onto the bed. She stared at Joanna.

"You have already felt it," she said in an awed whisper. "On your first night of practice, you have already tasted the sweetness of Heaven. Haven't you?"

Joanna didn't need to answer. Shi Po had surely seen the truth. But as Joanna watched, the Tigress's face grew hard, and her words rushed out in angry demands.

"What did you experience, barbarian? Tell me everything. Why does it come so easily to your kind?"

Joanna frowned, startled by the sudden change. Before she could answer, there came a commotion, a loud banging and the rush of feet outside. Seconds later the bedroom door burst open and a young servant stood there, her eyes wild, her breath ragged.

"What is it?" the Tigress demanded, clearly annoyed.

"Soldiers!" the woman gasped. "A general!"

Shi Po pushed to her feet, her face tightening as never before. "Serve him tea!" she snapped at the servant. "And send for Kui Yu. I am coming."

The servant nodded, then sped away. Zou Tun had gained his feet, but beyond a long, searching look exchanged with the Tigress, he said nothing. The Tigress said nothing, either. She seemed to dismiss him with a quick wave of her hand, her attention fixed on Joanna.

"Remain here," she hissed. Then, when Joanna dipped her chin in a wobbly acknowledgment, Shi Po stepped forward, her entire body rigid. "Hear this, ghost barbarian. If you wish to learn, it must be from me. And it must be here. Leave without my permission, and you will never touch Heaven, never gain immortality. Do you understand?"

Again Joanna dipped her chin in agreement. This sudden intensity startled her even as her mind wrestled with its meaning. Just what did the Tigress want? Why were there soldiers here? What had Zou Tun done? But there was no time for more questions as the Tigress spun on her heel and left. In the distance, the noise from the soldiers was growing louder, and Zou Tun looked more and more uncomfortable.

Joanna said his name, but he cut her off.

"We must leave. Now." He turned, quickly gathering what few possessions he had. With an almost casual movement, he tossed coolie pants and a loose shirt at her. "Get dressed. We will escape out the back garden."

Joanna's hand twisted, holding the coarse fabric of the pants. A strange revulsion hit her. She had just spent the last few days steeling herself to removing her clothes. She had just discovered something amazing: Putting clothing on felt like a step backward.

Yet Zou Tun obviously had no intention of remaining.

"Didn't you hear Shi Po?" Joanna asked. "We have to stay here. She is coming back for us."

"I heard," he said, as he rummaged through the single-drawer chest, quickly packing ointments and Joanna's stone balls into his bedroll. Then he paused, his hands hovering over the open Tigress scrolls. Before Joanna could say anything, he rolled them tight and stuffed them into his pack.

"The Tigress will send the soldiers away," Joanna said. "She knows you are hiding from them." She narrowed her eyes, seeing confirmation in the quick jerk of his body. Yes, he was hiding from the soldiers. And yes, he was very afraid. "What did you do, Zou Tun? What do they want with you?" *Are they really going to kill you? Kill us?*

She didn't speak her last questions aloud, but he must have understood them. He turned to her, the air whirling with the force of his movement. "She cannot send them away. Those are imperial soldiers in the front courtyard. They have tracked me down."

"How?"

He slipped to the door, opening it a tiny crack to peer out. "I don't know how. But it is not a large step. The abbot of my monastery was the Tigress's brother. Now please, *please* get dressed."

She shifted, pulling on the pants to calm him. "Was?" she pressed. "The abbot *was* her brother?"

He nodded, a quick slash of his chin. "He's dead now. As are all the others." He turned haunted eyes to her. "I am the last of Abbot Tseng's Shaolin."

His anxiety was infectious. She hurried her movements, pulling the loose blouse over her head with quick jerks. When she could see him again, she met his gaze. "Why, Zou Tun? Why did the soldiers kill everyone? Why are they looking for you?"

He returned to looking out the doorway, but his words traveled to her nonetheless. "They believe we are revolutionaries."

She straightened, pieces beginning to fall into place. After all, why else would a Manchu, a member of the ruling class, be running from his own government? Unless, of course, he supported rebellion. "So you are a Boxer."

"No!" His denial was vehement—and honest. He did not have the look of someone who wished to overthrow the government.

"But the others were," she said. "At the monastery. And so—"

"Yes. No." He ran a shaking hand through his hair. "I don't know, Joanna Crane. Some, yes, wanted to end the oppression. But they were just boys, talking as boys do." He pulled her to her feet. "Please, will you come with me now?"

"But it was a fighting monastery. So the government thinks—"

"Not now, Joanna. I swear I will tell you everything. But only after we leave here."

He meant to pull her out the door, but she dug in her heels, refusing to move. "The Tigress said if I leave she will not teach me. I will never learn the rest of this practice."

He paused, his breath catching in his throat. Then he turned his head, his eyes at last focusing completely, intently, upon her face. "But you are not serious about this teaching, Joanna Crane. You are merely a bored rich girl with uncommon intelligence, and this has been a pleasing distraction."

His words were as much a question as a statement, but she bristled nonetheless, her voice dropping to a low hiss. "If I am so frivolous a creature, then why must I come with you? Indeed, isn't it safer for me to stay here?"

He groaned, his body collapsing onto the bed. "I have insulted you, Joanna. I apologize. I wish to . . . understand." His eyes continued to roam, but not to the hallway and back. This time he searched her face. "Are you truly serious? Enough to devote your entire life to a foreign religion and life?"

She sobered, knowing he was looking for honesty. Knowing, too, that his doubt was understandable. She had trouble believing in her own passion. And yet it was there, undeniable and true. "I want this teaching more than anything in my life." She gripped his hands. "I want to stay here. Even if it means risking my life with those soldiers, I want to stay here."

He shook his head, his voice morbid. "Not the soldiers. The general."

She leaned forward, touching his face. "Can you not trust in the Tigress? Maybe she can turn them away."

He shook his head. "I have to leave. And I want you to come with me." It wasn't so much a statement as a plea. And it tore her heart to see him so afraid.

She wanted to go. Lord, she wanted to go simply because his eyes begged her and his hands trembled in hers. But she had just found what she wanted; she had just discovered something wonderful. How could she abandon it? Wouldn't that make her as flighty as he had just accused her of being?

"Do not make me choose," she begged. The thought of him leaving tore her heart. And the thought of finding a different partner was more than horrid; it was repulsive. But she needed Shi Po as well. Sacred scrolls were one thing, but they were steeped in imagery only Shi Po could explain. Joanna and Zou Tun had nothing without her. "Please, can't you trust Shi Po?"

"Do you?" he pressed. "Do you believe she has your best interests at heart? That she understands what it is she does?"

Joanna bit her lip. No, she couldn't say that. And yet . . . she could. She believed in Shi Po's ability to instruct. But the woman was much more complicated than that. Even Joanna could see that she was struggling to harness forces she did not fully comprehend.

"When countries are at stake, even religions get twisted," Zou Tun muttered. Then there came a sound: the noise of servants and feet, a man's loud protest and a woman's sob. Joanna couldn't identify the voices, but she knew the meaning. The soldiers were coming. If she and her monk were to leave, they had to do it now.

Joanna remained poised, undecided. The knowledge she craved or the desperation in Zou Tun's eyes? Shi Po? Or Zou Tun?

Phrased that way, the decision was clear. The monk. Always. Because he was gentle and kind and protective and honorable, despite this confusion with the imperial army. And yet Joanna still hedged, needing something—one last answer before she threw her lot in with him completely.

"Why, Zou Tun? Why do you want me to go with you?"

He looked at her, his hand poised on the door. "Because you are the only one I have trusted in three years," he whispered, and she could tell that the words caused him pain. "And because I need you."

That was enough. It wasn't everything she wanted, but it was enough for now. Before she could change her mind, she grabbed the blanket off the bed, using it to shroud her very Caucasian hair and face. "Do not forget you have promised to explain everything," she said.

"I haven't forgotten," he said as he checked the hallway. Then he grabbed her hand and together they ran.

Zou Tun cursed under his breath as he realized the truth: He had nowhere to take Joanna. He'd sworn to keep her safe, then pulled her away from her true passion. And it was a true passion; of that he was sure. It still stunned him to think of a woman—a *ghost woman*—with the strength to dedicate herself as any monk would at a temple. As he had done three years ago with Abbot Tseng.

And so he had one more sin to add to his growing list: taking a true seeker away from her place of study and worship.

He groaned, trying to focus his thoughts. His sins could wait. Right now he had to find a place in Shanghai where a penniless monk and a runaway foreigner could hide from imperial soldiers. Or more important, from the general, his father.

"You don't have a clue where to go, do you?" There was no accusation in her voice, just a weary certainty that he was a complete fool.

Zou Tun sighed, too ashamed to hide his incompetence. "I have never been in this city before." He tried not to wince as he spoke. The pain in his throat was like shards of glass cutting at his vocal cords. It was his punishment, he knew, for having taken away Joanna's voice. This malady would not go away until after he had atoned.

Joanna was looking at their surroundings with a knowing air. "This is my city," she murmured as much to him as to herself. "I know where we can be safe from the . . . the general." She gave him a significant look. "Then we can talk."

He nodded, though he wondered if he would have the voice by then to answer her questions. Still, he had promised to explain, and so he would even if he wasn't sure how much of his own inadequacy he wanted to expose. Why, above all things, he would worry what one ghost woman thought of him, he didn't know. But he was man enough to acknowledge his fear.

Yes, he cared what she thought of him. And so he would do his best to earn what honor he could in her eyes.

"Come on," she said, taking hold of his hand. "You got us out of the Tigress's compound. Now I'll get us out of Shanghai. Or more specifically, out of *Chinese* Shanghai."

It didn't take long. Not only did she know the way, but she got them a rickshaw and they were soon moving quickly through the crowded streets. Zou Tun didn't like the noise or the buildings. The city felt too cramped, too cluttered, and much too smelly. But even as he longed for his silent mountain crags, he blessed every unfortunate soul who clogged the city streets. The more people who squatted like beggars here, the more people there were to confuse and misdirect his father.

All too soon Joanna was taking off her blanket covering. Though the air still had the bite of winter, she wrapped it around her shoulders, allowing her white face and brown curls to shimmer bronze in the sunlight. She was indeed a beautiful woman, and Zou Tun was dazzled by it.

How had he not seen it before? And how had he not realized how commanding and capable a woman she was? She easily handled the guards manning the gate into the foreign concession. With a smile and an absentminded air, she gained passage for both himself and their rickshaw driver. She even cut off the guard's questions with a wink, as if it were her right to wander through China as she would. It was only after they were well inside the barbarians' territory that she leaned over and whispered into his ear.

"Just about every guard knows me," she confessed. "I've been going in and out of the foreign concession for years now, and I tip very well." She sighed. "Of course, there are problems with being recognized. It will take less than an hour for someone to tell my father I've returned."

He caught the note of anxiety in her voice and cast her a sharp look. "Will that cause a problem?"

She shook her head, though her words were heavy. "My father doesn't allow problems." Then she turned away from him, focused completely on giving directions to the rickshaw runner, who, in turn, was wholly occupied with avoiding the increasing numbers of horses and carriages that choked the streets.

Zou Tun could do no more than look about him in shock and awe. These barbarians lived like royalty! There was wealth everywhere he looked. Jewels. Gold. Horses. Towering buildings. It seemed he had stepped from one country into the next, though he knew he still remained on Chinese soil. And yet everything he saw was foreign to his eyes. Strange colors, strange food smells, and even worse, strange words.

Was *that* what Joanna's language sounded like? It was terrible. And yet perhaps it was musical in its own barbaric way. He didn't know what to think. It was appalling that these barbarians could adorn themselves with jewels and finery while in the countryside his people were struggling for even the smallest grains of rice. And yet he had been to the Forbidden City. He had lived in Peking. He knew what wealth adorned even the lowest eunuch there. He knew the extravagance of the generals, his own father included.

If those Chinese could adorn themselves with finery, why not these barbarians as well? Was not that always the way of men, to garner wealth at the expense of someone else? China was too poor for all to live in elegance, so those who could grabbed from those who could not.

The truth saddened him. This was not the Taoist way.

His thoughts were cut off as the rickshaw stopped before a mansion—a glittering monstrosity of stone and wood. In truth, it reminded Zou Tun of a grave marker. Large and ugly, it squatted on the land next to all the other stone edifices, monuments to man lacking harmony with nature and Heaven and everything else.

"My home," Joanna said softly, but there was no warmth in her tone.

He reached out, touching her hand. He could tell by the cold sweat on her skin that she was afraid to return. He opened his mouth, intending to suggest another place, any other place, but she shook her head.

"We'll be safe here," she said softly as she disembarked. Then she told the rickshaw runner to wait; a servant would pay the fare. Slowly she turned and began climbing the steps to the mammoth front door.

Zou Tun was beside her in a moment. He would not abandon her to face her father alone. He looked at her, seeing her smile encouragingly at him. The expression was clearly false. She was gripping his arm, her fear obvious for all that she tried to hide it.

"You are safe with me," he lied, doing his best to comfort her. He touched her fingers, knowing how inadequate was the gesture.

They never made it to the door. Within moments of their climbing the first of a dozen steps, the door was flung open. An elderly Chinese man stepped out, his face a wrinkled mixture of joy and fear. His words were unintelligible, but Joanna understood. She ran up the last steps, throwing herself into the man's arms. They hugged, their words fading into silence as they simply held each other. Zou Tun stood back and watched the unusual display.

The man was the butler. At least, he appeared so from his livery. He was head of the household servants, and yet Joanna was clinging to him as if they were friends long separated. Zou Tun intertwined his fingers, searching for a monk's calm as he stood to one side. But no peace centered him. All he felt was a hot surge of jealousy. Even if the two were servant and mistress, they cared for each other, and he envied their emotional reunion.

The pair soon separated, embarrassment coloring both their faces as they realized how public their display had been. The man then turned to Zou Tun, but Joanna stopped him from speaking.

"Someone must pay the rickshaw," she said quickly. "And we need baths. And clothing. We cannot appear before my father like this."

The man nodded, ushering them inside even as he began dispatching orders to other servants. Then all was accomplished in silent haste as they were shown to separate bathing chambers. Joanna did not say another word except to promise to see Zou Tun soon. And that they would talk later.

He did as she told him. He enjoyed the comforts of a heated bath in a copper tub. He used perfumed soaps and thick towels. Then he dressed himself in the finest silks, reminiscent of when he was a pampered and cosseted Manchurian prince. And though his Shaolin soul wanted to claim that the luxuries were repellent to him, he knew that they were not.

The water felt excellent, the silks even more so. And without even realizing the shift, he found himself walking and thinking once again as a Manchurian prince. He ordered the servants to get him fine foods and demanded that someone perfume his clothing. But when he watched a silent girl sprinkle costly scented water upon his person, he felt shame flood his soul. How quickly he had forgotten three years of learning. How quickly he had slipped back into extravagance and all the temptations entailed therein.

He reached to stop the woman. She looked at him, her eyes wide and afraid. He tried to reassure her with a smile, but she was truly frightened, and he wondered what type of household this was that had such anxious servants.

"You have done most excellently," he said gently, even as her hand trembled beneath his. "But tell me, is there any other clothing available for me? Something simpler?"

She bowed anxiously, her head dipping up and down. It was not an imperial kowtow, but it served the same purpose—demeaning one for the elevation of another. "You do not like your clothing? My deepest apologies. I shall find something else immediately. Something finer. Something—"

"No, no," he said, trying to catch her fluttering hands. "These clothes are fine. Just fine."

"But I can search—"

"No," he repeated. "No. You have done excellently. I shall inform the master of this house that I am most pleased with your work."

She bit her lip, obviously too frightened to know if he was sincere. "Thank you, great sir," she said softly. "Please just show me to where dinner will be served."

"But your sweetmeats are coming. They will be up in a moment."

He winced, having already forgotten that he'd ordered food. He shook his head. "No, miss." He used a formal address. "Those are for you and any you wish to share them with." Then, for fear she would misunderstand, he made his next words absolutely clear. "And I will not need your assistance any more tonight."

"Oh, but, sir!" she cried. "Please do not dismiss me. The master will be annoyed. Please." Her voice trembled. "Please allow me to . . . to . . ." She couldn't finish. Did she truly think he would require her sexually tonight?

He didn't have to ask. Some things, apparently, were universal. In both Manchurian and barbarian society, when a man was served by a pretty young woman, certain things were expected.

He sighed. "I will not dismiss you." But he had an idea. "Please go into the city and find out any information you can about imperial soldiers. Do not endanger yourself. Simply listen to what is said; then report back to me in the morning. Can you do that?"

She nodded, her expression lightening. "I know exactly what you wish, sir. I will learn everything I can."

"Thank you," he said, waving his hand in dismissal. However, it was interesting that Joanna's servants were well used to acting as spies. Yes, some things were common in all wealthy homes, and the very thought sickened him. He hated returning to a place where someone watched his every movement, and people spent hours every day planning and devising strategies for gain.

He had no head for playing those types of games. And no will to learn. The very thought was exhausting. And so with a weary heart he left his room, exploring as best he could, finally descending the stairs to the main floor in search of Joanna.

What he found was a formal room, designed not for harmony but display. At least the air seemed to move here; he did not feel so stifled. Then he realized that it was more than just air. It was the energy of the room that flowed, pulling one inside. It didn't take long for him to identify the arrangement. It was that of a merchant, a sucking tide of commerce such as one found in a canny businessman's shop.

It began at the periphery, with a single, simple piece near the door. The tiny tree was an exquisite carving of black ivory. It drew the eye inward to yet another piece, even grander, more beautiful than the previous. White jade like a bleached bone reached for the viewer, drawing him nearer toward a delicate etching of an immortal offering a peach of long life.

On and on one stepped, the flow ever stronger, the temptations grander, more stunning. Cloudy jade was followed by red jade, only to be followed by a pure jade so translucent a single candle flame glowed through the delicate fanlike design. One piece was carved trees, the next was immortals, then angels and deities. And in the end, what did one find? What was the vast sucking center of energy, the merchant's greatest pride and joy for which he would expect a treasure trove of gold?

Joanna Crane.

It was a painting, actually, that hung over a square fire pit; huge, overdone in oils, and yet still beautiful. Joanna sat in a flame-orange dress with rubies flashing at her throat. Her long white fingers held a flower Zou Tun did not recognize. He knew only that it was large and funereal white. A fitting match for her face, he thought, which was pale and frozen, without the barest spark of life.

"Hideous, isn't it?"

Zou Tun turned, seeing the real Joanna Crane standing just outside of the room, her warm bronze eyes a hundredfold more glorious than the glorious picture behind him. She was dressed as elegantly as he, though the style was barbarian. She looked uncomfortable, squeezed into her laces and silks that did not move or flow but held her stiffly in place.

He much preferred her in coolie clothing.

"I do not like the flower. Or your face," he stated flatly, referring to the picture.

She laughed, her voice was high and tight. "Trust a monk to avoid flattery."

He hesitated, wondering how honest he could be in this place. "I did not mean to offend," he finally said, resorting to his court manners. "It is a beautiful painting, but it does not capture the bright glow of your essence."

She raised her eyebrows, her face alight with stunned surprise. "My goodness, Zou Tun, when did you turn poetical?"

He shook his head. "As a barbarian you cannot know true poetry. My words are merely a monkey's chatter."

She was in the process of sinking into what he assumed was a barbarian curtsy. She stopped short at his words, straightening with a wry expression. "Now *that*," she said dryly, "is the Zou Tun I remember."

He frowned, feeling awkwardness settle between them as had not happened since they had met on the road so many days before. He had not intended to sound arrogant, but he had. "Joanna—" he began, wanting to bridge the gap between them.

She shook her head, cutting him off. "It doesn't matter," she said as she crossed the room to stare up at the painting. "My father had this commissioned two years after coming here. All the rich families have one, you know, and so he found an artist. My mother died soon after the crossing, and so it had to be me, sitting for hours on end, clutching that stupid white lily. The artist said it meant purity and majesty, and so I was to hold it like Queen Elizabeth, the Virgin Queen." She blinked, coming back to herself. "I'm sorry. I'm rambling, and you probably haven't a clue what I'm talking about."

"A queen. Of your people."

"A silliness, actually. Of my father's. But I'm his only child now, you know, so he told me I had to obey."

"As is appropriate for any daughter. It is her duty to obey her father."

Joanna turned, her eyes suddenly dark and intense as she focused on him. "Do you mean that, Zou Tun? Do you truly think it is my duty—my obligation—to follow my father's dictates, no matter what they are? No matter what I think?"

He froze, suddenly thrown into a quandary. It was easy to forget her place—and his—when they had been locked in a tiny bedroom in the Tigress's household. But now they were in the world. Her world, but society nonetheless. And he had the feeling her questions had far greater importance than was obvious. He had no answer.

"I was taught that women are happiest when they obey. When they follow the dictates of those whom Heaven has placed above them."

She snorted. "That's what you were taught. What do you believe?"

He sighed, his gaze torn between her living face and the large painting above her head, a frozen creature dead to all but her father's dictates. "This is what your father would make you, is it? A pale, virginal creature without intelligence or—"

"Life. Without a mind or a will, just a doll to hang on the wall and show off to his friends." She nodded sadly. "Yes, that is who my father wants me to be."

"And what do you want?"

She sighed, her entire body trying to shift but held in place by its huge cocoon of frilly fabric. "You know the answer to that, Zou Tun. I want to be a Tigress. I want to learn what Shi Po teaches." She once again pinned him with her dark gaze. "But I have chosen to go with you. So, Zou Tun, what does that mean? What do you want me to do?"

She had something in mind. He could see it in her

eyes, feel it in the room. She wanted him to say something. To do something. But he didn't know what. He was too disoriented by this strange home, by her strange customs. By the simple knowledge that they were in her father's house. He had no thought beyond that.

And yet he did: escape. He felt a burning need to leave her home and his. To go back to where he'd once been, a simple bedroom near a vast library. With a temple, perhaps, for prayer, and all the peace of wilderness surrounding him. That was what he wanted.

But how to tell her that? How to explain?

Before he could frame the words, a loud clatter interrupted them. It was a booming noise followed by a loud bellow in the language of the barbarians. Zou Tun spun around, his muscles tightening at the forceful sound. It took only a moment before he understood what it was. And when he did his body clenched even tighter, his thoughts becoming even more cluttered and anxious.

Joanna Crane's father had arrived.

Military force brings disaster. But sometimes there is no other alternative. In such a case, it should be carried out in a levelheaded manner, seeking to attain the goal but no more.

—Lao Tzu

Chapter Fourteen

The man did not look like Joanna's father. Given Joanna's sweetness, Zou Tun had expected a large man, fleshy and round. But Joanna's sire was tall and lean in the way of a snake. His eyes were sharp and clear, his skin freckled and ruddy and not at all ghost-like. All in all, Joanna's father was nothing like Zou Tun expected, and yet he was undeniably her father.

The man rushed into the room, calling her name in the way of all fathers who suddenly find a lost child. He enveloped her in his long arms and kissed her forehead, closing his eyes as he breathed her scent. Joanna, too, held on just as tight, just as warmly. Until her father pulled back, searching her face and body as if for some taint.

He looked at Zou Tun. His lip curled, and he spoke in his barbarian tongue. From his tone it must not have been a compliment.

Joanna pushed away, fire flashing in her eyes, but her father would not release her. He held her arm with bony fingers that dug deep into her flesh.

Zou Tun felt his body tense. A single well-placed blow could easily break the man's hold. But it was not his right to interfere. He had no claim on Joanna, and so she belonged to her father. If the man chose to beat her to death for her rash actions, Zou Tun could not stop it. He would not deny a man his rights, not even this skeletal barbarian.

Or so he told himself, even as he thrust his hand forward, breaking the man's grip. Joanna had also been jerking away, and so they appeared to have moved in concert, his blow aiding her escape.

Then they all stood apart, three points of a triangle, all eyeing one another with angry frustration—father and daughter because they were at odds, Zou Tun because he could not understand the words that boiled in the air.

Joanna spoke first, her voice starting low but quickly rising to a roar. Sound after sound crackled from her lips. Her father stared at her, his mouth falling open in shock. Clearly Joanna had never spoken in such a way to him before, but he quickly recovered.

All too soon he spoke, his voice louder than hers, his fists tightly clenched at his sides. But then those too began to rise, and Zou Tun tensed. He would not allow any blow to fall on her.

None did. Instead the father opened his right hand, cutting it through the air like a blade. He spoke one word, and it silenced Joanna.

Then there was no sound. No movement. Only dark, angry glares between father and daughter. Zou Tun wanted to intervene. The need to rescue Joanna—to take her away from this ugliness—drove him mercilessly. But he knew he could not. The most he could do was wait in silence and prevent violence.

And even that prevention was illegal.

"Marry me." The words came out in a quick burst,

rushed for fear he would change his mind. In truth, what he suggested was impossible, but he pushed the idea nevertheless. "Joanna, tell him we are married."

She jerked to look at him, her eyes abruptly washed in tears. "What?"

"Then he will have no right to you. And I can take you away."

"As your wife?"

He wanted to agree. His chin even dipped in acknowledgment, but the movement was cut off. The truth was too harsh, and he could not lie to her. "No. I cannot marry you in truth. It is impossible, Joanna. My family . . ." How to explain the complex requirements of a young Manchu bannerman?

"They will not accept me," she finished for him.

"You ask me to defy everything, Joanna. To give up my heritage and my name. To abandon not only my family but my country. It is not possible!" He stopped speaking, but his breath came in angry gasps, his heart pounding in his throat. Some part of his mind recoiled at his reaction. She had not suggested anything of the kind. It had been *his* idea. A storm raged inside his chest at the very thought.

Meanwhile it was the father's turn to talk, to demand answers in his barbarian tongue. Joanna merely sighed, stepping backward to drop onto a cushioned bench with obvious exhaustion. She said something to her father, something apparently intended to silence him. Then she turned back to Zou Tun.

"I have already told him I am married in the letter I sent yesterday. It was the only way to stop his search."

Zou Tun felt his chest squeeze impossibly tight. The storm still raged inside him, now in even less space. "He believes we are married?"

She nodded, and though her head dipped, her eyes

continued to hold his. The word *married* echoed in his mind.

Suddenly the storm abated, the pain eased, and his body relaxed. He could protect Joanna. "It is done," he said. "We will rest here tonight, then leave in the morning. Please convey my thanks to your father."

Joanna pushed up from her seat, obviously thrown. "No, it is not done! Because we are not married, you haven't explained anything, and I—" She cut herself off, her words stopped as if by an unseen hand.

Both Zou Tun and her father moved forward, wanting to help her. Both stopped, not understanding what had happened, what she needed. Especially as she glared them into immobility.

"Joanna?" Zou Tun asked.

"I want to eat," she said firmly. "And then I want answers. Everything, Zou Tun. You have to tell me everything."

"Of course," he answered immediately, knowing there was little choice. Knowing, too, what would happen when she finally did understand. They would part ways. They would have to. For even in this barbarian home, lost somewhere in Shanghai's foreign concession, they were not safe. His father, the general, would find them. And if any hint of an impropriety like marriage reached that man's ears—false or not—Joanna and her father would be killed.

Joanna grimaced. The meal was inedible. Her father and his kitchen had gone to great lengths to cook her favorite foods, but Joanna discovered she absolutely despised it all. How could she ever have enjoyed heavy cream, thick meats, and grainy breads? And how could her body have changed so quickly that these foods tasted overcooked, overdone, and mostly too greasy?

It didn't stop her from eating, though. She was incredibly hungry, and food was food, after all. Even though her palate rebelled at the taste, she ate. And she did her best to spin a ridiculous romantic tale so her father would accept her pretend marriage.

She talked about secret meetings, about chaste kisses and love long denied. She spoke about a sudden desperate flight to a priest and a wonderful honeymoon in Zou Tun's palatial estate.

Her father said nothing throughout the entire recitation. One glance at his face told her he didn't believe a word. He was too shrewd a businessman to believe in romantic tales anyway, but she liked her pretend story. She liked thinking—even for a moment—that Zou Tun cherished an undeniable passion for her. That his love leaped the chasm of bigotry and xenophobia that so plagued the Chinese. That she and he would live happily ever after.

Except the more she spun her tale, the more she spoke of undying love and purity, the more she realized it wasn't true. None of it was even remotely possible. Zou Tun still considered her a barbarian. And despite all they had shared, he had never even hinted at a single tender feeling for her.

So she was lying to her father and herself, while sitting directly across from her, her pretend husband picked morosely at his own food and looked exactly like a man who wished to be somewhere else.

Joanna fell silent, her words—like her food—dark, heavy stones in the pit of her stomach.

"Will you ever tell me the truth, Joanna?" her father asked.

She started slightly at his low, hurt tone. She glanced at him, seeing for the first time his haggard expression, his stooped shoulders. Her father was aging. And her disappearance and ridiculous story weren't helping matters at all.

And yet what could she tell him?

"I don't know the whole truth. Not yet."

"Are you hurt? Are you safe?"

She straightened in her seat. Across from her she could see that Zou Tun had picked up on the change in tone. On the sudden tension in the air. But he did not understand English, and so it was up to her now to decide the next move.

She could end it all right then and there. She still had her virginity. She could tell her father Zou Tun had abducted her. She could send for the general and pretend the whole last few days had never happened.

But they *had* happened. And she didn't want to forget. So she turned to her father, investing all of her passion in her next words.

"I am absolutely safe," she lied. "And I want to stay with him."

He swallowed his wine in a single gulp. This from a man who never drank any kind of spirits at all. Then he looked at her over the rim of his glass. "Are you really married?"

"Yes. Absolutely."

His eyes went flat. The color drained out of his face but he didn't speak a word. Instead he pushed up from his chair. Without so much as a backward glance, he walked from the room. A moment later she heard the front door bang shut.

The sound echoed through her body, reverberating in her mind. Her father had left the house. He had walked away from her as he would from an unpleasant odor or a plate of bad fish. He had walked out of the room, then out of the house. And she had done no more than tell him she was married.

She looked at her plate. She knew that Zou Tun was watching her. She could feel the weight of his attention like a warm blanket—surrounding her or smothering her, she wasn't sure which. Either way she wasn't prepared to deal with him, with his questions or even his answers. Her father had just abandoned her. And she felt very, very alone.

"You are not alone, Joanna," he said.

She jumped, startled that he had read her mind.

"Fathers have dreams for their children, plans that are etched upon their hearts and souls. It destroys them when a child does not fulfill those things."

"I didn't destroy him, Zou Tun. I got *married*. Or so he thinks." Amazing that she could even say the word without crying. Especially since the truth was so much harder to bear. In truth she wasn't a wife, and she was no longer a daughter. So exactly who was she?

"What do you want, Joanna?"

She shook her head. She didn't know.

"To sleep," she suddenly said. "I want to sleep."

She stood, intending to go to her room. But she didn't want to leave Zou Tun. How would she know he would be around when she woke? Would he leave as well?

"Will you come with me?" she asked. "Will you . . ." What did she want to say?

"I am tired as well. Perhaps we would both benefit from a rest."

She smiled, at once awed and disturbed by how easily he understood. Was it sinful to wish to lie with a man who wasn't her husband? Would she be damned to an eternity of fire and brimstone because she wanted to feel his arms wrapped around her as she slept? And would her father's curses add to the coals Satan poured upon her head?

She sighed, full of questions spun from hellfire sermons, collisions of her Christian teachings and the Tigress scrolls. What was real? What was true?

Zou Tun took her hand, and she gripped him as tightly as she would a lifeline.

He was real. He was true.

Together they walked to her bedroom. Gently he undid her clothing, slipping her gown from her shoulders and removing the restriction of her corset. She took her first deep breath in hours as all her undergarments dropped to the floor. And then he lifted the covers and helped her settle into bed.

She rolled onto her back, watching as he drew closed the curtains and shut out the afternoon sun. He turned to look at her. His face was in shadow, but she felt his gaze nonetheless.

Without a word she scooted to the far side of the large, four-poster bed. She pushed aside the frilly coverings and made a space for him. It took him less than a moment to strip off his clothing. Then, with a sigh that wrapped her in warmth, he settled into bed.

She snuggled backward, fitting her naked body to his, her back against his chest, her legs intertwined with his. She felt his breath, the heat of it and his body wrapping her in a cocoon of peace.

Did he feel delight or sorrow, joy or fear? She felt his lips touch her ear and his arms pull her tightly against him. Pressed flush against her bottom, his dragon stirred and swelled, but she didn't respond to its call. Her mind was on Zou Tun, not his dragon. On the man, not the religion.

He wanted to be here with her. And she wanted to stay right where she was. All the other things didn't matter. Her father, the Tigress, even the general who hunted them—none of those things mattered just then.

So long as Zou Tun held her, she had no questions and no fears. She slept.

* * *

She woke when he left her. She felt him slip away, creeping out of bed with a stealth only a fighting monk could achieve. She lay still, fighting tears and pretending she wasn't imagining the worst when she heard him open their bedroom door. But then he closed it again, and she heard him use the chamber pot. Heard him wash his face and hands in the basin. Felt him return to the bed, his body slipping slowly beneath the covers.

Only then did she release her breath. Only then did she begin to think rationally again.

"What time is it?" she whispered.

"Evening," was his response. "The servants have left a tray outside the door. Would you like some food?"

She wasn't hungry. Her mind was in too much chaos, her body still recovering from her last meal. And yet she sat up, pushing the hair away from her eyes as she reached for the tray he was already offering. "I'm starved," she said. "Why is that?"

"The yin tide takes a great deal of food to sustain."

She didn't answer. She was busy eating a mango and trying not to spill the sweet juice all over her covers.

When the fruit was consumed, the bread tasted and set aside, all that remained was the tepid tea in her cup that tasted like Heaven. "We must make some decisions, Joanna," Zou Tun said. His voice was coarse, and he winced as he spoke.

"Your throat still hurts. Why?"

He shrugged, trying to appear casual. "My punishment."

"But I forgave you."

He nodded. "It appears I have not forgiven myself."

She blinked, wishing with all her heart that she understood even a fraction of the mysticism he knew. "There is just so much to learn."

He reached out, stroking a finger across her cheek, his expression infinitely sad. "I would teach you, Joanna Crane."

"But . . . ?" she prompted.

He sighed. "But we won't have the time."

Joanna leaned back against the cushions, her eyes narrowing. She folded her arms. "All right, Zou Tun. I am sick to death of cryptic statements. What is going on? Why is the imperial army after you?"

His expression went flat, but his voice remained level. "I have already told you. The emperor suspected my monastery was training traitors, people who wished to overthrow the government."

"But you weren't, right?"

His shoulders stiffened in outrage. "Of course not!"

"So why—"

"Because they killed everyone, Joanna. Rebellious or not, they are all dead." His voice was heavy, and his eyes slid to the coverlet.

"Except you." She bit her lip, wondering if what she suspected was true. It couldn't possibly be. Zou Tun was a gentle soul. And though he was trained in the fighting ways of the Shaolin, she had never seen him kill. Certainly he couldn't have caused the death of innocents; it simply wasn't his way.

Unless, of course, the decision was taken out of his hands.

"You were a spy, weren't you? You were sent there to root out and destroy the insurgents."

He didn't deny it. He looked at his hands and they twitched—as if he were petrifying them by an act of will—and a single tear dropped between them.

Joanna stared at the darkened circle on his pants,

her breath catching in her throat. It stunned her to see him cry. She hadn't seen any man cry—ever. Not even her father when he was burying his wife and son.

But Zou Tun cried. He sat in silent misery, tears slipping down his cheeks.

Then she remembered his words. Monk's words, but true nonetheless: *Embrace the feelings, for they are part of you. And then allow them to pass through.*

Except, of course, the misery wasn't passing through Zou Tun. It was engulfing him. He was drowning in it.

"You didn't know about the attack, did you? You would never have destroyed an entire monastery."

"They burned everything. The temple. The holy artifacts. I saved three scrolls. But no one was left alive."

"Why didn't they take you? Why weren't you killed?"

He looked up, and for the first time ever she saw hell. Not the Christian hell of fire and brimstone. What she saw in Zou Tun's eyes was more than misery. It was agony and remorse and a guilt so huge it threatened to swallow her. It had long since consumed him.

"What happened, Zou Tun? You must tell me all."

He shook his head, his mouth open as if he wanted to speak but couldn't. She wrapped her arms around him, drawing him down to the mattress. Resting his head on her breast, she whispered to him. She told him a secret she had not even admitted to herself. But she said it to him, because it was true. And because he needed to hear it.

"I love you, Zou Tun. I will not abandon you now, no matter what happens. Or whatever has happened."

She felt his entire body still. He didn't breathe. He didn't even look at her. He simply froze. His tears dried.

"I know you think it's not possible," she continued. "After all, I'm a white barbarian. And a flighty one at that."

"No," he whispered.

"Why else would I have abandoned the Tigress compound? Why else would I have taken you here to my father's house and pretended we are married?" She lifted his face, turning it so he could see the truth in her eyes. "Because I love you." She tried to smile, but she knew the gesture was weak. "It doesn't make sense, I know. But I do."

"But there is no future for us," he said, his voice anguished.

"I know," she lied. "Because I'm a barbarian." She said the words, but inside her heart was breaking. In truth, she didn't know why it wasn't possible. Why couldn't an heir to the imperial throne marry a white woman? Why couldn't they find somewhere they could be happy together?

"You are not a barbarian to me. But to others, Joanna, you are an invader. I am a Manchurian prince. There are those who would kill you—kill us both—for being together even once." He pushed up. "Do you not understand? Our peoples are at war!"

"Not war," she defended. "We're—"

"The whites come into our harbor with gunboats and demand reparations and territory. You pollute our people with opium and preach your religion. Even the Fists cry, 'Kill the barbarians,' as often as they cry for the end of the empire. Is that not a war?"

She swallowed. Perhaps it was war. How easy it had been in the seclusion of their little bedroom to forget the vast differences between the Chinese and Americans, that he was part of a monarchy and she believed in a democracy. That this was his country, and her people were the ones who had come here with guns demanding open ports.

"What do you feel, Zou Tun? What do you want?"

He dropped his head wearily on the pillow, his gaze vague. "I want to forget."

She kissed him—on the mouth, as she had never done before. She pressed her lips to his, but with no understanding of what to do. She only felt his mouth as hard flesh and teeth so hot as to sear her skin.

Or at least so he felt. She knew it was the strength of his qi that burned. The heat from his yang fire had built up so strongly in him. But still, she did not expect it, and so she drew back on a gasp.

He pursued her. He pressed his body forward, following her down. And then there was nowhere for her to go. His mouth descended toward her, but did not quite close the distance. Instead she felt his tongue tease the edges of her lips, then slip into the small opening between them.

And all the while she felt his yang heat. She felt it build within him, surrounding her, until her yin began to answer the call. She felt her breasts begin to tingle, her legs begin to weaken.

And still he had done no more than tickle the inside of her lips.

Finally she could stand it no more. "Kiss me," she breathed.

He did. His mouth descended onto hers, his tongue shooting forward, opening her wider as it began to thrust and dance inside her.

It was a marvelous feeling; exciting, erotic, and amazing. She recognized the rising yin tide in her blood, the hunger that made her own tongue dart and duel with his. How easy it would be to join him in this forgetfulness. How tempting to simply let their yin and yang merge as they would, and leave the rest to the outside world.

How easy it would be.

But she shouldn't. They shouldn't. And most especially, he couldn't.

She pushed him away. It took a great deal of her strength, but in the end he pulled back, his expression dazed and confused.

"Do you remember my dream, Zou Tun? The one about your qi leaking out of you? How if you didn't stop it, you would die?"

He frowned and tried to return to her mouth, but she pushed him away.

"Do you remember, Zou Tun?"

Eventually understanding came to his eyes. They narrowed and focused before closing completely on his sigh.

"Joanna—"

"Tell me all of it, Zou Tun. For your own sake, tell me what happened."

"They captured me."

> *29 July, 1896*
> *Dearest Brother,*
>   *Father will delay no longer. My wedding will occur at the first moon. You must return home by then. All in Heaven and on Earth wish to see you then. Indeed, I fear for Father's health if you do not return soon.*
>
>   *In prayer,*
>   *Wen Ji*

Decoded translation:

> Dear Son,
>   Our situation grows most tenuous and I

must show the emperor progress. I will attack at the next full moon. You must show yourself as a loyal and devoted son. If you do not, I cannot guarantee your survival.

In anger,
General Kang

The best way to govern is through nonaction—allowing people to follow their natures and live in their own way. When everything is accomplished without people even knowing anything was attempted, that is when we can say it was naturally so.

—Lao Tzu

Chapter Fifteen

Zou Tun tried not to wince as he spoke. The pain was growing. His throat was parched and scratchy. But Joanna was relentless in her questions. She deserved much, this fiery woman, but he did not owe her this story, this explanation.

And yet, despite the needles in his throat, the words pushed to be released. Like dark pus from a festering wound, these words would come out one way or another. He only harmed himself by holding back.

But still it was hard. So very, very hard.

"It was at night."

"Were you sleeping?" Her words were a soft caress, a whisper that warmed his chilled skin. He closed his eyes, trying to isolate the feeling of her breath across his cheek. He succeeded but only partially, and the sensation was a welcome distraction.

"I was meditating. The sounds didn't reach me until too late. Much too late."

She reached out her long, slender fingers and caressed his neck. She was trying to take the sting out of her question, but he flinched nonetheless.

"Did you know? You were a spy there, right? So you must have known."

He shook his head, trying to deny it. "I wrote to my father. I told him not to come." But he had known the attack was imminent. When had his father ever changed his mind? So Zou Tun had gone to the abbot, tried to get him to put up a guard or some defenses. But Abbot Tseng was a good and holy man. He had no understanding of how politics could interfere with the search for enlightenment.

Abbot Tseng had not been raised in Peking.

"Your father? What did he do?" Joanne pressed.

"My father is General Kang." He lifted his gaze to look at her. "The one who is chasing me."

He felt the shock of his words in her. Their bodies were pressed so intimately together that he felt the muscles of her stomach tense, could see the shift of her shoulders as she flinched.

"Your father wants to kill you?" He could tell that she did not understand such a thing. The worst her own father would do—*had done*—was abandon her.

"My father is a general fighting a losing war against invaders from beyond our borders and insurgents within. There is no room in his army for a disobedient soldier."

"But—"

He cut off her objection. "And no place in his heart for a *bu xiao* son."

She frowned at the strange words, and he marveled again how these foreigners could imagine they understood the Chinese when they did not even comprehend the most basic concepts. "Unfilial. Disobedient," he explained. "The Chinese have no use for a man who disregards the duty of a son to his father, a man to his emperor. That is the correct order of things, and the only way a civilized society can survive."

"But you didn't follow it? You told your father not to attack the monastery?"

"I told him I would not go home."

He didn't dare open his eyes. He didn't dare look to see her reaction to a man who would abandon father and country to hide in a monastery. Except he hadn't been hiding. He had been studying. Learning. He had . . . "All I have ever wanted was to study the sacred texts. To learn and understand the Tao as taught by Lao Tzu, as championed by scholars and monks for thousands of years." He felt tears grow behind his eyelids, the weakness of a man who had no wish for warfare. "He knew. My father knew, and so he came and destroyed it all."

"My God," Joanna whispered. "He would destroy an entire monastery just because—"

"He thought they were insurgents!" Zon Tun hissed.

"He thought you were abandoning him." Her voice was cold and hard, crueler than he had ever heard.

"No. You don't understand."

She sighed, pressing her lips to his forehead. "Yes, Zou Tun, I do understand. Even we white barbarians have a hierarchy. A daughter obeys her father." Her gaze grew abstract as she looked away. "You cannot know the anger, the ugliness from my father whenever I disobeyed him."

"He would never kill you."

She shook her head. "No, I don't suppose he would. But then, your father didn't kill you."

"My father wasn't there." Indeed, he almost wished his father had been. That the general had killed him and ended the war between them. But that wasn't what happened.

"But if your father didn't spare you, who did?"

He shook his head. "You don't understand the Chinese. When a temple is destroyed, when a group of revolutionaries is discovered, they are all killed except one."

"You?"

He nodded.

But he hadn't been spared the ultimate betrayal. They'd pulled a beaten and bloodied abbot before him, dragged the last and the best of the Shaolin, too. They'd made Zou Tun confess that he had been the one to do this, to call the soldiers, to destroy everything the good Abbot Tseng had built.

"They showed him my letters, Joanna," he whispered. "They told him I had done this to him. Then they sliced open his belly. I held him as he died. As he whispered his sister's name." That was how he'd known to take anything that survived to Shi Po. That was why he had come to Shanghai.

She had no words to comfort him. Indeed, there were none to give. He had caused it all.

"It's not your fault, Zou Tun."

"But—"

She pressed her hand to his lips. "It is not your fault."

He kissed her fingers. Kissed them in thanks and in blessing. And then he sighed. "There is more."

She pulled her fingers away, setting her hand lightly upon his chest. He felt it there, a warm, soothing presence. It helped once again to distract him from the words he was saying.

"They left me alive to tell the others, to spread the word to any other temples who think to train warriors against the empire. That is how it is done in China. One is left alive to tell the tale."

"They didn't know who you were?"

He shrugged. "I do not know. But they treated me as only the last and weakest, the one left standing to spread the tale." His shame burned through him, leaving him weak and helpless. Weak until she kissed him. Helpless until she spoke.

"But you didn't go to another temple. You went to . . ."

"The Tigress's home. Yes."

"But—" She cut off her words, clearly afraid of what he might have done.

"She is in no danger. The general will not believe that women could be powerful enough to threaten the government. And Shi Po is smart enough to appear weak and subservient." He sighed. "Besides, the general is interested only in me now." Then his heart froze as he looked at her. "And in any distraction I may have from my duty."

"You mean me."

He nodded, unable to deny it. "I must leave you, Joanna. I must leave you here and never return. You are not safe until—"

She stopped his words again. This time she used her lips, not her fingers. Her kiss was strong and abrupt but no less stirring for its aggressiveness. But when he would have continued, she pulled away.

"I will not abandon you," she said.

"Joanna—"

"Tell me the rest, Zou Tun. There is more. I know it."

He stared at her, marveling. How could she know him so well?

"Zou Tun—"

"I went to the Tigress, Joanna, not to any of the other temples. Not to the ones they meant me to go to."

"But—"

"I will not tell the tale, Joanna. No one knows. No

287

one but you. And the Tigress, because the abbot was her brother."

She looked at him, her brow creasing as she struggled to understand. She couldn't, of course. As intelligent as she was, there were things in China no foreigner could understand.

"Nonaction," she whispered. "To rule without appearing to rule. You—"

He gasped, lifting up off the bed as he stared at her. How could she know?

"I have always loved philosophy, Zou Tun. And the works of Lao Tzu are famous throughout China."

"But how could you have studied?"

She shrugged. "I have lived here many years. A bored rich girl can buy many things. Even Chinese tutors."

She did understand. She knew that he had joined the rebellion in his own way. That he had indeed become one of the people who waited in silence for the corrupt empire to fall. And yet he did not. He could not.

How could he wish for the end of everything he held dear? His family? His country? His emperor?

Abruptly he sat up, pushing her aside with the coverlet. "I must leave, Joanna. It is not safe here."

"What?" She scrambled to her knees, her mouth open.

"I must go."

"Why?"

"Because—"

"Don't tell me it's dangerous. You're perfectly safe here. At least for the moment."

He shook his head. "My father—"

"—cannot come stomping through the foreign concessions. It would upset too many people. You know that."

He did. But how to explain the pounding need to move, to leave? To stop thinking.

"You're running away again. You're running from your father. From your temple. From me—"

"You make me think too much!" The words exploded out of him without thought. They were loud and painful in his throat, and made his eyes sting. Any other woman would have shrunk from his anger. She would have turned aside and made herself pleasing. But not Joanna. She was made of much sterner stuff.

She simply looked at him, her expression patient—and sad. "What do I make you think?"

He shook his head. "Do you know what it is to be without a name? Without a country?"

She almost laughed. He could see the humor sparkling in her eyes, but her voice remained deadly serious. "I have not lived in America for ten years. I have read all their papers that I could find. I have written letters until my hands were black with ink. And I try, Zou Tun, I try to remember what it was like there. But I cannot."

He saw the pain in her eyes and knew she understood in part. But not fully. "For a Chinese man family is everything. It is who we are."

"But you are not Chinese. You're Manchurian."

He sighed. "In this, we are one and the same."

"Except maybe more," she mused, her expression inscrutable. "After all, you are heir to the throne."

"No!" he gasped. Then he said it again more firmly. "No. I am only one cousin of many. Others could take the throne if the emperor dies. And I do not want the imperial throne."

"But your father wants it, doesn't he? Or he wants you on it?"

Zou Tun shook his head. "My father wants whatever he can get. If that is the throne, all the better."

She touched his cheeks, soothing him with a single stroke of her delicate fingers. "What do *you* want, Zou Tun?"

He shook his head. "In China, a man's wishes are less important than his family's needs and his country's requirements. How else can we hold back the barbarian tide?"

"With guns? A modern army? Or, here's a thought: Why not take Lao Tzu's advice? Rule through nonaction. Do nothing. Let the countries fall where they may."

"And if it means the destruction of China?"

She sighed. "Then it means the destruction of China."

He flinched at her bald statement, but she didn't stop there. She leaned forward, her eyes piercing in their intensity.

"You are only one man, Zou Tun. You cannot save China by yourself. Especially since . . ." Her voice trailed away. But he wanted to have it all. To have her say it all.

"Especially if . . ."

"Especially if you have no interest in politics and no aptitude for it."

There, she had said it—flat-out, with barely an apology in her eyes. He had no ability in politics. No aptitude, and even less interest.

"But I was raised to be a great general."

"And I was raised to be a rich, pampered woman. But I don't want to be pampered. And you don't want to be an undercover spy or a leader of armies, do you?"

He could not deny it. "No. I was successful only when I led monks. In prayer."

She shifted, this time tucking her knees up under

her as she rose above him. Her hair fell in glorious disarray around her face—a beautiful distraction—but she pushed it impatiently out of her eyes. "I have a question for you, Zou Tun. One that you may not be able to answer."

He nodded, curious and wary.

"What would Lao Tzu counsel? The founder of Taoism, what would he tell you was more important—the affairs of a nation, or of one man?"

Zou Tun frowned, having never thought of his religion in this manner. "I believe he would say that if the heart and mind of every man were in natural order, then there would be no need to govern the nation."

She grinned. "Exactly."

"No, not exactly! The hearts and minds of China are not in natural order. They are not pure or in harmony. In fact, the disharmony cries out to Heaven!"

"And how will causing your own disharmony help, Zou Tun? How will becoming exactly what your father wants—a political force—help anyone?"

He closed his eyes, his heart and mind torn in two. She was offering him everything he wanted, holding up Lao Tzu and the sacred texts as an example for him to follow. But no Chinese scholar or immortal ever proposed disobedience to father and emperor. None suggested that he should pursue his own ends at the cost of his father's. And perhaps the nation's.

She interrupted his thoughts, her voice persuasive. "What skills can you offer the emperor? Truly, Zou Tun, he doesn't need another bad general. What can you offer your country?"

He shook his head. At last the truth fell from his lips. "Nothing," he said. "I have nothing to offer."

"Oh, Zou Tun," she said, her eyes shimmering with tears. "That's not true. You can be a leader of men."

"I can't!"

"Yes, you can. You can lead men to be in harmony with their nature. You can teach the sacred scrolls. You can lead in prayer and bring the people back to a rightness with all. That's what you can do." She leaned forward, pressing a kiss to his forehead. "That's what you want to do, isn't it?"

How to answer when his mind was in chaos? How to think when her breasts dangled just above him? And how to believe he could still serve his country—and serve well—when he had always been taught the opposite?

He shook his head. "I don't know. I . . ." He closed his eyes. "I just don't know."

She sighed, and he felt her settle back beside him. "You do know. You just don't want to believe it is possible."

He opened his eyes to find her beside him, her lips a few bare inches from his. "What do I know of enlightenment? I know what Abbot Tseng taught, but it did not save his monastery from being destroyed. I know what the Tigress Shi Po teaches. But I cannot control my body. I cannot even look at you without thinking . . ." His voice trailed away, but she would not let him stop.

"Without thinking what, Zou Tun?"

"Without thinking that I have no control over my dragon whatsoever. And that to be a monk, I should. I must. Except, with you . . ." He reached up, roughly pulling her down to him, pressing his lips to hers, devouring her mouth with his own. And when he was finished, he relaxed his hold. "Except with you," he continued, "I have no control at all."

She blinked, and he was vain enough to be pleased by her dazed look. But all too soon she focused again. "And to be a good monk—"

"A Jade Dragon. In the tradition of the Tigress."

She nodded. "To be a Jade Dragon, you must be able to control your yang fire. You must be able to direct it, just as I need to learn to direct my yin tide."

It wasn't a question, but he answered it nonetheless. "Yes. But I have no faith that it can be done."

She nodded, her expression thoughtful. "Then we must find your faith, Zou Tun."

He almost laughed. She sounded as if she would discover it under the bed, or in a forgotten pair of pants.

"It can be done, Zou Tun. We just have to find a way." She began to smile, a slow, sensual expression that made his dragon leap in response. "Perhaps we should work on finding you enlightenment tonight."

He swallowed. He did not think he was proof against her determination. Certainly not when she looked so delighted by the prospect. Still, honesty forced him to tell her the truth. Before she could lean into him, before he felt her lips against his, he told her what would happen.

"We will do whatever you wish tonight, Joanna. But in the morning I will leave."

"But—"

He shook his head. "No. I will not endanger you."

She swallowed, her eyes stricken. "Where will you go?'

"Somewhere that is not here. Perhaps even to Peking to lay my case before the emperor. I could tell him everything and then let him decide."

She sighed, dropping her head onto his shoulder. "And if he should decide to kill you?"

Zou Tun shrugged, knowing death was a real possibility. "Then I will accept his judgment."

"And what of *your* judgment?"

He laughed, extending his hand to her beautiful

curls. "My judgment is faulty. Have I not just explained that to you?"

She sighed. "Your judgment is just fine. It is the rest of the world that is faulty." And so saying, she turned her lips to his. Then they began to practice.

Except that when they kissed, he felt a change. And when her hands stroked over his dragon, the caress was different. He had no name for it, only that her touch was warmer, her kisses more passionate.

Before she could do more than take hold of his dragon, he stopped her, his hand over hers, his eyes searching her face. "What are you doing? Why does this feel different?"

She froze, slowly lifting her hand away. "This is wrong?"

He shook his head. "No. It is better. But why?"

She looked down at him, her eyes unfocused. "I don't . . ." Then she bit her lip, extending her free hand to trail a fiery caress down his chest. "Yes," she murmured softly. "This is different."

He lifted her hand to his lips. "Yes, but why?"

"Because it is done with love. Zou Tun, that is the answer. That is what the Tigress Shi Po didn't understand."

He frowned. "Joanna—"

"You said it yourself—that she doesn't fully understand what she teaches."

"No one can. Not even the great teachers. That is the nature of the Tao."

She nodded. "Well, this is something Shi Po doesn't understand. That this"—she leaned over and kissed his chin when he would not give her his lips—"this is better when done with love."

He shook his head, denying it even though part of him wondered if she could be right. "They teach that you are *not* to get attached. That the Tigress uses—"

She pressed her finger to his lips. "Then they teach it wrong."

"But—"

She shook her head. "I am sure of this, Zou Tun."

He sighed, gently pulling her hand away from his mouth. "Only novices are sure. The masters know that nothing is permanent. Nothing is assured."

"The Tao is permanent. God is assured. And love is—" She cut off her words with a sigh. "You do not trust anything, Zou Tun. And so perhaps we should try an experiment."

He arched his brow, waiting and wondering what her incredible mind would think up next.

"Touch me, Zou Tun."

He grinned and reached out to stroke her breasts. They had been tempting him for an eternity. But she stopped him, holding his hand just shy of her flushed skin.

"With love, Zou Tun. Try, for a moment, to touch me with love."

He froze, his insides clenching. She could not be suggesting it. She could not ask for him to love her. It was impossible. He was a Manchurian prince. She was a white barbarian. He couldn't possibly love her. And yet, when she looked at him, her bronze eyes clouded because of his hesitation, his heart squeezed painfully in his chest. How could he hurt her like this? How could he deny her so simple a thing?

After all, he could touch a pet dog with love. A hurt animal in the wood. Even his fellow monks had been treated with a kind of love. Why not her? Why not allow himself to feel for her?

So he did. He allowed himself to revel in the wonder that was Joanna. He saw not only her rounded breasts with the dusky rose nipples, but also the warmth that was Joanna, which heated her skin and filled those breasts with pure, wonderful yin. He allowed himself to touch her white thighs, stroking them with a tenderness that had nothing to do with how beautifully firm they were, but with how her legs were strong because she made them so. And when he kissed her shivering belly, trailing ever lower, he closed his eyes, knowing that he was kissing the woman Joanna, and not the line between yin centers.

And then he found himself at the entrance to her cinnabar cave, smelling her spice and tasting her sweetness. And he froze in fear. It was a ridiculous place to be immobilized with terror, but he was. He had no explanation for it. Above him, Joanna's gasping breaths began to slow. Her body began to still. He knew now was the time to push her to the yin crest. Now was her time.

But he could not.

Because he wanted more. He wanted to be with her when she crested. To be inside her. To feel her around him, but most important, to give her everything he had of himself. Not the Manchurian princely part, not even the Shaolin monk, but the whole of him.

She had recovered her breath and was lifting her head to look at him, a question in her eyes. But he didn't answer. Suddenly he knew what he wanted. What he had always wanted. Perhaps he couldn't always have it. He would not likely be here longer than tonight. But for this one moment, this one time, he would do it all. As he wanted. As she wanted. For them.

He pulled himself off of her, looking down into her eyes, and said not the words she wanted, but the words he needed to say.

"I cannot marry you, Joanna. There are too many

obstacles. But I can give you everything I am. I can bind myself to you as I have to no other woman."

She blinked, clearing the yin haze to focus upon him. "I don't understand," she said.

"I wish to give you my child."

The underlying substance of the universe is nothingness.
From nothing came Heaven and Earth.
From Heaven and Earth came the myriad things.
Finally giving rise to the world as we know it.

—Lao Tzu

Chapter Sixteen

Joanna stared, unsure she had heard him properly. He obviously saw her confusion, because he went on to explain.

"This is not 'practice,' Joanna. This is . . . this is the most I can do to save you. To share myself with you."

"But . . ." She couldn't even form the words; there were too many questions.

"You are nearing your fertility. I can feel it. If I give myself to you now, you may conceive a child. I will declare you my concubine. If it is a girl child, you will have status and yet still pose little threat." He paused and sighed. "Of course, if it is a boy and my heir"—his expression grew tortured—"then you will be in even more danger. There will be many who do not want a half-white son as a possible successor."

He fell silent, thinking. Joanna could only stare, her mind reeling. A child? With Zou Tun? The thought sent her soaring into the heights of joy. She found she desperately wanted his child—a little boy with dark hair and serious eyes. Or a little girl with his exotic skin and intelligent mind. Such thoughts took her breath away.

"Do you understand, Joanna? I have two enemies: my father who would put me on the throne and my cousins who would see me barred from it. There is only one way I could become unfit to rule—"

"By openly taking a white lover?" she asked, beginning to follow his thoughts.

He nodded. "And what better way to prove that I consorted with a white woman than to sire a half-breed child? Should the Emperor die, even the most incompetent of my cousins would take the dragon throne before me."

"So your cousins would be thrilled, but what would your father do?"

He shrugged. "Girl children are unimportant. He would ignore such a thing. And my cousins would do much to ensure that child's safety. There is no better way prove my unfitness for the throne."

"But a boy?" she asked, her heart in her throat.

Zou Tun shook his head. "My father would not tolerate a half-white grandson heir. You and the child would have to die."

Joanna swallowed. It was bad enough to think of becoming an unwed mother. But to add such danger to her children would be inexcusable. She couldn't force that on them.

And yet she so desperately wanted to do this.

But she couldn't risk her son. Not even for love.

She sat up, pulling Zou Tun to his knees before her. She kissed him as deeply and passionately as she could. Most of all, she sent him her love. And when she was finished, she said the words aloud so he would truly understand.

"I love you, Zou Tun. With all my heart I want to have children with you." She swallowed her tears, forcing herself to continue. "But I cannot, not even for you, risk the lives of my children." She pulled away then.

He nodded silently, sadness in every line of his body. "You are wise, Joanna."

She shook her head, then called his name to force him to look directly into her eyes. "No, Zou Tun, but I am determined." She lifted her chin. "There will be no half measures between us. If you want to take my virginity, to give me a child, then you will have to marry me. You will have to stay with me forever and to protect that boy or girl child from whatever comes. You will have to do that."

"I . . . cannot." His voice was anguished. "I cannot abandon my family and my country. I am a Manchurian prince. I cannot give up everything I am. Even for love. Even for you."

"Then, my love"—she dropped her head against his forehead—"there can be no child. And no—"

"I will give myself to you, Joanna. I will give my soul to you in every touch, every caress. But . . ." He sighed. "But you are right. There can be no child."

So saying, he touched her. He began with her breasts, lifting them with his hands, drawing the nipples to a tight point with his tongue. Joanna felt her yin tide begin to rise, boiling through her blood and setting flash fires across her skin. Her body shuddered with the power, her breasts dancing in his hands.

He grinned as she moved, whispering directly against her right nipple, "That was your fear being thrown off your body. Let us see if I can help you purify even further." He pressed her down on the bed, his tongue roving in circles around her breast while his other hand continued to mold and tweak in echo of his mouth.

Joanna moaned in sweet hunger, but her eyes were

on Zou Tun, her hand caressing the softness of his nearly bald head. "I want more," she whispered.

He paused, then began to shift his hand down her belly. "More?"

She shook her head. "Not more for me. More of you." She abruptly sat up, pushing him down onto the bed as she moved. She shifted, placing her head lower on his body, in line with his dragon. She had easy access now as she gripped it. Extending her tongue, she began to play with him as he had done with her, swirling her tongue around his dragon head, cupping the twin houses of his dragon seed with one hand while she circled his jade stem with the other. He groaned, his body jerking in his own kind of shuddering response.

"Was that fear you just released?" she asked.

"No," he whispered against her thigh. "It was awe."

He began his own explorations, pushing his head between her thighs and they began to move in concert. As she sucked on his dragon, he pushed his fingers deep inside her. As she tongued the underside of his dragon head, he licked her pearl. She felt his yang power mixing with her rising yin all the while, for her yin poured a stream into his swirling yang. They were like a single circle, flowing into each other, power pouring between them. But they were not one, merely two joined together.

She felt him begin to crest. She knew he was close, just as she was. Her body was tightening. His dragon was pulsing. His fingers were hard and thick inside her, twisting and pushing, making those tiny circles that pushed on her pearl.

"It is time," he gasped, his breath sending shivers across her skin.

"Yes," she whispered. She gripped his dragon. She

knew what he wanted her to do, and her legs trembled with the force of anticipation.

"Now."

One word, and then they bent to their tasks. She wrapped her mouth around his dragon, sucking hard. He pressed his fingers deep into her, their tiny circles becoming a tight pinpoint of power. She extended her tongue, rolling circles around his dragon head. Once. Twice. A third time. He imitated the motion around her pearl.

"Now," she echoed.

And together, they tightened their lips and sucked. Once.

They exploded.

Together.

But it did not end there.

The crest continued. The yin tide raised her higher and higher as her body convulsed, and he continued to thrust.

They soared, higher, happier, more joyfully.

Heaven.

They were in Heaven! At least, that was how it looked to her. Dark black sky was everywhere, even below their feet. And there were tiny dots of stars swinging like lanterns all around them. Such beauty!

"Where are we?" she whispered.

"I don't know," he answered. Which was when she realized she hadn't really spoken out loud at all. She had thought the words, and he had apparently heard.

She took a deep breath, pulling her joy inside. And then she remembered.

"I know this place. I remember it. From that first night of practice."

Beside her, she saw Zou Tun turn. "You came here?"

She nodded. "For a moment. It felt . . ." She opened

302

herself to it, feeling the wonder fill her soul. "Yes, felt like this."

Heaven began to change. Directly before them the darkness grew lighter. It parted, and a being of impossible beauty stood before them. She was an angel. Joanna knew it with a certainty that left no room for doubt.

And then that glorious creature spoke.

"Welcome, Joanna. Welcome, Zou Tun. We have been waiting for you, and are so pleased you could come."

"We are dead, then." Zou Tun's horrible words did not sound frightened. Perhaps he was relieved. Perhaps he was finally at peace.

The angel laughed, a beautiful and joyous sound that made the heavens shimmer and vibrate. "No, Zou Tun. When you die, you will go to a much grander place than this. You will go to Heaven." She gestured to the side, and the darkness faded long enough for Joanna to glimpse something so much more than here. And yet, how could anything be better than this?

"This is not Heaven?" she asked.

"This is merely the first step—the Antechamber. You must have total commitment before you can attain Heaven. But now you are here, very much alive and very much in need."

Joanna wanted to step forward. She wanted to ask so many things. But she was held transfixed—not by fear, but by awe. So the angel came to her; she seemed to glide forward until they both were bathed in her radiance.

"We wish you to remember," the angel said.

"Remember what?" Both Joanna and Zou Tun spoke, both striving to please.

"Who you really are."

And with that, the angel touched them both. A single finger pressed into each of their chests, right above their hearts.

Joanna didn't know what she expected—a memory, perhaps, buried in her mind. A message disregarded. Something small but lost.

She was right. And she was wrong. This was not something small. It was big. Huge. And so fundamental that she could not believe she had forgotten. But she had. What she had forgotten was there, deep within her, but buried beneath a life's debris. And it was so simple, she couldn't believe she had forgotten it.

Love.

It was one word. But it was not just that she was loved—by God, by Zou Tun, by her father and friends. No, it was more than that.

She was a being of love.

All the tiny pieces of herself—her body, her soul, her heart and mind—all of those things were made up of love. That was the core of who she was; that was at the center of everything. She was a creature of love—created by love to embody love, and to express love in all its myriad forms.

She had merely forgotten.

As had everyone else. Because they, too—Zou Tun, her father, every soul on the planet—came from the same source. They all had the same center of love.

They all had merely forgotten.

She heard Zou Tun exclaim, a mirror of her own astonishment. In front of them, the angel smiled in such a way as to make all of Heaven sing.

"How—"

"We—"

Zou Tun and Joanna stammered, their minds reeling. Questions formed, only to be cut off, to surrender to the simple truth: They were creatures of love.

"We are so pleased that you remember," the angel

said. Then she kissed them both, a warm blessing on their foreheads.

And then it was over.

Joanna woke with a start, her body languidly at rest against Zou Tun's thigh. She felt him wake at the same instant, lifting up with a gasp.

They looked at each other. In his eyes she saw the echo of her awe, her confusion. And the memory. That beautiful memory was still shining through his entire body.

"Was it a dream?" she whispered.

He shook his head. "That was no dream. Was it?"

"No. It wasn't a dream," she agreed.

They moved as one, straightening, reorienting. She settled into his arms almost at the moment he opened them. She took comfort in the steady beat of his heart, but her mind remained in turmoil.

"It was real," she said.

He nodded, his arms tightening around her. He didn't speak. And so they remained while dawn lightened the sky.

"Lao Tzu didn't say anything about love."

Joanna lifted her head so she could look at Zou Tun's face.

"Lao Tzu," he continued, "the immortal who founded Taoism—he spoke about the myriad things. That the myriad things came from nothing." He looked at Joanna, and she could see anguish in his eyes. "He didn't say the myriad things are made of love. He didn't say we are beings of love."

"Maybe he didn't know."

It was a simple thought, and an obvious one. But it made Zou Tun shake, his body trembling with his confusion. "I cannot know more than Lao Tzu. I . . . He . . ."

"He is the founder of Taoism. And do you still feel his teachings are true?"

Zou Tun nodded. "Of course. Even more so. But—"

"But he didn't speak of love. And he didn't practice what the Tigresses teach, did he?" She shifted, sitting up to face him more fully. "We build upon what our forefathers knew. We learn more based on what they understood. Why can't we have discovered something that even the great Lao Tzu didn't know?"

His eyes misted as they looked at her. "Because we didn't discover it. We *remembered* it."

He wasn't making any sense. And yet he did make sense. Like her, he was reeling from the enormity of what they had just learned. "It is only our minds that are confused. Our hearts remember." She was speaking aloud. To herself. To him.

He responded, "My heart is so full. I cannot say it any other way." He looked down at her. "I love you."

Her chest squeezed tight. "I love you, too." She said the words. Felt the emotion. Knew that what she experienced was real. But his words didn't mean what she wanted them to. His love was the overwhelming love they both felt. For all things. At the moment she loved the trees and the birds and the squirrels as well.

What she felt for Zou Tun was different. It was more, and it was unique for him.

His love was not. She could see it in his eyes, in the abstract way he looked through her. He was not in love with her. He simply loved all.

And that thought cut a deep hole in her heart.

"What?" he asked. "Why do you look sad?"

She swallowed her tears, blinking as if coming out of a daze. "It is nothing," she lied. And with those words so much of her experience, of her memories, of their experience, faded. She felt it go, mourned its loss, and even knew the cause. Lies only buried truth.

She pulled away from Zou Tun, feeling ashamed of herself, saddened by her loss, and most of all confused and disoriented. She so wanted to return to Heaven. She wanted to feel all that love again. She wanted to be with the angels.

And yet she knew now that she didn't deserve such knowledge. Not when she abandoned it so easily.

"I want to go back there," he said. "I want to try again. Right now."

She nodded, agreeing with the sentiment. It was easy to agree, for she could hear in his voice that they could not attempt it right away. He continued, confirming her thoughts.

"But it is almost morning. I cannot remain here."

"What are you going to do?"

He took a deep breath. "I cannot be a general. I cannot join the military. Not now. Not after . . ."

"Not after remembering." No creature of love could lead men to kill other men. The very thought was repulsive.

"I will talk to the emperor. He must understand. He must remember."

She straightened, turning to look at him, to see if she guessed correctly. "You're going to tell him what happened? Who we are?" She shook her head, struggling with the words. "I mean . . . who we all are?"

He nodded. "Manchurian or Han, Chinese or barbarian, we are all the same. All the myriad things are the same." He looked down at her, his eyes still bright with the kiss of Heaven. She admired him for that. Admired and envied him for keeping what she had so casually thrown away. "We are filled with love."

But when he said it, she remembered. She felt truth again. "Yes," she whispered. "We are."

He looked at her, his eyes lingering long upon her face. She thought he would kiss her, but he made no move to do so. He simply looked at her, his entire being glowing with the force of his love.

She could not stop the tears that began to flow from her eyes. Was it wrong for her to want his attention, his wonderful love to be a little stronger for her? For him to love her a little better, more personally, more uniquely? Was it wrong for her to wish for that?

"Joanna, why are you crying?"

She bit her lip, unable to lie again and yet unwilling to diminish his joy. He still held Heaven's love; he still embodied it as she might never again. She would do nothing to take that from him.

She pressed her lips to his, pouring all of her needs and hopes and most especially the last of her heavenly love into him. He took it, returning it a thousandfold. But when she would have clung to him, when she would have pushed for deeper contact, he pulled away.

"I must leave, Joanna. I will return as soon as I can."

She nodded, forcing her mind back to earth, back to the mundane issues of travel and money and soldiers.

"I know just what to do," she said, and she pushed away from him. It took all her strength to leave him. Indeed, her knees buckled as she stepped onto the floor. Fortunately she was able to catch herself on the bed. And if she had missed, his arm was there as well, nearly touching her, nearly saving her.

She drew away.

"Leave the details to me," she said. She didn't look at him. And with a coldness that hadn't been inside her twenty minutes before, she straightened and walked away.

Zou Tun shook his head, his mind reeling. Joanna was an amazing woman. With no more time than it had taken for him to dress and wash, she had two horses saddled, and money and provisions pulled together. The servant who was supposed to tell him of his father's movements had reported to Joanna instead, and now Joanna was writing a letter to her father, her beautiful face pulled into a tight, blank expression.

He missed her smile. Already he missed her touch, her caress, and her generosity of spirit. After all he had done to her, she still could look at him with love. True love. For him.

Even his throat pain had ended. Because she loved him.

That thought overwhelmed him. Even his Manchurian arrogance was humbled by her spirit. But that did not mean he could take her with him, live with her in harmony and bliss. Yet he didn't want to start that argument just yet. He wanted his leavetaking to be sweeter than that. Especially as his soul was already crying out at the thought of leaving her behind.

"What do you write to your father?"

She looked up, and for a moment he caught a flash of pain in her eyes. Then she looked down at her letter, hiding her eyes from him as she folded the parchment.

"I told him that I have made my choice." She looked up at him, her expression steely, her voice flat. "I am going with you, Zou Tun."

He stepped forward, wanting to take her into his arms, but she was too far away. "You cannot. If my father catches you, he will kill you." The very words froze his throat.

"What will he do to you?"

Zou Tun shrugged, trying to appear casual. "He is my father."

"And what will your father do to you when he catches you?"

"He will not kill me."

She straightened, coming out from behind her

desk. "Tell me it all, Zou Tun. Do not lie to me. It . . ." She bit her lip. "It will damage you."

He frowned, wanting to know what she meant, but she shook her head. "What will he do to you?"

Zou Tun sighed, knowing she would not stop until he explained everything.

"My father has been positioning me to become the new emperor. He has spent his life with that single goal."

She leaned back, obviously stunned. "You are so close to the throne?"

He nodded. "I am the most logical choice if Emperor Guang Xu dies without an heir."

She blinked, her eyes widening with awe. "You're the 'crown prince'."

He simply shrugged. He didn't understand her English words.

"Then why were you wandering around the country unprotected? Why would he send you to that temple in the first place?"

Zou Tun sighed. "Do you know what it is to live under lock and key? To constantly suspect poison in your food, assassins at your door? I could not stand it anymore. And so I convinced my father to let me go."

"To root out the revolutionaries at the temple," she said. "But also to escape the threats on your life." She nodded.

"Yes, there were threats everywhere. Every morning I woke to fear, ate my meals and made plans rooted in terror, and went to bed in fear. I couldn't stand it anymore."

"Is that the life of an emperor in China?"

He shook his head. "That is the life of the emperor's possible heir." He sighed. "The emperor's life is much, much worse."

"And you hate it."

He shook his head. "It is much worse than just hate, Joanna. I don't *understand* it." He began to pace, his words like bandages finally lifted off a festering wound. "My father sees threats where I see people. My father sees nations and strategies, and I see only people. My father moves armies and conquers enemies; I see only people needing to be helped."

He folded his arms, wishing he could contain his incompetence, to hide it from her. But he wanted to explain this. He wanted to tell her. And so he sat down, letting his words flow in an unbroken stream.

"I understand that a single ambassador represents a nation. It has been explained to me many times. And yet he is one man. How can one man be so important? How can he choose the course of a nation? How can that be right? How can any one man see what should be done for the good of all?"

She tilted her head, looking confused. "But that is the duty of an ambassador. Or a president. Or an emperor."

He nodded. "Yes. That is true. But I would rule as Lao Tzu counsels. By nonaction. By living a moral life and expecting others to follow my example. People should choose their own way."

She frowned, and he could see that she was beginning to understand him. "And if they didn't choose wisely?"

He sighed. "I could not kill the men who attacked you, seeking to rape you until you died." He sighed. "How could I kill a man for simply believing differently than I do, for acting according to his desires and conscience?"

"What if those actions are wrong?"

He stared at her, wishing he could make her understand. "I cannot kill, Joanna. I just can't. I will not take responsibility for choosing the death of another." He saw her eyes widen and knew she was beginning to understand his weakness. So he finished, telling her all. "No ruler of China could ever guide the country with such a flaw. Certainly not now, not with foreign nations seeking to carve us into pieces."

"It is not a flaw!" she argued. "It is honorable and noble and right."

He sighed. "It is weakness in a ruler of a threatened empire."

She nodded, stepping forward to touch him. She gave a simple press of her hand on his arm, but he felt it nonetheless like a soothing balm across his soul's wounds. And he was everlastingly grateful.

"What will your father do if he catches you?" she asked again. "What does he wish to do?"

Zou Tun looked down at her hand, her beautiful white hand against his darker, yellower skin. "He will kill the emperor, put me on the throne, then systematically kill all the foreigners in China."

She gasped. "All that murder! And for what? China doesn't have the defenses. My people's gunboats will decimate your country. We have better guns and soldiers. We will send armies to cut your country into pieces, and there will be nothing left."

He could not deny it. "My father considers that a nobler end—for himself and for China." Then he gripped her hand. "And I would not be able to stop him. He would lock me away and rule in my name. Even if I die, he could keep it so no one would know. He could continue to rule in my stead, pretending that I am still alive."

"That's not possible," she said, but she knew the truth as well as he.

"It *is* possible. And it has been done before in China." She squeezed his hands. "And so you ran."

He nodded. "Without me he cannot assume power. He needs me first, at the beginning, while he consolidates his power."

Joanna kissed him, her lips tender. But then she drew away. "Why has he not already assumed power?" Why has he not put himself in position to—?"

Zou Tun sighed. "The emperor does not like him. And neither does the dowager empress."

"But they like you?"

He nodded. "Yes. For they do not know the extent of my father's ruthlessness. They do not believe that he would use me to gain power, kill them, then lock me away."

She straightened, a look of resolve on her face. "Then we must tell them."

He immobilized her by gripping her hand. "You cannot come, Joanna. I cannot risk you."

"You cannot *stop* me." She leaned forward. "Think, Zou Tun. I have money, horses, connections throughout Shanghai . . . I can get us out into the countryside."

"And then you will—"

"And then I will come with you to Peking, even if I follow alone. Zou Tun, you will not abandon me here."

He straightened, appalled by her suggestion. "There is no abandonment—"

"You are afraid to be seen with a white woman."

"Of course not!"

"You think I am a liability, a detriment to you and your task."

He shook his head. "No, that is—"

She reached out, stroking his cheek. "I am your partner, remember? I will stay with you."

She left no room for argument, and even though he knew it was wrong, he felt himself weakening against her. Her life was at risk as long as they were together. And yet she gave him such strength. Every time she looked at him, he remembered what they had shared. He remembered his time in Heaven and the message he had received.

With her by his side, he had no fear that he would be tempted away by the lure of power. And he had no fear that he would forget he was a creature of love, meant to share that message with all who would listen.

So, even though he knew it was wrong, he decided to agree. He would allow her to remain at his side despite the dangers. It was her right to choose. And he did not wish to be alone. Nor did he wish to forget.

Suddenly, he realized he loved her. And that, he knew, would lead to their deaths.

22 January 1898
Dearest Father,

Do you know that we are all creatures of love? Made of love, existing to express love, and when we die we return to love. It is the truth, and yet as I look at these words I know they convey so little of what I mean. I love. I love all, including you. Most especially you, my father, though when you left me last night you gave me such pain. Such horrible, cutting emptiness.

But I know much more today than I did before. So, despite what has happened, I still honor and revere you as my parent. I love you and always will.

Do you understand that, Father? Nothing you say or do can separate us. I will always love you.

But I will not live with you anymore. I cannot. My future lies in loving and helping a great man. His message is what I have been searching for. Helping him with his work will be my life's work. For we both have the same message, the same goals: to remind all of what we have forgot-

ten. Yes, we are creatures of love, created to express that love, and when we die we return to love. So what shall I fear, my father?

Nothing. Thus, I am leaving you today. I travel to Peking with Zou Tun. We will see the emperor there and help him remember what all have forgotten. I do not know where this path will lead, only that I choose it, and that I walk it with a full heart.

Please love me, Father. And allow me to walk where my heart wills.

In love,
Joanna

People always pursue the outward appearance of things, pursue wholeness and fullness, and because of this they invite contention. We should try to reside in humility and weakness, yielding and retreating. In this way we can attain a realm of noncontention.

—Lao Tzu

Chapter Seventeen

They rode like the wind, covering ground as if Heaven had given their horses wings. Zou Tun watched Joanna for signs of weariness or regret, but she remained a steady companion, neither complaining nor flagging. Truly, she was an amazing woman, and Zou Tun envied her strength.

He, on the other hand, felt his belly tighten with every mile they moved closer to Peking. He found himself eternally listening for his father's men behind him, fretting about the obstacles ahead, and worrying that he would fail Joanna when she most needed him. He knew there was little he could do beyond pushing them with all speed to the emperor's palace in the Forbidden City, but his mind still whirled with the dangers so near.

Even once they arrived in the Forbidden City there would be complications. He had been away a long time. He had no idea how the power now flowed between the emperor and his mother. He knew he must bring his case to the emperor, who had always thought the Western barbarians offered more than his mother acknowledged. But would the dowager empress allow her son to open up the country to more barbarian influence? He had no idea. And taking Joanna into such a politically charged situation was foolhardy at best, suicide at worst.

Joanna tried to soothe him, but he was inconsolable. His only peace came when he wrapped her tightly in his arms, feeling her yin call to his yang. But even that he could not allow, for they both needed rest. There would be no practice until he knew they were safe.

They made it to the capital city in better time than he expected. Joanna's horses were of the best quality, and she was an experienced rider. He wished he could show her the beautiful city in safety. He wished his countrymen could see her for the loving woman she was. But there was no safety for a white person in Peking. In Shanghai the ghost barbarians brought money and commerce; here in the capital, they brought only guns. So he counseled her to remain silent, to keep her face covered and her eyes averted.

She did so without comment, but he could see the pain in her eyes. As he did, she wished for a better world. A place where each man and woman could be who they were. Where every man, woman, and child remembered their heritage as creatures of love.

But that did not exist now. Not here.

They came to the gate of the Forbidden City, nearing the end of their path. For better or for worse. The palace eunuchs recognized him. His father had seen to that long ago. He was allowed to enter. And when they would have forbidden Joanna or killed her where she stood, he stopped them with a single word. They could see his anger, knew his potential power, and so allowed the heresy.

A white woman would be given audience with the

emperor because Kang Zou Tun wished it—unheard of! But such was the fear that his family engendered. Or rather, such was the fear that his father engendered.

Zou Tun and Joanna entered, palace eunuchs scrambling to keep pace. Zou Tun held Joanna tightly to his side as they began to cross the city within a city. He could see her eyes were wide, absorbing everything she could. But she spoke Shanghainese, not Mandarin. She would not understand what was said here.

It was probably just as well. The things said of white barbarians would not be complimentary.

They moved through building after building in the Forbidden City—through the Hall of Supreme Harmony, then another courtyard before the Hall of Perfect Harmony. He'd long since noted the irony of the structures' names. There was no harmony in China, no matter what the ancestors called their ancient buildings.

Next came the Hall of Preserving Harmony, and he made a hard left to head toward the emperor's palace. There they were stopped.

Two eunuchs cut off his approach, while more came from the side. He did not remember these men, did not know to whom they pledged allegiance. And inside the Forbidden City, such ignorance could be lethal. There was nothing he could do but tuck Joanna close behind him while eight eunuchs surrounded them.

They remained respectful, of course; courtesy was everything here. But even as they kowtowed before him, they made it clear he had no choice. He would not be seeing the emperor. Another exalted person requested his attendance.

The dowager empress.

"What is it, Zou Tun?" Joanna whispered.

He tried to smile, but she knew him too well.

"Don't lie to me," she said. "Just tell me the truth."

He nodded, even as the eunuchs began ushering them to an entirely different palace—one he had entered only once before.

"The dowager empress wishes to meet us."

He heard her gasp, but he could tell she did not fully understand the situation. Fortunately they were speaking in the Shanghai dialect. The palace eunuchs likely could not understand, though he was sure the empress would have a eunuch to translate. Here, though, he thought it was safe, so he spoke openly, though he kept his words low and quick.

"There are two main powers in China, and most especially in the Forbidden City. Guang Xu is the emperor. He favors modernization, and though he dislikes the barbarians, he understands their superior weapons."

"But we're not going to see him, are we?"

Zou Tun shook his head. "His mother, the Dowager Empress Cixi, hates what her son has grown to understand—that the foreigners have something of value. One cannot blame her. The barbarians have taken everything from her. She wishes most fervently to see all of them expelled from China."

He heard Joanna sigh, her shoulders drooping. "Then we are finished before we have begun. She will side with your father, for he appears to side with her. She will not hear your words." She swallowed. "She might even kill us outright rather than expose her son to my Western presence."

He nodded, startled that she understood so well. Still, it pained him to expose such bloody realities to her. Assassinations, poisonings, and unjust imprisonments were commonplace within Chinese politics. It had appalled him before he ascended to Heaven's Antechamber. Now he utterly reviled such truth.

And yet he had brought Joanna to the very center of Chinese bloodlust.

"Perhaps she will see your goodness and become an ally," he said.

"Or perhaps she will take one look at my ghost face and scream for the executioner."

He had no response. It was indeed a possibility. But before he could speak, she lifted her head, her eyes stricken.

"No, Zou Tun. Don't listen to me. I have lost my faith. I shouldn't have lied to you, and I have lost Heaven because of it. But you are still there. Hold on to your love, hold on to what we knew. Believe and then I can believe, too."

He frowned at her, trying to understand her words. Her distress was obvious, but he could not entirely comprehend it. All he heard was that she had lied to him and lost Heaven. And yet he saw Heaven in her eyes, felt it in her body. She was as much a creature of light and love as he. And yet she looked so lost.

"Joanna . . ." he began, only to be cut off. They had arrived at the palace of the dowager empress. The eunuchs were announcing their presence, and Zou Tun could hear only Joanna's last rushed words.

"I love you," she said. "Whatever happens, remember I love *you*."

He heard her emphasis on the last word, knew it was important, but they were already being presented. The dowager empress would expect a response. So, with a rising sense of frustration, he turned to the woman who had ruled China for two decades while her son grew of age.

She was dressed as was appropriate for a woman in her station, including white face paint, a red-dotted lip, and an elaborate gown sporting the most auspicious embroidered symbols. Her black hair was wrapped around a heavy board to support an array of fresh flowers and painted butterflies. And yet, for all that she dressed in the finest Manchu style, he saw the weariness in her—and the flash of cunning in her eyes.

She was not looking on Joanna with favor.

He dropped into a full kowtow, pleased to see Joanna mimic his action. It would be awkward for them to remain on their knees before the empress during the entire interview, but such was customary. And he knew Joanna would follow his lead, even though it required her to kiss the floor.

The empress spoke, her voice commanding despite her age. "Why do you come into my presence in such a disreputable state? And in such company?"

Zou Tun looked up, seeing the woman's lip curl in disgust as she looked at Joanna. His soul wanted to leap to his lover's defense, to explain to the empress that the barbarians were as much creatures of love and deserving of honor as she. But that was not his place. Nor would it be helpful. So he merely dropped his eyes and spoke an apology.

"My gravest mortification, empress. I had not intended to enter your exalted presence; otherwise I would most certainly have dressed myself to honor your divine beauty."

"To seek the emperor in such a state is even more heinous, Kang Zou Tun. You shame yourself and your father."

"The shame is entirely my own." He swallowed, rapidly reviewing his options. He understood enough of court politics to know that he would not be allowed to see the emperor. Not until the empress was satisfied as to his purpose. He could think of no convenient lie to explain his presence. Especially with Joanna at his side. And besides, he could not form the dishonest phrases. Knowing no other option, and realizing that his appeal to the antiforeigner empress was doomed, he began his tale as best he could.

"Indeed, most heavenly empress, I come here fleeing my father." He lifted his head, trying to speak clearly, with all the force of his soul. "He wishes me to rule China, Empress."

Her eyes narrowed. "Do you bring the emperor news of a plot against his life?"

Zou Tun frowned, wondering how to explain. "Plots against an emperor are legion, and a son's loyalty to his father knows no bounds. I could never suggest that my father would so betray his vow to China."

"Such sentiment demonstrates your worthiness as a son."

Zou Tun winced at her words. Indeed, he was anything but a filial son, and his next words proved it. "Empress, if I may speak plainly." He straightened slightly, lifting out of his kowtow. "I have no wish to rule China. I would do it very badly."

She said nothing to him but simply watched, and he felt the presence of her intellect as a physical force. He'd seen the empress be charming and effeminate in the way of all women, especially in the way of concubines to a Qin emperor. But here now was the true woman behind the pretty clothing, the mother of the current ruler, the one who had guided China for so long.

How odd that he felt her power paled beside Joanna's. Not because the empress had any less intelligence or force of personality. Indeed, he thought them equal in that regard. But now, with the gifts of Heaven still in his soul, he could see what others perhaps did not.

The empress was afraid, and Joanna was not. Because Joanna remembered who she was and where her soul would go after her body died. It would go back to the love that had created it, the Heaven that awaited them all. The empress, for all her power, did not remember.

"What do you see when you look at me, Kang Zou Tun?" the empress demanded, oddly seeming to sense his thoughts.

He dropped his head, his forehead once again touching the floor. "The empress of China."

"And?" she prompted.

He straightened his arms, raising himself to look directly at her. "And a woman afraid."

She stiffened, her eyes narrowing. "Are Shaolin monks not afraid?"

He was not surprised she knew of his training. And, since he had determined to tell her all, he lifted his head off the floor. "Not the Shaolin. The Dragon immortals." At her frown, he explained. "It is a form of Taoism. One that I have learned with this woman here." He straightened further, rising up until he was on his knees. "I understand little of court politics, of my father's plans, or the direction of a nation at war." He took a deep breath. "But this thing I do know." He reached out and lifted Joanna, drawing her up to rest on her knees like him. "With this woman, I have entered the Antechamber of Heaven." He paused for a moment, taking the time to invest qi energy into his next words. "I will not give her up, Empress. Even should China fall about my ears because of it."

He heard the startled hiss of the eunuchs surrounding them. He even felt Joanna shift, obviously aware he had said something momentous, even if she could not speak this dialect. But the empress did nothing. She merely stared at him.

They waited there, on their knees before the empress. They waited in silence while the eunuchs shifted impatiently on their feet and the wind rushed unsettled through the trees. But from the empress, Zou Tun, and Joanna, there came no movement.

Finally the empress sighed. She turned to her nearest eunuch. "Where stands General Kang's party?"

The eunuch bowed. "In the city. He will be here within the hour."

Zou Tun flinched. His father was so close?

"And the barbarian men? Led by the birdman, Crane?"

At the mention of her father's name, Joanna canted a quick glance at Zou Tun.

The eunuch answered, "The barbarian is being brought to us. He will arrive sooner, but can be delayed."

The empress nodded, her gaze returning to Zou Tun. "So you have seen Heaven through a ghost woman's thighs," she sneered. But there was doubt in her eyes. And a fear that she was making light of something she should not.

To further her fear, Zou Tun remained silent, neither denying her crude statement nor acknowledging it. And in time, her fear made her speak. "You have seen Heaven?"

He nodded.

"And what did it show you?"

"That we all come from love, were created of love, and are deserving of that love." He spoke the words honestly, without intent to shame or instruct. The effect was startling.

The empress's eyes began to tear. And Zou Tun, a Shaolin monk, knew what the others could not see. This empress, this cold concubine that all reviled as evil or praised as heavensent, was merely a woman like every other. And the purity of her yin tears revealed just how deeply she felt the agonies of her position as ruler of an impoverished country.

But when she spoke, her voice was hard and cruel. "And who among us receives what we deserve, be it love or hate?"

He shook his head. "I do not know. But what I have found, I will not relinquish. And what I cannot hold, I have no wish to have."

"No, you cannot rule the country with a barbarian pet. And I do not wish such perversions to infect the Son of Heaven."

Zou Tun nodded, knowing she referred to her son. And that Zou Tun had just given up his place as an heir to the throne. He would have been relieved, except that most people in this situation were killed as an example to others who would abandon their duty. The empress's next words would be to order his and Joanna's deaths.

To his surprise, she did not. Instead she leaned forward, her eyes narrowing. "Your father's power grows daily. It becomes increasingly difficult to manage unruly generals and misinformed ministers. Your death, Kang Zou Tun, would only strengthen his position." She frowned, slowing rising to her feet. When she spoke next, it was with the weight of her entire nation, her words as official as if they were written on an imperial decree.

"I do not believe you, Kang Zou Tun, about Heaven or this woman. I believe that your father has sent you here to tempt my son into deeper consort with barbarians. In this he was mistaken, because you have come to me and not my son." She moved forward, towering over Joanna, her words like an executioner's ax. "Yes, your father has erred. He has trapped you in the net he meant for my son." She twisted, turning away from

Joanna as she would from bad meat. Her gaze fell hard and heavy upon Zou Tun. "*You* will have this union with this woman now. Or you will die."

Zou Tun meant to leap to his feet with joy—he even surged forward—but the eunuchs were there before him, their hard hands heavy upon his shoulders, blades pressed deep into his back. So he swallowed, using the time to clear his thoughts. "You wish me to marry Joanna Crane? Now?" He fought back his astonishment.

She nodded. "Yes. Now. Where your father will see it. Where the emperor himself will see. And then you will live with your shame before all."

He blinked, at last understanding her logic. Zou Tun's father was a threat to her and her son's power. But no one would support his ascension to the throne if a half-white grandson might one day inherit the empire. So long as Zou Tun remained alive and openly consorting with a white woman, the entire Kang branch could never take the throne.

But only if it were proved that Zou Tun consorted with a white woman. And only if that woman were to bear a child.

"Tell me, Shaolin monk," the empress asked. "Is she fertile?"

Zou Tun swallowed, his gaze moving to Joanna. "Yes," he said. It was true. He could see these things.

"Then you will be joined."

Zou Tun looked up at the empress, wondering at the rush of emotions whirling through him. He recognized anger at being forced, and fear of the empress. He also felt surprise and grief at the shame he was about to visit upon his family. But above all was a new terror: What if Joanna refused? What if she had no wish to wed him now? And certainly not in so public a fashion?

But if she agreed, if she said yes, then he could have everything he wanted. He would be free of the insidious corruption that was the Qin imperial court. He would be able to openly practice his religion with the woman of his choice. And he would have Joanna beside him at night, greeting him every morning.

It was too much to ask. Too much to hope for. And yet the empress was not only offering it to him; she was demanding it.

"Kang Zou Tun!" the empress exploded. "Will it be done, or do you die now with your honor intact?"

He lifted his chin, shrugging off the eunuchs' restraint. Straightening to his full height, he drew Joanna up as well, tucking her protectively against his side. Then he gave his answer.

"My honor and my life are in her hands, Empress. We will let Joanna Crane decide."

Benevolence and righteousness, knowledge and intelligence, filial piety and parental kindness, loyal ministers—these concepts all came about after the Tao was forsaken, after simplicity was destroyed. Their presence is an indication of moral bankruptcy, of the degeneration of people's hearts. They are evidence of a regression rather than a progression of society.

—Lao Tzu

Chapter Eighteen

Joanna blinked, startled when everyone in the room turned to stare at her. Despite all attempts, she had been unable to follow the shifting currents within the conversation. All she knew came from guesses about Zou Tun's expression. She knew he wasn't happy. Indeed, she guessed he was becoming very afraid, though all that showed in his face was a quiet resolution. Purpose and faith seemed to surround him in light. It was so bright, she wondered how the others couldn't see it—but they clearly could not. Certainly not the eunuchs who surrounded them, who even now menaced them.

But something had changed in the room. Before, Joanna had been treated as vermin. The eunuchs would have happily slaughtered her, the dowager empress could barely look at her without curling her lip, and even Zou Tun ignored her, his attention on more important matters, though he'd tried his best to keep her shielded from the scarier eunuchs. But now they all stared at her. She heard their gasps, saw the shocked stares, and finally felt the heated touch of Zou Tun pulling her slightly away to look directly into his eyes.

"Zou Tun?"

"Will you marry me, Joanna Crane?"

Joanna's heart constricted painfully in her chest, her eyes tearing from pain. Part of her wanted to leap into Zou Tun's arms. Part of her wanted to sob out in joy and relief at his words. But she didn't. She couldn't. Because his eyes did not show her love or desire. They were flat with fear. And with everyone else's attention riveted upon her, she knew he was being forced to ask, forced by some devious political scheme to pretend a love he did not feel.

She blinked back her tears and took a deep breath, speaking in quiet Shanghainese. "Why do you ask me this? What is going on?"

Zou Tun opened his mouth to answer, but the dowager empress interrupted in Mandarin Chinese, her voice sharp. Joanna saw a flash of irritation cut through Zou Tun's expression, but it was quickly masked as he turned and bowed respectfully, speaking to the imperious lady in a calm tone.

Joanna had no idea what he said, but apparently it worked. The lady huffed in annoyance but did not speak, waving her hand in dismissal. Then she nodded to a eunuch who slipped to the side, opening a doorway in the audience chamber. But the eunuch did not go through. Instead he simply stood there, standing beside the opening that led off into darkness.

Joanna frowned, her gaze slipping back to Zou Tun. "What is happening?"

He swallowed, then began speaking in the Shanghai dialect. His words were low and rushed, as he obviously hoped to get as much said before the empress lost her patience.

"They wish us to marry, Joanna Crane. My father's power grows, but he will lose all support if I openly consort with a white woman." He looked hard at her. "The empress wishes you to bear my child—a boy child if possible. No man will support the general if a half-white grandson might gain the throne."

"But won't your father kill the child?"

"The Empress will protect him and us. As long as we live together, my father will not move against the emperor. Without me to sit on the throne, he has no support."

"So she wants us to marry. And if we refuse?"

He glanced uneasily at the guards. He didn't need to answer.

"They will kill us, won't they?"

He nodded.

"So we have no choice. We will marry." How easy to say the words. How easy to simply take what she wanted and forget the reason, to focus on the fact that she was marrying a great man and ignore the truth that he didn't truly love her. Not in the way a man should truly love his wife and the mother of his children.

He shook his head, clearly frustrated because she didn't fully understand.

"What am I missing? Tell me it all."

He lifted his gaze, pointedly looking at the darkened doorway the guard had just opened. "We must openly consort with each other, Joanna. We must do what wedded people do. There are ministers who will require proof of my"—he swallowed—"my perversion."

She stared at him, her mind temporarily frozen. They had to consort, to make love. Publicly? "In front of witnesses?" she gasped.

He nodded.

"To prove your *perversion?*"

Again he nodded. "They know of the Tigress religion. They know I have . . . practiced."

This time she could not stop the tears that flooded her vision. She wasn't sure what she'd expected. She knew the Qin court had no cause to love white people. She also knew that they considered the whites barbarians. Bestial animals. There was no greater perversion for an heir to the imperial throne than to openly embrace a white woman.

Part of her mind embraced these political consequences. She knew that it would only advance the foreign political cause if the imperial heir loved a white woman. Even if that man lived in disgrace for the rest of his life, he would always be an example of unity for their two peoples, of peaceful coexistence between the races.

But she was not a political cause, and he was not a nation. They were two people. Two hearts. And hers was the one in love.

Of course, they would be killed if they didn't comply. They had no choice. They had . . .

Her eyes narrowed. Zou Tun had once before told her that they had no choice. That they were forced to comply with Shi Po's demands. But he could have escaped then. She looked around. There were a great many eunuchs around, but they were lax in their appearance. Truly, their swords and big fists were impressive, but she doubted they had much true fighting experience. After all, merely the appearance of their threat was likely enough to intimidate most people. Plus, she had seen Zou Tun. She was positive he could fight a path to the door so that they could escape. They could probably still fight their way to see the emperor if he so chose.

So why had he not simply done that? Why was he acting as if he were forced into this marriage? And forced to bed her in so public a fashion.

"Zou Tun, do you wish this? Do you wish us to wed?"

He opened his mouth to answer, but no words came out, only a strangled sound that might have been the "I . . ." But it didn't matter. She saw the panic in his eyes, the desperation and the fear. And somewhere beneath, something else.

"Don't answer," she whispered. "I can see the truth." He didn't love her. Didn't want to disgrace himself in this fashion.

He gripped her arms, not in a bruising grip, but in the way a man holds the only solid thing in his life. The way her father had held Joanna just after her mother died. The touch held anger and fear, but also love and tenderness in a conflicted mass.

"I will die with honor, Joanna Crane. If that is what you wish."

"Of course I don't want that! I'm trying to find out what you want." She snorted in disgust.

And at the rude sound, the dowager empress lost her patience. With an angry gesture, the eunuchs sprang into action. They drew their swords, and suddenly Joanna and Zou Tun were ushered through the darkened doorway.

Zou Tun did not fight. He went quietly, his only resistance in order to ensure that his body was between the sword points and Joanna. He was protecting her, but since she had no wish to see him skewered, she moved as she was told, walking anxiously down the darkened hallway until they came to . . .

A bedroom. A glorious sunlit bedroom with elegant tapestries and stunningly beautiful furniture. But most of all it held a large bed with silk sheets and open curtains.

The dowager empress followed, her power obvious in every line of her diminutive body. She was the one in control here, and the eunuchs leaped to follow her next command—to remove the hangings surrounding the bed.

Joanna stared in shock. Did the empress intend to stand in the room while they did the deed? The thought was horrifying—though she supposed no more so than the entire bizarre situation. And still, Joanna had no idea of what Zou Tun thought. What *did* he want?

He, apparently, didn't want to tell her. His face gave nothing away, even as he watched the eunuchs' progress.

Then they were gone. The guards left, and the dowager stood before them in the imposing bedroom. She said nothing but stared hard at Zou Tun, who in turn stared hard right back at her. It was a standoff. The two glared at each other, eyes hard and cold. Joanna merely watched, unable to understand, much less interfere.

And then, abruptly, Zou Tun dropped to his knees, his forehead pressed to the floor. He spoke to the empress. Joanna had no idea what he was saying. Begging for their lives, perhaps? Pleading with the empress to change her mind?

Whatever he said, it didn't work. The empress merely stared at his prostrate form, then flicked a dismissive glance at Joanna before turning on her heel and leaving. The door shut behind them, and the silence reigned long and horrible.

Joanna looked about the sunlit chamber. There was no escape. Even the windows were covered with beautiful laticework that barred exit. And Joanna was not fooled. She had stood behind a tapestry and seen Little Pearl perform her service. She knew that the room likely concealed dozens of peepholes. Zou Tun had said they would be watched. She had no doubt they were.

She looked at him then, his body still on the floor in his kowtow. Indeed he had not moved since his plea to the empress. Not knowing what else to do, Joanna knelt beside him, reaching out to stroke what she could of his pale cheek.

"What did you say to her just now? What did you say to the dowager empress ?"

He raised up, but only enough so that Joanna could see his face. He still looked at the ground. "I told her I was a loyal Manchu. All I have ever wished to do is serve my country with honor." Then he looked at her, his eyes wet with tears, his expression stricken. "I have striven all my life to be an honorable man—one who brought joy to his parents and glory to his country. How is it . . ."

His words were choked, and but Joanna finished them for him.

"How is it that you have come here, been forced to bed a white barbarian to the dishonor of your family and the horror of your emperor?"

He did not answer, but she saw acknowledgment in his face.

"You do not want to marry me. You do not want to bed me." She swallowed, forcing herself to say all her fears. "You do not want to father a half-white child."

"No!" he cried, and the word echoed in the room. He reached for her. "That is my shame, Joanna Crane. I do want those things. I do. . . ." His voice dropped to a whisper. "I do wish to join my body with yours. I have wished it from the very first moment we met. I just did not think . . . I did not believe. . . . I did not know . . ."

"What?" she asked.

"That my desires would necessitate such shame."

Her eyes dropped. Her heart fell also. "You are ashamed to be with me."

"No," he said, the word pained. "I have learned how foolish I was. I am honored to be with you. The shame is my father's. My family's. This will destroy them." He lifted her chin, drawing her close enough to press his lips to hers. "No, for me the shame is nothing at all." Then he kissed her, his lips seeking hers with an honesty she had to acknowledge. He desired her. She felt it in the very air they shared.

"But what of marriage, Zou Tun? Do you desire it?"

He didn't speak at first. Instead he stroked her cheek as he struggled. In time he spoke, his words coming out in a halting whisper. "In China there is no such thing as desire. There is only proper and improper, honor and dishonor."

"And what you desire is improper? Dishonorable?" She looked into his eyes, praying he would answer clearly. "Do you desire me?"

Again he kissed her. Deeply, penetratingly, he filled her mouth and soul with his hunger. Her yin tide surged in recognition, even as her heart trembled in despair.

She broke off the kiss. "You desire me, but there is no love, Zou Tun." She didn't know why she was pressing the point. She didn't understand this perverse need to torture herself. They would be killed if they didn't marry. Why did she need to hear him say it, to state out loud for all to hear that he did not love her?

"My father will be here soon." His voice was low, his words rasping. She could tell that he was speaking as much to himself as to her. "The dowager will bring him here. To watch us. To watch me so all will know that his hopes and dreams are ashes." He raised his eyes, letting her see the pain that haunted him. "Do you know what it is for a good Chinese son to shame his father so? Do you know what will happen?"

She shook his head.

"He will kill himself, Joanna. Himself, and my mother who bore me. And my sister who is not yet married. The house will burn. And the servants as well. They will all die because of my shame. Because my father will order it."

She reared back, choking on her horror. Still, he spoke.

"*That* is the cost, Joanna." He pressed his lips to hers. "That is the cost of my love for you."

She didn't know how to react, didn't know what to say. Her mind was reeling from his words. Could it be true? Could he truly love her? And could his love cost so much? Her mind could not grasp his meaning, could not separate truth from hope, desire from fear.

Looking in his eyes, she saw the same bizarre, twisting confusion in him.

"You love me?" she whispered.

"Yes," he answered, agony in the word.

"You want to marry me? And love me? And raise our children together?"

"Yes. Oh, yes."

"But to do so will mean the death of . . . of your entire family. Even the servants?"

He nodded, the single slash of his chin more potent than any word.

"Are you sure?" She shook her head in awe. It couldn't be possible that a man would order the death of his entire household because of the choice of one son. "This cannot be true."

Zou Tun closed his eyes, as if hiding from himself, but his voice was clear and firm. "I have never understood my father's choices. Some are political. Some are from fear. But mostly his choices come from ambition and vanity."

She frowned. "You know this?"

His eyes opened with surprise. "Of course."

"And yet you allow him to dictate your actions?"

He frowned, his expression wavering on the edge of true confusion. "My disobedience carries a cost. How can you not understand this?"

She swallowed. She did understand. And yet . . . "But to kill everyone. Would he truly do such a thing?"

He didn't want to look at her as he answered, but she took hold of his face. She lifted it so that she could read his expression, see the truth in his eyes.

"My father has a great deal of pride," he finally said.

So yes, the general would indeed kill his entire family out of shame.

"But what if you were honorable? What if you performed a great feat, if you did something far beyond—"

"Ruling an empire?"

She nodded. "Yes, something even greater than that. Then he wouldn't be dishonored. He wouldn't kill everyone, would he? He couldn't kill everyone out of shame, could he? He would have to acknowledge your greatness. And there would be no cost. No shame." Her voice dropped to a whisper, her soul barely able to voice her greatest wish. "Then we could live together in honor."

His gaze brightened with hope, but doubt still plagued him. "If you could do such a thing, Joanna Crane, find a way for me to save my family, then you are a far greater prize than I deserve."

She leaned forward, dropping the most tender of kisses upon his lips. "I am no prize, Kang Zou Tun. I am simply a woman who will risk everything for the man I love."

Before he could respond, she stood up, directing

her words to the nearest tapestry and the most likely location of peepholes. "Empress Cixi! Empress Cixi, I beg to speak with you! Please, great empress, there is something you must hear."

"What are you doing?" Zou Tun gasped. He too took to his feet. "One does not call for an empress like calling for your boots!"

Joanna sighed, impatient with protocol. They were in desperate straits. Surely the empress would understand. Surely . . .

The empress did not. She did not appear. Her eunuch appeared, his face contorted with anger, his sword in his hand. Joanna did not give him the chance to speak.

"How dare you treat the immortal Kang Zou Tun this way? China is truly barbaric if it treats its holiest men in such a fashion."

She spoke in Shanghainese, so she doubted the man understood. But no woman could rule an empire without people around her who spoke all languages of her country. One of the empress's eunuchs would speak Shanghainese. One of them would relate her words. And with luck, the empress would be superstitious enough to not risk offending Heaven. She would come investigate the claim. Even if it was the claim of a barbarian woman.

In the meantime, Joanna and Zou Tun had to wait out the angry, sword-wielding eunuch before them.

Fortunately, the single guard was little threat. Zou Tun's fighting skills could easily defeat the man. So they waited in stillness, praying the empress would hear.

And in time she did. Cixi entered slowly, in a stately fashion, preceded by two other guards. She spoke to Zou Tun, discounting Joanna completely. But Joanna did not wait; she spoke in the only Chinese she knew, trusting that one of those guards would translate.

"Great Empress, I apologize for my loudness, but I meant no disrespect. I merely sought to inform you of this man's status. His humility forbade him to tell you of his greatness, but I am here to relate what even a white barbarian has seen. Kang Zou Tun is an immortal. He has walked with me in the heavenly realm."

Beside her she felt Zou Tun stiffen. They both knew that she had just made an extraordinary claim. That, in truth, they had *not* made it all the way into Heaven. They had simply walked in the Antechamber. They might never pass beyond that gate. But Joanna could not allow doubt to creep into her voice or thoughts. She pressed on, preventing Zou Tun from contradicting her.

A small man, a clerk by the look of him, stood just behind the empress and whispered into her ear. He was translating. Excellent, Joanna thought. The empress was indeed understanding her.

"I know that for many, Kang Zou Tun's glory cannot be seen. But naturally the act can be repeated for those with eyes to see." She bowed slightly to the empress. "For those who daily view the glory of the Son of Heaven . . ." Joanna placed special emphasis on the emperor's other name, the one celebrating his direct descent from the divine. "You, of course, will be able to know."

It was a big gamble. The Chinese were not predisposed to listening to a white woman. But they did honor their religious leaders. And they did believe that any man—no matter how humble his origins— could become an immortal. How much more likely was it for the near cousin of the current Son of Heaven?

Joanna waited, praying that the empress would believe. Praying, too, that the woman had heard everything spoken. That she understood men's pride, believed in the possibility of true love, even if it was between an American woman and a Manchurian prince. But would she believe enough to make a happy ending possible?

Cixi spoke two words. They were in Mandarin, so Joanna did not understand. But she saw Zou Tun bow, dropping his head in acknowledgment while the empress and her retinue once more filed out.

It was not until she and Zou Tun were again alone that Joanna finally asked, "What did she say?"

Zou Tun turned to face her, hope shining in his eyes. " 'Prove it.' "

The only lasting satisfaction is that which is found in know-ing when enough is enough. If everyone were contented, the world would be a peaceful place.

—*Lao Tzu*

Chapter Nineteen

Prove it? Prove that they could reach Heaven? While others watched to see if what they claimed was true? The very thought was obscene, but they had little choice. And every reason to succeed. Zou Tun's family and their lives depended upon it.

Joanna turned to Zou Tun, drawing him to the bed.

"Joanna," he whispered. "It cannot *be* proved."

"Of course it can. They will be able to see it in us," she guessed. In truth, she had no idea whether they would or not. But she could not afford doubt. They had to believe. Zou Tun had to believe.

She kissed him, long and slow. Or so she tried. She tried to be calm and sure. What she expressed instead was fear and doubt. But he was reassuring. His kiss did what she'd wanted to do: It calmed her, eased her panic.

He'd centered her!

Her breath caught as the realization fully crystal-ized. She had a center. It was him. It was Zou Tun, and she would be lost without him. So she closed her eyes.

She forgot about everything but Zou Tun. She ignored the room and the people who watched. She released the future and the past. All that mattered was him. And her. And right now.

The words came easily, without forethought. Merely because they were true.

"I love you," she said.

He stilled against her breast, his lips curving into a smile on her skin. She thought he wouldn't speak because he was so still. But then he lifted his head, looking directly into her eyes. "I feel your love," he whispered. His face was filled with awe. "I feel it like the power of the sun." He swallowed. "You give me such power, Joanna."

She smiled because his eyes spoke to her. Only to her. But he had not said he loved her. Not as a man loves a wife. When he looked directly at her, the words had not come. And so she dropped her eyes, looking away.

"What has happened? Joanna, what are you doing?"

At his alarm, her gaze jumped back to his. But the words would not form. And when she didn't speak, his expression grew frightened.

"Do you not know that what we do must be done honestly? Openly? Why do you close yourself off to me?"

She bit her lip. He was right. She had to tell the truth if they had any hope of climbing to Heaven.

She swallowed. "When I say I love you, Zou Tun, I mean *you*. Not everyone else, but you—because you are strong and smart and you try so hard to do the right thing even when an entire empire conspires against you. I love you, Zou Tun. With all my heart. You are my center, and I will abandon my family, my culture, and everything I know just to be beside you."

His face softened, his eyes misting as he kissed her. "You honor me beyond words," he said, his voice choked.

She kissed him back, framing his face as she pulled him closer, touching him with all the hunger and love in her heart. But he pulled away, his expression growing somber.

"Why do you pull away from me?"

"I haven't—"

He stopped her words with a kiss. "No lies, Joanna. You said yourself that it damages you."

She nodded, resolved to tell him. "I have such love for you, Zou Tun. It hurts to know that your love is not . . . not for me alone. That you love me in only the most general of ways."

He stilled. It was not the silence of peace and meditation. This was a cold quiet, an absence of movement that came from a frozen soul.

"It's all right, Zou Tun. I understand. And you know what? I'm not sure it matters," she lied. But this time her lies were for herself. She so wanted to believe it didn't matter. That her love was enough. "I will take all of you that I can have and not wish for more. I love you that much."

He shook his head, the movement forced. "No," he whispered. "No."

She shifted away from him, the touch of his body feeling wrong. If he wanted to have this discussion, they would. If there was to be truth, then she would have all of it.

"Why, Zou Tun? Why can't you love me? How am I wrong?" It was a ridiculous question. No one could force love, even if they wanted to. But she could not shake the feeling that he could love her, if only she were different. If only she changed.

His eyes grew stricken. "You do not understand."

She had been reaching for him, needing to feel a connection even if it was wrong. But at his words her hand fell still. "Make me understand."

"Do you know what it is for a Chinese man to love?" He shook his head. "We love our fathers and honor their position. We love our country and emperor, for he is the Son of Heaven and the ruler of us all. We love our sons, for they are our future and the blessings of our old age."

"And your daughters? Your wives? Your empress?" she pressed, beginning to understand. "What are they to you?"

He shrugged. "They are nothing. They are the holy vessels of our sons."

She nodded, at last beginning to see where the difficulty lay. "And I am an imperfect vessel. A white barbarian who can give birth only to a flawed son—a half-white boy."

He looked down at his hands. "I do not wish to feel this way, Joanna."

"But you do. And because of that you have held yourself back. You have not been able to love me."

He nodded, and she read misery in every line of his body.

Now she understood. In his eyes there was something wrong with her. She was white. And she was female. And both counts damned her.

She straightened, slowly moving off the bed. "I wasn't raised that way, Zou Tun. I was raised to be a person. A valuable person, an asset to my husband, my country, and myself. And I don't think I can live any other way."

"Where are you going?" he asked, his voice tight with fear.

"Love can be stopped, Zou Tun. Did you know that?" She stepped off the bed, turning to face him. From the corner of her eye she caught the ripple of a tapestry. There was someone behind it, watching. It was death, but she ignored it. There was too much at stake here for her to worry about who overheard what. All she cared about was Zou Tun's love and their future. So she focused on him, blocking out all else.

"I love you. Completely. Totally. I could have told myself I didn't love you. I could have blocked you from my thoughts, created reasons to hate you. And in time I think my love would have grown cold and hard. I might never have forgotten it, but it would have become a bitter thing, twisted and ugly." She shook her head. "I didn't want that. So I chose you. I choose to let my love flow freely. To you. And I will give up everything to be with you."

He pushed off the bed, coming to stand before her. "You humble me," he said.

But she held up her hand. "You have to choose the same thing, Zou Tun. You have to throw away everything, my love. You have to discard the thought of me as a flawed vessel; you have to step away from your country's demands and your father's wishes. You have to choose *me.*"

He stopped, his eyes growing wide. "I have given up my throne. I came here with you," he snapped, "at the risk of both our lives. What more do you want?"

"Your heart. Freely given. To me." And with those words she risked all. Even knowing that they were watched, that they were not alone, she did it and held up her head with pride.

She pulled off her dress. She was wearing Western clothing—a riding habit that stripped away easily despite her fumbling fingers and pounding heart. Dress, corset, shift, garters—everything came off.

Zou Tun stood and watched, his mouth hanging slack with shock. "Joanna . . ." His voice was thick with emotion, but she shook her head.

"I understand your culture feels different, but this is my decision. I will not let you touch me until you choose."

"Joanna. There are people watching. We will die. If they believe I have forsaken all that—"

"We will die if you don't," she interrupted. "Because I cannot help you to Heaven if I am just a vessel, interchangeable with another."

He swallowed, his Adam's apple bobbing in anxiety. "I could never replace you with anyone. Barbarian or Manchurian."

"Choose to *love* me, Zou Tun. Open your heart to me."

He didn't. He couldn't. She could see it in his eyes and in the twist of his body. He wasn't looking at her. He was looking at the tapestry and thinking of the people standing behind it.

"This is my country," he said.

She didn't answer. She simply stood there, her heart and body cold from her nakedness.

"This is all I have ever known," he continued. He paused, then: "But as a child grows, he learns new things. And so I have grown. And I have learned." He abruptly stepped forward, facing the tapestry and the people hidden behind it, simultaneously blocking their view of Joanna.

"I am Kang Zou Tun, onetime heir to the imperial throne and a Shaolin monk. And this I say to you: We are wrong. Our women are not vessels. They are not useless creatures without thought or will." He took a deep breath, his next words spoken with more power than she had ever heard from him. "And the white barbarians are ahead of us in that thinking, for they have educated their daughters with pride and skill. Indeed," he said, as he twisted slightly to look at her, "I think their women are superior in every way. Which means their children—boys and girls—are also superior." He straightened, his eyes going back to the tapestry. "And so it is that I, Kang Zou Tun, choose this woman—this white woman, Joanna Crane—as my wife. It is what I *desire*."

He turned then, looking to her with a hope and a love that made his entire body shine. "Will you marry me, Joanna Crane? There are ceremonies, but if you say so now, out loud, then the empress has the power to make it so."

She nodded, barely able to believe it was true. That he would forswear everything—his country, his throne, and his home—all for her. For the love of her.

"Yes," she said, her voice gaining strength as she continued. "I will marry you. With great joy."

He wrapped her in his arms then, kissing her with the full strength of his love. And when their lips parted, it was only so that he could whisper into her ear. "I never knew," he said. "I never knew that love could be so freeing. I feel . . . I feel light. I feel joyous. I feel . . ."

"Love," she finished for him. "Great, overwhelming, wonderful love."

He pulled back so he could look her in the eyes. "Yes. Thank you for making me choose. Thank you for making me release the chains that held me."

She went to kiss him then, but he would not let her.

"We can go to Heaven now, Joanna. I am sure of it. Together, with our love to make us light and free, we belong there. Will you go with me now?"

She grinned. "Of course."

He led her to the bed, lifting her with reverence onto the mattress. Then he stripped out of his clothing, his beautiful body flexing, his dragon already eager.

She felt her yin tide surging, buoyed by the love that flowed freely between them.

"I feel it," she told him. "The yin is so strong. And your yang . . ."

"White-hot. We have enough, Joanna. We have enough power—"

"Love," she corrected. "It is love that makes it so."

"Yes. We have enough love. Heaven will welcome us now."

And so it was. One kiss on her mouth and the yin tide began to surge. One caress on her breasts, and her cinnabar cave opened to welcome him. She was ready, and yet he took his time. His mouth worshipped her, his tongue swirling around and around her nipples until he drew them into his mouth. He suckled her, pulling hard and rhythmically, heating her yin tide until it boiled.

She touched him as well, caressing his dragon, kissing the whole of his body. They twisted their positions naturally, using their mouths to fire their blood, to help their bodies soar.

The circle of power flowed so strongly now, their love making his yang like a river and her yin like the ocean, each pouring into the other.

Her contractions began immediately. Those wonderful pulses within her cinnabar cave pushed her ever higher, ever closer to Heaven.

She brought him to the same place as well, bringing his dragon to the edge of throwing its white cloud. And then she stopped, pressing on his *jen-mo* point, helping him keep his seed inside.

He lifted her up, drawing her to his side so that they lay together, facing each another.

"You are my love," he said. And then he echoed her words back to her. "I abandon everything for you—my family, my culture, and all that I know, because you are everything to me. I love you."

She smiled, rolling and pulling him atop her. His weight was gloriously heavy. Her legs slipped open and his dragon stretched for her.

"You are my center, Zou Tun. I have never felt more whole, more at peace, than when I am with you. I love you."

"I love you."

They spoke at the same moment. And then, as the meaning of those wonderful words still echoed in her thoughts, he thrust into her. His dragon buried itself deep in her cinnabar cave. She felt the barrier of her virginity stretch and break. But before she could cry out, before she could protest the fullness of his presence, its heaviness and sheer size, she began to feel his yang. The river of energy pumped even faster now, flowing deep into her body. And the wonder of it far exceeded any discomfort.

She was stretched open, filled to her center, had become a link of yin and yang that was beyond anything she had ever experienced. He began to withdraw, but she didn't allow it. Wrapping her legs around him, she drew him forward, the impact of his body like a great pulse pushing her higher.

"Don't leave me," she gasped.

"Never," he answered. And then he pulled back, looking into her eyes. "We will go to Heaven now, Joanna."

She nodded. "Yes."

They did not need to speak any more. Whispered phrases of love were instead tender caresses of joy. The bright spark of passion burned eternal. Nothing was spoken aloud, but they saw forever reflected in each other's eyes.

His dragon pushed again and again into her cave.

She saw the moment coming in his eyes. Dazed wonder took him—a gasp of power and the release of joy.

His dragon released its yang cloud.

Her yin met it with a surging tide.

And as they cried out their joy, their souls ascended to Heaven and passed through the gate.

From her seat behind the tapestry, Dowager Empress Cixi released a long sigh. She knew she should be thrilled. The Kang boy had solved one of her great problems, and that should make today a good day. Beside her, General Kang twisted in shame, while beside her stood the white father of the barbarian. Mr. Crane was his name. And he had turned his back on his daughter rather than witness her coupling.

The new husband and wife were still now, their bodies intertwined while their souls danced in Heaven. She might have thought them dead if she hadn't been able to see the telltale rise and fall of Kang's breath. No, they were in Heaven—the white woman, too—while a half-dozen men and eunuchs watched in awe. Even her own son—brought in to see this heir's perfidy—had no words for the sight.

Two new immortals, and one a white woman.

Cixi shook her head in sadness. She would have declared them immortal even if they had done nothing more than couple with lusty abandon. She needed General Kang's troops, needed his skill, and this was the only way to spare his pride. Yes, she would have declared the Kang boy an immortal to prevent his father's suicide. That these two had accomplished the task made all her reason cry out.

With envy.

Once she had loved another with such abandon. She had loved with such totality that a single kiss felt like Heaven. She'd gotten a son from the process and become the ruler of an empire. And yet her lover died, leaving her surrounded by greedy hands on all sides—from within and without the country.

How she envied this young barbarian woman.

"They are rousing," whispered a eunuch. The two had danced in Heaven for nearly an hour, but were now beginning to stir, coming back to themselves with smiles and soft whispers. Their eyes still glowed. Even General Kang could not deny the accomplishment.

He turned, facing the emperor with calculating eyes. "My son is an immortal," he said with obvious pride. "No better man could serve as your aide. With him by your side, China will be undefeated."

Empress Cixi did not give her son time to answer. "With a white woman by his side, the peasants will revolt and finish off what the foreigners have begun. The Qin Empire will end in disgrace."

General Kang's eyes narrowed in anger. "A coupling does not make a marriage."

Beside him, the barbarian father stiffened in outrage. His translator had voiced the previous interchange. "Harm one hair on my daughter's head, and all of America and Europe will rise up to destroy you. I will see to it."

It was no idle threat. The ghost people were already waiting for a reason. And her son knew that.

With a sigh, the emperor shook his head. "Your son *has* married a foreigner, General Kang. Even I can see the love that surrounds them."

"That is the glory of Heaven," the general protested.

"Even so," responded the emperor. "No, we must give our newest immortals a temple in which to preach, a place where they can raise children and instruct a new generation." He waved a negligent hand to the nearest eunuch. "Show me the empire."

Within moments a map was brought forward and unfurled. The emperor pointed at a small dot.

"What is this?"

"Islands, Your Majesty. The largest is called Hong Kong."

"Very well. Send them there." He sighed and stood. "Love and Heaven," he spit. "And who rules the country?"

I do, thought the empress as her son wandered off. She saw to the threats and eliminated them. She protected his power and saw that what could be saved of China, would be.

But unlike the white barbarian woman, she had not been raised to demand respect, to force the men around her to see her value. She ruled from behind the screen. She disposed of threats without acknowledgment. For that was the life of Chinese women.

Her gaze wandered back to the couple still embracing on the bed. She would build them their temple in Hong Kong. And she would send guards to protect their lives and the lives of their children. Not because it protected her son from the machinations of General Kang. Or because it showed her enemies that she had the power to do so. And not even because the coming of two new immortals would be seen as an auspicious sign for China.

No, she would do this because in Zou Tun and the barbarian she saw hope for the women of China. Hope that one day her country would raise women who stood side by side with their men, wielding their own strength and intelligence freely. That was the promise she saw in this couple on the bed.

And that was the reason she would make sure that they lived long and happy lives.

Empress Cixi stood, leaving her seat and drawing the rest of the men along with her.

"Let them rest there as long as they require," she instructed. "They can leave for their new home tomorrow." Then she turned to both fathers, her voice cold. "Go and do as the Son of Heaven has ordered," she said firmly. "Announce this glorious union to your people. I shall see them escorted to their new home."

There was reluctance on both men's part, but neither could thwart the empress's will. In the end, both bowed and withdrew. The emperor had already returned to his work, and so Empress Cixi turned her attention to the next political threat.

Yet the couple did not leave her thoughts. *One day,* she whispered to herself. *One day all women will stand beside their men, beloved by their mates, and blessed by Heaven.*

One day.

White Tigress
JADE LEE

Englishwoman Lydia Smith sailed to the Orient seeking her fiancé. She finds treachery instead. In seedy Shanghai, she is sold and made a slave to a dark-eyed dragon of a man. But while her captor purchased her body, is that what he truly sought? He demands not her virginity, but the essence of her ecstasy, and there seems no choice but to consent. What harm, Lydia wonders, is there in allowing him to pleasure her and teach her until she can flee?

It is the danger—and reward—of taking the first step on a journey to heaven, and her feet are already on the path to becoming a radiant and joyous…

Devil's Bargain
JADE LEE

The death of her father made Lynette a penniless relation. Rather than burden her family, she resigns herself to the inevitable: selling herself into marriage. But to whom? Viscount Marlock—a dark devil, carnal and unrepentant—offers to arrange her match, but for a price. He will teach her all she needed to know about ensnaring a man; will use his touch, his tongue, to open her to the pleasures of the flesh. She, in turn, will obey him without question, trusting his whispered promises. But in this game, who will be caught, and who saved?

TIGER EYE

MARJORIE M. LIU

He looks completely out of place in Dela Reese's Beijing hotel room—like the tragic hero of some epic tale, exotic and poignant. He is like nothing from her world, neither his variegated hair nor his feline yellow eyes. Yet Dela has danced through the echo of his soul, and she knows this warrior would obey.

Hari has been used and abused for millennia; he is jaded, dull, tired. But upon his release from the riddle box, Hari sees his new mistress is different. In Dela's eyes he sees a hidden power. This woman is the key. If only he dares protect, where before he has savaged; love, where before he's known hate. For Dela, he will dare all.

CHRISTINE FEEHAN
DARK DESTINY

Her childhood had been a nightmare of violence and pain until she heard his voice calling out to her. Golden and seductive. The voice of an angel.

He has shown her how to survive, taught her to use her unique gifts, trained her in the ancient art of hunting the vampire. Yet he cannot bend her to his will. He cannot summon her to him, no matter how great his power.

As she battles centuries-old evil in a glittering labyrinth of caverns and crystals, he whispers in her mind, forging an unbreakable bond of trust and need. Only with him can she find the courage to embrace the seductive promise of her . . . *Dark Destiny*.

Connie Mason

The Laird of Stonehaven

He appears nightly in her dreams—magnificently, blatantly naked. A man whose body is sheer perfection, whose face is hardened by desire, whose voice makes it plain he will have her and no other.

Blair MacArthur is a Faery Woman, and healing is her life. But legend foretells she will lose her powers if she gives her heart to the wrong man. So the last thing she wants is an arranged marriage. Especially to the Highland laird who already haunts her midnight hours with images too tempting for any woman to resist.